The
Ash Tree

Printed in the United States of America

Cover art: Painting by Jeanette Arax-Melnick

Armenian poems translated by Diana Der Hovanessian, Marzbed Margossian and Aram Tolegian

Book design by *the*BookDesigners

A CIP catalog record for this book is available from the Library of Congress
ISBN-13: 978-0-9818547-6-2

First Edition

The Ash Tree

a novel

Daniel Melnick

Fresno, California

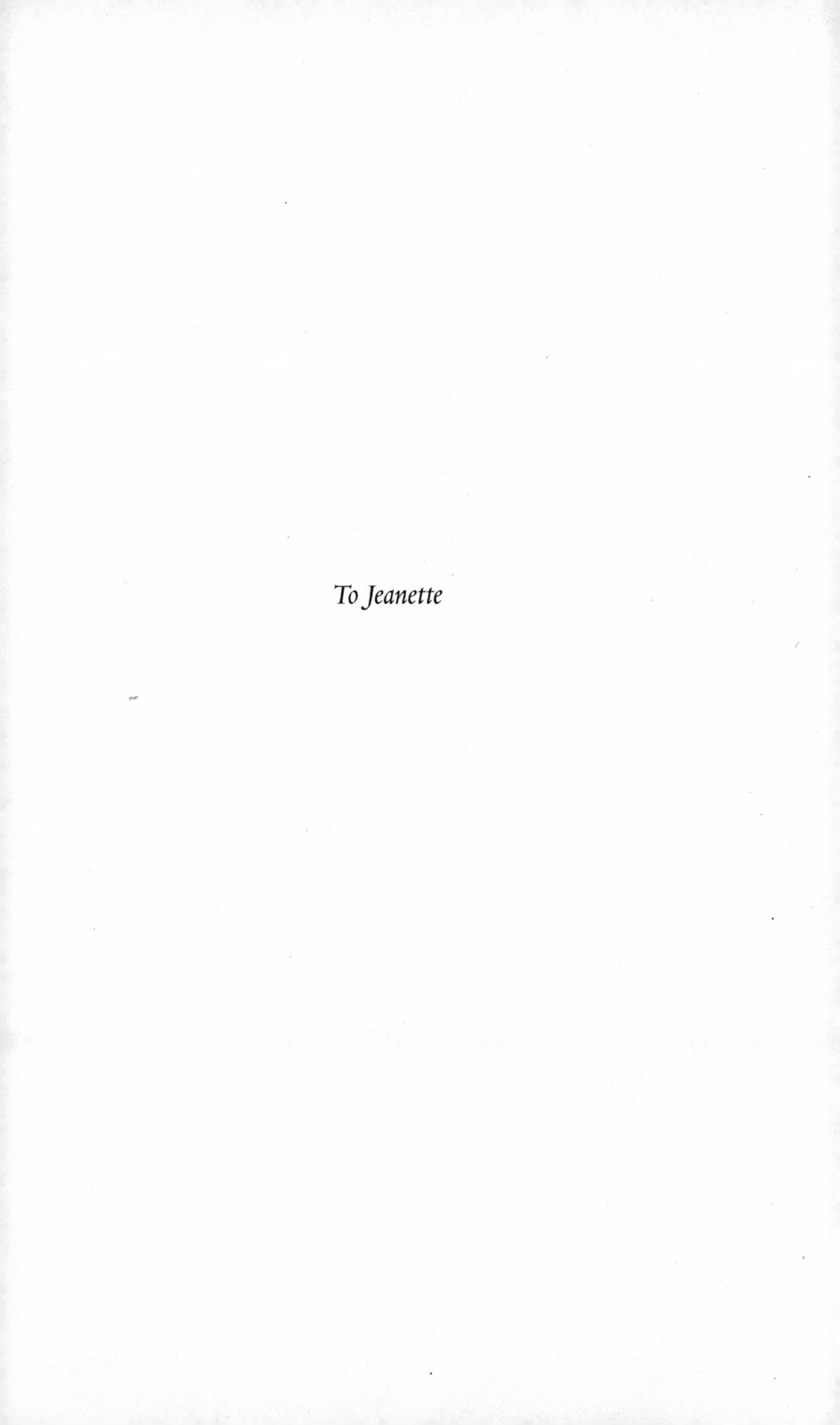

To Jeanette

I love the taste of the sun in their words:
The Armenian laments, those ancient airs,
Are like the burning scent of blood-red flowers.

—Yeghishe Charents

Contents

Prologue: A death in the family—January 2, 1972 1

Part One: *The Afterlife of Genocide*

1. Armen—February 8, 1925 9
2. Artemis—November 6, 1928 23
3. Tigran the Great—April 1, 1930 39
4. The burning house—June 20, 1938 53
5. Wartime—December 7, 1941 69
6. On the bridge—March 12, 1944 79

Part Two: *A Daughter in Diaspora*

7. Juliet as a child—September 3, 1946 93
8. A trip to the country—May 30, 1952 105
9. Independence Day—July 4, 1955 119
10. First grandson—December 31, 1957 137
11. Poetry—August 15, 1958 155
12. The blinding sun—July 29, 1959 169

Part Three: *American Lives*

13. Fathers and Sons—December 24, 1960 183
14. Genocide Commemoration Day—April 24, 1962 199
15. Armenia—October 26, 1962 213
16. Juliet in Berkeley—November 11, 1962 223
17. Garo's Garret—October 26, 1964 233
18. Honeymoon—June 19, 1965 247
19. A daughter's daughter—June 5, 1969 261
20. Christmas—December 25, 1970 275
21. In the end is my beginning—January 2, 1972 295

Prologue

A death in the family

JANUARY 2, 1972

—●—

A car drove out of the foggy darkness and parked in the driveway. From the family room, Artemis heard her husband, Armen, shuffle about in the foyer; a key clicked in the lock, and the door opened. It was Tigran, their oldest child. His voice and Armen's met in the entrance. When Tigran mumbled something, a strangled cry came from Armen. Then Tigran walked in, his face hard and colorless. Artemis felt her own face freeze and her shoulders and chest tighten. The tightness made her shake.

Tigran mumbled something again."What?" she said. "I can't hear you. Why do you mumble?"

"Garo..."

She could not hear the rest.

"What?" she spit out, stern and urgent.

"Garo, Ma. Garo is dead."

"You're talking gibberish," she said.

"Garo was shot at his bar," Tigran said.

"You're lying! Don't you dare speak such lies!" She spoke in a high-pitched rasp and felt the acid of her stomach rise into her throat.

"Ma, Garo was murdered. He was shot. He's dead!"

She stared at him, and then she screamed. She beat her fists against his chest.

"No, no, no."

A spasm shook her. She could not bear to be breathing, to be standing, to be living when her younger son was not. She shrank to the floor, lowering herself to her hands and knees. She crawled across the family room to the hall and into her bedroom. A high thin acid wail rose from her, a continuous howl. Her arms and legs and back were wracked with pain. She crawled to the mirrored door in her bedroom, slid it open, and hid deep inside the closet among clothes she pulled down over her. There she howled, her body bent into a ball.

Tigran flickered above her. She saw his hand reaching toward her. Buried in the clutter of clothes and useless shoes, she screamed and sobbed. The thought of her 40-year-old son shot and murdered – it seared her to the bone. Her gall rose with horror at her loss and at her failure, her terrible failure to be vigilant, to protect her son, to fend off the forces that boiled you alive, sliced you open, blew you to bits, or shot you to death.

Tigran wavered before her again, his face distorted as if under water. She could hardly hear his words. She saw her husband cowering at the door. Armen must have seen her looking at him, for as she cried and whimpered, he began to approach. His eyes were red, his lips lax, his lined face no longer a seventy-one year old mask, but sagging and tortured and human. It was a vulnerable child's face. Her back and limbs were in agony as she began unbending herself, rising now, oblivious to Tigran's helping hands. She reached for Armen, and they stood in the bedroom holding each other without words, sobbing and wailing at how infinitely empty the universe was.

Slowly she became aware that Tigran stood in the doorway to the hall and held his arm around his thirteen-year-old son, Adam.

They had moved in with her and Armen after Tigran's divorce. The boy stood in pajamas; he was crying and staring at her. Suddenly, the images of Garo's children – Pauly and Annette and John John – loomed before her.

"The children!" she cried out. "Armen, we must go. We have to be with the children." Walking up to Tigran and Adam, she reached to her grandson and hugged the crying youngster. "My sweet Adam," she said. Then she stared suspiciously at Tigran, as if her surviving son might bear more terrible news.

He turned away from her hostile gaze. "There are things I have to do," he said in a bitterly efficient voice. "I need to call Juliet, for one. Then I'll drive over with Adam."

Through the foggy night, Armen drove slowly north and west to Van Ness extension. She sat in the middle of the Ford's front seat, needing to be near her husband now. Occasionally, they exchanged short sentences, each repeating what the other said, always in Armenian.

"We must help the children."

"What?" Artemis asked.

"We must help the children."

"We must."

"We are all they have now."

"All they have."

Armen said these poor children were harmed now like the children in the Genocide. But this happened here in America, where there was so much politeness, so much deception, so much money.

Then Artemis said maybe Tigran had lied. Garo would wake up, would burst forth alive, breathing and bent on vengeance.

Garo and Lily's house appeared out of the fog. All the exterior lights were on, and she could make out a dozen cars in front. She took her handkerchief and dried her eyes; she smoothed her hair with her hand and held her coat tightly around her breasts and her aching back. The two of them walked through the fog as if through a storm. Frail, their arms linked, they stood at the locked side door. Armen pressed the ringer.

Lance Fetzer opened the door.

"Oh, Mr. and Mrs. Ararat," the huge bouncer said in a small, honeyed voice, "I'm so sorry Garo's passed."

Artemis ignored him and pushed her way through the door.

There were many people sitting and standing in the open kitchen and the big family room. She could not see the children anywhere. Suddenly there was a piercing cry from nowhere.

"Artemis!"

It was Lily, and she reached for Artemis and clung to her. They cried together. Lily's body felt terribly thin, cold, on the verge of collapse.

Someone – it was Lily's brother-in-law, Gene – helped Artemis and Lily to one of the couches in front of the massive adobe fireplace.

"I told him," Lily began, but Artemis hardly listened as her daughter-in-law broke again into sobs.

Around them everyone was talking in hushed voices. She realized that Big Mike and Zephur Arslanian stood across the room, and there was their son Ronnie, button-holing Lily's brother-in-law a few yards away. "It's a cruel world. I may be an S.O.B., Gene, but there are much worse in this city, and Garo thought there was nothing he couldn't tackle."

Suddenly the psychologist Dr. Hopper sat down beside her. Teary eyed and grey-headed, he said, "He fought for his life, Artemis! It took six bullets to bring him down. I was at the hospital." She let the doctor hold her hand.

"He fought and fought until the last drop of blood drained out of him."

She turned abruptly away and faced Lily.

"Artemis, I'm so worried about Pauly," the widow said. "I told him Garo was dead, and he ran out of the house. He ran and ran through the fog. He's back now, but I don't know where." Artemis said she would look for him.

In the murmuring room, the grandmother rose to look for the children, but for a moment she stayed near the couch, watching the knots of people, everyone affected by the grief in the room. Armen was talking to the Balians about how he had once lived in Paris after the Genocide and how the Parisian-Armenians had greeted him with tears in their eyes and a feast of barbequed lamb under the palms; she thought maybe Armen was cracking under the pressure, for her poor husband had never lived in Paris. But she saw that everyone's words were strange, and it was as if they were all huddling together in a lashing winter wind. But then she felt hot and sweating; the family room suddenly seemed filled with the unspeakable heat of a Fresno summer. She struggled to keep her bearings, standing on the verge of collapse, as if on a field of ash, scorched by the sun.

Finally, Artemis was able to flee into the hall, and she walked past each room – the dining room, the living room, the master bedroom – looking carefully into each. John John was in his own bedroom playing with one of his cousins. Artemis hugged her husky eight-year-old grandson. She told him she would always help him. He said, "Okay, Gramma," in a detached and polite voice.

Annette was in her pink room. Two young cousins sat on the bed, looking at magazines. When Annette, almost thirteen now, saw her at the door, she dropped some clothes she was somberly folding to place in the top drawer of her chest. She rushed into her arms, and moaning hopelessly she buried herself against her. Artemis kept patting her granddaughter's hair, and over and over she said, "Annette, Annette, we love you, our sweet Annette." Finally the girl let go. In a thoughtful voice Annette asked whether she could get something for her grandmother, a glass of water even. Artemis' heart broke. "No thank you, honey," she said.

She walked further down the hall to her oldest grandson's

room and opened the door. The walls were covered with the teenager's posters of Jimi Hendrix and the Rolling Stones. Pauly was not there, not in the bathrooms, not anywhere. She retraced her steps, searching through the big house.

In the dining room, she saw a foot protruding from behind the curtains. She approached slowly. The boy whimpered there, and she kneeled down and pulled the curtain away. Pauly crouched, bent into a ball against the window. He wore an unbuttoned, man's white dress shirt, which he must have gotten from his father's closet. It enveloped him like a shroud. He wailed quietly.

The sound shattered her. She stood frozen by him, all her vigilance failed and her world demolished. It was her punishment to hear these sounds, to bear the death of her beloved son, to live beyond all natural boundaries. Time could not regain the power to heal the wound, and she would never again be the Artemis she had been. Suspended in this hell, how could she begin to draw her stricken Pauly back to life? Kneeling, she reached toward him, and he let himself be held. She gathered him in her arms, and her lips began whispering. Her poor Pauly, her beautiful Pauly, she and Grandpa would always help him, would always, always love their beautiful grandson, their dear grandson.

For a long time, Artemis and Pauly sat this way on the dining room floor, her grandson sobbing in her arms.

PART ONE

The Afterlife of Genocide

Chapter 1

Armen

FEBRUARY 8, 1925

Armen Ararat dreamed that he ran parallel to the train, peering in, trying to keep up. He wondered where it was headed as it accelerated across the plateau. Straining with the last of his will to keep up, he looked into its compartment. He could hardly make out what was within, but just as it was about to surge down the tracks, he saw. He himself sat there, eating chocolate. On the seats all about him were the bodies of the dead.

He sat up in bed. Someone was knocking at his door.

"Armen, it's time to wake up," Mrs. Hagopian, the landlady, said outside.

"I will get up, Madame Baroness," he said in formal, polite Armenian. He knew he had dreamed and could remember only a feeling of breathless distress. He had lived with the sensation for a decade, since he was fourteen, when he saw and heard things about which he could not feel at peace.

Armen unbent his sleepy limbs, rose, and dressed. As he walked to the bathroom near his room, his small, attentive landlady disappeared down the stairs to the first floor. Then, in his room, he thought of his early morning appointments tutoring freshmen at the university. As usual Madame Hagopian had kindly awakened him. She ran her boarding house in Berkeley with the genteel efficiency she had possessed a decade before while reigning over her haute-bourgeois household in Constantinople. Armenians sometimes called her the red baroness, out of respect for the refinement of her upbringing and the passion of her leftist politics. Now, in America, Armen was drawn to her idealistic socialism partly because he felt such an allegiance to the new socialist republic of Soviet Armenia, which was so vulnerable next to Turkey. And reading The New Masses and other left-wing papers, he found an indignation at injustice like the bitterness he poured into some of his poetry. This month he had written "In exile, I cannot forget" with its last lines:

Under the blinding sun, passing alien grain,
I ride the hurtling train of my black fate.
The other exiles and I weep in rage and pain,
For with us sit the beloved bodies of the dead.

Madame Hagopian was a short, thin-boned woman with delicate shoulders, and she always held herself with her back straight. Her thick brown hair was pulled carefully into a bun, prematurely peppered with gray, and her drawn face possessed an intensity that seemed a vestige of the pride and elegance of her years before 1915. After the death in that year of her husband, an esteemed lawyer for the sultan, she had gathered all she could of the family's savings and fled with her children from their regal home, traveling across the globe to San Francisco. Now she owned this large Victorian house in Berkeley, renting out the second- and third-floor rooms and living on the first floor with her son and daughter. His landlady's spirit had been tempered into an unblinking graciousness in the decade since her husband had been arrested at midnight on April 24, 1915.

Later that morning almost a decade ago, on April 24th, Armen had been taken by a teacher to Constantinople's Galata district to visit the great poet Varoujan. When they arrived, there were rumors that something was happening across the Golden Horn in Beyazit Square, the huge public space in the center of the city. "Go home," his teacher, Oshagan, had said. "Hurry!" Yet he delayed, and alone he began to walk down Galata Hill, through the crowded labyrinth of streets. Groups of Turkish Muslims milled about the dusty byways; most of the Christian Armenians, Greeks, and Jews who normally filled the quarter had locked their shops and homes and were nowhere to be seen. He hurried south to Galata Bridge, where the passage became thick with people; his pace slowed, and he felt paralyzed in the hostile element, as the water of the Golden Horn sparkled below in the April sun.

He burst out of the bottleneck on the bridge and sprinted down a wide, palatial avenue to Beyazit Square. He must see what was happening, but the vast public space was packed with men. There was the smell of dust and sweat from the multitude, as well as an odd odor of metal, of damp rust. A loud hum arose, curses and catcalls, prayers and rants in choppy, surging waves of the city's languages. He slipped closer and closer, but always he saw before him a wall of backs, which towered over him. Some were clothed in coarse cloth and others in nicely cut European suits; some heads wore fezzes or bowler hats, and others were bare – some bald and others with hair scruffy or carefully shaved at the neck. The sea of heads churned before him, the bobbing heads allowing him only brief glimpses. There seemed to be a gallows set up for a public execution in the center of the square, and then suddenly he saw the phalanx of gendarmes and soldiers standing at attention below a score of hanging men.

A bloated ripeness had stiffened the bodies, and a crowd of flies hovered around the corpses. Some had been sliced, and the blood had set and darkened the clothing where the knives had slit. His eyes were raw and fixed in place. All the executed seemed to be Armenians, twenty men hanging before him. He saw one of his teachers suspended in the middle of one row of gallows; it was his history professor, mutilated and dead. And then he recognized the contorted face of Baron Hagopian. The lawyer's fine European suit had been slit in several places, and the blood had splotched and thickened.

The wall of backs closed in on him. The milling crowd in this sweep of public space seethed with a peculiar lust. He had been reckless to come here, and stealthily now, he dodged away from the crowd. He could hardly breathe, yet he ran and retraced his path back to the Galata Bridge. He must report the horror he had seen to Oshagan, whose writing would tell a new generation of the catastrophe.

He ran and ran but made little progress as he crossed the bridge again and stared at the fetid water below. He ran through the maze of dusty streets and past the knots of Turks standing around, as their children played in the guttered lanes. He gasped for each breath as he clambered up through the steep neighborhood and finally strode around the corner of Varoujan's street. There he halted. A half block away, at the poet's door, nearly a dozen gendarmes gathered. They surrounded Varoujan, grasped him, and forced him to march down the boulevard to a waiting cart. Two officers had followed, arms akimbo, chatting and smiling as if they were at a fair.

Now he knew he was late. He took his notebook and a book in French from the desk and descended the rooming house stairs two at a time. Passing the dining room, he glanced in.

"You had no breakfast," Mrs. Hagopian called to him. He said he had no time.

The big Victorian house was covered in dark-stained shingles and had a large turret, a curved bay window, and a wide porch. Armen bounded down its high steps into the February fog and ran to

Telegraph Avenue. There he began walking past the small one- and two-story shops clustered in the blocks approaching Sather Gate, the entrance to the university: a pharmacy, tobacconists, cafés and food stalls selling American food, and a scattering of bookstores. None of it was as impressive as the student district in Constantinople. But his sense of that city was ghostly now, and fleeting memories floated in and out of his awareness as Armen ran across the bridge at Sather Gate. The fog was slowly lifting, and he hummed a bittersweet folk-song: "Alakyaz sarn ambel az" – clouds are shrouding the mountain. He took the steps up two at a time in front of Wheeler Hall, the new building for the humanities departments.

"Bonjour," he returned the greeting of the head of the French Department as he passed her office on the second floor. The gray-headed woman had interviewed him last spring and arranged for him to work as a tutor to first-year students. He had been exempted from lower division courses and admitted to the upper-level French major. In Constantinople, he had translated Verlaine and a novel by Anatole France into Armenian. Armen had hoped to go to Paris and attend the Sorbonne, and he had cousins in France. But when he was nineteen and about to depart, his Uncle Haig had written from Central California to summon him: come work with him there for a year on the farms near Fresno, and earn enough to bring his brother, his sister, and his mother, who was Uncle Haig's sister, out of the cauldron of Turkey and to the safety of America.

So he – and then his family – had come and had worked themselves to the bone picking grapes day in and day out under the burning sun or packing apricots and peaches in the stifling sheds. He remembered driving with his uncle to pick up his family at the Fresno train station and then, on the way south to Delano, stopping in the town of Yettem near the Sierra foothills; the little Armenian church there was the oldest in the valley and was right next to the cow pasture. Incense came through the open doors and mixed with the farts of nearby cows. Mama began to cry. It reminded her so much of the village. And now five years later, it was 1925, and here he was in Berkeley, a student and teaching assistant at the University of California. His old teacher Oshagan – in Beirut now, writing a chronicle of his and Armen's village and its fate – might be proud, if only he knew.

Armen was late, and he headed down the wide hallway to the corner lounge, used for tutoring and TA office hours. The new hall's wooden floors were shining, and the resinous smell of wax and wood flooded his nostrils. He opened the lounge door and saw a blonde freshman sitting next to his desk – an eighteen-year-old American girl.

"Bonjour, Mary Ellen," the tutor said.

On Wednesday he had met her for the first time and planned their course of action. Today was Friday, and she would be reciting for the first time a poem she was preparing to memorize, one of Verlaine's brief "Romances sans paroles." Mary Ellen was like the rosy-cheeked well-fed girls he had first seen in New York's Grand Central Station when he had boarded the train and surveyed the other passengers headed west. He had stopped at the candy stall, pointed to the bars of chocolate, and laid a dollar down on the counter. The attendant asked incomprehensibly, "You want a whole dollar's worth?" The bars were all he consumed during the days and nights on the train to California. Other passengers would board and depart in waves all across the country, tall, short, friendly or gruff. The American women, whether bourgeois ladies or country girls, looked alike for the most part: they looked like Mary Ellen. She was pretty, but was this really a woman, with soul in her eyes, mystery in her body, knowledge in her brain?

"Mary Ellen, récitez le poème de Verlaine, s'il vous plaît," he said.

"Le poème...de Verlaine," she repeated with an American twang. "Il... pleure...dans mon...cœur...Comme il...pleut sur...la ville...."

Her smiling hesitations told him that no rain fell in her heart as it fell on the city for Verlaine, no causeless pain penetrated her soul.

Sorrow did not threaten to swallow her whole. He did not blame her, though he would have liked to dismiss her. Instead he painstakingly corrected her pronunciation. Armen remembered how Oshagan had led him patiently through the poems of Verlaine and Baudelaire. Oshagan was a born teacher, but not Armen. A second student arrived in the TA's office, and so his Friday morning proceeded.

After tutoring students, he had a cup of coffee and a chocolate bar. Then at 11 in the morning, he attended a seminar on renaissance French drama for seniors and graduate students. The old professor droned on in French about versification in Racine's "Phèdre." He never acknowledged how the language captures her tortured sensuality, or how moving is her tragic passion. Armen's whole soul was intoxicated by the singing of the verse.

The California sun had already burned off the fog and the clouds when he walked down the cement steps of Wheeler Hall, through Sather Gate and then by the same shops he had passed before. When he was a block away from Mrs. Hagopian's, he looked carefully at the distant driveway. A yellow car was parked there.

Through the window, his brother sat alone at the long table in Madame Hagopian's dining room. He must have driven their yellow Dodge up from Fresno. The two brothers had bought the roadster together a few years ago, just after their break with Uncle Haig. Ervant was nineteen and had been only a child in 1915 and had not seen or suffered so much. It had taken Armen time to trust his brother, but he did now, even with their Dodge. Suddenly Ervant looked up, leapt from his chair, and shouted his name.

"You're here!" Armen cried, and then as he always did, he assumed the worst. "Who died?"

"No, no," Ervant said. "No one died. I just wanted to surprise you!" His brother reached out to hug him, and they kissed each other on the cheek.

"So what is it that draws you from forlorn Fresno to this magnificent city?" Armen said in Armenian, and his brother smiled.

"I had to drive up. I hear Gloria whispering to me from North Beach," Ervant said, quiet and deadpan, but then he couldn't help grinning and flashing his hooded eyes.

Armen grinned, too, but he could not forget the warnings against syphilis pictured on Red Cross signs and in public offices, the grim reaper descending on unsuspecting couples. Ervant never seemed to feel ghostly or numb, and so he could indulge himself. He could invent stories at will, become wild at a moment's notice, and even lie, sometimes. Armen felt so high-spirited only in his poems; that was the one place where he felt his blood surge – and, of course, also occasionally in his political speeches.

Mrs. Hagopian swung the dining room door open and entered, carrying platters of lunch foods. It was after one, and there were no other boarders at the table. "Please, sit down," she said to them. "I hope you are hungry." She brought them a decanter of strong coffee and filled their cups.

"Thank you so much, Madame Baroness," Armen said.

"Yes, thank you so much, Madame Baroness," Ervant repeated. She poured a cup for herself and joined them as they filled their plates.

Armen sat eating, and he felt a familiar strangeness, as if he were separated from both the past and the present. His memories were always there, but he felt somehow barely present in them. And in the present, he felt the same separation. His face was stiff and furrowed, and his compact twenty-four-year-old body felt thick and numb. As he sipped the black coffee his landlady had poured, he took all the care he could to show his respect for the extraordinary woman sitting next to him, and she seemed to feel great pleasure in helping Armen, who as a teenager had been a part of the cultured Constantinople Armenian life she so missed.

On the two brothers' plates were slices of lox on crusty Italian bread; there were also sliced oranges, blue-veined Roquefort, and large Greek olives. Mrs. Hagopian said in Armenian, "The smoked salmon is from the delicatessen – not as good as in the old country."

"It's a brave new world" Armen said in English. Ervant, with his pomaded hair, silently hunched forward as he ate and sipped his coffee.

Reverting to Armenian, Armen said: "We used to eat plump, oil-cured olives in Constantinople. Anchovies, the brine washed off, had the savor of a kiss. And oranges tasted of sunlight and the tree." He extended his hand in a wistful gesture over the table.

"Yes," Ervant said, without looking up, "a beautiful country, Turkey - beautiful food and beautiful sun - but not so beautiful when they massacre more than a million of you. We're lucky. If we had stayed in our village, we'd all be dead. They would have murdered us without question."

His brother was right, Armen knew, but he had to change the subject for Mrs. Hagopian's sake. "Ervant, I was just thinking about when you came to America."

"Sure," Ervant said, "when Uncle Haig brought us to America – and why? To use us."

"We worked for Sun-Maid and Del Monte," Armen said. He saw that his landlady was listening, though he was not sure that this emissary from their lost world quite understood. "We were paid very, very little."

"But what a buck could get you!" Ervant smiled slyly, "Even a couple of very nice nights in San Francisco."

"It's important not to live for the dollar," Mrs. Hagopian said with polite fervor. She was objecting to Ervant's excess, and Armen restrained his smile as he remembered his brother's bravado as a child. When he was nine, at his entrance exam for school in Constantinople in 1914, the boy was asked about Roman history, and he spoke extemporaneously for twenty minutes. The examining professor said, "That is the most fascinating account of Roman history I have ever heard. Unfortunately, not a word of it is true."

But Ervant was admitted, probably because of his performance.

"It's true, baroness," Armen said now; "you can't count on money. Anyway it soon became scarce for us."

"Right, and soon there was no money at all," Ervant said, "because we stopped working for Uncle Haig."

"That was your fault," Armen teased in a suddenly neutral voice, as if they were playing cards.

"Somebody had to call his bluff, so I did! Uncle Haig would dress up in his clean white shirt and spiffy tie and spend his days at the Armenian coffeehouse, and one day after we all came in dirty and worn out from the fields – even Mama, his own sister – I asked him: 'Uncle, how much is in the savings box now?'"

Ervant was now stretching his hands out dramatically in front of Armen and the landlady. "Haig flew into a rage. Mama kept apologizing for me. She begged him to calm down. But he kept shouting how ungrateful we were. He never should have brought us from Turkey! He would have been better off bringing sacks of wheat! 'I'll give you the money – sure!' he yelled. 'And I'll hang myself. Will that satisfy you?' With that he stomped out, and we never got a dollar from him. We began working for ourselves. And now you're at Berkeley! And I'm on my way to Frisco."

"What's important is the family survives," Mrs. Hagopian said. "What can we do after all that has happened? We say we are fine, so we can seem fine or at least pretend."

As she talked in Armenian, Armen felt their conversation was itself like the food before them, nurturing them. He felt like singing a folk song – about good wine and good food – but now his landlady began talking about the fate of Armenia after the Genocide. In 1920, Turkey had threatened to invade across the Arax River near Mount Ararat, and Lenin saved their homeland by sending Russian troops to the border.

"It was the only way we survived," Mrs. Hagopian said.

"The only way," Armen said, "as a Soviet republic."

"There's hardship, even starvation, I know, but there is hope," Mrs. Hagopian said.

"Okay, okay. But what a cost!" Ervant said. "How many people did Lenin murder when he created the Soviet republics? And who knows how many Stalin will kill?"

"The Soviets," Armen said too loudly, "saved Armenia from extermination."

But now another student boarder wandered into the dining room, looking surprised. Mrs. Hagopian got up to greet him in her clear, slightly accented English.

Ervant whispered urgently, "Brother, I have to talk to you, alone. Right away." In English, Armen told his landlady they needed to talk privately.

As they rose to go into the living room, he glimpsed a forlornness in her face. He felt tears unbidden rising in his eyes. It was as if their leaving the dining room were some sort of grave farewell – it was irrational, he knew, for they were just doing what everyone did in America, hurrying on their way from point to point, one collision to another. Talking with his brother was one such collision. Ervant's ebullience made Berkeley seem unreal, and Armen, weighted down by his obligations, was drawn to his younger brother's sense that reality was a crapshoot, where you had to watch for the advantage and take pleasure when life allowed, where chance reigned and fate could always intervene.

"Armen, something has come up," Ervant said as they sat on the couch in the empty living room. "We don't have much time. We must decide this weekend, or we're lost. I'm telling you, it's our only chance to get rich: I can get a one-year lease on 320 acres, twenty miles outside of Fresno, prime land – raisins and peach. But I can't do it without you. If you go in, Arsine's husband will go in, and we can't lose if Nubar works with us. I need you, Armen. It's why I drove up. Mother and our sister, we all need you."

Armen was stunned.

"I'm not asking you to decide right now. Anyway, I'm itching to spend the evening with Gloria. You tell me tomorrow."

"Ervant, do you see what you're asking?" He could hardly speak.

"Listen, Armen. Just think about it. I'll come back by noon tomorrow."

They walked in silence onto the porch. He saw his brother to the yellow Dodge and watched him drive down Channing Way through the crisp February afternoon.

In the boarding house, Armen climbed the stairs to his small room with its bed, desk, chest, and stacks of books. There was a photo of Lenin that Madame Hagopian had placed on the wall. Sitting mechanically at his desk, he started to imagine abandoning his life here and returning to the San Joaquin Valley for a life on the land near Fresno.

From an envelope in his desk drawer, he took some photographs. Among them was one of big Uncle Haig and himself, taken when he first arrived in California. Haig wore a pinstriped suit, a shimmering tie, and two-tone shoes. The handsome man sat on an elegant chair with claws carved into the end of the arms. One of his big, powerful hands held a claw in its grip; the other rested in a loose fist on a crossed leg. Next to him, Armen stood dwarfed and wide-eyed, dressed in a corduroy suit, with his thick wavy hair combed but barely under control. He rested his hand on the shoulder of his seated uncle, who seemed twice Armen's size. Haig had pale, expressionless, Northern European-looking eyes. One of them squinted as if it were taking aim at you; the other was open and unblinking. This was the man who met Armen in the train station in Sacramento in June of 1920 and greeted him by reaching up and knocking away the beret that Armen had worn for years in Constantinople. Uncle drove him downstate, past Fresno to Delano, where he and the other workers taught him how to labor in the fields, how to cope with the ache and sweat, how to conserve his back as he leaned to work, and how to bathe his swollen hands in vinegar at night. This was the giant who, like a Turk, slammed a co-worker up against a tree one afternoon, holding him there, one large hand tightening around the man's neck, as if he would rip out his throat or, if an axe was handy, hack off his head. Uncle Haig was always ready for violence, but he was blind to his own brutality; he said proudly that he had killed a man in a knife fight in Bulgaria, when he first fled from Turkey. Always he was on the verge of exploding.

Yet Armen understood his Uncle. He remembered his first days in the fields when he felt the blinding sun blast his consciousness. At night on this reclaimed desert, the temperature dropped from 110 to 70, as the flatland descended into darkness. Suddenly you were almost invisible and bathed in numbing air. It was a blasted desolation you felt, reducing all the life you knew to your body and its basic functioning, breathing and sleeping, eating and excreting, killing or dying. Your mouth was silenced, and your eyes stared blankly at the blackened endless moonless fields. A year ago, the great Armenian General Andranik Ozanian had talked with Armen about the ruthless Fresno sun and the cruelty of life. Asthmatic but unbroken, Andranik had recently moved to Fresno. Sitting with Armen at the coffeehouse, the steely man with strangely kind eyes had said: "You're a fine, well-spoken young man, Armen. But life is a vicious dog, and it will sink its teeth into you if you let it."

Yes, he understood Uncle Haig. All of the Armenian immigrants here had been permanently scarred by what they carried with them from Turkey. They had been cast out of their homeland and ended up here in the Wild West, this vast vacant sunbaked land where they were all one step away from being gunslingers, their outrage always close at hand. You had to be ready for someone to murder or be murdered. "Did someone die?" was always the first question you asked.

How could such knowledge fit into a student's life? He remembered the hours he had spent translating Anatole France's "Thais" into Armenian, his tremendous effort to capture its voluptuous asceticism, and yet his goal – to become a poet, an intellectual – seemed unreal and false now. All the learning from his apprenticeship with Oshagan and all the poetry he loved by Verlaine and Mallarmé – how could his awareness of all this fit into the life of an immigrant in this savage world? Finally, it was idle to try pursuing an American profession, for it would involve the unimaginable labor of remaking himself completely. And what profession would let him enter it? Anyway, his fate was to float between worlds, among languages. He was an Armenian in America, in this land halfway around the globe from Anatolia. So words – whether Armenian or French, English or Turkish – became unreal; they could only bob and float, ungrounded and almost unspeakable. Words would not survive unscathed after the murder of a million and a half Armenians and the exile of another million.

"Sickdir pesavang!" The Turkish obscenity exploded from him. He was not sure to whom he directed it: fate, the Turks, America, himself, or his brother for making everything clear. It echoed hopelessly in the empty room.

Armen opened the French-Armenian dictionary on his desk, and the pages of words seemed all at once seductive and untrackable. He would take his books with him back to Fresno, and they would be a lifelong reminder of literature and its temptations. As he was closing the dictionary, he looked at the flyleaf. In the fall when he first came to Berkeley, he had copied a sentence there. "Je cherche toujours pour trouver un maison favorable pour moi:" I try continually to find a favorable abode for myself. For him, there was no favorable place. He felt, too, his lack of any true companion. The image of a small, beautiful, golden woman entered his mind, not a seductress like Thais, not a bearer of the syphilis he feared. No, rather, she was the muse he yearned for, a muse and soul mate.

Chapter 2
Artemis

NOVEMBER 6, 1928

—•—

The gravel crackled under foot as Artemis Haroutian walked down the driveway. An autumn wind blew over the hardpan fields and stirred up the dust at her feet. She would be exactly on time to open the store at 7:30, when she had opened it almost every morning since her eighteenth birthday. That was a year and a half ago, just when the letter arrived admitting her to Fresno State College. As she walked, Degas' paintings were on her mind, especially his paintings of ballerinas. They had fascinated her ever since she saw them last year in her Freshman Introduction to Art. The instructor was interested in the latest trends, even in the new cubism, but what most attracted Artemis were the prints he brought of Degas. The ballerinas inspired her. Sometimes they were really contorted, yet always they were floating in a pure, balanced world. Degas showed their reality, she thought, but he also gave them a beautiful place in what her teacher called "the order of things." Seeing them, she felt much joy.

Unlocking the grocery store, she quickly shut the door against the wind and turned on the lights. The scents of cinnamon, cardboard, and produce filled the empty store. Two non-Armenians soon entered. One was a gray-haired stranger in a shabby jacket and the other a young woman, who brought a glass bottle of milk and a loaf of bread up to the register.

"I heard your mother is sick," the sandy-haired woman said, handing her a quarter.

"No, she's fine," Artemis answered in a clear, unaccented voice. She smiled at the pasty woman, gave her a nickel in change, and bagged her groceries.

"No? Well, you tell Lucy be well from me. She's such a sweetie."

The paper bags were low, and she reminded herself to restock them from the supply room. She took a brown bag, placed the gray-haired man's bottle of sherry in it, and carefully rested it on the counter. The man put his coins down and eyed her coldly, staring at her hazel eyes and light reddish brown hair. His icy look conveyed such contempt that she wondered whether he might rob the store or even assault her. She was worried, but she offered him a cool, courteous smile.

"You people can't vote today, can you?" the man said.

"You people?" she said.

"I hope Hoover wins and sends you dirty Armenians back where you came from!" he snarled.

"I was born in Connecticut," she said coldly.

"Sure, and I'm the King of England," he said before he rushed out.

Outrage and bitterness welled up in her. She tried to steady herself. Slowly she inhaled the scents of the store – the citrus, the spices, and the old wood floor. She wished her sister would come to relieve her. It would be a little while yet, but soon she would be at the college. She walked to the back room to restock the bags. Then three more customers came. She swept the store, and other customers entered.

Finally, there was a lull. She took a book from her purse and placed it on the counter. "Poetry of Byron" was assigned for her sophomore English class this afternoon. She loved the slim volume, the silken flyleaf over the poet's image, curly haired and handsome, and the small sturdy pages with their clear, intensely black type. She loved the Romantics and especially this poet, for Byron fascinated her. She loved the fact he had been a great leader, fighting like a general, in the Greek war of liberation against the Turks. Also, he had said that Armenian is a beautiful language and had arranged to learn it at the Armenian monastery in St. Lazare, Venice. She was inspired by Manfred and Childe Harold: "I live not in myself, but become Portion of that around me." And she was deeply moved by the poet's adoration of women in "She walks in beauty, like the night," and the grace and nostalgia of it:

So we'll go no more a-roving
So late into the night,
Though the heart be still as loving,
And the moon be still as bright.

His poetry was so musical, and Artemis imagined him as a great troubadour like Sayat Nova, the classic Armenian poet with his lute. In Turkey, there had been musicians in her mother Lucine's family. Lucine's brother had played the lute in Harput where the family lived, and the two of them had been very close, for they had been orphaned when Mama was six, during the Turkish massacres of Armenians in 1896. Then when Mama turned sixteen, Papa had met her. Artemis' father-to-be had traveled back to Harput from Connecticut in order to arrange a marriage with Lucine. Mama's brother had threatened to kill Papa, but Lucine had left anyway. She voyaged to America with an Aunt in 1908, and as soon as she arrived, Dikran had married her. A year later, Artemis had been born in the Hartford General Hospital. And six years later, in

1915, Mama's brother was murdered by the Ottoman Turks, who destroyed Harput's Armenian Quarter with its beautiful boulevards and lovely restaurants.

"So you're reading on the job now!" an abrasive voice said in Armenian. It was Uncle Zorab. She immediately stiffened and closed the book. "You'll wreck your eyes," said her uncle – one of her father's stepbrothers. He lumbered up to the counter, his large stomach protruding above his belt. His hair was straight and brown and framed a big cow-like face.

"Hello, Uncle Zorab," she said respectfully.

"What are you reading?" He grabbed the Byron off the counter and held it upside down. "What's this? For college? You'll never marry! Who would ever marry a girl who goes to college?"

Artemis stared at her uncle and said nothing. He dropped the book on the counter. Maybe he resembled a pig more than a cow.

"What are you squinting at – you must need glasses already. Why don't you get off your ass and sweep the store? Everybody says you're lazy."

"Look around. I already swept the store," she said, looking down at her book. She heard the terrible hum of gossip in her uncle's voice, and her whole body tensed.

He let out a dubious grunt and said, "People say you're still going around with that Bolshevik. If you don't stop, it will bring shame to all of us – horrible ahmot down on you especially, the worst you've ever known!"

Artemis had heard Uncle Zorab say such things all her life, along with the echoing voice of her other uncle, Souren. They even criticized her father – their own half-brother, who was older than them by a dozen and more years.

"We told you to never see that Bolshi again!" He walked out of the store with a bag of red apples in hand and without saying goodbye.

He meant Armen Ararat, who was educated and artistic, like no one she had met before. He was the opposite of her uncle, for he was a brilliant man, an idealist, a socialist, and what was more, a successful raisin farmer, ever since returning from Berkeley three years ago. People at the Labor Day picnic or in halls loved to hear him give speeches, and he was friendly with the older Armenian intellectuals – Zarafian the actor of Shakespeare in Armenian, Kalfayan the composer, Moradian the great singer, and Lulegian the publisher of Fresno's leftist Armenian weekly. And Armen loved poetry. He would take her to Roeding Park, and they would sit on a bench surrounded by a semi-circle of Greek columns and a ring of ash trees. The thick-haired young man would recite Armenian and French poetry from memory in his expressive baritone – especially Verlaine and Mallarmé. "La chair est triste, hélas! Et j'ai lu tous les livres – the flesh is sad, alas, and I have read all the books. Oh, to flee and be among the spray and breeze, the sky and sea."

He was beautifully spoken, and he possessed a sort of grandness she had never encountered before. He was so kind and admiring toward her, and yes, there had been tenderness between them. He would call her an angel. Two or three times kisses had been exchanged in the park. It felt almost like an extension of his wonderful voice – how could she have stopped him? Insouciant, maybe a bit selfish, but always kind and worshipful, he seemed to dodge the traps of shame she knew too well.

And yet she had hoped never to have a suitor who was born in the old country, let alone one nine years older than she. Artemis had always wanted a suitor who was free of the agony of 1915, an American free to soar in America, not weighted down by foreignness and history. One summer, when she was twelve, the family had taken a trip back to Connecticut, and she had seen the big buildings rising tall in Hartford. What was it like to be the wife of the chairman of the Hartford Insurance Company! That was the life she wanted to lead, for she was born in America, and she could help her husband achieve anything, even become the president of the United States.

"Hi, Artemis," her sister Satenig said in her sunny way as she came through the door. It was already 9:40 a.m.

"You're late! You're so selfish."

Her sweet, red-headed sister frowned, and Artemis regretted her words.

"That's a nice green ribbon you're wearing," she said. "It's so pretty with your hair."

Her sister smiled and said, "Thank you, it's new." Satenig had just turned sixteen, and her temperament was serene and accommodating, a little like their mother. Of course, Artemis loved her other siblings too, but for Satenig, who now stood a head taller than her, she felt such fondness and solace, especially after what had happened when Artemis was five.

The two girls exchanged places, with Satenig taking up the post at the counter. Artemis got a quart bottle of milk to take home and said goodbye. The store stood at the edge of a twenty-acre farm east of Fresno, on the corner of Kings Canyon and Chestnut. She walked back toward the house over the gravel driveway. It was rocky and hard-packed, like the soil of the entire farm. The farm had failed soon after they moved there, and only the grocery store they opened had kept them solvent. Her father and mother had bought the twenty acres of hardpan because Uncle Zorab had browbeaten them into doing so. Artemis was two years old then, and she had an infant sister, Lucaper, who had been born, like her, in Hartford.

Then, three years later, in early 1915, her parents had taken baby Satenig out in their Model T and left little Lucaper and Artemis in the care of Uncle Zorab's wife. Auntie was washing clothes in a low, steaming trough of boiling water, which was on the path between the driveway and the house. When the two sisters in their little wool coveralls heard the Model T returning, three-year-old Lucaper jumped and toddled down the path toward the rocky driveway, and suddenly she stumbled and fell into the trough of blistering water. Lucaper screamed only once and turned purple in her steaming wool jumper. Artemis' mouth and throat and stomach had risen up. Her lungs had exploded in horror.

From then on, she knew that terror and death could descend at any moment. Yes, there was nothing she could have done, but nothing could lift the load of shame and terror that weighed on her, bending her shoulders and her legs, scarring her memory, and making her vulnerable to all fault-finding. Her stricken mother had withdrawn to her bed. Unable to walk, she crawled to the bathroom, and she did not speak for weeks. In the spring, when she finally got up, they told her that her brother had been killed in the Genocide. Artemis was five years old, and only her baby sister Satenig was some solace. She felt responsible for her, and so throughout their childhood, she had stood guard over her.

Now, Artemis stepped onto the porch. She opened the screen door and saw her mother standing at the glass-topped inner door and smiling calmly. Lucine's face was so placid, a wide oval, with slanted doe eyes which they called Kirgiz eyes. Her luxurious hair was dark and carefully bound in a wide bun on top of her head. Mama had a serene beauty that seemed French, though she was not.

The living room was dark because of the wide porch roof and the curtains that kept out the daylight. Artemis said hello and handed her mother the bottle of milk. From down the hall, Uncle Souren, Papa's other stepbrother, was playing the violin in his room. It was a sad folk melody called Groong, or The Crane. She knew it had been transcribed by the wonderful Armenian composer Gomidas. Though Souren's bedroom was down the hall and his door was closed, the sound of his violin filled the house with the melody and its yearning for a lost homeland.

"Artemis!" her father grumbled from the dining room.

"Papa, I'll be there soon," she answered, giving her mother a pleading look.

"Come here right now!" his high, irritable voice called out, and her mother waved her into the dining room. Her father was fifty-eight, twenty years older than her mother, and Dikran had suffered a stroke on his fiftieth birthday in 1920. It happened during a passionate argument about Armenian independence. Papa had been a colonel and a compatriot of the great hero General Andranik in the Armenian militia, which had risen up after the Sultan Abdul Hamid's massacres of Armenians in 1896. Papa knew firsthand how much courage was needed to fight the Turks. Eight years ago, at the Asparez coffee house, he was shouting about the danger that Turkey would overrun the new Republic of Armenia, and suddenly he could not shout, could hardly speak.

Now he sat partially paralyzed at the head of the dining room table. In front of him were plates of flat lavash bread and eggplant with peppers in her mother's rich Harput tomato sauce. Even in repose his face looked on the verge of speech, his eyes slightly bulging. With his good hand, he carefully wiped his mouth. His thin waxed moustache was worn expressively long at the ends.

"Zorab was here. This morning," he said. A sense of being wronged simmered in each word. "He said you disrespected him. But I know you did not disrespect him. He disrespects you. He says my daughter should not go to college. What right does he have to say you should not ..." The words would no longer come, and he stared in silence at Artemis. She watched him quietly, for there was no placating Papa when he was in a state. And she needed to get to school; she did not want to be late for her art class at 11 this morning.

"He says you are still seeing Armen Ararat. He says people talk about you and the Bolshevik! Are you bringing ahmot down on this family, Artemis? On me!" he said, and his eyes screwed in on her.

"Papa, I would never bring shame to you," she pleaded.

"Then how can he say it? He disrespects me – a colonel! I fought shoulder to shoulder with the great Andranik, God rest his soul. I fought to protect children like you."

She had no time to hear the stories he would spin again, yet she did not want him to be troubled. "Papa, I must go to the college.

I'll be back, and I'll explain. I must go to my classes now," she said. With that she scurried out of the room. Her mother called for her to eat something, but she had no time. First she went out the kitchen door, across the back porch to the outhouse nearby. Then she walked through the house to the bedroom she shared with her sisters. She thought her period might have come early, but it had not. When she was twelve and began to menstruate, she felt only shame. Her uncles had found out. "It's time to get her a husband," Uncle Zorab had said in front of everybody. "What's a woman for when she gets breasts? It's the way we do things, just like in the village." She was enraged by Zorab's cruelties. Like in the village! This was the 1920s in America, and she was an American.

On the back wall of the bedroom was a framed picture of Mt. Ararat she had drawn from imagination and with the help of the encyclopedia. She glimpsed herself in the foot-long rectangular mirror; she was well proportioned, but her rounded shoulders and her back looked as if they held up a heavy burden, and her small, pretty body felt oddly battered. Why, she wondered, but her face stared back from the mirror without an answer. She had her mother's round face and golden complexion, and her father's widow's peak and silky hair and his alert, brooding, slightly bulging Renaissance eyes. She put on a nice gray dress and gathered up her coat, notebook, and sketchbook.

"Are you ready to go?" she heard two voices say almost in unison through the bedroom door: her mother and her uncle. "I'm ready to take you," Souren said impatiently. Artemis opened her door and swept past them through the hall. She was already in the passenger seat of their Dodge when Souren opened the driver's side door. With his long violinist's fingers, he turned the key in the ignition and held the steering wheel as they drove out the crackly driveway. It always surprised her that the tense man's strangely elongated fingers could make such beautiful music. They passed the store and headed west on Kings Canyon toward town. Mama had asked Uncle Souren to drive Artemis to her classes. He was unmarried, in his forties, with thinning hair and sad eyes like her father, though he was slight and had neither Papa's physical intensity nor Uncle Zorab's piggishness. Also unlike Zorab, he had encouraged Artemis' painting, though slyly, never in front of other family members.

"You must be kind to your mother," he said in a soft yet oddly threatening tone. "Don't you dare get her into trouble."

"I would never do that, Uncle Souren," she said anxiously.

"Wouldn't you? They say she's too lenient, and they're right."

She would not answer him, and in silence they turned north now on Blackstone, toward the state college campus. If they had turned south and headed downtown, they would come to Armenia town, filled with immigrants living in the neighborhood surrounding the Armenian churches. Last year, Souren had driven them to the massive funeral there given for General Andranik, the great Armenian national hero and her father's commander. They had to park blocks away and walk to the church – Dikran with his cane, Lucine, Artemis, Satenig, Souren, Zorab and his wife. People said there were four thousand mourners, all of them survivors of 1915 in one way or another. Artemis saw only an ocean of heads and backs. They never got into the church. In the hall after the burial, though, her father had positioned the family at one of the tables for the Hok-e-jash – the "soul meal" – and they heard speech after speech. Across the hall sat her friend Armen Ararat with his family – his mother with her upright posture and striking white hair, his brother Ervant with his hair slicked back, and his sister and brother-in-law. When Armen stood and spoke about the General, everyone was riveted by his words.

All the while, her father sat, crippled and seething with paralyzed intensity, unable to summon the voice to tell his story to the assembly. In 1903, Dikran had been responsible for stockpiling rifles in Harput's Armenian cemetery; he was thirty-three then, and he could not bear to see a repetition of 1896, when Sultan Abdul Hamit II's troops massacred hundreds of thousands of defenseless Armenians. That autumn, General Andranik sneaked into Harput, contacted Dikran, and asked him to give half the weapons to his fighters. Andranik was a somber, noble man of immense physical courage, who could not be disobeyed, and in 1904, he used those rifles in his defense of Mush a hundred miles to the east. After the Genocide, Andranik had spent his last years in Fresno, struggling to cure his worsening asthma.

In those last years, Andranik had come to their house. Dikran and he would exchange stories of fighting in Turkey, and her father would listen to the handsome General's laments. Artemis had been allowed to sit at the dinner table the last time General Andranik visited. Lucine made him her famous manti – meat dumplings with yogurt – and kufta burgers in her rich Harput tomato sauce, with buttery pilaf. Artemis was hypnotized by the stern grandeur of the general's presence, the sweep of his authority as he daintily ate the tender dumplings.

"I've traveled half the world, Dikran, and I've never before seen a place like this. Do you understand? I have seen massacre and carnage. I have led armies into battle and with my bare hands killed those who were destined to die. But now I spend my days with petty, empty men who have little knowledge of life and death." His breathing was labored, yet his shoulders were stiff with power and pride. His fine eyes seemed kind and deeply sad, and Artemis thought of all they had seen. "The Armenians in Fresno are half-men. They know neither what they've lost nor what they're about to lose. In America, the sultan is not a person but a thing; its name is Money. It will swallow the Armenians whole, Dikran, and spit out their bones."

Andranik seemed to lead an alternative life to the paralysis surrounding her and her family. Artemis wished that a woman could lead such a life, could achieve such grandeur and sweep of spirit. If she could, Artemis too would become a general. Whatever adversity she met, no matter the challenge, she would never give up, even in the face of death. She would be ready for anything.

"Well, are you getting out?" Uncle Souren said to her.

"Oh, yes," she said. His car was parked on McKinley near the entrance to Fresno State College. Its walkways were lined with newly planted trees.

"Thank you, Uncle Souren," she added respectfully." I'll see you at four."

Once out of the car, she walked down a path through the arbor of plum trees, whose leaves still clung to the branches in the slanting November sunlight. It was a path she loved. She began to think about the prints her art professor had shown them; there were new images of Monet's meadows and Degas' dancers, and they gave her that joy she found nowhere else in life. She passed a small sign posted on the lawn and pointing the direction to a voting station in the college library. It was Election Day. Eight years ago women had been given the right to vote by the Nineteenth Amendment, and in two years when she was twenty-one, she would vote. Then she noticed a short, stocky young man slouching by the art building entrance. His hair was slicked back with thick pomade.

It was Armen's younger brother, Ervant, and people always said he was cocky and wild. He wore a fancy long-sleeved shirt, embroidered white on white, and it made him look oddly formal. It would be years before she put it together: that Armen and he had devised a brilliant plan.

"Artemis," he said in a hoarse whisper. She stopped by him on the steps. "Armen is sick. You have to come with me and help him." He stared earnestly into her eyes.

"I have a class," she said, upset and confused. "How can I help him?"

"He's in the car, Artemis. He's very ill," Ervant said, and then added dramatically, "Please, you must help me take him to the hospital!"

She was swept up by his urgency, and she followed him down the path past the plum arbor with its few, last clinging red and brown leaves rustling in the wind, which picked up now.

His 1924 Ford was parked in an alley across the street from the college. Armen was lying down in the back seat. When she approached, he sat up, bending forward as if he were in pain. He looked like he had been crying. His wavy hair was wild and unkempt, but he, too, wore a beautiful, embroidered white shirt.

Ervant touched her arm, and she glanced questioningly at him, as he opened the back door of the car.

"He's sick," Ervant said very softly. "He's sick with love for you."

"My angel," Armen said worshipfully as he reached to hold her hand, "my angel goddess, I can't live without you. Please, will you marry me?"

Panic gripped her, and she was unable to speak.

"Artemis," Armen cried out, "please, angel, I will die without you. Please marry me." He was watching her with anguished adoration, as she still stood speechless at the open door of the car. "I will hang myself if you don't marry me. You don't know how desperate I am. Please, angel, I love you." Suddenly his anguish penetrated her resistance.

"How can I marry you!" she cried out. "What would my family say!"

Ervant whispered, again very softly, by her side: "They already know. I had a letter delivered to them just now, telling your family that you're eloping with Armen."

She could not breathe. Her face felt simultaneously icy and hot, and her legs began to buckle.

Armen reached for her and helped her sit by him on the back seat. At a distance, it seemed, she heard his voice explain his plans. They would be married at one p.m., he said. Arrangements had already been made at the courthouse. And they would drive north to stay a week with John and Lucaper Hatchaturian, mutual friends in San Francisco. Then she would move into the house on his Fresno farm. She was outraged, but she was also amazed that this brilliant man was so deeply in love with her.

For the next two hours, she remained in a daze – during the drive to the courthouse, signing the official document, the brief ceremony in a judge's chambers, and later the drive north in the Model T borrowed from Ervant, who would use their old Chevy truck for the week.

Forty miles out of Fresno, they were driving through downtown Madera on 99, and she suddenly awoke.

"Stop here, Armen. I must send a telegram to my parents." So they parked by the Western Union office in the little farming town. She opened the creaking door. Standing in the dim office, she felt completely alone. The man in the cage asked her what she wanted. She wrote out her fifteen words on the form he handed to her: "Armen and I got married. Going away for week. It is my fate. Don't worry." Yes, she had been grasped by fate and had been forced to consent.

Armen was smiling broadly when she returned to the car. "Angel," he said. She sat in the passenger's seat, and the car rattled onto northbound Highway 99. From the corner of her eye, she kept glancing at him as they drove, seeing the smile flicker on his face and his now combed hair tremble in the breeze from the window, which was open a crack. This man had just destroyed her secret expectations of what life could contain – to lead a new, fully American life. And yet she was drawn to him, to this young genius. What was more, he adored her.

At the wheel, Armen began singing. It was a sweet folk song. "Kele kele kelit mermen: You walk and walk, and I would die to walk with you. I die for your beautiful spirit, my quail, my lovely little quail."

He sang loudly, above the car's motor, and she wondered at what had brought her to this moment. What were his motives, his faults, and his virtues? He called her his angel, his goddess, and she realized that his imagination had transformed her, Artemis Haroutian, into something like an icon, like the statue of her namesake, the classical goddess of the moon, of the hunt, of fertility itself – or maybe an icon like one of Degas' beautiful ballerinas. It moved her despite all her resentment, and she began to feel tenderness toward him. But then she wondered if he was deluding her. Perhaps he was the sort of rake who attracted an innocent girl to use her, to trap and exploit her. She had been tricked. Yet listening to him sing, she could not believe that he was so ruthless.

They reached San Francisco at 7 p.m., and Artemis was famished.

She had skipped breakfast, and they had eaten only a light picnic lunch with Ervant in Roeding Park – a celebration under the ash trees, during which she was mostly silent. But now she was delighted with the dinner that their friends the Hatchaturians served the newlyweds. There were the mezes of sour tourshi and string cheese and lavash, and then roast lamb and wedding pilaf with almonds, raisins, apricots, and dates. She even drank a single shot of strong, anise-tasting Raki with the others. She looked out the window of the small dining room, and she saw the fog-choked street and the yellow dots of isolated street lamps. Lucaper had kindly prepared the little back guest room for them with flowers and a special nightgown in a package on the bed, which had been made up with thick blankets and white sheets beautifully embroidered with pale gray leaves.

Initially she felt flattered by the adoration he expressed for her – her face, her skin, her breasts – and even a reciprocal attraction. Then there was the oddity of his organ against her and the uncomfortable moistness of their first lovemaking, though no pain. This, she thought, was what all the fuss was about. His gentle entry into her was touching, and she did not feel nothing. There was tenderness she felt and an irresistible impulse to protect, to care for her genius. After he finished and withdrew, he whispered "my angel, my angel," and then fell quickly to sleep. Slightly damp, she was bothered by the knot of feeling inside her, and for a time she remained awake beneath Lucaper's beautifully embroidered, stained sheets.

Chapter 3
Tigran the Great

APRIL 1, 1930

—●—

Armen wandered out the kitchen door of the farmhouse, and he immediately lowered his eyes against the blinding glare of the sun. His body ached from a sleepless night. The signs were not promising. Artemis had tossed and turned all night, waking him every hour from three o'clock on. "I think it's begun," she would say, lying on her back next to him in bed. She would turn away and stare blankly into the darkness. Her distended stomach was a small mountain beneath the blanket. She had become some other being than the beautiful shy angel he had married with her pale skin and hazel eyes, so other-worldly that touching and loving her had been a privilege and a joy. No, his twenty-one-year-old wife was now another species, whose shape and appetites and needs were alien to everything he knew. He felt so much gratitude for the new life within her, but he had not expected this peculiar feeling of shock. He could not help it, his strange detachment.

The gravel path crackled beneath his shoes. He saw that a timber from the driveway gate had come loose, and one end was sticking into the loose gravel. An animal or the wind must have knocked it free of the gate. He walked out the drive and squatted, bending his knees to pick it up. He had learned how to bend and stoop when he began working in the fields in 1920; the Mexican workers had told him not to use his back, but to bend his knees instead. It was a blessing, one of the first lessons he learned in America from his fellow workers, and it saved him from the lumbago that afflicted his uncle and other farmers. He wedged the timber back in place and walked toward the house, glancing out across the flatness of the landscape and the acres of fruit trees and the occasional Fresno ash. Some of the fruit trees were late-blooming and covered with flame-like buds, like a phoenix flaring pink and white. In a few weeks a uniform green would cloak all the living twigs and branches. Yet he would not prune this year. There was no point; even if he planted the fields or tended the vines or pruned the fig or apricot trees, nothing would sell. The long stalks of the grapevines remained uncut, and spiky sappers branched from rows of fig trees, looking like spidery tree roots struggling toward the indifferent sun. Figs were called tooz in Armenian, and today was Tuesday, April 1, 1930: it was fig day.

Armen felt restless and uncomfortable; he wanted to go back to bed. But he also yearned to leave. He could take the car and drive to Los Angeles, two hundred fifty miles to the south. He would not, of course; he would stay nearby because Artemis needed him. But he would have preferred going to visit his old friends in L.A., who had abandoned their farms around Fresno when the Depression struck last fall. There was no place for him now, Armen felt. The markets had disappeared, and there was no more demand for what the small San Joaquin Valley farmers produced – grapes, raisins, hand-fruit. In the last six months, thousands of Armenians had fled from Fresno.

"Armen," a matter-of-fact voice called from the kitchen door. It was Zarouhi Hagopian, the daughter of his distinguished old landlady in Berkeley. Short, with a thin pretty face and curly brown hair, she was like her mother, though more pert and energetic, a smart and gracious young woman. Zarouhi had come to visit from U.C. Berkeley where she was on break in her sophomore year, and she was helping out in the last days of a pregnancy. "Artemis says don't be absent minded. Stick close to the house, in case you need to go get Dr. Charles."

Armen clicked his tongue in an irritated tsk. He knew, he knew. He strolled across the gravel, past the vegetable garden they had planted in March, and toward the stand of spidery fig trees. No, the signs were not promising. The Americans called today April Fools' Day. Now that all the money was gone and capitalism had collapsed, he thought, what was the American Dream but a fool's dream? For ten years now, he had felt the unreality of life in America, the charade that money was; now the money had dried up, and the charade was exposed for what it was. He worked for almost nothing now at the Del Monte packing house.

Earlier in the twenties, when the market for raisins brought $200 a ton, he had mastered how to harvest three tons an acre, twice what other farmers produced. When he got married two years ago, he had picked his three tons on each of his twenty acres, though the price was a quarter of its earlier value. Still Artemis had been happy, and he was glad; the big harvest was a sort of wedding present for her. They had begun to think of moving to a larger farm with a nicer house since she had become pregnant. Now though, raisins were almost worthless, and they would have to sell this farm to survive, except that so far there were no buyers. Even Sun-Maid had gone bankrupt. But money seemed a charade to Armen whether he had tens of thousands of dollars in the bank or now when he had almost none. What counted as real was Armenia, its culture and literature. Two years ago, he was twenty-eight and as rich as he ever thought he would be, so he decided to join the Communist Party USA – to support the Soviet Republic of Armenia, of course.

He stood among the spiky trees and looked out across his acres of abandoned land; the soil lay uncultivated, weed-infested and hard, the vines wild. A fine dry dust had begun to cover the fig and ash and fruit trees. Under the burning sun, the land would revert to the desert it had been before. Even weeds would wither and turn to dust. He had felt how hard was the poor workers' lot, laboring under this sun, and he had always paid them more than the other farmers did. But now there was no money. The men had pleaded with him when he told them in early winter that there would be no work this year. He knew that all workers must have rights and protections, that socialism was the only answer. And he knew as well that he had exploited his Mexican and Filipino workers, but what choice did he have?

In his childhood village, the entire family had worked so hard in the fields, and then his father would take their harvest of silk or walnuts or hemp to the city. After 1912 when his father had died of typhus and they moved to Constantinople, his earliest writing was about the contrast between the nobility of the Armenian village and the greed and rancor of city life. The memory came again to Armen that his teacher, the wonderful writer Oshagan, had complimented him on one of those biting sketches in an Armenian newspaper in 1913, and had taken up the youngster, initiating him into the richness of literature, the poems by Verlaine and Baudelaire in French, and Shakespeare's sonnets in translation. It was a year later that he had introduced him to the new Armenian writers, to the class-conscious prose of Zarian and the beautiful poetry of Varoujan, which inspired his own poems about village life.

Of course, now, Armen knew that farm work broke the body, yet he felt that there was no finer vision of such work than Varoujan's "Tillers of Wheat:"

The sun flecks their faces,
Coursing like liquid light in their veins,

And the earth pulses and throbs under their strength.
As the tillers tread, the earth trembles, but not a shoot is bruised.
What if froth from the oxen's mouth is on their skin
And their ripped pants reek of the stable,
The living seeds sprout in their hands.

Oshagan had worked with his fellow writers, including Varoujan, on a new literary magazine: Mehian, which meant the pagan altar.

In March of 1915, Oshagan – with his curly moustache and his wire-rim glasses – had for the first time taken Armen to meet these men, and they walked through the neighborhood surrounding Galata Tower, north of Galata Bridge, trudging up the hilly maze of streets. At the top was a broad avenue, where rows of four-story European-style buildings had shop signs in Armenian, Greek, and Hebrew, and they heard the passersby talk in those languages and Turkish, Arabic, German, French, and Russian. They stopped at an anonymous door and climbed four stories to an apartment at the top.

Armen had imagined Daniel Varoujan as a brawny giant of a poet. A father, a husband, a poet, a farmer, the man must have big callused peasant hands, though he must have a depth and kindness in his eyes, like his teacher.

Oshagan knocked, and the loud voices within stopped. As they entered, Armen heard a woman's voice and children in the inner rooms; it was Varoujan's apartment. Outside the windows across the room, he saw Galata Tower loom up like the leaning Tower of Pisa among the rooftops. Beyond, the hilly city stretched out in the late March morning light.

"Daniel, this is Armen Josepian," his teacher said.

Waving gently to him was a short, thin man, and Armen could not believe that this incredibly slight man, who hardly filled the easy chair next to a small table stacked with books, was the poet. He wore a narrow moustache above sensitive lips, and his thinning hair was sleekly combed in the French style. The eyes, however, were classically Armenian, dark and almond-shaped, looking like deep reservoirs into which the world poured its sights. There was another man sitting on the couch, who looked like the Daniel Varoujan Armen had expected; he was introduced as the poet Rouben Sevag, and the warm bear of a man stood to shake the youngster's hand. By the double windows, which framed Galata Tower outside, another man sat at a desk; he smiled quizzically when Oshagan introduced Armen. This short fat man was Gasdan Zarian, the satirist, recently returned from Paris. He said now: "Please, Daniel, your poem, let us hear it once more."

Varoujan sat quietly in the stuffed chair; his hand held a small, decorated Iznik cup of coffee; the pungent smell filled the Galata living room. Armen sat between his teacher and Sevag on the couch and listened, rapt, as the poet began reciting. With his wisp of a moustache and sparse hair, Varoujan looked like a thin Baudelaire. He spoke a poem, clearly not for the first time, in a lyric nasal voice:

In a bowl on my worktable
There's a handful of earth taken
From my homeland. This sponge of wounds
Drank up life and the light of the sun
And turned blood-red, being a slice
Of Armenian earth: nothing
But the pure element preserved.

The poem said that the rust-colored, iron-rich earth of the Caucasian mountains in ancient Urartu – where Armenian was first spoken – had turned a darker red from the blood of Armenians, massacred first by Scythians and Persians, then by Greeks and Mongol hordes, and recently by Ottoman Turks. Varoujan's hand lifted his finely decorated porcelain cup of coffee, and it was as if he lifted the bowl of the blood-red earth. "Here, I hold it toward you," and so the poem ended.

In a thin lowered voice then, Varoujan had said, "The rumor is that they're rounding up Armenians once again in the outlying villages. The Turkish army is so efficient, no?" The other men began speaking immediately.

"Well, we have no army to oppose them," Sevag said.

"There is our Andranik," Oshagan said. "But he has only a small band of partisans. And of course we have no Lenin."

"We certainly have no Lenin, whom I met once in Brussels!" Zarian said, not for the first or last time. "I remember he said without an army there can be no effective opposition. But, my friends, here in Constantinople we're safe – here among the Orthodox." Armen knew that the Orthodox meant the residents of Galata, the Armenians, Greeks, and Jews, the doctors, lawyers, shopkeepers, artists, and bohemians.

Zarian turned then to Armen and smiled at Oshagan's promising young pupil. "Of course, we could all flee to Paris, Armen. Next year, let me take you there and introduce you to Picasso and Cocteau and Stravinsky. And you'll study politics and literature at the Sorbonne."

"I would like to," Armen said, but he thought of his mother; maybe his family could move with him to Paris

"You write cutting little sketches, don't you?" Zarian continued. "I liked your piece in the newspaper. You have some nerve."

"I hope so," the boy said, with bright assurance.

"But, Armen Josepian, you need a new name," Varoujan said in his high and thoughtful voice. "All our names are made up."

"My name is a pen name," Zarian said. "Armen is not bad, but we must do better than Josepian."

"It should be a classical Armenian name," Varoujan said.

The youngster stood, small and proud, among these writers, who were more than twice his age. He had thought about the names he wanted to call himself. "Aslan," he said, "I've thought of Armen Aslan, the Lion."

Zarian had laughed. "You may have the lion's bite, but not his roar or his mane. Let's think of something less predatory. You need a name right out of ancient Armenia, from Urartu. What about Ararat? Armen Ararat."

"Armen! Armen!"

The screams came from the little farmhouse. Young Zarouhi stood anxiously signaling at the kitchen door. "Armen, come! Her water broke! Come quickly!"

He ran to the house, dodged through the kitchen to the bedroom. There Artemis sat up rigidly in bed, her angelic face drained of blood, looking as if she had seen a ghost. Her swollen body was still, but she bunched her hands up in fists. Zarouhi stood next to her, kindly and fidgeting.

"Armen," Artemis said, exhausted, "My contractions, they've begun. Go now. Go pick up Dr. Charles, like we said. Go right away."

"Right away," he said. He suppressed an edge of fear in his voice, but he could not move. "Will you be all right, Angel? With Zarouhi?"

"Just go!" the two women said.

He drove his old Chevy pickup out of the gravelly driveway onto the highway, east toward the city. He sped anxiously past miles of abandoned farms, dusty and dilapidated. Soon, he passed Kearney Park toward downtown. Fresno seemed like a ghost town to him; it had shrunk in six months to two-thirds its size. It was midmorning Tuesday, yet there was no traffic. Where were the fifty thousand people who remained in this landlocked town? It was the opposite of magnificent Constantinople, which the Turks had renamed Istanbul. He read last week in the newspaper that they were transforming the city into a military zone, with the army everywhere on the streets. When Zarhoui Hagopian screamed "Armen, Armen," he had remembered the April morning fifteen years ago in Constantinople when he had seen her distinguished father hanging from the gallows in Beyazit Square.

There was suddenly a honk, and he instinctively put his feet on the brake and clutch. A car rushed around his truck, the driver gesturing furiously for him to hurry up. Without realizing it, he had slowed to a standstill, for he had passed Dr. Charles' office on K Street. He pulled into a driveway, drove back, parked, and walked into the brick building. After fifteen minutes, as arranged, the doctor in his suit and tie scrambled into the passenger seat of the truck. Dr. Charles was an awkward, impractical-looking physician, a tall gray-haired non-Armenian, an odar, whose air of distraction made Armen wonder how competent he was. Artemis liked him, though, and would hear nothing negative about him.

The two men spoke little as the truck rumbled past Kearney Park toward the Ararats' farm. He did not really know much about Dr. Charles, but he sensed that his Armenian patients remained a mystery to him, even after the decade he had spent in Fresno.

"You're from back east, no, doctor?" Armen spoke up.

"Philadelphia," he replied in a deliberate voice.

"Yes?"

"There were food riots in Philly recently. Rough times."

"Yes, rough times."

Then the doctor turned to face him as he drove. "Have you read about the new planet?" he asked.

"Yes. The astronomers have discovered..."

"Pluto. The astronomers named it Pluto."

"God of the underworld."

Dr. Charles looked surprised that his patient's immigrant husband was not illiterate, but he still maintained his patronizing air. The two men fell silent. The doctor seemed to be studying the abandoned fields they passed in the speeding truck.

Armen wondered why Dr. Charles remained in Fresno. Of course why really were any of them here? Why was Armen driving down this dusty road instead of living in Paris and studying at the Sorbonne? Of course, Uncle Haig had written from California, but in any case, how could he be an intellectual when bare survival was at stake, when all of his family lived in jeopardy ever since 1915? That May, he remembered, two bone-thin cousins from their village across the sea had knocked on their door in Constantinople. Under warm blankets, they kept raving: "The Turks are at the door. Don't you hear? Don't let them in, Auntie." Mama, Daddy, Grandpa, Grandma, they were all burned alive. Uncle was beheaded.

Now he drove the truck up the gravel drive. Zarouhi opened the farmhouse door and gestured for them to come quickly. There were pots of boiling water on the stove in the kitchen. The two men stepped into the hall, and Artemis was crying out on the other side of the bedroom door. The doctor put his hand up.

"You wait in the kitchen, Armen, or better yet outside." At the kitchen table, he sat frozen as Zarouhi came in and out with steaming pans of water. Finally, he could no longer stand the muffled screams. He went outside and started pacing back and forth on the gravel of the drive. It was already afternoon, and he was hungry, though Zarouhi was too busy to make him food – and of course Artemis could not.

After a while, words came to him, echoing the rhythm of his pacing. He yearned to write a poem to be a garland of words for their first-born child. The fruit trees were in bloom, the tooz trees sprouted their figs on this blossoming Tuesday, and here now was Tigran the tiger. Yes, if it was a boy, that was the name they would give the baby.

He thought of all the Armenian writing he had done in these past fifteen years, and he saw that much of it was one long lament: "In exile I cannot forget," "Sad Songs of the Village," "Bat Cries in the Mosque." In recent years, he had written poems about love in the village of his youth; then a year ago, in the first spring of marriage, there was the love poem, "Krung" – Spring – which he had written for his beloved wife:

At the door, she waited in the sun and handed me a cup
Of cool water to slack my thirst on a warm spring day in May.
I have never seen such a smiling love, such lively eyes,
Such a fragrant sweet embrace, like the first rainbow of May.
Spring breathed in each tulip kiss, and innocent delight filled
Her stormy chest with proud love on this flowering May day.
In English, the shy Armenian girl with pomegranate cheeks spoke
Her marriage oath, filled with fervent love on this May morning:
A fragrant wreath of flame-like buds, red and pink and white,
Circled her forehead, shining with holy oil and the promise of life.

Finally, last November he had written "A Worker's Faith," a poem he would use in his speech this April 24th at the Ramgavar commemoration of the fifteenth anniversary of the Genocide and the tenth anniversary of the founding of the Armenian Socialist Republic. The poem spoke of the great betrayal that was the Depression, a barbaric assault on the workers of the world. This new capitalist genocide of the common man, was it so different from the Turkish massacres of their martyred people?

But what was he thinking? He must not shed bitter tears on the day their baby was being born.

"Armen," Zarouhi called at the kitchen door. It felt like an hour had passed.

"It's a boy!" she said, her face a palely smiling flower. "Artemis is okay. I'll tell you when you can come in and see them." And she rushed back in.

Clouds filled the valley sky all the way to the horizon, the spring wind whipped up the dust, and patches of sunlight broke through the clouds, making the trees glitter in the wind. He imagined the perfectly formed infant with his face a flowering white bud, smiling with joy; on his tiny forehead there was a garland of green laurel leaves, foretelling achievement and success. He paced again slowly over the gravel, beginning to hum a folk tune. Zarouhi appeared once more, and he went inside.

The doctor was washing his hands and arms at the sink.

"Thank you, Dr. Charles," Armen said with fervor and stepped toward the bedroom. But the doctor began to speak with cool objectivity.

"I had to use instruments. There's some bruising, some injury, but time heals all wounds."

"Time heals all wounds?" Armen said.

"She must have been in labor all night, and still it wouldn't be born easily. You heard her, I'm sure. She's been in a lot of pain."

Armen had had enough of his talk. He walked into the bedroom and saw Artemis holding the tiny bundle to her breast. She had dark circles around her eyes as if she had been punched, and the skin of her cheeks and forehead was paper white.

"Come here," she whispered sweetly.

When he drew close, he saw dark purple bruises covering their baby's face.

Worry and rage gripped him, but he showed no sign. "Angel," he said and reached to touch his wife's forehead and their baby's soft bruised cheek.

"Our Tigran!" she said out loud, and tears formed in her eyes. The infant stopped nursing and began to cry. "He will be okay," she said. "Now go. You haven't eaten; Zarouhi will feed you something."

In the kitchen, the doctor was waiting, dressed and ready to go; Armen would drive him back to town and eat when he returned. Within an hour, the early April sun would be setting.

In the truck, they talked very little at first, and then Armen spoke up.

"Doctor, we cannot pay you right away. I will have to pay you later."

Dr. Charles was silent for a while and then said, "It's rough times."

"This is what America has come to."

"Yes, it's rough times, all around."

Armen no longer listened. He thought about tomorrow morning and having to go back to work at the Del Monte packing house, side by side with his brother and his mother. He thought about his new son, bruised but alive, who would be like his namesake Tigran, the great king of ancient Armenia. Tigran the Great must never lead such a life – the hard-pan, hand-to-mouth, back-breaking life that Armen now led.

Chapter 4
The burning house

JUNE 20, 1938

—•—

She lifted herself off her side of the bed. Armen was still asleep and snored away. It was 6:30 a.m., and already it promised to be a scorching day. She put on her slippers and her coral robe, and walked to the bathroom and into the living room where she raised the windows and swung the front door open. It was stuffy, and the house had to be aired out, now when the temperature was still below 70. Outside their cinder-path driveway, bleached and dusty, wound out to the highway. A slight wind stirred little eddies of dirt, which moved steadily across the dry fields. It was like their previous two farms, except that the smell of charred wood rose from the plowed-over rectangle of ashen earth where their two-story Victorian had stood. Next to the grave of the house was a stand of fig trees; their wide leaves were blackened, and their scorched limbs curved toward the earth or grasped at the sky. The fields where Armen had irrigated were all shades of green. Where he had not, the land had the uniform parched gray-brown pallor of dead skin, stretching out to the horizon. Haze obscured the light from the newly risen sun.

In the kitchen she opened the back door and raised the window above the sink. Through it, she caught the smell of garden mint and basil. By nine, she would close up the house, pull the shades, and hope that the temperature outside would not reach as high as it threatened. She had not yet fully mastered how to cool this old, one-story house. It was a month since they had moved in, making their Filipino foreman take his family and leave. She felt sorry for them, but how could they help it? They could no longer afford to pay him and needed to occupy this house after theirs burned last month. She used to believe that she could escape from all this loss and meanness. With energy and imagination, she wanted to develop a sweeping authority that would connect her to the larger world. But she was reduced to living in this ramshackle house from which they had kicked out the foreman's family.

Artemis paused at her sink. She slowly drank some refrigerated water from the blue mug she kept for herself. Then she took a cantaloupe from the bin in the icebox and placed it on a wooden board on the counter; in a kitchen drawer she found her sharpest knife, and she proceeded to peel, clean, and slice the melon for the family's breakfast. Stacked against the wall by the kitchen table were a few boxes she still needed to unpack, possessions saved from the blazing house.

It was the second house of theirs to burn in ten years, since she and Armen married in 1928, and this was the third farm to which they had moved since the price of raisins had fallen in the Depression. Even after Franklin D. Roosevelt ended Prohibition, the price had not risen. Roosevelt was her hero; she had voted for him in her first presidential election six years ago. His picture was framed on the living room wall, between Armen's portrait of Stalin and her painting of Mt. Ararat, its rounded shapes gray white against a cloudy blue sky. Stalin was there because he was Armenia's protector, though Artemis wondered at what a tyrant he had become. But socialism was the only hope for their shipwrecked lives, now that almost everyone was drowning in poverty. Yet their family endured, despite the horrible Depression; they even survived with some integrity. She remembered how Armen drove down to the Election Board to register the Communist Party for the local 1936 election. It was a courageous thing for him to do, but bitter too, for in these years they felt there was nothing more to lose.

At least they had kept this farm. Other than that they lived hand-to-mouth. Most of their friends had left for Los Angeles and San Francisco, the fog-bound seaport where Armen and she had spent their first nights together. It was a temptation to go there, but they had decided to stay in Fresno. They could have bought land dirt cheap that others had abandoned if they had had any extra money. Of course, some of their relatives were buying it up. There was the farm on Shaw, north of the city, which was bought by Nubar and Armen's sister, Arsine, who was so proud and penny-pinching. And there was the land far to the south of the city that her sister Satenig's greedy husband, Nick, had bought, boasting all the way. Resentment filled Artemis, even though she was uncomfortable about feeling so vindictive.

She heard Armen's mother open her bedroom door, walk into the living room, and close a window.

"Zabel, leave it open," Artemis called out in Armenian, for her mother-in-law spoke only a few words of English. "I'm cooling down the house."

"But it's cold."

"Put on a robe."

Entering the kitchen, Zabel wore a white terry cloth robe over her nightgown, and her white hair was let down. She was a strong, thin woman with large gnarled hands, and she always stood with her back and shoulders straight; Zabel was an inch or so taller than Artemis.

"Cantaloupe," she said. "It smells good." She reached for the blue mug on the counter and began rinsing it at the tap.

"That's my cup, Zabel," Artemis said, as she had for weeks now with more and more irritation. "I'll get you a glass."

The white haired woman placidly watched her as she rinsed and dried her hands, got a glass from the cupboard, and poured water from the icebox.

"Thank you," Zabel said and sat down at the kitchen table. "It was so good yesterday for the two families to get together. Arsine made a nice Sunday dinner."

They always said Arsine made such a nice this or a superior that. According to Zabel, her daughter was perfect, and Armen seemed to agree, poker-faced as he was. His sister was two years younger than he; she was proud, tall, and already gray at thirty-five years old. Arsine possessed her mother's rigid posture and formal ways, inherited from Constantinople, a polite formality so unlike good manners here in America. It was the bond of the Old Country that connected Armen to his sister and mother. Living in Turkey in 1915, they had witnessing horrible things. But Artemis thought that the bond among them was based on false pride. The favoritism toward Arsine enraged Artemis, who cooked her own mother's delicious Harput recipes as well as mastering her mother-in-law's Istanbul recipes, certainly as well as Arsine; she was considered such a fine cook and a superior character, mostly because she had a big house and more land than Armen and Artemis. So why didn't Zabel move in with Arsine and her husband, Nubar? Why did she prefer living with her son and daughter-in-law? It was galling to Artemis that she, twenty-nine years old and the daughter of a colonel, had fallen into just the trap she had hoped to avoid: a life of resentment, powerless and petty. She was the servant of all, the leader of none. Her hands began to tighten into fists. And she hated that so much tension and anger welled up in her.

Tigran and Garo raced into the room, energized and loud: "Mama, Mama," they called out, and they took seats at the kitchen table, which was laden now with plates of melon, feta cheese, yogurt, olives, and flat crackery lavash, which Artemis had sprinkled with water to soften slightly.

"Good morning, Grandma," Tigran said politely in Armenian; the boys spoke English with Artemis and each other, but whenever they were in Zabel's presence, they spoke Armenian out of respect and necessity. She greeted her grandson and leaned over to kiss him. Tigran was a small sturdy eight-year-old, with alert blue eyes and a shock of wavy dark brown hair.

"Good morning, Grandma," Garo echoed – the younger by a year and a half but already as big as his brother. His hair was blond and curly. Even as a baby he had dreamy, hazel eyes like his mother's, and Artemis could not help herself, she loved him so. When he was born, he had been huge, weighing 13 pounds at birth on the family cheese scale. It was as if he had gestated a full year, and his face had been fully formed and beautiful. Now, he sat lamb-like and eager on the other side of Grandma, and Zabel kissed him too, on the cheek.

The youngster reached across her to take a piece of melon from the platter in front of Tigran, who grabbed Garo's hand.

"Be polite, Garo! Say please pass it," Tigran said with a slight frown; he had said this before, and Garo had not heard more than once.

They all began to eat and occasionally to talk. Watching her sons, she felt a pang of affection deep within. She loved and trusted Tigran, who was tough and already understood what life was about. And she adored Garo, who was a dreamer, with his innocent energy and his intensity and his wide owlish eyes like hers. She remembered over a year ago, when Armen could not start the car, and the little boy had walked up to them. He had helped Papa, he said; he had put sand gas in the car. Even now at six-and-a-half, it was possible he still believed such silliness, for Garo was ethereal. He lived in a world of dreams and high hopes, just like her – except that she had known early on how terrible the world could actually be. She hoped Garo would never learn to be as wary as she was.

Now she heard Armen walking down the hall, and then there he was. He had already dressed in polished shoes, formal pants, and a short-sleeved white shirt, open at the neck. At five feet five, her husband was only a few inches taller than her, but Armen was still an impressive man, especially when he wore the clothes she picked out for him. He looked so calm and dignified, she thought. She still felt drawn at times to her thirty-eight-year-old husband, though she kept all that to a minimum, only when he seemed most forlorn and in need, which was rare for he seldom approached her now; certainly she wanted no more children. She respected his intelligence and his brilliant public speaking, for he made fine speeches at gatherings of leftist Armenians, though now he seldom wrote his beautiful poems. Here he was, dressed up as if he was going to make a speech, and she wondered why. She would not ask, though, not yet. Armen was really very private, even uncommunicative. He had so much on his mind, but there were many times when she felt he owed her more than he gave.

"Good morning, Mother. Boys. Angel," he smiled briefly, sat down to breakfast, and Artemis filled a plate for him with cheese, olives, and lavash.

"Pop, they say Jesse Owens is going to visit Fresno next month," Tigran said, in Armenian. "You know... the runner who won the Olympics?"

Armen raised an eyebrow and let out his characteristic tsk, tongue against teeth.

"I can run faster than anyone," Garo said, eyeing everyone at the table.

"Could we go see him?" Tigran asked.

"We'll see," Armen said in a noncommittal voice, and in the same voice, he spoke politely to his mother. "I saw Mr. Issakian at the Asparez. He sends his regards."

Zabel did not respond. Artemis knew Mr. Issakian wanted to marry her mother-in-law.

After a minute, the boys got up from the table, as did Zabel.

"Thank you," they said as they left the room. As he ate, Armen began reading a People's World, the communist daily newspaper, which he took from a pile on one of the unopened boxes. She too began to eat some of the pungent melon and a little of the tangy feta with the cracker bread.

"They say," Artemis said about her mother-in-law's friend, "that Mr. Issakian is from Bitlis – he's dark skinned. Hard working and penny-pinching."

Armen raised an eyebrow and directed a tsk at her. Always he was like that, suggesting with a single sound or a glint in the eye that he had thought of everything you thought plus a million things beyond. It did not matter to her if he thought her gossipy, though his superior manner did sometimes bother her. It was as if he felt the shocks he had absorbed in the Old Country entitled him to a sort of arrogance. She understood that, and yet his taciturn air disturbed her, especially because he depended on her so. The man she had married ten years ago could be self-indulgent, impulsive, and terribly restless, always on the move from farm to farm. Sometimes he would disappear for a week, calling from L.A. to say that he was staying with their friends.

From the beginning, his impatience had scarred them both. After the marriage, her family had refused to see him. One day, Armen came home somber and completely silent, as if he had witnessed an atrocity. She found out that her Uncle Souren had stopped him on the street and said: "You're a scoundrel, Armen Ararat, a man without honor." After Tigran and Garo were born, only her mother had treated her with occasional decency or kindness.

Now Armen took out his pipe, filling and lighting it, and he got up from the table. Freshly shaved and his black hair nicely combed, he looked as ready to meet the world as when they stood before the municipal judge in 1928.

"Where are you going?" Artemis asked. "You're all dressed up."

"Out."

"You're all spruced up. Where are you going?"

"I must see someone, Angel," he said in a slightly pleading tone.

"But who?"

"Someone. You'll find out," he said, tsking and walking out the open back door. She watched him. Pipe in hand, he went to smoke under the grape arbor, inspecting the garden and the dusty fields in the distance.

Withholding information was not unusual for him. But the efficiency was strange, the fact that he had bothered to look so neat and pressed. Usually his appearance was clean enough but sloppy, for often a sort of languor would set in, and he would say, "Angel, I am dying," and retreat to his bed. The doctors were unsure about what to think and what to do – as usual. They guessed that it was the aftermath of some disease he had contracted in the Old Country, some malaria or anemia associated with the Mediterranean region. This disease had no symptoms except exhaustion, and headache.

Now, through the kitchen window, she watched Armen pull away from the house, down the long dirt driveway; his mother sat in the car passenger seat, on her way to the packinghouse. The children were at the back door, and Artemis went out with them. The deep irrigation ditch bordered one edge of the farm's wide yard, and it carried the swift, audible flow of Sierra water.

"Stay away from the ditch; you could drown," she told the two boys as she did every day during all the years of their play here. Under the grape arbor by the house, she leaned to take the hose and pull it over to the garden to irrigate the plants – tomatoes and peppers, eggplant, basil and mint, and a pale, soft-skinned Armenian gutah cucumber. The cantaloupe and watermelon were in a bed of their own to prevent the gutah from cross-fertilizing. The sky had become a vast blue oval and the sun a blinding white disk. It was already almost eighty degrees, and she had forgotten to close up the house to keep in the cool.

"I have to go in," she told her sons.

The boys were racing back and forth in the driveway, holding their hands up to eye level with two fingers pointing together, as if they aimed guns.

"Stop, or I'll shoot."

"Too bad, Garo. Bang, bang! You're a slow shot, stupid."

Artemis was glad Tigran had an acid tongue. Though he did not look like a general, still he was willing to put people in their place. He would be a good corporal or sergeant, skilled at keeping people in line.

She reentered the stucco house, closing the door behind her. She walked through its one story, lowering windows and shades, shutting the front door. In her bedroom, she went to the toilet and then put on a shapeless, flowered housedress. In the kitchen, she filled a pail with hot water and added some Hexol to it. She took the steaming, strong smelling water, along with mop, sponges, and other equipment, to the end of the house. She was going to work her way forward from the tiled shower attached to the house and then down the hall, from room to room. Every Monday she cleaned the house until it shined. Of course, they always boasted that Arsine's house was so clean, but she had two daughters to help her, and they treated her like a queen. Artemis deserved compliments, too, she thought. She was a strong, efficient hard worker. And unlike Arsine, she was loyal. They were selfish – that was the problem with the Ararat clan, and especially with her sister-in-law. A cold stubbornness could descend on Arsine at any time, and if it served her interest, she was always capable of cutting a person off.

"Bang, bang."

"Quit it," Tigran said. "You can't shoot anymore."

On her knees cleaning the bathtub now, she heard their voices outside the window.

"Yes, I can."

"No, you can't. You're already dead as a doornail."

In their play, she heard echoes of what had happened to Armen's younger brother, their poor confused Uncle Ervant. She had forgiven him for his role in Armen's plan to marry her; if there was any blame to assign, it was her husband's. Since that time, Ervant had often gotten into trouble with the law, and when he was on the run, it was Artemis who had hidden him, not Arsine, his own sister, who had washed her hands of Ervant.

But Artemis knew and felt for what had happened to the poor man. He had charm and a gift for inventing stories, so when the Depression hit, he used these to make money, for what could he do then other than employ those cons? He had a short, disastrous marriage in Oregon, even a son somewhere. But things got only worse, and soon – poor injured soul – Ervant felt threatened by enemies, people who exploited him, as if the world were full of Turks. That was what his lawyer said at the trial – it was Aram Saroyan with his flowing white hair, Willie's and Daisy's uncle. Soon Ervant became a sneak thief and finally a bank robber. Almost caught four years ago in San Francisco, he fled to L.A. From a wanted poster, a policeman recognized him and followed him to his hotel. There was a shootout, and Ervant fled again, but the policeman died of his wound.

Late at night, he had knocked on their door. Zabel screamed when she saw him, and she collapsed in his arms. Artemis nurtured him and listened to him; they gave him money, and he disappeared into America, but he was recognized again and captured. At the trial, the Armenian attorney dressed him all in white – long-sleeved shirt, pants, and even shoes. With his lawyer's magic, Aram Saroyan painted the picture of a person quite unlike her brother-in-law, and it saved Ervant. The judge, bitterly disappointed, spoke from the bench: "You deserve the death penalty! But this jury has decided differently."

Saroyan's summation to the jury was even more forceful than any speech she'd heard Armen give: "Ladies and gentlemen, whether you are a Yankee or an immigrant, can you imagine losing over a million of your people in a matter of months? That was what happened twenty years ago to the Armenians in Turkey. Can you imagine being ten years old when this happened? What if you saw your government gather together the leaders in your community, the most distinguished doctors and businessmen and authors and politicians, and hang them publicly on gallows built in the downtown square, as the Turks did where young Ervant lived in Constantinople on April 24th, 1915? And what if you were a fine sensitive ten-year-old like Ervant, and you saw your government send its army into every town and village where your people lived and herd all of them into the public squares? There the Turkish Army shot or enslaved all the men and made the old people, women, and children walk – yes, Ladies and Gentlemen, I said walk – out of Turkey. Few survived the thousand-mile ordeal through the burning desert under the blinding sun. Little Ervant heard that his grandma and grandpa died tragically in this way. All his aunts and uncles from the village where he was born were killed in this way. Can you imagine the impact this would have had on you when you were ten? Poor little Ervant was a victim of the Armenian Genocide, the most terrible systematic massacre in history. Take pity on this poor man, Ladies and Gentlemen, for he bears the terrible wounds inside him to this day."

Ever since the trial, Artemis and Armen and Zabel had tried to help him. They drove up each month to visit him in San Quentin, on the northern edge of the Bay Area, and they would talk with him in a room through a big wire fence stretching from floor to ceiling. But not his sister Arsine. Loyalty and kindness were not words in her vocabulary. Poor Ervant was a sweet, lively man, and it was in self-defense that he had murdered someone. Was there such a clear line between goodness and crime? Her sister Satenig's Nick was a good citizen, yet his greed and bluster led him to do shady things.

"Mama! Mama!"

Outside, Tigran kept screaming, and she dropped her sponge and ran down the hall. Her whole body was bent with terror. The old horror gripped her. It always waited for her, emerging with each possibility of death ever since her little sister drowned in scalding water. She burst into the yard, scanned the scorched earth where their house had been, and ran toward the seething water of the irrigation ditch.

"Mama!" she heard again, but it was from the vegetable garden. Fifty feet away, Tigran was standing among the flourishing leaves. Garo was getting up from the dirt. A tomato plant, which had been as tall as he, now lay crushed next to him.

She came toward him and heard Garo's English words. "I'm sorry, Mama. I'm sorry. I'll never do it again!" Her arms unfurled toward her son and held him to her breast. "My sweetie, my sweet Garo, you're okay." He nodded in her embrace, and she reached to hold Tigran too, as her hips and back relaxed.

"I told you, Garo, it's stupid to run in the garden!" Tigran said, but his impulse to be critical was softened by his relief that Artemis was not angry.

She frowned as she pushed the tomato leaves away to reveal the broken central stem. "Garo, from now on be careful! Take the broken plant to the garbage," she said seriously, as if it were an important responsibility she assigned him. "Then help Tigran cultivate the vacant space. And think about what you are going to do for Papa to make up for this."

Sweating from her run in the extreme heat, she walked back to the house. Inside the cool, darkened living room, she sat on the couch. Her fists were tightly clenched on her lap, as if she held a knife in each hand.

It was the same scream that had summoned her out of their two-story gray Victorian last month, the same run out toward the ditch beneath the blasting sun, to discover that Garo had sprained his ankle as he played. Except, that time, the rats in the walls of the old house had dislodged wallpaper by the stove. She had been frying batches of fresh, flour-dusted sardines in olive oil and a piece of the paper fell and flamed up in the hot oil. The whole wall caught fire, and then the house. She hosed water onto the blaze; neighbors and finally a fire truck came. From the flaming house, she kept running in and out, grabbing whatever she could, until the fire was too much. Gulping for breath amid the smoke and ash, she had been able to save only armfuls of their possessions. At the end, she had fallen to her knees on the rocky drive, coughed and wept. All her hopes lay in ruins. What had her dreams gained her, kneeling there sunblind and coughing on the cinder path?

Now she rose in the darkened room. Never would she be caught defenseless again, never would she let her fists unclench.

She must take care of the remaining boxes, still unpacked here and in the kitchen. There were built-in shelves on each side of the fireplace, and she had worked hard to clean them, to remove the dust and ash and microbes left by the previous inhabitants. She opened the cardboard boxes. One contained a warm, blue comforter her mother had knitted for Tigran when he was born; she laid it out over the back of the couch. Assorted papers were at the bottom of the box, and she placed them in the drawer of the desk Armen and she shared. From a second box, she took the few books she had saved – Armenian literature, a handbook of Marxism, her books of English poetry, a history of art.

One of the books she placed on the case by the hearth caught her eye. It was Armen's French-Armenian dictionary. During the first year of their marriage, she had looked through it and found in the flyleaf a sentence written in Armen's beautiful, regular printing. There the words were still, and she read them once more: "Je cherche toujours pour trouver une maison favorable pour moi – I search always to find a favorable home for myself." It broke her heart. Then she looked at another line just below his, from the same Mallarmé poem, but written in her flowing script in the first year of their marriage:

"La chair est triste, hélas...the flesh is sad, alas."

Her face was parched, and yet she felt that tears flowed from her eyes as she stood frozen by the bookshelf and read these interlocked lines, struggling to converse. Finally she was able to place the dictionary back on the shelf.

There was so much work to be done. She went back to washing the floors and cleaning the rooms. Then she entered the kitchen, washed her arms and hands, and began preparing lunch. She looked out the kitchen window and saw the boys playing in the green shade of the grape arbor and drinking water from the hose tap. She heard the car drive up outside before she saw it. It must be Armen, back from his appointment.

Maybe it had to do with a Ramgavar meeting and Armenian politics. She knew a summit meeting was to be held soon in Cairo between the progressive, pro-Soviet Ramgavars and the anti-Soviet Dashnags, who had never given up their fantasy of an independent nation and whose name meant knives. Five years ago, Fresno Armenians had been horrified by the murder in New York City of Archbishop Tourian from the Holy See in Soviet Armenia; he was performing the Mass, and several Dashnags rose from their seats, took knives from beneath their coats, and stabbed him to death right there on the altar. Of course, Stalin was not very kind to the Mother Church in Armenia either; it was said that the Holy Father in Echmiazine, Catholicos Khoren, had been murdered this spring by the Soviets, but how could they believe such rumors?

"Garo! Tigran! Come here." Armen's voice came through the kitchen window. "Boys, let's practice." She watched as he lined up his two sons in front of him. They stood in the green shade and mottled light of the grape arbor, the boys in shorts, tanned and shirtless now, Armen in his clean white shirt and holding his pipe up as if he were a conductor.

"Comrade brothers, let us sing the Internationale," he said, and the three of them began singing in Armenian at the top of their lungs. Garo's beautiful, high voice slurred the words; Tigran knew the lyrics but couldn't quite get the tune. Armen sang his steady baritone accompaniment with a delight that made Artemis smile.

"Arise, ye prisoners of starvation
Arise, ye wretched of the earth
For justice in revolt now thunders
At last a better world's in birth."

It must have been a party meeting he just attended. Just after they were married, he had joined the Communists; devoted to Soviet Armenia, he had risen in the party all the way to the California State Committee.

"No savior from on high delivers
No faith have we in prince or peer
Our own right hand the chains must shiver
Chains of hatred, greed, and fear."

She frowned. There were such dangers now with the fascists on the rise everywhere. Some of their party friends in Los Angeles had gone to join the fighters against the fascist rebels in Spain. And in the Soviet Union there were rumors of anti-fascist purges in the party ranks; Trotsky was in exile, and Bukharin – Stalin's right-hand man – had been executed. What was Armen planning now, and why did he draw their small sons into his affairs, having them walk onto the platform at Armenian halls and with their high little voices lead the assembly in singing the Internationale?

He opened the back door, and a wave of superheated air eddied into the kitchen. The boys, red-faced now, greeted her noisily and scrambled through the house. Armen shut the door against the heat, and he looked at her as she chopped the tomatoes, cucumbers, onions, parsley, basil, and mint for a summer salad. She was frowning as she worked.

"Ah, Mademoiselle Frou Frou is upset about something," he said. He sat down at the kitchen table. "Angel," he said sweetly, "may I have a glass of cold water?"

She put down her knife, rinsed her hands at the sink, took a glass from the cupboard, and poured refrigerated water from a pitcher in the icebox into the tall glass.

"Sit down," he said when she brought it to him.

"I have to finish making lunch," she said irritably and returned to the counter.

"There's a buyer for the farm," he said off-handedly. "I've agreed to sell it. We are moving to San Francisco."

"What!" she snapped.

She stopped chopping a red onion at the counter and held the kitchen knife tightly in her hand. She was enraged that Armen had again sprung such news on her. It was too much to bear. Once more she had the sensation of fate's sudden, arbitrary descent on her.

"Hatchaturian has his flower cart outside the St Francis Hotel," he continued in his neutral tone, as if he were a lawyer reading a will. "He said he'll get me a fruit cart, that it's a good living. Think of our living on one of those hills, breathing the fresh sea air. It will be like Constantinople ... Angel, farming isn't a life anymore!"

In the last words he spoke, she heard a sad bitterness. The vituperation that had flooded through her mind gave way, replaced by a pained cry.

"Oh, Armen," she called out, laid down her knife, and went to him. Her hands – smelling of onion and parsley – grasped her husband, and she held his head against her breast.

Chapter 5
Wartime

DECEMBER 7, 1941

—•—

Through the store window, he watched the cars pass by on Solano in the late morning glare. The staticky radio was on, and the news kept repeating the stories of the carnage in Hawaii: bombs and airplanes had attacked an entire fleet of ships, blasted open now and sunk to the watery floor in Pearl Harbor. The harbor aflame and demolished with so many dead and missing: he had known of such things before in Turkey in 1915. Last summer, there was Hitler's bloody invasion of the Soviet Union; Moscow had been attacked, but worst of all was the ongoing siege of Leningrad. London was on fire from the Blitz, Paris was occupied, and war was arcing from North Africa up through the Middle East not far from Armenia. It was a terrible, threatening arc, and anything could happen, he thought, sitting on a stool by the cash register as customers came and went in the claustrophobic store. Continually, now, he felt that everything was floating and unmoored around him.

His new friend George Stringer had just called to lament the news. But, he said, there would be a panic, which meant there would be property to buy from people who feared a Japanese invasion of California. He knew of a market for sale across from the naval station in Richmond, and he wanted Armen to buy it cheap with him. George, a non-Armenian, was the first odar to be a close friend of his. The new market would be a goldmine, he said. Anything was possible, Armen had replied, now that the war had begun. Fortunes could be made, George said. As he talked to his friend, Armen felt how strange the panicky voice was on the radio, as if it was expected that the world would collapse and unrecognizably reassemble itself. Armen told the stock boy at the back of the store to take over the cash register for a while. Ray, sixty years old, shambled up. "Okay, Mr. Ararat," he said, and Armen left for lunch. It was 11:30, and around noon his sons would be coming across the street from school for their lunch break.

The door in back of the store opened directly into the Ararat living room. Shutting it behind him, he heard the radio from the kitchen where his wife was making lunch.

"Artemis," he said as he walked in. She mumbled a greeting, preoccupied with cooking. He sat down and watched her at the counter. The smell of freshly chopped vegetables was in the room. She glanced momentarily at him and then focused her green owlish eyes back on her chopping. Curls of red-brown hair were loose at the back of her neck, and there was an air of softness about her, though she possessed so much more energy than he, especially since his debilitating Mediterranean illness had descended. An hour ago, the radio had first blared the news, and she had rushed into the store to tell him about the surprise attack. With her need to control and her rage for order, she was sometimes impossible to handle, and he had to put up with her anger and entitlement. After all, she was not a soldier taking orders or a wife from the village, but an intelligent, American-born Armenian woman.

She brought to the table a bowl of tuna salad, Armenian style with lemon, parsley, onion, and mayonnaise, another bowl with white bean salad, and a round of tasty bread, peda. She poured him a glass of tangy yogurt drink.

"Thank you, Angel," he said and drank the cold tahn slowly, savoring it. Little Juliet was sleeping in a basinet in the master bedroom, nearby with its door open. Now Artemis sat down across from him.

"How is the baby?" he asked.

"She'll be waking soon," she said, her voice distracted above the radio. Husband and wife began eating the lunch before them in their Albany apartment on Solano just northwest of Berkeley.

All at once, Artemis began talking fast and fluently. "Roosevelt tried to buy time so he could build up our armaments. Stalin tried the same thing with Hitler, and Roosevelt's gotten six more months than him. But now the Japanese surprise attack!" Even with her sweet high voice repeating things he had said to her before, he thought she sounded more like a general than he ever could. She said now that the criticisms of Stalin's pact with Hitler were unfair. "It was his pact with the devil, so the Russians could gain time." A strange, floating sensation gripped him once more.

He let out a curt tsk, but Artemis continued reciting her views of the new World War. Otherwise, he remained silent, for he did not want to think about Stalin's strategies. What was important was Armenia, and its survival required Stalin's protection, so what Russia did had to be accepted. Since before the Genocide, the Germans had been allies of the Turks, and like the Turks, they were a fiendish adversary. But the unstoppable flow of Artemis' comments still impressed him. If only he could harness her energy, he imagined that together they would do a lot of good for Armenians and Armenia – if only they could join his ability to write and speak Armenian with her reservoir of outrage and her amazing capacity to become indispensable to the people she cared for.

Finally, there was a pause as Artemis got up to bring a plate of sliced oranges to the table, but then she began again. "Your sister and your mother, they would never help us if there's an invasion! Arsine has never lifted a finger for us, even when Juliet was born. They say she keeps bags of silver dollars under her mattress."

The radio kept up its blare.

"I love gossip," he said.

Juliet could be heard softly crying from the bedroom.

"Okay, okay, Juliet," Artemis said mechanically. "Here's lunch for the boys," she said, gesturing at the table full of food and leaving to change and nurse their new baby. Armen was going to get up to see his tiny new daughter, precious Juliet about whom he felt so glad, but he thought better of it and remained seated, filling his pipe from a pouch of Half and Half tobacco. He sloughed off stray tobacco from his pants onto the floor and then began to smoke. In a week, Artemis was going to have an operation to correct some female problem, and his mother, Zabel, was coming to help out with Juliet. Their daughter had come into existence only because Artemis had been caught unaware, for they had not been together for many weeks as the world situation exploded around them. Later she said she had forgotten to use her diaphragm. For Armen, the pleasure of loving his shy and masterly wife was nothing compared to the immense joy of Juliet's birth, the infant's gentle yet animated presence.

"Hear about Pearl Harbor?" Tigran yelled as he pushed open the kitchen door.

His brother, in fourth grade now, clambered into the kitchen, saying "Yah, heard about it?" The radio was spitting out the noon news.

Armen tsked. "Yes, yes. Sit down, and eat," he said, and the boys sat and started talking at once about what they had heard. His lively sons were always sparking one another, so different were they from each other. Tigran was still short and stocky; his hair had grown darker, though his eyes remained blue. Already he was so responsible, helping out in the store and babysitting his infant sister when there were political meetings his parents had to attend. Garo was the opposite; still dreamy and wild, the nine-year-old was now taller than his older brother. Whenever Tigran frowned on some silliness his younger brother said, Garo would fume or laugh, but always he would react.

"Where's Mama?" Tigran said.

"With Juliet," Armen said as he listened to the radio voice describing once more the devastation in the Pacific.

"Juliet is bad news."

"Yah, bad news," Garo repeated with a smile.

"When she was born," Tigran said, "I knew something bad was going to happen. Now the Japs pulled a surprise attack at Pearl Harbor. I knew she was bad news."

"You knew?" Armen said and let out his tsk. He was about to correct Tigran, but then he let it go and tried to focus on the radio news. His son's capacity to disapprove, not unlike his own, was equipment he needed in order to survive. Also, Armen knew, he was echoing the negativity he heard from his mother about the little baby.

"I must tell you, Armen," the obstetrician at Herrick Hospital had said to him last October, "your wife gives every indication of not wanting this baby. At best, she ignores her; at worst ... Have you discussed giving Juliet up for adoption? For the sake of both mother and child." Armen was horrified. He told the doctor that Armenians never gave away their children, but he knew then that there was something wrong.

Everything around him was strange and weightless. Tigran seemed to float by him as his blue eyes focused on his food or on Garo. A snatch of Gomidas arose in his mind, a chant about a crane, and he was about to hum it when he realized he was dizzy with headache and could hardly hear his sons or the radio news. He sat there silently as his sons chatted away. War distorts also the bystanders' lives, he thought, and a host of memories from twenty-five years ago came to him, immediate and palpable.

In 1916, in Constantinople, war had descended on the whole region. He had to live in the attic of their apartment building, one of twenty thousand Armenian teenagers, the Army of the Attics, who had fled into similar attics and cellars; they were all escaping from army service which would have meant almost certain deportation and death. Armen was sure he was especially in jeopardy, for his last newspaper article on April 1, 1915, had called for Turkey's Armenian minority to be granted its own flag. In order to go outside, he had to wear his sister's dresses so that the Turks would not seize him in a police sweep of the city, hunting young Armenian males.

Under the eaves of the third floor attic garret, Armen lived until the end of the year, stashed away with his books and clothes. While there, he read all he could of Armenian and French literature – Racine, Moliere, Voltaire, and Rousseau; Balzac, Flaubert, Zola, and Anatole France, whose novel "Thais" he began to translate. And he read the poetry of the nineteenth century, intoxicated by Lamartine's dream of rural childhood, by Baudelaire's nightmare images of the city, and by the beautiful extremity of the Symbolists. Paul Verlaine was his favorite, and Armen heard echoes of the poet's beautiful intensity in the poems of the great Varoujan and Siamanto, whom he tried to imitate in his own poetry.

Yet how could he truly escape into poetry? Death was everywhere. Among the writers who became his mentors in 1915, only Oshagan and Zarian, the satirist who had proposed Ararat as Armen's last name, were still alive. On the morning of April 24, after Armen had seen ascetic Daniel Varoujan being arrested, the poet had been thrown into Istanbul's central prison for weeks and then had been herded with scores of fellow prisoners onto the main highway east, heading into the interior. After a week of walking, a Turkish officer on horseback singled out Daniel and directed Kurdish peasant troops to take him into a grove. They stripped the thin man naked and tied him to a tree, where they proceeded to dismember him with knives. "This Armenian soil, a rust-colored sponge of wounds, turns red before our eyes."

A month later, the great poet Siamonto was similarly bound, tortured, and murdered at Chankere prison in central Turkey. And there the beloved composer Gomidas, who had been Armen's choir teacher, was held for months and then released to wander through the Galata district of Constantinople. In 1917, Armen had left the attic and was working in Constantinople at Babigian's Bookshop, housed in an elegant old building. The brilliant composer would shuffle past the shop, and Armen would step outside and try to talk with him. The great man's beard and hair were matted, dirty, and overgrown, his cloak dusty and ripped. Gomidas, who had been a fastidious and demanding choirmaster, gazed at Armen with blank uncomprehending eyes.

Then, early in 1917, Oshagan had knocked on the door of their rented apartment on the first floor of the Shamlians' building in Constantinople. He had endured months in the army and was hiding from the police. He stayed with Armen's family for the first months of the year. In their living room, he talked endlessly with Armen about the literature he had read in his attic room. Oshagan counseled him to flee Constantinople and go to Paris; he would write his friend at the Sorbonne. Their landlord, Baron Shamlian, who had so far successfully used proxies and huge bribes to keep control of his railroad, heard of his plans, and he offered to pay Armen's way for the three years at the University of Paris. Then, one day someone was rapping on their courtyard door, and when Armen's sister Arsine answered, the police burst in. They searched but found no sign of Oshagan. His beloved teacher, with his wise eyes and fragile glasses, had jumped for his life out the back window and escaped.

When Oshagan was forced to flee, Armen realized that, except for his mother, sister, and brother, he had nothing left. The last two years had deprived him of everything else. Even the conversations with his teacher, he realized, had been somehow ghostly, for they were unable safely to touch the ground of this city, unable to live their lives. The same sensation shadowed the feverish talks at Babigian's Bookshop where he worked in 1917 and 1918 – discussions of the Russian Revolution and the possibility of a new Armenian republic. And the sense of strangeness beset his unit of the Armenian Boy Scouts, where he had risen in the ranks and in 1919 written their regional anthem.

The same unreality arose when he talked in halting English with the American woman who directed the city's Red Cross and had hired him in 1917. Signs were posted on the whitewashed walls of the office, which listed services, sought donations, and warned of health risks – influenza, tuberculosis, and syphilis. One day, a German colonel visited. As he talked, the director kept glancing at Armen with embarrassment because the officer kept dwelling on Turkish atrocities against Armenians. He spoke as if the cruelties were nothing very unusual.

"Look closely," he held up a string of worry beads, "this is made from the nipples of Armenian women."

After the colonel left, the director had told him: "You must leave Turkey. Leave and go to Paris if you can. There is nothing left for you here. Leave, Armen."

Now Armen rose from the table. His sons had just closed the back door, returning to school. He washed up in their single bathroom, and he stopped in the bedroom to say goodbye to Artemis. He gave a kiss to Juliet, who was burbling in the bassinet, "Anoush," he said softly, "Sweet" – and then he said "Angel" to his wife. Artemis seemed calm and intent as she leaned now to carry Juliet, in her little bassinet, into the kitchen. As he opened the door from the apartment to the store, he mumbled, "There is nothing left."

"Nothing left of what?" Ray said; the man was a Communist Party member, and the job was a favor to him. He had a son and daughter, both of whom wanted to join the Army to fight fascism, and now they certainly would.

"Nothing," Armen said as he replaced Ray at the cash register.

Sitting there, watching the cars float by on Solano, Armen thought about being the only Armenian member of the party's state board. He was respected as the voice of the loyal cadre of Armenians in California. In board meetings and in the local Berkeley cell meetings, his party name was John Harris, though people knew his name was Armen Ararat. When he learned the names of his comrades – Slavic, Jewish, Irish – he would rename them with a dual-language pun. Mr. Somer became Mr. Melon because someroog meant watermelon in Armenian. But nothing would lighten the spirit of those meetings. It was as if everyone – professors, janitors, and bureaucrats, Negroes and whites – were all undergoing an x-ray, which exposed the essential bones of their thoughts and loyalties. With everyone so exposed, it was such a betrayal that there were FBI informants among them. With the war, though, everyone in America would be feeling vulnerable and exposed, as if anything might happen.

A man in a suit entered the store and disappeared down an aisle. The face was oddly familiar, perhaps because it was so ordinary, except that the man had a close-cut military-style haircut. Armen began to feel agitated, and he stared into the aisles from his perch by the cash register. Suddenly the man emerged from the back of the store, and Armen realized he looked like an FBI agent. The man came up to the counter, placed a bottle of milk there, and dug his hands deep into his coat pockets.

"Stick 'em up," he smirked and pointing something in his coat pocket at Armen, who thought he held a gun in the pocket. Armen grabbed the counter in front of him as the room turned upside down.

"Don't shoot me, comrade. I understand. You feel desperate and poor."

I have lived forty-one years so far, Armen thought, and what has my life been that it should end here, now, like this?

"It's the system, comrade, it's the system's fault!"

Suddenly the stranger pulled his hand from his pocket and wiggled it in the air. "Only kidding, mister," he said. "You were staring at me as if I was the devil! I couldn't resist."

"You shouldn't do that to a person," Armen said coldly. "You could get hurt." He carefully controlled his hands as he took a half-dollar from the man and went steadily through the motions of giving him change.

"Sorry, mister," the crew-cut man said. "But why were you staring at me like that?"

"Nothing," Armen said and looked out at the street through the store windows. The man let out a harrumph and left.

Sitting stock still, he felt on the verge of collapse. He had not felt so assaulted for many years. Then he remembered a moment a few months ago with Artemis, when he drove her to Herrick Hospital in Berkeley – she was in the passenger seat and having contractions, and Juliet was about to be born. If it was a girl, he was insisting on a Russian name, Sonya, to honor the Soviet protectors of Armenia. It was a beautiful name, but Artemis objected, so he suggested a French name, Juliet, a compromise. On the verge of a contraction, Artemis suddenly turned to him as he parked the car in front of Herrick. "Why Russian?" she said contemptuously, "why French? Why not an Armenian name! You used to be a proud Armenian, proudly writing poetry in Armenian. After twenty years here, suddenly you don't want an Armenian name for your baby. And how many poems in Armenian have you written lately? Who are you, Armen? A fraud?"

"No, Artemis!" he began to protest, but she screamed from the agony of the contraction. He had followed the attendant wheeling her into the hospital, and he felt the same inner assault when the FBI agent just now said "Stick 'em up." How could she have called him a fraud? How could she attack him like that! Yes, she was distraught, overwhelmed by her pregnancy, but she knew that he was a devoted father, husband, and party member. She could not have been serious. He remained seated now on his stool, alone and reeling, as the radio kept up its talk of war.

Chapter 6
On the bridge

MARCH 12, 1944

—•—

She stepped down the three stairs from the back door of their apartment to the street. There were dark clouds in the morning sky, and on the sidewalk she felt she stood in a tunnel of darkness. Her hand carried a packed suitcase. To the left was a stucco house, pale yellow in the gray March light. In the yard, a black dog barked and lurked, and his snarling echoed in the street. This morning, she knew the neighborhood and all the world crouched and lurked like that.

She turned away and took automatic steps toward Solano, walking past the windows of their corner grocery store connected to the apartment. It was Sunday now. The store was closed, as was their new Richmond market. The family sat around idly in their small intolerable apartment. Glancing back, she saw Tigran descending the apartment steps and holding little Juliet's hand. Why were they following her? He should have known better. She remembered after Christmas overhearing Armen tell their son, "You can't go back to school. Mother is sick. You must help in the store."

She turned her face away from Tigran. Why hadn't he brought Garo, her sweet younger boy, instead of her daughter? The girl, who was two-and-a-half years old, was a terrible mistake! But Armen had gotten the daughter he wanted. She remembered how they argued over her name, for the Russian name he wanted was impossible, and so finally she had to accept his choice of a French name, Juliet. A few months after her birth, Tigran said she was bad luck: she had caused the attack on Pearl Harbor. Then, late last year, there was Artemis' operation. What had fate wrought for her? Not only her – the darkness was everywhere. Millions of soldiers were dead. The Jews in Europe were being murdered, though no one knew for sure how and how many. The Japanese had disappeared from Northern California, and they were in camps now. London was in flames from the Nazi rockets, and there were pictures of Axis cities on fire from Allied bombing.

At the corner now, she turned west, crossed the deserted street, and began to take short quick breaths. Tigran and Juliet followed several yards behind. Cornell school on this block of Solano passed as if in slow motion. She could not tell whether she was walking or standing still.

Maybe she was sleep-walking, except she was awake. She was unable to breathe deeply. Her lungs would not allow it, only short, quick breaths. It had been like this since the operation in November on her private parts. She had begun to feel a strange pressure down there soon after Juliet was born. Something was wrong, but she lived with it for all those tense hours spent at the cash register in the store or cleaning the apartment and cooking and caring for the new baby, the boys, and Armen. Suddenly, just before Thanksgiving, she became terribly anxious, aware something was growing inside her. It was a tumor, the doctor said. As the operation approached, there were odd changes in her breathing, and when she complained, the doctor looked at her as if she were a crazy Jane. But she was not crazy. No one admitted or understood that something terrible was happening to her; she felt how idiotic everything was, the doctor, her illness, her blind family. The anesthesiologist had pushed a breathing tube down her throat. She fought the coma which descended, breathing rapidly, shallowly, with a dwindling awareness that men gathered at her vagina to enter and remove her uterus and the fibroid cyst within it. After the operation, she never felt the same. The doctors said it was just allergies. The men had no idea what harm they did with their scalpels and their indifference. She could no longer breathe normally, her voice rasped, her pulse was painfully erratic, and her skin felt raw and feverish. What did men know of such things, what right did they have!

"Mama," Juliet called, running a few feet behind her now, "Mama, stay here. Don't go." The little girl's voice was plaintive, and the mother swung around to face her.

"Go away," Artemis said. "Go back home." Her stare zeroed in on her little daughter's dark brown curls, her olive skin, and her penetrating, dark brown eyes. Juliet reached toward Artemis and pulled at her sleeve. A glut of fury filled the mother. A flash of rage filled her and the street, the school nearby, the sky above. A wail came from deep within her throat, and she found herself saying: "Don't touch me. Or you'll never see me again."

Juliet faded from her sight. Artemis heard her shower of tears, and everything seemed so remote to her now. Tigran came forward, standing on the vacant sidewalk of Solano Avenue. She knew he would not mention Juliet and her crying; he would be above that. "Your birthday, Mama," Tigran said, "we wanted to give you an early birthday. It's Sunday, and we're all free."

She heard a bus chugging down the street; today it came only once an hour, and she thought of her plan – to get to the train station and go to stay in Visalia, a farm town south of Fresno, where her sister Satenig and her brother-in-law Nick lived. But suddenly she knew she would not; she could not. The suitcase was heavy in her hand, yet she felt detached from its weight, from her son, from the tunnel of unbreathable air through which she was walking.

"Go home, Tigran," she said in an empty voice. "I'm taking a walk." She wheeled about with her suitcase in tow and trudged down Solano. The bus roared past, all grinding metal and glass, which would have taken her away. At the pharmacy, the clerk leaned his face close to hear her as she asked him to keep her suitcase until she returned for it. She walked past cafés and little shops. She glanced in the open doorway of a bar. The raucous band music of Glenn Miller (who had disappeared over the English Channel) poured out into the late morning air, and she stared into the bar's open doorway. In the obscurity, she could make out the jukebox and the patrons, smoking and drinking. She knew their ways, their lack of responsibility, their escape from everything.

Now a dead glare of late winter sun penetrated the clouds and seemed to blank out everything she passed. The grinding sound of cars on Solano invaded the air she walked through. It was cold for March, cold enough to kill the new leaves on trees and the budding flowers. She heard band music from another bar she passed and then from one café, "A kiss is just a kiss." Everything she heard was dead, empty – there was so much death.

For a moment she felt weightless in the dull light, and everything here seemed fake. Solano Avenue was just one more stage set of a city, and behind the façade were most likely the rubble of a fire-bombed city and a horrific stench. It was all a charade, the life she led, the fake city blocks, the apartment up the street, the grocery store, and especially all of Armen's foolish schemes. Responsibility or even the future meant nothing to him. And with his passion for Soviet Armenia, it was the past he really loved and his elegies for all he had lost. As for the future, he thought he was entitled to be as erratic as he wished, always planning to move to Armenia or disappearing to see his comrades in Fresno or L.A. But for her the past was a cruel hoax. Her life was destroyed, and the future was menacing and unknown.

She heard a distant scream, and she could not determine whether it came from a building, or maybe it came from inside her. When she was young, she had imagined using her wits and strength to soar above the scorched world, to succeed as no one she knew had done. But now only deadness surrounded her; there were no choices left for her. It was her husband who felt able to soar above everything, while she with her larger soul and deeper hopes must always be chained down, always be responsible for them all and insulate them from any harm. And what was left of her but a scream?

She reached the corner of Solano and San Pablo; the bay was a few blocks away, and she smelled the bracing breeze blowing from it. The sun glared now, and she could not make out any water. She was lightheaded and hungry. Tigran would be laying out a spread for his brother and sister and their father. She began to walk back the dozen blocks to their store and home. It would be her birthday, her thirty-fifth. In four days, one day after the Ides of March. Always after, everything for her was always after, too late. Yes, "beware the Ides of March" was from "Julius Caesar." Tigran was like Antony, smart and shrewd. "Friends, Romans, Countrymen, lend me...." But she liked Brutus best. The truth was, though, that Brutus, as brooding as he was, did not understand what life was really about. Or he understood too late, always too late, like her, and so more death came into the world.

"Sit down on the couch," Tigran called from the kitchen when she opened the apartment door. "You'll see." She sat in the cramped living room. Her tired feet rested on the Oriental rug, a bargain that Armen had brought home one day; stuffed easy chairs and the green couch she sat on circled the red and brown geometric rectangle. There was a commotion in the kitchen, and she heard all their voices, subdued and combative as they prepared something there.

"You can come in now," Tigran said. She drifted into the kitchen. They all sat at the round table wedged into the breakfast nook; there was a vacant seat for her between her sons. Tigran had gone to so much trouble, and suddenly she felt so sorry for him. And her beloved, distracted Garo – twelve years old now – smiled at Artemis, and she realized that she was smiling back, that the outside of her face was cooperating with her sons. She lived only for them, her two beautiful boys. They were the future.

"Happy birthday," they called out in rough unison. She surveyed what was set before her: jajuch made of cucumber, mint and yogurt, the lamajun she had made yesterday, with peppery ground lamb toasted on rounds of dough, baklava with honey and nuts, which the Hatchaturians had given them last weekend.

"Thank you," she said softly. She automatically reached to serve them, and Tigran let her. Their patter of teasing and complaint surrounded her, and she too began to eat. Once she heard a distant barking from the street, and she looked up briefly.

After the boys left the kitchen and she began to clean up, she saw her husband staring at her as he lifted his pipe from the ashtray by his plate. She stared coldly back at him, at his lined, inexpressive face, his foul pipe, his blunt thick hands, and the crusted skin flaking from the psoriasis on his arms. She would never again accept his interest in her body, the urgency of his organ! And she could not believe that he had actually wanted to uproot them all and go to Armenia, that he would even have gone without them; thanks to the party's opposition, he gave up his plan.

"Happy thirty-fifth birthday, Angel," Armen smiled.

She did not reply. She felt fifty-five, not thirty-five. Halfway through the journey of my life, Dante had written. He knew what life was, an inferno.

"Angel...," Armen said. She flinched, sensing that once again something was about to befall her. "George and I found a nice home, near the Richmond store. Next month, we move."

She could hardly breathe, and she quickly sat down opposite him at the table. As if it were a birthday present to move! Never did he consult her. Always he was thinking up schemes with his American friend George Stringer. George had psoriasis, too, worse than Armen. Always they imagined they were on the verge of enriching themselves, but it never happened! First, in 1942, they decided to buy the grand old Claremont Hotel in the hills overlooking Berkeley and Oakland, available for $75,000 because the owners feared a Japanese invasion, but no sale! Next year they intended to buy a large farm in Manteca. Their current investment in the new market next to the Richmond Naval Base was their only success. It brought the two greedy leftists a torrent of cash. Now to move again after only a few years on Solano! But what disturbed her the most was how casually he imposed his decisions on her and how suddenly.

She kept staring at him, but he sat there smoking, apparently content that she did not complain. She heard the children playing in their bedroom, and she sat across the table, mute and paralyzed by her anger. But she sensed he was still not finished, and she girded herself for more.

"Angel," he said, tapping tobacco from his pipe and beginning to clean it with a new pen knife, "I have to go to San Francisco today."

She could no longer bear holding her silence. "We were just there!"

"I have to go. Come with me."

"For god's sake, why?" she cried out. "You never tell me why you do anything!"

"To visit the Hatchaturians. To see John."

"But why!"

He held up the new knife. "I borrowed it last week to clean my pipe. I forgot to return it, and he needs it. Let's all go."

She held her hands to her face even as she kept staring back at him. He was an idiot, yet it was impossible to laugh at him. She could hardly speak to him, and anyway something was wrong with her breathing. She went to the sink and began washing the dishes.

They all gathered in the living room. She threw on her shapeless oversized coat; and they went out to their Chevy station wagon with its wood panels. Suddenly sound exploded around her: the children teased and bickered in the back seat about the war and baseball, about Musial, Lombardi, Stephens, Boudreau – with Tigran behind Armen, Garo behind Artemis, and Juliet with her doll between the boys. Armen sang at the wheel – first "Allons enfants de la patrie," then "Garmir kini" – an old Armenian drinking song – and finally "Arise Ye Workers of the World."

They approached the new Bay Bridge arching up from the shore beyond the end of San Pablo in Oakland. She glimpsed San Francisco across the Bay water, tiny and bleached by the blank sun. In 1939, he had taken her and boys to see Charlie Chaplin address the Longshoreman's Convention in Masonic Auditorium there. "Comrades," Charlie Chaplin had said, "and I do mean comrades." The comedian, with his moustaches, black suit and white shirt, spoke before thousands of workers, waves of them applauding, standing instead of sitting. The little man began the Internationale, and tens of thousands joined him. "Arise ye workers of the world." Tigran and Garo sang along, their little mouths open and their eyes wide. She had shuddered at how loud the crowd was, its power.

They drove onto the sweeping span of the Bay Bridge now, and she looked at Armen. He held his pipe tightly between his teeth. What sort of comrades were they really, he and Hatchaturian? The party had assigned Armen Ararat, a man with a fake last name, a new fake name: John Harris; it was a fake name for a fake leader of the Berkeley cell, comprised of Jewish professors, black workers, immigrant intellectuals, and unionists. All these idealists and humanitarians did was talk, talk, talk, while the real world was a seething mess in which tens of millions were killed and hundreds of millions hurt. At what cost had the Red Army relieved Leningrad from the Nazi siege, after years of bombardment, death, and starvation? Now there were rumors that the Nazis were systematically murdering the Jews. Another genocide was occurring, and the same thing could happen again to the Armenians. Yet all Armen and his comrades did was talk, talk, talk. Again she thought of his abandoned plan to move to tiny Soviet Armenia, his mad failed scheme! How dare he think of endangering the family! A wave of rage poured over her.

"You're so white, Mama," Tigran said from the back. "Are you okay?"

She had turned ghostly white, she knew, and she wondered whether it was due to the terrible changes in her body or to rage.

"No, Tigran, I am not okay," she heard her voice spit out.

Armen took the pipe out of his mouth and put it on the seat next to John Hatchaturian's knife. She took up the knife, and her fist closed over the handle, cool and powerful in her hand.

"Angel?" he said. His hands tightly gripped the steering wheel as he drove.

"Why are we on this bridge?" she said bitterly. "You're always taking me where I don't want to go." She unfolded the blade from the knife she held. "And for what? For this idiotic knife." She put the open knife brazenly in front of his face.

"Artemis, no," he warned. Cars sped by them on either side.

"For this!" She began to slice the air between his face and the windshield. She did not care. Let him realize how much rage was in her.

"Artemis," he shouted again, and with his free hand, he twisted the knife from her. The car began to swerve in its lane.

"How dare you hurt me!" she shouted back and began hitting his arm with her fists, tearing his shirt and ripping it. Armen lifted his hand to avoid her blows, and she heard the car tires squeal. At a great distance, there were cries behind her from Juliet, her Garo, and Tigran. She was waging a life and death battle, and frightened though they were, the children had to be her witnesses.

"Do you want to kill us all?" she snapped. The car steadied in its lane. "Don't look at me with those black eyes, those evil eyes. I can't stand it. Armen! We can't be together anymore."

"Angel," he pleaded softly.

"What did you say? Don't you dare call me Angel. After all you've done to me. Abducting me. Making me live on god-forsaken farms. Leaving me for weeks on end. Always putting the party first. Dragging me to San Francisco, away from everyone I love. Moving again now! And making me pregnant with Juliet – a child I didn't want! I can't stand it anymore!"

"Angel, the children are listening."

"Let them listen. They should know. It's reality," she shouted. "You have always been selfish, always self-pitying, always getting your way. Always shitting on me!"

Bile tasting like death flowed through her. She knew she had lost control, but she could not help herself. She began screaming in earnest. She reached to pummel Armen again, and her fists hit his arm, his shoulder, and then his face. The car careened now into the side lane, narrowly missing other cars. His hands tried to protect his face, and suddenly the car swerved up over the curb and was screeching against the outer railing above the bay. She did not care. Let them all die, if that was their fate.

There was a crunch of metal, and the car came to a halt with its right side wheels on the curb and the front bumper lodged up against the edge of the bridge railing.

Artemis was able to open the passenger door just enough to squeeze out of the car. The children's cries rang horribly in her ears, and she stepped to the metal railing and grasped it. The wind was violent; it whipped and buffeted her hundreds of feet above the seething water of the bay. It numbed her face so that nothing could touch her. Across the sparkling water, she saw the grey green El Cerrito hill near Solano Avenue. There was a terrible beauty to it and to the blank canopy of sky above her. She thought of what it would be like to jump to her death from this bridge, to soar in the wind and plummet into the water of the bay. She could die here and now, if she chose.

She felt someone's hand cover her hand on the railing. It was Tigran.

"Come back, Mama," he called to her above the wind. She saw his face staring at her in dismay, and suddenly she was brought back to the reality of the moment, the pavement, the rushing cars, and her family staring at her through the side windows. Tigran's face came close to hers. "Come with me, Mama," he said, unsmiling and deeply serious. "Don't worry, Mama. Come back." He drew her hand carefully into his.

They returned in silence to the car.

PART TWO

A Daughter in Diaspora

Chapter 7
Juliet as a child

SEPTEMBER 3, 1946

—•—

Her eyes were on the big, deep red strawberries. The other boxes of fruit were beautiful, too. The apricots had cute freckles on their pale orange skin. The peaches were yellow orange with little touches of red and streaks of pink; they were the prettiest fruit, but she loved the strawberries best of all. No, she took that back. She loved all the fruit equally, stacked there in the back of the station wagon. She loved the station wagon, too, with those brown wood panels and yellow fenders and the windows open to the warm breeze.

This was Tuesday morning. They were living in Fresno now. Daddy had a market, and he had taken her with him to buy fruit and vegetables for the produce aisle.

"Juliet, let's play hooky," he said in Armenian, when he was driving her to nursery school. So they drove downtown, and he sang her a nice song in Armenian: "Beautiful Yerevan, bountiful Yerevan, sweet Yerevan." Yerevan, she knew, was the capital of Armenia.

Of course, she missed nursery school a little bit. It was so different from home; she loved to play with the other children in the bright sun and to do all the projects in the classroom. But she thought maybe the teacher did not like her. Her parents said people in Fresno did not like Armenians, and they had to stand up for their rights. Once the teacher had said to draw a big O and make a face from it, and Juliet had drawn a mouth with lips and pretty hair and big eyes, but the teacher had said to her, "You didn't follow directions, Juliet. You should have drawn an O first!" In her fist, Juliet took a black crayon, and scowling, she had scrawled a big O around the face she had drawn. She was almost five, and Mama said next year she might skip kindergarten and go into the first grade.

Daddy parked the car and held her hand as they walked by dusty warehouses and big smelly sheds. They came to the stands of fruits and vegetables that farmers had brought for the grocers, and Daddy stopped to talk to the farmers and taste pieces of the fruit.

He bit an apricot and smiled. "I can taste the sun in it," he said. He offered her a bite, and it was so sweet. He bought a big bag of them.

The grocers bought wholesale and sold retail. That meant they were going to arrange all the fruits and vegetables in pretty pyramids and bins in their stores.

"Here, tsakis," Daddy would say; tsakis was his word for her, and it meant a little baby lamb. "We eat tooz on Tuesday," he said, handing her a fig. She tasted the sweet flavor in her mouth and smiled.

When they were finished, they drove a few blocks, and Daddy said, "I will just be a minute." He had parked the car in the shade of a tree downtown by the Asparez Club, where there was a special café – a Surgeron – where they drank smelly coffee and yelled when they played tavloo with noisy backgammon pieces.

Now she faced backwards in the car, standing on the backseat and looking at the fruit in boxes. The strawberries were within reach, but she did not want to be naughty. She thought of how her mother would tell her how she was bad and selfish. "You are char!" Mama would say, but Daddy would smile and say "Charagigi!" She knew Daddy would not mind if she ate one or two berries. She reached over the seat and took a big plump one with the deepest red color. When she bit it, she smelled the sweet aroma and tasted the delicious red and pink juices. She felt like singing. Her hands dripped, and she reached for another. She felt the burst of juices drip down her cheeks.

"Juliet!" Daddy cried through the open window and swung the door open. "Your face is bleeding!" He drew her out of the car onto the sidewalk, holding her carefully.

"I'm not bleeding, Daddy," she said in Armenian, and she held up a half-eaten strawberry.

"You ate strawberries!"

"It's delicious," she said. Uncle Nick stood behind Daddy.

"Char!" Uncle bellowed like a bull. "Char! You are a naughty little girl!" he shouted. "What do you think your Mama will do when she sees you!"

"Everything will be alright. We'll take care of it," Daddy said.

"Artemis will have a hemorrhage when she sees that dress!" Uncle Nick snorted and waved goodbye as he walked down the sidewalk.

"Let's clean you up," Daddy said and began walking her to the parking lot of the surjeron.

There was a faucet with a hose in back. She unbuttoned her stained organdy pinafore. Underneath, her little yellow cotton dress was clean. She rubbed her hands together in the stream of water, and her father gently rubbed her face with the edge of the stained pinafore. The clear water from the hose made steam rise from the black asphalt.

Then they drove home on Maroa. Right by the big buildings of Fresno State College there, they turned left. Daddy said that someday she would go to college and be educated. They parked in the garage of their new home on Normal; they had moved in just four days ago, on Labor Day weekend. Mama had worked to unpack and arrange everything on Saturday with the movers and on Sunday with Auntie Satenig and Uncle Nick. Everybody loved the new house. There was the big front porch under the eaves, which were the beautiful wide upside-down V of the roof. They had moved from a big two-story farmhouse in Manteca; Juliet liked the new house more because it was all on one story, nice and cozy, and it had cool rooms. She remembered the farm house, the old furniture with big gnarly feet, and the farm yard where her little lamb lived; in the farm yard, Grandma Zabel would catch a chicken by the neck and cut its head off just like that, with a hatchet. The chicken would race around the yard flapping its wings, and blood spurting from the neck. It was strange. She vaguely remembered the houses they talked about in Richmond and Albany across the bay from San Francisco, but this Normal house in Fresno was the best.

She knew Mama would be mad about the strawberries and her pinafore, and so she walked quickly down the hall to her room. There was the unpacked box with her Raggedy Ann and her other dolls and her bears, her little tea set, her crayons and paper, and her favorite books. She loved to draw and to read. There was the Golden Book of Stories. Its beautiful endpapers had little flowers printed on thick black paper, and there were the Golden Almanac and the Tall Book of Nursery Tales.

Down the hall she could hear her parents' voices. Ever since they got home yesterday from the Labor Day picnic, they had been like this, talking back and forth, mad and sad. Something had happened just a few minutes after they came home from the picnic yesterday. There had been a knock on the door, and Mama said she would get it. Men's voices were there; they were not Armenians, and Mama was inviting them in to have some coffee, but then she came to the kitchen where she and her father were sitting. Mama was very pale and had an upset voice: "There are some odars at the door. They want to see you. But they won't come in."

Daddy and Mama went, and Daddy said, "What do you vant?" "Vant" was funny, like his "veddy" for "very." That was the way an Armenian person spoke English.

One of the men had some pages in his hand, and he started saying something like: "We have a petition here that the whole block signed. It says you can't live in this house and you can't live in this neighborhood. There's a real estate law says Armenians can't live here. We mean to uphold it."

"We're American citizens," Mama said in a polite but high-pitched voice. "The government gives us the right to live anywhere we chose."

"Well, you're dead wrong about that. It says here in black and white: nobody of Turkish descent can live here," he said, pushing the petition at the couple.

"And we are not descendants of Turks!" Daddy said, taking the petition being held up to him. "We have a right to live here, as much as you or anybody else."

Daddy ripped the paper in half and pushed it back in the odar's hands. Then he shut the door on the men. Mama stood by him. She was very white, but she did not object to what he had done.

"Those are very bad men," Mama whispered. "It's horrible to come to a person's house with a petition like that. It's illegal."

"It's inhuman!" Daddy said. They walked to the kitchen and sat down at the table.

"You should have warned me!" Mama said, still very quiet, but her voice had become strange and raspy now. "You should have told me there were horrible people in this neighborhood. You should have known this would happen!"

"How!" Daddy said. "How could I have known the whole neighborhood would sign a petition? They are idiots!"

Then she had said in a suddenly commanding voice, sounding like a policeman, "The government will protect us because we are American citizens. I was born in Connecticut."

Now Juliet walked into the hall. Her parents kept arguing in the kitchen. Maybe now it was about her pinafore stained with strawberries. The smell of a struck match came down the hall and then

Daddy's pipe smoke, a sweet campfire smell from his Half and Half. That was a funny name for tobacco, she thought; it smelled nothing like cream. Juliet was holding her red and blue Raggedy Ann, and she began to take the doll on a tour of their new house. Here was the bedroom where her brothers, Garo and Tigran, lived when they were not at school, and here was Mama and Daddy's room. There was the bathroom where they washed and brushed their teeth and the potty where they did kaka and chish. The beautiful little tiles on the bathroom floor were white with six sides, all fitting together and dotted with little black ones. She walked down the hall past the dining room and the kitchen, into the living room, and she showed Raggedy Ann the green couch and the big easy chairs, and the brick fireplace where they would burn wood in the winter.

"The pipe is such a bad habit," Mama was saying in the kitchen; it was what she always said. "Now, again in this nice new house, I'll have to follow you around, cleaning your ashtrays, sweeping up behind you."

In the living room was the Oriental rug, and there were zigzags all over the blue border. Red paisleys filled the two brown center diamonds.

"What's wrong now?" Mama said. "You look like a ghost, all gray and cold. Is it Juliet's pinafore? No, it's those horrible odars with their petition!"

"It is no good here, Angel."

"Please, Armen, we just moved in. Not another move, no more changes!"

Juliet sat Raggedy Ann in the exact center of the rug's upper diamond; it was like a room, with brown walls covered in red wallpaper. "This is your room, tsakis," she said.

"I am moving to Armenia, Angel. I must. They need help to rebuild the country. I must go..."

"How dare you say that! I can't raise these three children alone! And the party already told you no."

"That was for the whole family. I am leaving, Angel."

"The party will not separate us," Mama said in a terrible raspy whisper. "First those horrible odars, and now you want to leave me!"

Juliet scrambled up from the rug, leaving her Raggedy Ann slumped on the field of red paisleys.

"Don't go to Armenia, Daddy," she called out and hurried into the kitchen.

Mama stood ironing at the ironing board, and Daddy sat smoking at the kitchen table.

"There is the char girl who stained her pinafore by eating strawberries without asking permission."

Juliet ignored her mother and cried out, "Don't leave me alone, Daddy."

Daddy put down his pipe. He stretched his hands out to Juliet, gathered up his little girl, and held her in his arms. She felt as if she was going to cry.

"Don't worry, tsakis," he said, and she saw there were tears in his eyes too. "I didn't know you listened. Don't worry, sweetheart, don't worry." He kept patting her head and rocking her, just like last month, when Mama suddenly took scissors and cut Juliet's long beautiful curls. "I have bursitis!" she had said. "I just can't comb it anymore." And Daddy had cried then too and held her.

"You naughty girl, you should be ashamed of yourself," Mama said. "And now you just want your Daddy to hold you."

"You are hot, tsakis," he said.

Mama came over to them and put her cold hand on Juliet's forehead. "Your face is flushed. You're sick. I bet it's the strawberries you ate. Maybe Daddy made you sick when he washed you off in the hot sun."

"Don't worry, tsakis," Daddy said.

"I'm not sick," Juliet said, frowning as she sat on her father's lap.

"Don't frown at me," Mama said angrily. "Everybody notices that you're always frowning and talking back."

"Don't worry, tsakis," Daddy said again.

"Here's the thermometer," Mama said. "Put it in your mouth. You have a fever. You're sick."

"I'm not sick!" Juliet repeated loudly, but Mama stuck the glass rod in her mouth. It was just like when Mama would force the enema tube into her rear end, when she had a stomach ache. But Juliet knew she was not sick. She was sad. And she was so angry that she began to scrunch up her face. Suddenly she bit the thermometer in half.

"Bad girl!" Mama shouted as she lifted her up off Daddy's lap with both hands and shook her. Then she cleaned her mouth with a soapy cloth. "You stubborn girl, go to your room right now."

Juliet ran from the kitchen, and in her room she climbed under the covers on her bed. She knew she was not sick, and she cried. At the same time she felt angry and afraid.

After a long while, Daddy came to the door. "Come and have lunch," he said.

They sat at the table. Mama had put before them a bowl of zucchini dolma, reheated from Sunday night, garlic yogurt, and red tomatoes cut up with parsley and red onion. She was talking about how good the produce was in September, the ripe tomatoes, the tasty peppers.

"Eat, Juliet," she said brightly, "have more dolma." Without any mention of what had just happened, there was only Mama's warmly talking about food. It was so confusing; Juliet did not know what her Mama would do next. It was hard for her to breathe. Barely looking up from her plate, she kept eating and eating.

Then Mama brought out some freshly sliced figs and a quart of vanilla ice cream for dessert, and she served a big bowl to Juliet.

Daddy began singing. It was something like a nursery rhyme he made up: "On Monday we drink tahn! On Tuesday we eat tooz! On Wednesday..." Juliet laughed, and there was air to breathe in the room again.

After lunch, the house was quiet. It was cool and dark in her room, and she took a nap. As she fell asleep, she thought about the Labor Day picnic yesterday, how angry Mama got, and again how confusing it was. As the picnic was ending, Juliet did not want to leave. It was so much fun playing with the other children, and so she went to hide on the other side of the bandstand where she watched the musicians packing up their instruments, the ouds like long guitars and the violins, drums, and a doudik like a big flute. She kept hearing her name called.

Suddenly someone grabbed her from behind. Mama dragged her across the dance floor, squeezing her arm and calling her a char little girl, and Juliet thrashed and screamed. It was as if she did not know how else to behave with Mama.

The sad thing was that she had loved the picnic so much and playing in the sun and the hush of the crowd before she heard the beautiful deep sound of Daddy's speech in Armenian, and then the old ladies serving shish kebab and pilaf, and afterwards everybody coming onto the cement floor to dance in the open air. On the drive home, Daddy had said he saw two FBI agents there, taking notes in the shadows of the smelly eucalyptus trees bordering the picnic grounds.

She could not remember her dreams when she awoke.

In her room, she gathered her crayons together and drew a pretty rug like the one she had shown Raggedy Ann in the living room. Later, she went to Mama and asked if she could go outside.

The summer sun was no longer as hot as it was at noon; she loved feeling it warm her through her yellow cotton dress. She was nearly five years old, and this was the end of her fourth summer. Four summers were so many. Four and a half years ago was Pearl Harbor, too. Her brothers always said, "It was your fault, brat," and she would cry and get mad whenever they said it. Her tricycle was in the backyard, and she rode it down the driveway to the sidewalk. She turned left toward Maroa and soared down the walk. She loved to ride fast, lifting her little feet from the pedals and coasting to a stop at the end of the street. Across Maroa was the state college. She could see rows of fir trees and big plum trees on either side of the main walkway; the wide green lawn with all those trees reminded her of the park where they had celebrated Labor Day. She turned around and rode back down the block to her house.

Coming toward her was a blond boy, whom she had met four days ago when they moved in. Freddie Hough was his name, she remembered, and he lived two doors down. He was in the third grade and wore his school clothes. Right in the middle of the sidewalk, he stopped and waved his hands, as if he were shooing away flies.

"Get off the sidewalk," he said in a high, piping voice.

"Why?"

"Because."

"Because why?"

"Because Armenians aren't allowed on the sidewalk."

Juliet felt angry, and tears began to form in her eyes.

"Yes, they can," she said in a defiant voice, and she rode her tricycle right up to him.

"Cannot."

"Can."

"No, they can't!" Freddie cried out and turned bright red.

"Yes, they can. The sidewalk belongs to the government."

"No!" Freddie piped in a high voice. His fist shot out at Juliet and landed on her nose. Blood burst from her nostrils, and she began really to cry.

She ran from her tricycle to the front porch of her house. Tears came from her eyes, and blood poured from her nose onto her yellow dress. Mama was at the door.

"Juliet," she cried out. "You're bleeding!" She led her quickly to the bathroom and had her lean over a white porcelain pan, which began to fill with blood. Crying and frightened, Juliet looked at the blood – it seemed like a huge amount, maybe a quart or a gallon.

The bowl was placed on the white and black tile floor.

Mama brought a cold dishcloth, and she kept saying, "Poor Juliet, poor tsakis." She softly petted her little forehead and cheeks.

Then she asked what happened.

"Freddie hit me!" Juliet said.

"What! Why?"

"He said Armenians weren't allowed on the sidewalk."

"Oh," Mama said in a whisper.

"I told him it wasn't true," Juliet said defiantly, "because the sidewalk belongs to the government."

Suddenly she felt her mother's hands grab her arms and shake her.

"Why didn't you just keep your mouth shut!" she shouted.

Before Juliet could get her balance or her breath, she felt her face being slapped, back and forth. "You troublemaker! That will teach you. There's a time to shut up!"

She began to gulp for breath, and she collapsed on the floor, next to the reddened dishtowel and the porcelain bowl brimming red. In front of her face she saw the little white floor tiles patterned with little black ones in an endless design spotted with blood.

Chapter 8
A trip to the country

MAY 30, 1952

—•—

They were driving through open country, heading an hour south of Fresno to her sister's new ranch house. It was Satenig's fortieth birthday, and Nick was giving her a big barbeque dinner. On the front seat next to Artemis was a small box wrapped in green tissue paper, and inside was a turquoise necklace, a present for Satenig to complement her reddish brown hair and her kind smile. The children sat in the backseat bickering, but Armen began to sing one of his folk songs, something about lowing cows mooing in the field. That would distract them, and anyway Artemis was too tired to intercede.

It had taken so much to get them all ready and out of the house. She made Armen change his shirt, for the strange purple one he chose was so dark it would have absorbed too much heat from the sun beating down on her brother-in-law's ranch. Then Garo had dawdled after his shower; his curly hair wet, the nineteen-year-old stood in his shorts in front of the mirror and kept swinging an imaginary baseball bat. An aura of health and youth radiated from him as she passed the open bathroom door and nagged him to hurry up. Tigran had gotten home at 4 and, of course, got ready immediately, dressing in a crisp white shirt and his beautiful brown corduroy pants. She had sent him down the hall to hurry Juliet, who was the worst.

When Juliet had walked home from elementary school at 3 p.m., she began complaining about having a terrible headache and about Mrs. Kelsey being mean again. At the beginning of the week, her fourth-grade class had written a page without signing it about what they wished for most in the world. They were not supposed to write about general topics like world peace, but Juliet said she wished most of all for just that. Today, the teacher gave her back her essay, but it was not hers – it was one about becoming "the richest lady in Fresno, with a big Cadillac." Juliet had told Mrs. Kelsey it was not hers, and the teacher had said, "I won't have you people talk back to me, young lady." Artemis knew Mrs. Kelsey was prejudiced, for there had been an incident earlier in the year; Juliet had found a photo in Garo's anthropology book from USC, and the caption talked about infants born with tails; when she told her teacher about it, Mrs. Kelsey had said, "Maybe some of your people have tails, but none of us do. We don't believe in evolution in this class." Artemis had complained to Mrs. Kelsey at Open House, but she had realized it would do no good.

Now she glanced around at the three children sitting on the back seat, her two big boys talking baseball on either side of Juliet, who was napping between them. Poor thing did have migraines. She was so much like Armen, so unpredictable and selfish, and she could tease like him, too. Last year, they had people over, and one of their friends – Gladys – had begun a silly dance, singing in Armenian: "I can't dance; no, I can't. My hair is too heavy, my hair is too thick. I can't dance, no..." Juliet had stood behind her, imitating her swaying arms and little hand gestures. All the men had laughed, but poor Gladys had thought they were encouraging her to dance. Still, though, it was true that Juliet had terrible migraines. She had first suffered from them three years ago, falling down from faintness and vomiting. Artemis had taken her seven-year-old to the bedroom; she thought an enema would help to get rid of the poisons. When she gave her one, she had kissed the poor thing's head, though it did no good. But headaches were no excuse for how badly she behaved. She was impossible to raise, so difficult and sloppy like her father, and she was talking back more and more. When she did not like the hominy served at the school cafeteria, she wrote a note to the cook telling her to stop serving it. When she went to the school nurse because of a migraine, the overweight nurse had noticed Juliet was plump and asked her to get on the scale; the ten year old said, "Only if you weigh yourself first."

Artemis heard about all this at Open House last February. She patiently listened to Mrs. Kelsey's complaints and realized how mean-spirited the teacher was. But it was certainly true that Juliet could be impossible. As she sat listening to Mrs. Kelsey's diatribe, she felt the same distress that for the last decade sometimes gripped her, body and soul. But she made a decision as she sat there: she decided to act truly like an American, because she was as much an American as the teacher, and she certainly knew how to be as proper as anyone.

"I hope you're not being prejudiced against Juliet, Mrs. Kelsey," she said in a soft but very pointed, confident voice, "just because her family is Armenian." Suddenly the teacher seemed preoccupied and started to mumble her words. She no longer looked at Mr. and Mrs. Ararat, and soon she ended the session. Artemis had been angry, but she would not let Armen say anything when he began to speak up. He wanted to complain about the A-bomb drills – that it would do no good to have the children crouch under their desks. No one would survive a nuclear attack, and they were just trying to frighten the children about the Russians. But Mrs. Kelsey was a hopeless case, and Artemis knew it would do no good to speak of it. And she knew, too, that Mrs. Kelsey was not alone.

Everyone said it was getting worse and worse in America. There were rumors of a hydrogen bomb, so much worse than the A-bomb. And there was the terrible Un-American Activities Committee witch hunt; they had just thrown Dashiell Hammett in jail for claiming the Fifth and not being a stool pigeon. When the Rosenbergs were convicted, friends said, "Armen, you could be next; you could be deported!" It was a dangerous time, and everything was out of control. It had gotten to the point that a woman at Open House had handed her a pastry, saying, "It's – if you'll pardon the expression – a Russian tea biscuit." Artemis had been sure the woman was laughing at her, but then she saw that the woman had looked sincerely apologetic.

"Conejo Avenue," Garo suddenly shouted in back of her. They passed the country road intersecting Highway 99.

"That was a no good farm," Armen said.

"It was good," Garo said. "There were so many fruit trees. I loved it."

"There just weren't enough of any one variety to make a profit," Tigran said.

"But there were so many different types," Garo began. "Peach, plum, nectarine, almond, pear, oranges, and lemons."

"Grapes!" Juliet piped up.

"And the trees! Eucalyptus, ash, cypress."

"Quince," Armen added, puffing at his pipe.

"Pomegranate," Artemis said. "But it was so far from the city, especially after living on Normal. It's better for us to run the market, and in the city you boys make so many more friends."

"We have enough friends, Mom," Garo said.

"You have such nice friends, Garo," she said. He was so idealistic, her beautiful boy. When he went to USC last year on a football scholarship, he made lots of friends there, too. Too bad he just did not like it, neither the classes nor the way the college coaches gave preference to the big city athletes over the small town ones like

Garo. Anyway he was so much calmer and happier on the farm. When she and Armen had driven down to L.A. last year in January, they had asked him to come home to help them out on the Conejo farm, and he had leapt at the chance to leave that mean college.

She gazed out at the dusty groves and sunny fields they passed and thought about her special boy with all his energy and goodness. Someday she knew he would soar in his own private plane high above his fields, which would stretch to the horizon, green wherever he irrigated and golden yellow where he had not. He would be like a colonel reviewing the terrain and planning his victory. Someday her son would be so wealthy and powerful that he would reroute the flow of Sierra water to irrigate his vast holdings, erase a lake here, create a reservoir there, and reshape the San Joaquin Valley according to his vision. And she knew Garo would never do some of the evil things the big ranchers did: he would never drive the small farmers out of business, as had just happened to them on Conejo, if truth be told. And he would not leach all the value from the land, or turn rivers and valleys into a wasteland. Garo could never be so selfish and ruthless.

"DiMaggio is a conceited s.o.b.," Garo said now in the back seat

"But DiMaggio is the number one player in history," Tigran said. "Maybe Lefty O'Doole was a nice guy, but they say he was a Nazi spy."

"No, he wasn't!" Garo said with intense seriousness, almost with anger.

Juliet said, "Lefty O'Doole was a Nazi spy?"

"You shouldn't joke about the Nazis," Artemis interrupted in her soft, cracking voice. "They were like the Turks – they did horrible things. Rounding up innocent people and shooting them. Burying people in mass graves. The Turks would douse little Armenian babies with kerosene, light a match, and throw them burning into pits."

"Mama, my head hurts," Juliet said.

"That's history. You should know what history is all about," Artemis said irritably. It was as if her sons' sniping had tapped a well of distress in her. "It's reality. I had to watch my own baby sister die before my eyes when I was four years old. How do you think I felt when little Lucaper stumbled into a cauldron of boiling water and turned all purple and puckered!"

Yes, they had heard the story before, but they needed to hear it. They needed to know how much a person had to steel herself against the world.

They turned off the highway and headed down a long gravelly boulevard with fields and fruit trees on either side. Nick had bought this farm in the thirties, held onto it, and expanded it for two decades; now it covered hundreds of acres east of the city of Visalia. It had been Armen who advised him to hold onto this property and then, when the time came, to subdivide and build close to the city. It was all advice that Armen himself, restless and erratic, had never followed. But Nick had heeded Armen's words, which in any case suited his inclination to stay put and stick with a thing.

As the Ararats' car approached, Nick and Satenig and their four children poured out of the new ranch house; the sprawling five-bedroom home had just been finished, and Nick boasted that it would be the first of many homes he was going to develop on the land.

"Armen!" Nick bellowed. Nearly a foot taller than his brother-in-law, he reached a hand toward Armen. Everyone knew that Nick was a stubborn bull of a man, but that was what helped him weather the hard times.

"How are things, Nick?"

"Always busy season here. Working like a jackass," he said, grunting at the surrounding groves and the lowing barn animals and the fowl fluttering just a few hundred feet from the main house.

"Thanks so much for coming," Satenig said graciously and warmly embraced Artemis, who felt the thick arms of the tall woman hug her tightly. Yes, Nick was a crude, boastful, ignorant man, but Artemis still felt proud and glad that her sister was well taken care of.

Juliet was walking with her cousin Sue toward a horse corral near the barn. Robbie, another cousin, began passing a football back and forth with Garo and Tigran. Artemis glanced at Nick walking with Armen over to a barbeque pit where a whole baby lamb was sizzling, skewered on a spit. She quickly turned her eyes away from the horrible sight.

She watched her sons playing ball in the spring sun. Garo was a big, fine athlete, fine enough to get that football scholarship. Tigran was shorter, fast, and slender; he could have been a pro baseball player if he had not broken his leg last year while sliding into third base during a game for their state college team. It had been a triple compound fracture and took months to heal, leaving that leg a little shorter than the other; now one of the polished shoes he wore had to have a thicker heel than the other. During those months Garo had really tried to help his brother, but it had not always been that way. Three years ago, she had seen them fighting on the front lawn, and when she went outside to check on them, Garo was standing over Tigran, who was stretched out on his back, almost unconscious on the grass. Ever since, Tigran had seemed wary of his younger brother. So now she was glad to see her two young men throwing and sprinting in the sun's glare. Armen had been talking to them about his latest plan to manage a new supermarket opening up in Bakersfield, a hundred miles south of Fresno, and the thought of another move exhausted her. Already in twenty-five years, Armen had made her move ten times. When would it stop?

Now Satenig walked with Artemis into the new house and showed her all the food Sue had helped her father make for the birthday dinner. She waved her sister to sit at the kitchen table while she stood by the stove and began melting a whole stick of butter in a pot for making pilaf.

"How's the A and B Market?" Satenig said.

"It's doing okay," Artemis said. Her voice was higher pitched than she expected, and she consciously lowered it. "The Balians are good partners. Mike's a hard worker, and Sirun is nice, though she spoils her kids. And she spoils Juliet too, when she sees her. She says things like 'I think I see a little girl who wants ice cream.' She tells me, 'Artemis, maybe someday my Joey will marry your Juliet.' Silly things like that. Their older daughter Gloria thinks Juliet has talent."

"Juliet likes art, doesn't she?" Satenig said in a jolly but doubting tone, as if art was a bad idea for a sloppy unruly ten-year-old girl to undertake.

"Do you remember I was good in art?" Artemis said.

"Of course," her sister said and smiled

"The Balians spoil Juliet with ice cream and compliments."

"Your little girl is putting on weight, no?" Satenig said as she cut up a loaf of white bread and ate the thick end piece.

There was a commotion at the door. Juliet entered and said, "Uncle is cooking a whole little lamb on the barbeque! I feel so sorry for it, Auntie."

Artemis saw her sister roll her eyes. Why did Juliet have to say that! This evening the family would be eating it, so why did she have to call attention to it? She was so thoughtless. It was just like when she came home this afternoon from school; Artemis gave her a bowl of ice cream as she did daily, and all the girl did was complain about school. Juliet just thought of herself. This afternoon, she had chosen a horrible bright yellow pinafore to wear to Satenig's.

"That color is so bright, it'll make a person blind," Artemis had said. "Go put something else on!"

"But I love yellow, Mama," she had moped.

"Everybody will laugh at you, Juliet."

Then, as Garo came in, he had teased Juliet: "Why so glum, kid?" And Tigran had followed, "Cheer up, Juliet."

It was the same when her daughter had wanted to paint her new room yellow. It would have been so glaring and unhealthy. Juliet always wanted what she wanted without thinking of what Artemis had to say. It was not how things were supposed to be, and Artemis had to tell the headstrong girl that yellow would cause cancer, which she vaguely remembered reading. It was not exactly a lie, but that did not matter; people need to see what the world looked like to another person, not from their own selfish viewpoint!

The men walked noisily into the kitchen, bringing a bottle of home-distilled Raki. Nick set up small juice glasses with ice for Armen, Tigran, Garo, himself, and his son Robbie.

"This is when a man can drink, when you're barbequing over a pit," Nick boomed out as he poured. "Want some, ladies?"

Artemis and her sister demurred.

Armen held up his glass of cloudy pungent anise-tasting liquor to propose a toast.

"To world peace," he said in his resonant baritone, "and an end to the immoral war in Korea."

"I don't want to hear no Commie propaganda," Nick said.

Armen took a swallow and then went right on, reciting a poem now. Artemis wondered for a moment whether her husband had returned to writing, but then she realized it was a poem by Varoujan, which he was changing and updating as he spoke.

"The strange blood color of this soil
Is not due to a chemical reaction.
This earth is a sponge absorbing lives and blood:
Armenian blood, but now Korean
And American blood, like slaughtered lambs."

Artemis could not believe her ears: How could he say such things, about lambs no less? Why would he do that with Tigran and big Nick, who stood next to her, and both of them intolerant of Armen's leftwing politics? One morning their son had joined the Marines to fight in Korea, after he had stayed out all night with his friends. After a few weeks of basic training, Tigran had been honorably discharged because he was allergic to wool. It was good luck that he had inherited her allergies.

Suddenly Nick leaned over to Artemis, and her brother-in-law whispered, "I'd give a million dollars to speak like that."

Later they all sat at the dining table for dinner. The fragrance of the apricot and peach trees filtered in through the windows. Artemis liked the salad, but thought it was a little vinegary; the lamb was charred but delicious and succulent, though she was disturbed when she saw the pools of blood in the serving platter. The rice pilaf was delicious, but it was made with too much butter.

When Juliet ate a mouthful of rice, she frowned and said, "The pilaf is so oily."

"No, it's not," Artemis interceded. "It's buttery."

Nick was a silent and efficient eater, consuming huge quantities of meat and rice. Armen was quiet for his part, but Garo and Tigran joked with Robbie, and Satenig kept telling Sue how perfect everything was on her birthday, and Artemis said so, too. Even the late spring weather was beautiful, not too hot. As Artemis ate and spoke and listened, she thought about all the voices around her and how she needed to interrupt any conversation that became awkward. She would always distract people with different stories; and she needed to be careful about Nick's anger and envy. She had been surprised to hear him praise Armen's gift with words. She wondered again why her husband had ceased to write poems. If she were to write, she thought it would not be poetry but plays.

"Hey," Nick bellowed at the young men, who had just risen. "You don't ask to be excused no more? Big men on campus too good to say excuse me?"

"Excuse us, Dad," Robbie said in a mechanical voice. Nick was too tough on his son, but Artemis did not say anything to Satenig; she had only to wait for her sister's laments to start.

"Excuse me, Uncle," Tigran and Garo echoed and turned to leave.

"Tigran," Nick said, "I hear your Dad's taking you guys south to Bakersfield. You'll be giving up coaching, I guess."

Juliet spoke up, "Mama says the coach is exploiting him."

"I don't know about that," Tigran said irritably, and he walked out of the dining room.

It was too much. She felt so tense she thought her bones might snap. Why had Armen told Nick about their maybe moving, when it was just a possibility? And why had Juliet blurted that out about Tigran? She had to intercede.

"There's a new supermarket," she said, a little too loudly and glancing at Nick. "It's a big opportunity, and it could lead to good things," she said, putting mysterious meaning in her voice. "But it's just a possibility."

"At least it ain't no farm," Nick said, looking at Armen. "You can't farm worth a damn."

Garo had lingered, and he said, "Yes, he can. He gets bigger harvests than anybody." Then he and Robbie left the room.

Nick hit the dining table with his big fist. "That's not the point! You gotta tough it out, take the bad times with the good. You can't just drop everything when you get a little bored, or things hit a snag. You can't go off at the drop of a hat visiting friends in L.A. or San Francisco. And you can't just leave your fields and trees for others to take care of, while you spend hours gabbing and drinking coffee downtown at the Ramgavar Club."

Armen sat saying nothing and calmly smoking his pipe. She would not intercede this time because sometimes people needed to hear things like that, even if it came from a big bull like Nick. People needed to know there was a view other than their own.

"To make a thing last," Nick continued, "you have to be strong and tough and put years of blood and sweat into it. But Armen, you're so restless and a born loafer. You make Artemis work her hands to the bone, while you go around making speeches all over the place, spouting your wacko Commie propaganda!"

She looked at her husband's frozen face; it seemed as if he might never speak to Nick again, and she knew she had to speak up – this was something that could end more than their visit. But then she heard his tsk, and she saw that Nick's words had rolled right off of him, as if they were just noise and verbiage.

Armen struck a match to relight his pipe, and with a mocking glance, he said, "If you only had a brain, Nick, I might take you seriously. But as it is, you speak goddamn bullshit." There was a silence in the air, and Artemis did not know what would come next from her husband's mouth. "So, do you think you can beat me at tavloo?" he asked. "Or are you not up to it?" He stood up from the table.

Nick lifted his bulk from his chair. "I'm just telling the truth, goddamn it," he harrumphed as he followed Armen to the backgammon board in the living room.

Artemis was relieved. He could have taken it further – beyond the tavloo table – and they would all have had to leave. Satenig began to apologize and commiserate about how hard her sister's life was. Artemis heard the new TV turned on in the living room and Nick changing the channels. "Goddamn it, where's the wrestling?" he was saying. Satenig and her daughter were beginning to do the dishes, and Artemis said she would go outside for a moment to smell the fragrant orchard.

On the porch, in the warm twilight she stood listening to the sounds from inside the house and looking out over the darkening fields of fruit trees and grape vines. She remembered another evening, far away and far in the past. She had been just Juliet's age, and her parents had taken the family by train back to Connecticut, to visit relatives and old friends in Artemis's birthplace. She remembered the big Hartford insurance company buildings downtown, and she thought that was what America should look like. But when twilight came, she stepped out onto the porch of her relative's house, and she saw something she had never seen before or since in the dry California evenings. Floating in the humid air were small globes of light that flickered on and off. Suddenly one of the tiny bulbs drifted close, startling her, and she had seen that it was not a bulb at all but a fly, with strange bare legs and a skeleton body. The small bent lit-up insects would never survive here in the valley heat.

Finally the Ararats piled into their Ford sedan and drove home through the warm darkness. Tigran and Garo were sleepy, and Armen began softly singing an old Gomidas song,."My heart is a house in ruins – Seerdus numan eh en puladz duner."

Simultaneously Artemis talked in her soft voice going over the whole evening in detail, what everyone did and said and ate. She carefully avoided Nick's criticisms of Armen, though she was disturbed not so much by them as by Nick's arrogance, for she could not abide anybody acting superior to others. Everyone had gone too far today.

She darted a glance back to Juliet, sitting awake between her two big brothers, who slouched sleepy and quiet. So many things her daughter had said today bothered Artemis, and she began to feel angry. She only vaguely fathomed where it originated, but that only increased her bitterness. She hated being subject to feelings she could not control. Her rage – at Juliet, at herself, at how unjust things were – crowded out her other thoughts.

"Why do you say the things you say, Juliet!" Artemis began. "Why do you mock people? And you mentioned Tigran's coach! And you complained about the butter in the pilaf. And you said you felt sorry for the little lamb on the spit. Why do you do such things! You are always hurting people's feelings. No wonder nobody likes you."

Chapter 9
Independence Day

JULY 4, 1955

—•—

*Garo rang up t*he pale man's groceries at the cash register, and Juliet bagged them. He was the last customer of the day, and he bought a couple of oranges, a loaf of bread, a quart of milk, and a bottle of sherry. Bagging the groceries was the job her brother had assigned her, along with neatening the supermarket shelves and occasionally relieving a cashier. Since she was twelve, almost two years ago, he had let her work once in a while at the cash registers. The word KING was printed on the outside of the brown paper bag, above a wide smiling mouth. Below the mouth was a phrase: Eat like a king at discount prices. Garo had thought all that up, and it was really his smile on those bags. He brought such energy and warmth to everything he did; she decided that he was just hyper. He loved the markets more than he had loved Daddy's ranches, more than anyone else did in the family. She wanted to help in the store, of course, despite the craziness among the workers there and the strangeness of the customers themselves, like this last customer with his puffy face and his grayish clothes. Garo followed him to the front door, unlocked it to let him out, and jovially said "Goodbye, buddy" to the old man.

"Ready to go, kiddo?" Garo asked, as he returned to lock up the one register he had used. It was his idea to open the store from 9 to 3 on July Fourth, and she and he had been the only workers. Already it was 3:30, and they had promised to be home to help with the party. Mama and Daddy were having a house-warming for their friends this evening at 6. At 3, Juliet had said, "We have to go home, Garo." But he had his own sense of time, and anyway he never hurried a customer. Also, there was a lot on his mind now that he had married Lily last April; the newlyweds lived with the Ararats on Garland Avenue.

He never hurried except when he was irritated or mad, and then everybody got out of his way, for he could become really angry and unpredictable. If he thought an employee was complaining about him behind his back, he could be viciously nitpicking. More than once, he shouted, "You're fired!" at an employee he relied on, and an hour later when the storm had passed, he would rehire him. And from the workers he liked or maybe pitied, he accepted so much craziness – drinking, gambling, absence, tardiness, even grossness in the freezer room. He always talked idealistically about workers' rights, but he raged like a wild man when King's employees tried unsuccessfully to organize. Sometimes Garo was very kind to Juliet and really to everyone, and generous to a fault, but then sometimes he acted so temperamental, spoiled, and distracted. She once told her mother, "I think Garo's mind is fuzzy or something." Later, during an argument, Mama cruelly told Garo's new wife, Lily, what Juliet had said, so for a week everyone in their Garland Avenue house didn't speak to one another.

"Let's go," Garo said now, and they walked out of the King Market to an old red Chevy pickup truck. He had grabbed two Almond Joys from the candy rack as they left.

"I'm hungry. Have one," he said, handing her a bar and unwrapping the other for himself.

"Thanks," she said. She smiled at her brother and began eating the bar as they drove out of the parking lot. Garo was big and tall with close-cropped dark blond hair and a full face. He was always going off the diets he put himself on. She understood how he felt, for she had been struggling with her weight for a couple of years. Since the spring, though, something had changed for Juliet, and she had been losing weight. She had begun letting her dark brown hair grow longer, ever since Garo's wedding. Mama had cut it short years ago because she had bursitis and would not comb it anymore; Daddy had cried. She remembered when Mama had come toward her with the scissors, and it had taken her a moment to realize it was to cut her hair; that had been when she was four or five years old. Ever since, Juliet had worn it short. Now, though, it was almost down to her shoulders, and she was a little anxious about how long it was and about her new slimness and especially about her newly developed body.

Mama's moods were a little like Garo's. She could be very generous, especially with food, but Juliet always had to watch out in case her mother's mood changed. Last October, a week after her thirteenth birthday, she had seen Mama suddenly turn on Grandma Zabel, who was old and frail and wore her very white hair pulled back in a bun. She was staying with them on Garland then, and one Sunday morning she had walked into the kitchen where Juliet sat eating breakfast. Mama's face was oddly drawn and pale, and she abruptly turned from working at the counter and began shouting in a thin voice, as if she were continuing some earlier, interrupted argument.

"You selfishly assume I'll do everything for you, just like your son. You're a terrible person, just like Armen and Arsine!"

"Not in front of Juliet," Zabel had said with calm dignity.

"Yes, a terrible person, with a cruel son and a cruel daughter!" Artemis was screaming, and suddenly she walked over and struck Zabel's shoulders and chest and pulled at her housedress with both hands, ripping it open near the shoulder, revealing the top of the woman's tired breast. Zabel screamed in terror. Juliet, who had been speechless and frozen, leapt up from the table.

"No, Mama, no," she cried and threw herself between her mother and her grandmother.

Artemis faltered and began to moan, "No, no, no, no, no." Then she walked out of the kitchen and in the living room slumped on the couch. Juliet reached to hold her Grandma's hand, as they stood there terrified and amazed that Artemis acted so crazy, that she must have felt she had a right to act that way. Juliet was afraid, but she also felt defiant and resentful. It all was so typical of her mother, and it seemed so unnatural to Juliet.

Now Garo drove the two of them down Kings Canyon Boulevard. That was the origin of the first market's name, and they had decided not to change it to Ararat. The 100 degree air blew in from the open windows, and Garo was talking non-stop about the market – how the oranges Daddy bought were so sweet, how great were the pyramids of produce Garo set up, how nobody appreciated how much work went into making the stores look good. He turned north on Blackstone, and as he talked he fiddled with the radio dial, moving it from one pop station to another. This was the way Garo always was, both frantic and distracted, she thought as she sat in the passenger seat and was inundated by his talk and the radio noise. They passed Olive now, where the family had bought a second supermarket last year. The first King they had bought two years ago, when they returned to Fresno from Bakersfield, and now they were expanding. Last year, Tigran had quit as assistant manager at the Bank of America on M Street in order to help manage the growing chain. He had been the first Armenian to be hired as a teller in the Bank's Fresno branch; that was partly because he was blue-eyed and had no final *ian* in his last name. In the markets, Tigran worked with the suppliers and did the books, while Garo worked as floor manager, hiring the employees and making sure customers got what they wanted.

Many of the workers were pretty strange, but he hated to fire them even if they were caught stealing or even having sex in the freezer room. King was a madhouse, Juliet thought, but nobody ever tried to change things. Chick Leone had worked at the Kings Canyon store since the beginning, and he always lied, but Garo would never fire him, or rather he would fire him and then rehire him a few minutes later. Chick boasted of being a banker, a farmer, a longshoreman, a bartender, and a professional ballplayer, yet he said he was twenty-nine years old. Juliet heard Tigran call Chick a bullshit artist, and Garo said he had to be as old as Methuselah to have had so many jobs. They caught him stealing a case of liquor, and when Garo fired and then rehired him this time, he promoted him to assistant manager.

"There's our billboard," Garo said, and his monologue came to a sudden halt as they turned left on Shields. There, elevated above the major intersection of Blackstone and Shields was a wide grinning mouth, lips slightly parted, about to eat like a king. It was Garo's idea to rent the board for a few months. Billboard after billboard had recently been built on Blackstone; passing them was like reading a magazine full of junky ads.

"What do you think?" he asked.

"It's good!" she answered and smiled at her big brother. He was the strangest combination of a man and a child. She had been feeling a headache coming on. She wondered whether it was caused by breaking her diet and eating the Almond Joy on an empty stomach, or the July air pouring its heat over her face and body, or maybe just the six or so hours spent non-stop with her brother.

Garo turned north and then took a side street by the ditch to get to Garland where they lived. The ditch they passed loomed on the right, where the slanted wall of earth six feet high was one side of a narrow, cement-lined canal. It held cold Sierra water coursing through Fresno toward farmland south of the city. Mama warned everyone not to walk on the path at the top of the canal with its silent rush of melted snow from the mountains ready to grab your hand if you reached to touch the cold, or ready to catch your foot and suck you in and pull you to the bottom and drown you, as had happened to a neighbor boy a few months ago. Artemis repeated this many times and in great detail. Of course, her mother had so many fears that Juliet could not take them all seriously. Just the reverse, to cope with all the anxiety Mama spewed out, Juliet struggled to be indifferent. But the truth was that her mother's fears had taken root in her, at least some of them and particularly the fear of unexpected violence.

Garo's truck pulled into the driveway of the big ranch-style house. He and his new bride had moved in with the Ararats three months ago. He parked behind Daddy's new white Plymouth, and an old black Chevy was parked next to it in the carport. That had to be the Hatchaturians' car; they were driving down from San Francisco for the house-warming, and they must have arrived early. Every month Daddy and Mama drove up with Juliet for a weekend at their house; it was one in a row, elevated on one of the city's smaller hills. Its back porch overlooked a small Japanese garden and then, when the fog lifted, all the undulating neighborhoods toward the Pacific, and from the front window you could see Coit Tower and Russian Hill. That was the city she wanted to live in when she grew up, not L.A. where Daddy drove them on occasional weekends, to visit friends. Los Angeles was so big and monotonous, but San Francisco was always changeable and so hospitable. Maybe she felt that because of the Hatchaturians. John was such a jolly host, and he loved talking politics with Daddy. Lucaper was a little woman with a tired face and the sweetest round eyes, always making sure Juliet was feeling well and had things to do.

She and Garo walked into the ranch house now, just as a yellow Cadillac pulled up to the curb in front, behind an old blue Ford. Maybe their parents' friends had been asked to come early.

"I called the store, but you weren't there," Mama said in the entry; she held her hands on her hips, a dishcloth dangling from one hand and her elbows pointing out authoritatively. People were talking in the living room, but Artemis hurried them to the back hall.

"Where were you?"

"Huh?" Garo said vacantly.

"Did you go somewhere?"

"Sure," Juliet said in a deadpan voice, "on the way home, we took a detour to San Francisco."

"It took so long."

"For Christ's sake, Ma," he glowered, "it took the same time it always takes!"

"Do you want something to eat, my boy?" she said. "But both of you look horrible. Better wash up and change first."

Garo was already walking down the hall. Juliet frowned and turned to go as well. On one side of the long hall were high windows letting the glaring light in from the front yard; on the other side of the hall were four doors. The first opened to a big bathroom, the second was Juliet's small bedroom, the third Mama and Daddy's bedroom with its two big beds. At the end of the hallway, the fourth door led into Garo and Lily's room with its own bathroom; wood-lined and sunny, the bedroom had been converted from an attached garage by the previous owner.

She walked into the bathroom, closed the door, and checked in the mirror to see how horrible she looked. Sure, she wore an irritated frown, but otherwise, what she saw was her wavy, dark brown hair and her almond-shaped brown eyes, a developing, very young woman. At five feet four, she was two inches taller than her mother and just an inch shorter than her father. Mama had said nothing to her about puberty, but one day she found a bag on her bed from one of the Fig Garden clothing stores, with two new bras in it. Her friend Gloria, eight years older than she, had explained to her about having periods and what she needed to do.

Juliet was wearing a light green cotton dress, and she was slimmer than she had been for years, even though there was so much food in the house since Garo and Lily had moved in with them. They had moved here because the Ararats had spent the money they would have given them for a mortgage on Lily's diamond ring and on their huge wedding. Mama's attention had shifted over to Lily, and Juliet felt better and had started to lose some weight. Lily had worked at the Bank of America, in back, when Tigran had been a teller there, and he had introduced her to Garo. With her sleepy dark Armenian eyes and bobbed hair, she was very cute. She had been born in France, but when she was a child, her family had immigrated to the United States. What was upsetting for the Ararats, though, was that her father was the fiercely anti-Soviet Dashnag priest, while Armen was a leader of the pro-Soviet Armenia Ramgavar faction of the Fresno Armenians.

She went to her room and changed into a clean, summery yellow dress, and then she walked down the hall to the living room. The men sitting on two couches said hello, and John Hatchaturian even gave her a kiss on the cheek. Besides him and Daddy, there were the two Mikes: Mike Balian, Daddy's former business partner in the old A & B Market, and Big Mike Arslanian, who was another old friend. She could hear that the women were in the kitchen, probably sitting around the big table there.

"Tsakis, would you bring me a glass of cold water," Daddy said in polite Armenian.

"Okay," she said and walked through the adjacent dining room with its long table set with Mama's best silver and porcelain.

In the kitchen, three friends were helping Mama. Lucaper Hatchaturian rose, saying "Dear Juliet!" and hugged and kissed her. So did sweet Sirun Balian, little Mike's wife. Big Mike Arslanian's wife, Zephur, was the third helper; she was Sirun's sister, and she sat with an air of dignity at the kitchen table, finely chopping parsley to help Mama. She blew a kiss to Juliet. These women – Lucaper and the two sisters Sirun and Zephur – were Artemis' best friends, and they were helping her with the last stages of preparation; it was strange, for Mama never let Juliet or, now, Garo's wife cook in her kitchen.

The family tie between Zephur and Sirun had been strained, and the sisters had not spoken for years, when finally Mama interceded. In the last two years, since opening the supermarkets, the Ararats had become close to Zephur and Big Mike Arslanian as they had years before to Sirun and Little Mike Balian, their A & B partners. They all played cards now mostly at the ranch house on Big Mike's sprawling farm between Shields and Shaw; it had a three-car garage for his Cadillacs. It was two years ago when Mama had a long talk with Sirun. "I can't remember what happened," Sirun had said, "but it was around when we opened the A and B Market. Zephur has never called once since. How can a breach like that be mended?" Mama's answer was, "That was five years ago!" And so she had invited Sirun and Zephur to lunch, without telling each the other was coming, for she hated that her friends argued and did not speak with each other. The two sisters faced one another, and they burst into tears; neither could remember what wrong had been committed.

Juliet filled a glass with cold water from a beaker in the refrigerator. Through the kitchen window, she could see Garo lighting the barbeque in the backyard; some of his friends sat at one of the patio tables set up for the party. Now she placed the glass of water on a dish, which she thought wasted a dish, but it was expected, and she carried it back for her father. John Hatchaturian asked her politely in Armenian to bring him a glass as well, and she repeated the task.

"Get me one too, sweetie," Big Mike Arslanian said in English when she returned with the glass on a tray and sat down in an armchair.

"The glasses are in the cabinet above the stove, and the cold water is in the refrigerator. Get it yourself, and while you're at it, please bring me one too," she said in flawless Armenian.

The four men began to laugh, even Big Mike, though his heavy face turned bright red.

"That's the spirit, tsakis," Daddy told her as he laughed.

"The Ararats are a feisty clan," little Mike Balian said to his reddening brother-in-law. "They're capitalists and they're communists at the same time."

"I'll never forget in the mid-thirties," John said, "when Armen marched down to the city election commission and registered the Communist Party for the Fresno ballot."

"Last summer," Armen said, "the FBI paid me a visit. Better late than never."

"Don't joke about them, Armen," Big Mike said pointedly. "They are nasty bastards!"

Juliet felt the odd intensity in Big Mike's voice, and as the men continued to talk, she remembered when the agents had come here last summer; she had been twelve and a half. Her parents had said these were bad years for the world, 1952 through 54. H-Bombs had been tested on both sides. China and America almost came to war over the Formosa Straits. Stalin had died, Charlie Chaplin was driven into exile by Senator Joe McCarthy, and the Rosenbergs had been executed.

Last summer, she had tried to save Daddy from talking with some FBI agents; they had knocked on the door on Garland, and Juliet went to answer. Two men with bland American faces and dressed in grey suits stood there.

"Is Mr. Ararat in?"

"Why?" Juliet had asked matter-of-factly.

"We'd like to talk to him. We're from the Federal Bureau of Investigation."

She was frightened, but she answered.

"He's out right now, at a friend's. You'll have to come back later." She quickly shut the front door on them and stood frozen as she listened to them shuffling their feet on the doorstep and walking away. Dazed, she walked through the hall to the kitchen. Mama and Daddy sat at the kitchen table; he drank coffee from a mug.

"Hello, tsakis," he said brightly, but then he reached to touch her hand. "Are you all right? You're trembling."

"The FBI was here."

"The FBI was here?"

"Two men came to the door. They said they were from the FBI, and they wanted to talk to you. I said you weren't here."

"The FBI!" Mama had said, her thin voice rising to a high pitch. "Armen! This is horrible. The FBI came here! How can you let this happen? Just when things are getting better, you have to make the FBI come and threaten us!"

Juliet had walked from the kitchen through the dining room to the living room. Still trembling, she went to the bookshelves near the fireplace and examined the books, standing on tiptoes to see the top row. She began to remove from the shelves the books by Russian authors including Turgenev, Chekhov, Dostoyevsky, Tolstoy, Gorky, Lenin, and Stalin, as well as all the books by Marx and Engels. Her friend Gloria had told her how good "Anna Karenina" was, so she had kept it out to put under her bed, but the others she had put in a box she found and placed it in the storage room.

Now the party was getting noisier. The front door swung open, and there was Tigran and his new wife, Betsy. Behind them were Betsy's two boys from her previous marriage and some friends and co-workers. Tigran and Betsy had gotten married in Las Vegas, a month after Garo and Lily's huge church wedding; she was not an Armenian, but a pert white odar.

"Hi, Pop," he said, and then to Juliet: "Hi, kiddo." Betsy followed and gave them each a kiss, and she did the same to Armen's old friends, carefully leaning over each of them. There was something attractive about her as she moved about the circle of men, making them take notice of her, even though Juliet thought she was basically a very conventional pale-looking American woman. Her sons waved vaguely from the middle of the living room; their father had died years ago in a drunken motorcycle accident. Everyone who entered now went on to the kitchen, but soon Tigran returned and sat on an easy chair next to Juliet, who tensed a little in her chair.

"Pop, how many times did you die today?"

"I'm good today, Tigran."

"Good. No headaches. You're not dying."

"Not today, I don't die."

"You sure got some big-ass oranges for the stores."

Big Mike Arslanian said, "I bought some yesterday at the King on Olive. They're sure sweet."

"How's the new Caddy, Mike?" Tigran said.

"That ride is smooth as silk, Tigran, and no trouble so far – they're reliable cars."

"It's a beauty. You know Joey DeMelto expanded his business last year – well, he bought himself a Cadillac. But a few months later he bought himself a sharp little Triumph. And now he's bought an Alfa Romeo. So I ask him how he likes his latest acquisition, and he says he's already sick of it. He's going to buy himself a new Porsche. Either business is very good, or he's just fucking nuts."

"After dinner," Armen interrupted, "we have some of those sweet oranges."

"They sure weren't cheap," Tigran said. "You paid nearly retail."

"Top quality. People will come in to buy it."

"I don't know. What draws in the sheep are sales on milk or coffee, but oranges just don't hack it, Pop."

Armen's tongue clucked his characteristic tsk, and he raised his eyes toward the set of bookshelves across the room.

Juliet did not like Tigran's puncturing tone, and she got up to leave.

"Kid," Tigran said, "get me a glass of water, would you?"

"Why don't you get it yourself?" she said, and all the other men burst out laughing.

There was more knocking at the front door. Juliet frowned and went to answer it. On the doorstep stood a group of King employees including Mr. and Mrs. Chick Leone; Garo's assistant manager at the King's Canyon store wore a garish yellow bowtie. He nodded, pushed past her, and headed for Tigran in the living room.

Juliet looked from the open door at Gloria and Joey, Little Mike Balian's children, as they got out of Gloria's new Plymouth down the street. In the entryway, one of the workers she had not seen before stepped out of the crowd there and tapped her on the arm.

"Hey, cutie," he leered, "I can see your panties through your dress."

She pulled away angrily and was going to complain, but the young man disappeared in the flurry of everyone saying hello at once. The house hummed with the voices from the entry, from the kitchen and the backyard, and in the living room – altogether almost thirty jangling voices. For a moment it seemed more like an out-of-control carnival than a house-warming. Daddy had brought out shot glasses and the Seagram's Seven.

After a few minutes, she walked back to her room with Gloria Balian, who was twenty-one years old, and her brother Joey, who was – like Juliet – almost fourteen. She went to the closet and brought out some new work she'd just finished; it was a small mosaic table made with ceramic tiles which formed a brown horse surrounded by a halo of white tiles, like the images she had seen in Byzantine or Armenian art books.

"It's beautiful," Joey said.

"It's a gift for the teacher I had this year in eighth-grade Art," Juliet said.

"It's like one of those Armenian illuminated manuscripts," Gloria sounded more competitive than complimentary, but then she said, "You have so much going for you, Juliet."

Gloria always seemed happy to spend time with Juliet, even though she was seven years older. Years ago, she used to babysit her and Joey. "You have a brain," she would say, and Juliet felt supported by her talking with her. She would always have something to say about the novels Juliet was reading, about "The Grapes of Wrath" and "Gone with the Wind," which the younger girl loved, especially Scarlet O'Hara for her terrific spirit. Gloria even let her brother Joey and Juliet tag along with her and her friends when they went to the movies to see "The Wild One" with Brando and "From Here to Eternity."

"It's a little like the mosaics in Ravenna," Juliet said.

"Yes," Gloria smiled and started talking about how beautiful those old mosaics were.

Someone knocked at the door. Startled, Juliet thought it might be the leering young man who had arrived with the Leones and the other King workers.

"Come in," she said coolly.

It was Gloria's cousin Ronnie Arslanian, the son of Big Mike and Zephur. He was a dark-haired, handsome young man with a classic Armenian face and Roman nose; he was a little older than Gloria and always wore perfectly pressed white shirts.

"Come on in, sweetie," Gloria said.

He smiled and said, "Artemis says dinner is ready." He looked around the room and pointed to the mosaic table next to Juliet.

"That's nice, kid," he said and walked out. It was more than her brothers ever said about her art. They claimed Ronnie was a hanger-on and a BS artist, but he had always been decent to her, and she wondered whether there was any truth to the rumors that he and his father were in the rackets. When her parents played cards at the Arslanian ranch and brought her along, she would swim in their pool. Once she came in after a swim and fell asleep on their rumpus room couch; Ronnie had put a knit vermag over her, and she heard him say, "You don't want to get a chill from the air-conditioning."

Now they all followed him down the hall; he walked through the kitchen and out the side door to the backyard where there were two patio tables and fifteen people busy eating – friends, co-workers, and the four newlyweds, Garo with Lily and Tigran with Betsy and her sons.

"Come," Mama said, following them and holding a bowl filled with yogurt flavored with mint, garlic, and cucumbers. "You three eat with us in here."

"No, Mama," Juliet complained, "we want to eat in the backyard!" She did not really care but knew that Gloria and Joey would want to be with the young people.

"There's no room outside! Come with me," Artemis said and headed for the dining room.

"No! No!" Juliet's shout resounded in the kitchen. "You're so mean!" She began to stamp her feet in front of her friends but then gave up and followed Gloria and Joey into the suddenly quiet dining room where the Hatchaturians, the Balians, the Arslanians, and some other friends sat with Daddy. The long table was laden with Mama's specialties and the shish-kebab Garo had helped barbeque. Juliet felt embarrassed as they sat down in the empty places, but then everyone started talking at once. There were patties of raw meat khema to eat, kneaded with fine cracked wheat and tomato sauce, covered with chopped parsley and red onion; there were little artichoke hearts braised with carmelized onions; there was a summer salad with cut up ripe tomato, peppers, gouta – the Armenian cucumber – and red onion, parsley and basil; and there was rice pilaf. (Unlike the others, Juliet had no pilaf; maybe it was her diet, though probably it was because she preferred Auntie Arsine's pilaf with just the right amount of butter and its strands of perfectly toasted vermicelli, but she would never tell Mama, who resented any compliment to Auntie.)

At the end of the evening, there were portions Mama packed up for people to take home, and by ten o'clock, the long day's twilight gave way to an eerie phosphorescence in the darkening air; it was as if this reclaimed desert glowed with a radium haze in the warm late evening air. A strange edge of green seemed to hover over the dark backyard barbeque and the ash tree and bushes. Juliet had gone outside to pick up the last empty plates. Garo's and Tigran's friends and employees were in the house, leaving, and her attention was drawn to the iridescence in the warm air. In the distance, there was the pop of late fireworks.

"Freaky, isn't it?" someone said from the dark yard.

She looked and recognized the obnoxious worker from one of the stores; he was about eighteen or nineteen years old, and she did not know his name or even whether he was Armenian.

"Yes," she said curtly.

"Come on over, cutie," he said. "You can see it better here."

"I have to go in."

"Aw," he said from the darkness.

She quickly stacked the dirty plates and was about to pick them up when she felt herself grabbed from behind. She let out a gasp of surprise.

"Quit that!" she called out into the night, "Stop it!"

He gripped her upper arm and wrenched her away from the lighted patio. Time stopped: she did not understand how this could be happening, and suddenly her voice disappeared. His mouth came at her, and she felt his body press against her. Up close, his features were grotesque – like an ape's. One of his hands ripped open her blouse. Suddenly she was able to move.

With a tightened fist, she punched him as hard as she could in the mouth.

"Bitch!" he spit out, releasing her and holding his face. "You bitch!" He rushed away and disappeared through the side gate.

She felt she was about to fall to the grass. Terrified, she walked through the dark yard and across the patio. Through the kitchen window, she could see Mama washing dishes. How could this have happened? It was not her fault, but she realized now that she was more vulnerable than she ever imagined. Maybe her hair was too long for a girl almost fourteen years old. She did not know. And she had never thought that an acquaintance of her brothers would do such a thing. But she could never tell Tigran or Garo; they would kill him, and it would be her fault. And she could never tell her parents that she had been attacked like that? The shame of it – amot! It had been horrible, the man's mouth and his hands mauling her and his body pressing against her. She felt awful. And he had torn her blouse. She would have to lie about it and say she had caught her blouse on something. She could never tell anyone.

Inside, her mother was still washing intently at the sink. Juliet went to pick up the stack of plates from the patio table, and holding them in both hands, she walked back into the Ararats' new house.

Chapter 10

First Grandson

DECEMBER 31, 1957

—•—

The Armenian parsley was wilting; it was because the bunches of flat leaves had not been properly watered. Garo needed to tell Chick Leone or one of the teenagers working at King to water the parsley – and the lettuce, too. She wheeled her cart further down the aisle of vegetables, and she saw torn paper littering the floor. What a shame! Usually, they prided themselves on keeping up the store. It was because Garo was overworked, but still he needed to pay attention; the vegetables needed watering, and the floor needed sweeping. Like an inspector general, she navigated her cart among the other shoppers, wheeling it now to the fruit aisle. The winter pears and apples and oranges were all prettily stacked. It was clear that someone had been assigned to spruce up the fruit. Starting last month, they had quince, pomegranate, and persimmons. It was wonderful that the store had such an abundance of fresh fruit and vegetables, and she felt soothed now by thinking about it.

"How are you, Mrs. Ararat?" Chick said behind her. She turned around and smiled stiffly at the thirty-year-old Italian man, with his soft, dark face.

"I'm well, thank you, Chick," she said in her purely American voice, and she asked him how he was.

"I'm good, Mrs. Ararat," he replied respectfully. She knew how to speak to Americans, and that had an impact on the odars. It was due not only to her accent-less voice, which to tell the truth was a little thin. It was because of what was behind the voice. She was a knowledgeable and intelligent person, and she knew that was what made the odars pay attention. She bristled if people thought she felt superior. Not at all, it was just that she knew how things ought to be, and she was sure people realized that.

However, she decided not to mention watering the lettuce and the parsley to Chick. She would leave those things to Garo, even though he had so much on his mind. There were rumors that the Italian assistant manager drank on the job, and at the employee's party, for which she had cooked for days, Chick had gotten drunk. She saw him try to kiss Lisa, a cashier. "Knock that off!" Tigran had snapped at him; "not in public – you're married!"

Chick wandered away, and she spied one of their private investigators by the liquor aisle. She could not help but notice things like that – what was happening around her, what things were really like.

The oranges were arranged according to size and quality. The large pyramid of the best was still intact, and she reached up to take a dozen of the big fragrant fruit from the top, filling a paper bag with them; most would be for a recipe she was making. Nearby were the cheaper oranges, which were on sale. Some customers were filling bags with them. It was just past 9 a.m., and the sale fruit bin already needed to be refilled. That was because King always offered sharply discounted specials, and sometimes people would come in to buy only the sales. Even owners of small markets came to buy and then resell at a profit. Such people were criminal. Of course, you had to run specials, and the really cutthroat competition came from the big market chains – especially Safeway. She knew that in the world of business the Ararats had terrible enemies, and it took all the family's strength to be successful, let alone expand now to Clovis and to the west side, where poor Mexicans and Negroes shopped and where the Armenians and Italians used to live. The Golden West, Garo called that store, because it generated such profit – it was a funny phrase, but it made its point. Garo and Tigran, with Armen's advice, were always coming up with strategies to counter the big chains' sales and to use manager's specials and advertising to draw in customers. So far they had succeeded.

"Hey, Ma," Garo walked up to her and hugged her. At six feet, her son loomed over her.

"Hello, Garo boy," she said, and then without a pause, "how's Pauly?"

"Great."

Pauly was her first grandchild, and she could hardly contain herself about him. That she was a grandmother to such a beautiful baby filled her with pride. She was forty-eight years old now, and it moved her deeply that her beautiful boy had now a beautiful boy of his own. Pauly's birth had also healed the little rift she had had with Garo's wife. Over a year ago, Lily had insisted the two of them leave the Garland Avenue house, and so the couple had ended up bringing the newborn home to a house of their own, which was fine with her, for lately she had felt unfazed about such things, almost invulnerable, and she felt that a sense of authority came from her now, even from her sturdy arms and hands and her face full of steadiness.

"What about his teething?" Artemis said. "You should put your finger in raki, and rub it on his gums?"

"It's not needed, Ma. We can't give him liquor."

"But it works."

"We'll see you tonight," he said. "His first birthday!"

"The parsley needs water, Garo."

"I know."

"Someone should spray it with water."

"I'll have Chick do it."

"Something's wrong with him. His skin is dark like wine. He drinks too much."

"Aw, Ma, you don't know that."

"I know what I know. He drinks too much."

Snippets of Armenian floated toward them from two women talking at the end of the aisle and filling bags with sale oranges. One of them pointed at Artemis and Garo, and said, "There are those rich Ararats."

Artemis looked up and smiled at her handsome son. His brown eyes were tense, and he ran his hand through his thinning dark blond hair, but then a grin lit his wide face.

"I wish!" he said quietly and then waved goodbye to his mother, who wheeled her cart toward the baking supplies. Most Armenians now came to King with spite in their hearts, and they bought only the specials – she had observed it many times. Maybe Armenians tore each other down in Armenia, too. It was absurd that they thought the Ararats were rich. Armen and she were socialists, and all they got from the chain was enough to give a middling income to each of the three families, Garo's, Tigran's, and Armen's. Competition made their profit margin very small, and it certainly did not go far compared to how much the land developers and the other new millionaires had. But now, with everything you saw on TV that you could buy, it was impossible to tell who had money and who didn't. People pretended all the time, out of envy and competition. She even saw it in Garo's Lily and Tigran's Betsy.

She put a bag each of flour and sugar in her cart and headed for the busy checkouts. The checker Lisa stood around on break; she was a cute blonde, and she waved Artemis over to a free lane and punched in her groceries on the cash register. The three Ararat families did not pay but instead signed for their groceries after they were rung up, just for accounting purposes. As Lisa chatted with her and worked the cash register, Artemis glanced at the stairs to the second floor manager's office. Tigran would be there and Armen, too, helping with the account books. Six months ago, when they had discovered some thefts by employees, the boys did not want to be bothered, at least at first. Especially Garo would not believe his parents' warnings. "It's not that bad," he said; the people he hired might be a little weird, but they were not thieves. The problem only got worse: food stolen, liquor missing, registers not rung and the money pocketed. To identify the culprits, she had suggested hiring a firm of private investigators, and now they posed as shoppers in all the stores. So far a cashier and a few stock boys had been caught.

Of course, things would get better if Tigran and Armen would come down stairs more, instead of leaving the floor managing to Garo. Her Garo boy was overworked, and he had the responsibility now of a beautiful son and a demanding wife. But Tigran, like Armen, was bored with that side of the business. So her oldest son and her husband between them did the buying and the books; neither cared as much as Garo for meeting customers, keeping up appearances, or directing the employees. In his engagement and involvement with people, Garo was like her. However, she would do some things differently if she were in charge of the stores, for she knew what needed to be done. She would force Tigran and Armen to be more engaged. She would take charge and bring more decisive authority to managing the store. Of course, she knew that, as a grandmother now and the mother of these sons, any influence her sense of authority had over her sons and her husband was bound to be indirect. Anyway, she could not really complain too much, for the stores were thriving.

Tigran's problem was only that he had not found what he really loved to do. She was sure that his wife, Betsy, had captured him when he was on the rebound from a terrible affair in Bakersfield. Once Betsy had even told Artemis she had never found it difficult to find a man, and Tigran was after all her second husband. He knew that nothing in life was perfect, and that you had always to carry your strength at the ready because of the horrible things that could happen to a person. Armen understood some of this in his way, but he did not face things head on. Tigran was really more reliable than her husband.

She drove their beautiful Ford sedan, one year old – like Pauly – out of the parking lot, and she turned the coral and white car north on Blackstone. At the corner of Shields there was the new King billboard, with a crown added now next to the slogan "Eat like a King at discount prices" and the trademark mouth open below. The winter sun was low in the sky, and its glare made it hard to drive as it poured over all the new houses she passed, unlandscaped and stretching as far as she could see. Their Garland Avenue ranch house was built on county land, with a Fresno zone number but without city streetlights and sidewalks. The houses on those blocks ranged from one-story bungalows to two-story haciendas, but that unregulated variety was the neighborhood's charm. So many other blocks had only uniform tract housing. To tell the truth, it was just the luck of the draw in Fresno, whatever developers and builders decided from block to block.

The city was the Wild West now, no longer the sleepy little farm town she had grown up in. New shopping centers were built nearby – Manchester Center and Fig Garden at Palm and Shaw. Big Mike Arslanian and his son Ronnie were among the developers cashing in now. Soon, in the afternoon, Artemis would be seeing Zephur Arslanian at their sewing group luncheon. The Arslanians owned many acres of land in the path of northward growth, and they had begun to develop big tracts.

For a while, Armen and she had owned – along with the Kings – 160 acres on the northern bluffs beyond the San Joaquin River, but it would have taken decades for the city to grow that far, and she could not imagine Fresno stretching so far north, to Herndon

Avenue and beyond. She was so glad when Armen sold the land last year. There had been some foolish plan for Garo to live on the farm with Lily, and for digging deep wells against the possibility of drought, but then the barn had burned to the ground. When Lily drove out Blackstone to look over the acreage, she saw the scorched plot where the barn had stood, and she said "Are you kidding? I'll never live so far out of town." The land had reminded Artemis of all the farms she had lived on during her forty-eight years and all the fires and droughts she had lived through; she had cried from happiness when Armen had sold it.

Now she drove into the driveway and parked in the carport next to a fir tree rising a dozen feet on the edge of the lot. The Ford's clock already read 9:30 this morning. She took her groceries into the house, and she turned on the oven to preheat it. She measured and sifted the flour and sugar in a large bowl, adding salt, baking powder, and an extra pinch of nutmeg. The kitchen became such a comfortable zone for her, where she felt assured and efficient. Her special enhancements to the recipe – a way of stirring or an amount of spice beyond the indicated ingredients – she always added with unconscious consistency. She attached the white, translucent mixer bowl to her Hamilton-Beach and beat the egg yolks, corn oil, orange juice and zest into a smooth thickened froth. She carefully poured wet into dry, stirring them until all was smooth. In another mixer bowl, she beat into stiff peaks the egg whites with cream of tartar and more sugar as the machine whirred away on the counter. Then she folded the whites into the big bowl of fragrant batter and poured the mixture into two oiled circular pans. She placed them in the hot oven. At noon, once they had baked and cooled, she would ice them with orange butter cream frosting.

The recipe for this chiffon cake was from the twenties, but it appeared in print only ten years ago. When she began making it for friends, they thought she was so modern. They loved it, and so did Garo and Armen too, who called it 'Pan d'Espagna.' She was making one cake for her sewing group friends meeting this afternoon, and one for the family at Pauly's first birthday party this evening. This chiffon and her sweet Easter cherag were all the bakery she made in her stove, for usually she disliked baking desserts. It was Juliet who loved to bake, but she was so messy that Artemis seldom allowed it. Anyway, the best dessert was fruit just picked and refrigerated – a slice of watermelon, especially the sweet heart, which tasted of the sun. But at times Juliet would insist. She was just sixteen, and somebody said she was full of piss and vinegar. Sometimes Artemis just had to give in. There would be flour and sugar all over the counter and kitchen table, and Juliet would not even notice the mess. No matter how good the chocolate chip cookies or the pies she baked, it was not worth all the cleaning up after her.

Sometimes she could not say no to her daughter, as much as she wanted to. If Juliet could be so stubborn, she could also be vulnerable. What right did she have to be so sensitive? Artemis did not like to think about it, and she grew agitated now, for it occurred to her that everyone around her was vulnerable and unstable in one way or another. As for Juliet, she was as willful as she had ever been, and yet she had been strangely morose lately, keeping more and more to herself, and she had gained weight again. What a terrible combination of stubbornness and misery? Maybe she was like Armen and Arsine and their side of the family, with all their delusions of grandeur. Suddenly the image came to her of Juliet as a little girl, screaming and flailing like a demonic cat, with blood streaming from her nose onto the bathroom floor. Lately Artemis had found a nice psychologist for her, Dr. Hopper, and she was convinced that he would help.

Just after noon, she drove the mile down Shields to Big Mike and Zephur Arslanian's ranch home, surrounded by the subdivided acres of smaller tract homes Big Mike had developed in northeast Fresno. She drove into the circle drive of the new home and parked behind one of the Arslanian's matching Cadillacs. When she rang the doorbell, Big Mike came to the door and welcomed her in.

"I'm leaving you ladies on your own," he said, "so you'd better behave yourselves." His voice was warm and hearty.

"That's nice, Mike," Artemis said, and she carried her cake into the kitchen where she heard her friends' voices. Yes, she thought, that was the man they played cards with each week, so powerful and at the same time so nice and sweet. There were rumors about Big Mike, about his youth and theft and even a murder in Detroit where, they said, he ran with racketeers. But she did not believe them; she knew how false rumors could be. It was true, though, that he and his son Ronnie were the sharpest businessman among their friends, buying land all along the main artery, from east to west on Shaw. Someday, she thought, they would be two of the most powerful men in the whole Valley. Yet Big Mike was so nice to her, and handsome Ronnie was always polite and wore such beautiful, cream-colored shirts. He even taught Juliet chess a few years ago, in the living room while the parents played Pinochle in the family room. And Big Mike and Zephur were so nice to their friends, always finding something to compliment about them. He raved about the quality of produce at King, he loved Artemis' tasty Armenian cooking, and he admired Armen's speech-making. When he would see sad movies from the thirties and forties on their new television, tears would silently course down his heavy cheeks.

Now, her friends sat around the big kitchen table where in the evenings they sometimes played cards with their husbands. There were the sisters Zephur Arslanian and Sirun Balian and three other women, including Armen's tall, aloof sister, Arsine, who lately had befriended sweet Sirun. After lunch, the six women would sit sewing or knitting on the nearby couches and upholstered chairs. Now, though, they ate and talked. Two years ago, the sewing group began by serving just coffee, tea, and little cookies, like almond-butter khourabia dusted with powdered sugar. But in recent months, every meeting was a feast, and Artemis enjoyed the new spirit of the group. They discussed the recipes for what they ate, the eggplant, the rice with leeks, the dolmas, the orange chiffon desert Artemis had brought. And they discussed their children and showed each other photos of grandchildren.

"How's Juliet?" Zephur asked in her polite, genteel voice. "She's not come with you to cards the last few times."

"She's been a little nervous lately, but she's okay," Artemis said.

"She has so much talent," Sirun Balian said.

"Yes, she's good in art," Artemis said. She thought of how the birth of her children had prevented her from pursuing art, and so she had not been able to succeed – but Juliet would not be able to succeed either. Her nervous daughter had talent, but not the needed dedication. You had to have drive, and without it, you could never overcome all the things that stood in your way.

"She designs her own clothes," Sirun said sweetly. "My Gloria says she could really be successful."

"That's just her opinion," Artemis said in an objective voice. Sirun always had a soft spot for Juliet and always tried to spoil her. And Gloria had become a strange Bohemian, smoking in public and wearing mostly black. "Armen and I talked with Juliet's Art teacher, at Open House his fall. He said even if she were the best artist in Fresno, even the best in California, she wouldn't be able to earn a living at it." Of course, she could have added that Juliet was a weak, erratic person – impossible to guide or even to predict.

"You never know, Artemis," her sister-in-law said in her coolly superior voice. What right did Arsine have to act so haughty! She always managed to make Artemis feel small-minded and even physically small, because Arsine was the tallest woman she knew, and now at the sewing group her height was accentuated by her conservative grey dress. Artemis was wearing her own favorite dress, a beautiful suit and skirt of dark red and black chambray, but at the moment she felt small and undistinguished and inferior. How dare her sister-in-law say you never know!

Always Arsine acted as if she knew best, but the truth was that she did not. She was not so perfect. Like when she cut relations with poor Ervant, her own brother. The sad man could not help it that the police had chased him; he had shot one, and he had been given a life sentence. She remembered when Ervant had escaped when he was on a work detail from San Quentin, and at midnight he arrived at his mother's back door on K Street. Zabel had pleaded for Armen and Artemis to give Ervant money. Of course, Arsine and Nubar had already refused.

"And how is Pauly?" Arsine asked. She sounded so cautious and cold. And yet the mention of Pauly managed to transform Artemis' mood.

"Oh, Pauly is one today!" she said. "Garo is so proud of him. You should see how long his beautiful auburn hair is getting."

"And Lily? Is she still touchy?" Arsine asked.

How dare she – Artemis almost said it aloud – bring up her difficulties with her daughter-in-law!

"Of course not. She's a very nice girl. What about your girls?" Artemis' voice was angry. "You have no right to criticize Lily. Are you having trouble with your daughters?"

"Now, now," Sirun said in a soothing voice, "Artemis, Arsine." Zephur and Sirun quickly began talking about their own children.

Artemis would have asked whether Arsine's two daughters still smoked in the bathroom. Of course, her own daughter-in-law did that too, though that had not been the cause of the terrible argument she had had with Lily. Over a year ago, Artemis had complained to Garo when Lily exchanged her wedding ring for a bigger diamond, paying the difference with savings from her job at the Bank of America. Artemis had said, "Those people – she belongs to a greedy family." Garo had repeated his mother's criticism to his wife, and Lily had said she would not spend another night under the Ararat roof.

Finally, at 3 in the afternoon, Sirun had to leave, thanking her sister for such a nice time; Artemis followed soon after. When she drove into the Garland Avenue driveway, Juliet was just going in the front door, and she was holding a stack of her high school books. Artemis checked the mileage on the Ford's odometer, as she habitually did, and she rushed into the house. In the kitchen, the light coming through the window above the sink shone on her daughter's creamy white skin and her mahogany hair.

"Don't eat that orange," she said as Juliet took one from the refrigerator. Usually she gave her a bowl of ice cream when she arrived home from school. "That's the last one."

"There's one more left. Why didn't you buy more?"

"That was all they had."

"That was all they had?"

"And I used the rest in an orange chiffon cake, for tonight."

"Oh," her daughter said coolly, putting the orange peels in the garbage can under the sink. "Would you like some of this?"

"Of course, not!" she said emphatically in her thin voice. "Why would you want an orange now when you know that you'll have the orange chiffon this evening?"

She expected Juliet to say something mean to her, but instead her daughter just gave Artemis an icy stare. It was so much like Juliet to be suddenly cold and silent. Why did she always act so superior, and how dare she patronize her mother! Artemis followed her down the hall to the back bedroom, and she noticed the shoes she wore. "Why would you wear white tennis shoes to school?" Juliet always insisted on wearing odd things like jean skirts, ponchos, and now white tennis shoes. "People will laugh at you, Juliet."

"Oh, Mama!" she said and went into the bathroom next to the back bedroom. Garo and Lily had slept back here in the first nine months of their marriage, before they left in such a hurry.

"You'll lose your friends," Artemis said at the closed door. But Juliet did have friends. Though who were they really? There was that pasty looking odar girl Sue – and Gloria Balian and now her new best friend, Edie. Artemis looked around the bedroom. Clothes were spread over one side of the double bed. "Sloppy Suzie," she mumbled. More than once, she had threatened that she would call the Salvation Army to pick up all these clothes flung around the room. And last summer she had gathered as much as she could carry of her daughter's clothes from her bed and floor, carried them out, and dropped them in a pile on the front lawn. But it had no effect. Her daughter had never learned. She just did not understand the need to take charge of your life.

A low bookshelf stood against the wood paneled wall, and there were novels on the shelves by Tolstoy, Dickens, the Brontes, Howard Fast, and Steinbeck, "Gone with the Wind," and the family's Shakespeare with those Rockwell Kent illustrations. Above the bookshelf was a cork board fixed to the wall, and a strange new print from a magazine was tacked there. It was a woman dressed in black standing rigidly to the right of two seated boys dressed in red sweaters playing checkers; behind them was a mantle with flowers in a vase and a small statue, and to the left was another woman seated on an orange couch. The strange thing was that all the colors, all the shades of red and orange, seemed to run together. And everything looked flattened and two-dimensional, including the chessboard, the mantle, the upholstered couch, and even the beautiful Oriental rug on the floor. There were no boundaries, and red was everywhere. That must be how Juliet saw the world. Everything melted together. There was something wrong with art like this, and her daughter did not need to have it staring at her all the time. One of the tacks was loose, she pulled at it, and the print began to fall. She pulled out the other tack and held the print behind her back when Juliet came from the bathroom.

"What are you doing, Mom?" the girl asked, looking around.

"Just cleaning up, Sloppy Suzie."

"Where is my Matisse print?"

"What?"

"What's behind your back?"

"Oh, that. It had fallen on the floor. You'd better get ready, Juliet. You're seeing Dr. Hopper at 4." She began to leave, not wanting to talk with her daughter any more. What had she done to deserve such a critical girl?

"May I have it back?"

Artemis handed it to her and went down the hall to change. What did the stubborn girl see in that painting?

In the master bedroom, she opened the mirrored sliding door of her wide closet. She took a coral housecoat from among the clothes hung on hangers and some comfortable shoes from the pairs on the floor there. Once dressed, she walked into the hall. She heard Armen being dropped off by Tigran, and she rushed out past her husband in the front yard to remind her son about tonight. He was already down the block.

When Armen drove Juliet to her appointment with Dr. Hopper, the nice psychologist, Artemis had the house to herself for a while. She called Tigran's number and told Betsy the time to come for Pauly's birthday at Garo's, and then she sat on the family room couch. The room had been converted last year from Juliet's former bedroom; now it had a sliding glass door looking out on the backyard; there was a beautiful, overgrown ash shade tree to the right and on the left the small swimming pool. Last summer, it had been dug by hand because their side gate was too narrow to let in heavy machinery.

This last year, remarkable things had happened not only for Armen and Artemis but in the world, too. In the Soviet Union, Khrushchev had denounced Stalin and put reforms in place. It was called a thaw, and she was glad about it, though she still admired Stalin for turning the Soviet Union into a truly industrialized nation. Now the USSR had even launched the world's first satellite, Sputnik, and the first ICBM.

Also, last January first, the day after Pauly was born, she had found a poem on her night table, and it was written in Armen's beautiful printing. It was the first poem she had seen of his for years, a love poem full of regret for having retreated like a hermit to some lofty mountain, and it was full of longing that she would search him out there. He wrote that he had been wrong to withdraw to his hermitage and that he must return now to her, to this house, to this family. During the year, it was true that Armen had become more tender, though they only held each other. That was enough, she felt, and it was more than had happened for years. Armen would have to be content; it was all she would accept.

With Garo's marriage, Pauly's birth, and the markets' success, everyone's spirits seemed somehow restored, except Juliet's. Of course, it was her own fault, but Artemis still wished Juliet could be happier. There was a sports car, an MG, she wanted so badly, and in the New Year, maybe Artemis would help get it for her. There was Dr. Hopper, who was helping in a different way; when she spoke to him on the phone, he seemed like such a nice man. Garo was seeing him, too, at Artemis' urging. Several times, her son had called, panicky and breathing fast, from a gas station or the drugstore, and he would say he could not drive his old Buick another inch and needed a ride home. Lily put him under so much pressure, poor thing, but Dr. Hopper was helping.

Armen and Juliet finally arrived back at 5:15, and while they were getting ready to go to Garo's, Artemis went outside to check the car's odometer. Five miles had been added, just enough for the trip to Dr. Hopper's in the Tower District. She had to be sure, for she still wondered about Armen, about how unreliable he seemed, how lazy and withdrawn he was despite everything.

At a quarter to six, they drove south and west to Garo's street. The three of them would eat with Garo, Lily, and Pauly, and then the rest of the family would come to celebrate Pauly's birthday – Tigran and Betsy, who was six months pregnant now, and Lily's mother and father, the Holy Trinity priest, and her brother Eddy, nineteen years old. Artemis knew that Eddy and Lily would hover around their parents, both to prove their superior status and to protect them from the left-wing Ararats! By nine, they would all head for their various New Year's Eve celebrations. On the phone, Lily had told Artemis that she was not staying up, but Garo was going out later; a friend had just opened a new bar in the Tower District.

They drove up to the ranch-style tract home, and Lily came to the door when they knocked; she was a very pretty woman, with the olive complexion and the beautiful almond eyes of a certain type of Armenian and the petite build and dainty insouciance of a young Frenchwoman.

"Ooph," she sighed and then smiled. "Pauly is grumpy," she said and embraced Armen, Artemis, and Juliet, as they all said hello. She took the plate with the orange chiffon cake from Artemis. "Thanks," she said, "we can use it." Of course, she could use it, because it was Garo's favorite, but she was too competitive to mention it. Still, though, things had improved between them, and Artemis felt a generosity toward Lily, because she loved little Pauly so much.

"Where is he?" Artemis asked.

"In the living room with Garo," she said in a tired, long-suffering voice, raising her sleepy eyes to the ceiling.

Garo's voice was yelling from the living room: "Good boy!"

They all entered, except Lily. Little Pauly was squatting in diapers on the floor. Garo sat across the room, holding a plastic ball; he pumped it frenetically in the air, then held it on the floor, and suddenly released it toward his son. But Pauly began crawling toward Artemis. She picked him up and hugged him with all the warmth stored in a forty-eight year old grandmother for her first grandson.

"Hi, Mom, Dad, kiddo!" Garo said.

She held the auburn-haired baby to her breast, and her eyes and ears were filled to overflowing. The softness of his skin intoxicated her, the sweetness of his odor, the delicate miracle of his eyelashes, the beauty of his fat dimpled face, smiling into her own, the timeless power and tenderness of his brown eyes. She yearned to protect him from what the world would do to such innocence. She wished she could hold the infant for eternity, as if she were the statue of Artemis, not the woman herself.

Chapter 11

Poetry

AUGUST 15, 1958

—•—

Armen held the columns of figures in his mind, and without the aid of a pencil or pen, he carefully computed the collapse of King's. The books began to go into the red a couple of months ago; now, it was clear that the business would fall into debt and worse. There had been a terrible price war with the big corporations for months now, and it forced the Kings to sell groceries below cost: sugar, flour, coffee, bread, milk, eggs. Safeway and Savemart colluded with each other and the suppliers. Unflappable as he was usually, Armen felt worried that his family's future was in danger. He and Artemis wanted the boys to file suit against the giant chains' monopolistic practices, but he knew it was already too late.

This summer psoriasis had again begun to appear across his stomach and back, his arms and legs. And his headaches had grown almost impossible to bear. One threatened him this afternoon as he sat finishing the day's accounts in the upstairs office on Clinton Avenue. The signs were all there. The light bothered him, and without warning exhaustion emptied him out, like a malarial fever, except his temperature did not rise, and then the pain began to tighten around his head. When all this would happen, he retreated to his bed after dinner and woke up at midnight, restless and unable to sleep. Very quietly, he would leave Artemis snoring in the full-sized bed next to his and drive alone to an all-night diner like Big Boy's or Sambo's, order waffles, and sip coffee for an hour. He had always enjoyed the atmosphere of a coffee shop, a surjeron like the Ramgavar club, but the old, progressive Asparez, located now in the second story above a pool hall downtown, had fallen on hard times because so many Fresno Armenians had moved to the northern suburbs.

King's was going to collapse. The boys would feel bitter, but he did not feel it, only worried. Lately, he was very focused on writing poems, and he spent hours composing in his mind. When he woke up at midnight or at dawn, he had returned to the pleasure of writing poetry in his clean, careful script, which was like the handwriting in the ancient Armenian illuminated manuscripts. He had begun to write again soon after Garo married Lily. His "Wedding Wish" to them had been the first poem he had written in years, and then ten months after the wedding poem, on the night little Pauly was born, he had composed his poem for Artemis, with its recognition that their lives were intertwined like vines. Poems about Armenia had followed. He would sit at the kitchen table or in the booth at Big Boy's, and it felt as if he sang a new song to himself.

It was 3 p.m. now as he drove home from King's. When he turned north on Blackstone in his usual route, the sun poured in through his side window. He had begun to wear sunglasses against the glare because of his increased headaches, but he loved the sun warming the crusted skin of his exposed arm. As he drove, he began to chant his new political poem as if it were an Armenian folk song, an ancient one like those Gomidas had set, "Groong" and "The Crane." His poem was titled "Armenian Crane," and it would soon appear in New Age, the Ramgavar paper published in Boston. It had been sent in by Mariam Saroyan, who was no relation to William, the writer, though she was very literary and so helpful to Armen. There were so few weekly papers left trying to keep Armenian alive. For Armen, the Armenian language was like the warm sunlight, just as the great Charentz had written, before he committed suicide: "I love the taste of my sweet Armenia's sun-flavored speech. No other language tells my want." And even though Armenian was disappearing here in America, Armen felt that his latest poetry was finer than anything he had written decades ago. And this new poem about the Armenian crane, praising Armenia, still had the bite of his earliest writing.

Almost home now, he remembered his first story, which was written in 1913, when he was thirteen. It was about his work as a young bookkeeper a few afternoons a week for an Armenian merchant in Constantinople. One winter evening, the merchant asked Armen to help him carry some bags of produce across the Galata Bridge to the merchant's home in the Armenian, Greek, and Jewish neighborhood north of the Golden Horn. On the bridge, a swift wind blew off the river into his face, and as he hurried across, he walked in front of the merchant, who carried only a briefcase. Each time he tried to walk in front of the merchant, Armen was pushed back. "Walk behind me," he spit out like a Turk, "three paces." Irritated, Armen had quickly written his anecdote almost like an improvisation and titled it "Walk Behind Me." He sent it to the largest Armenian daily in Constantinople, and to his surprise, it appeared as a letter to the editor. Armen was delighted by the sudden magic of publication, though revenge was not sweet in this case, because the merchant immediately fired him. But that day his love of words truly blossomed into a love of writing.

The other stories he had turned out were similar exposures of arrogance or of life in poverty. One piece was about his first day at Adamian School in the fall of 1913. When he applied for a scholarship, he had refused at the interview to say, as he was required to do, that his family was poor; his beloved teacher, the great writer Hagop Oshagan, had needed to intercede. For the first day of classes, his mother had altered the single, black suit of his father, who had died of typhus the year before. Steeling himself with pride, he walked before his fellow freshmen, who said: "Did somebody die?" and "A suit fit for a corpse!" and "Your Excellency, Baron Armen, would you wear something a little less shabby tomorrow?"

Now as he drove into the driveway, he saw his daughter going in the front door. He briefly glimpsed her glowing face and the beautiful dark-brown curls falling to her shoulder, and his heart lightened at the sight. From her earliest years, she had been a great comfort with her spontaneity, her alertness, and even her wayward irritability. She was his ally in the family, her father's daughter, though she did not really know what went on in his mind, which was probably for the best. She could get very mad and very sad, and he wished he could give her as much comfort as she had given him. Now at seventeen, she still saw things according to her independent lights even in this materialistic society of America. Of course, she was also like him in wanting to have things they desired at once. Three years ago he had brought home a surprise for Artemis, a new Ford Fairlane he had loved at first sight. And last winter Juliet had asked her parents to help her buy a British sports car. He had wanted to please her, and to his surprise Artemis had agreed, and so this spring, they had signed for the loan on an MG. Almost immediately it had needed the mechanic to work on it, and even today it was in the shop with a broken axle. Of course now they would not be able to afford to keep it.

He walked into the house and heard mother and daughter bickering. It was such a waste of energy, an unwinnable war. He hoped Juliet could go away to college; that way she could escape. Her high school English teacher had encouraged her to apply to Berkeley next year, and he wanted her to go as well, to the university where he had spent a little over a semester as a French major almost forty years ago.

"One of us is going to have to drive her!" Artemis said in an exasperated voice as he entered the kitchen.

"I can," he said to his daughter. She looked up from her bowl of ice cream and smiled.

"Daddy, I saw your cousin Manoug, when I was walking home from school," she said. "He drove by and gave me a ride. Or maybe it was your cousin Isahag. I can never tell them apart."

"That's because..." Armen began.

"That's because," Artemis interrupted, "all you care about is yourself, and you don't even notice the difference between people."

"Mama!" Juliet said.

"Manoug and Isahag are twins," Armen mumbled.

No one listened, so he walked out of the kitchen, and a little later, he found Juliet in the family room.

"Let's go, tsakis," he said. He used the endearment, little lamb, instinctively with his daughter, just as he had always called Artemis Angel. The words were like talismen against any bad feelings hovering in the air.

As he drove her to the appointment with her psychologist, Dr. Hopper, they were quiet. Juliet was preoccupied, as she often was, and he was thinking about visiting a friend during this hour. After he let her off at the psychologist's, he drove to Mariam Saroyan's house, which was near the Tower District. Mariam was a widow, whose husband had been a crude, unworthy soul. She had been born, like Armen, in a village near the city of Bursa, which was southeast of Constantinople. A literary, educated woman, she too carried with her terrible memories of the Genocide and knew the ancient litany of massacres that made up the history of the Armenians, starting with their first sun-worshipping Neolithic settlements, which had been overrun and incinerated by Bronze Age conquerors. Armen imagined a giant God of War holding a torch in one hand and a saber in the other, and trampling across Armenia's fields and cities, reducing them to ashes.

After the flood in the Bible, it was said that Hyak, who was a grandchild of Noah's, had led the surviving Hyes of Urartu to rebuild their cities on the plain surrounding Mount Ararat. As he once more recalled, this new Armenia, Hyastan, was repeatedly conquered and then rebuilt. Byzantium absorbed the Hyes' Christian cities and villages into its empire, which were in their turn conquered by Central Asian tribes and then by converted Muslims, and finally starting in 1915 – forty-three years ago, when he was fifteen – the Turks' Ottoman Empire slaughtered one and a half million Armenians: burning, hanging, shooting, stabbing, and the fatal long march of deportation.

He parked now in front of Mariam Saroyan's house. Walking to her door, he wondered once more at how brutal their people's history had been and what a terrible effect that had even on their language, which was dying now here in America. He rang the bell and waited.

"Armen!" Mariam said, surprised and pleasantly smiling as she opened the door. "How nice of you to stop by." She spoke such refined Armenian, and she never complained about his unannounced visits over the last two years.

Miriam Saroyan kept an archive with copies of everything he had written and everything of his she had sent to the Armenian newspapers on the east coast. She was his supporter, and Armen felt grateful for the admiration of this smart, well-read woman and all the work she did for him. He sat on the old brocaded couch in the dark living room and savored the tea and almond cookies and polite talk she offered with her Old World graciousness.

She sat at the other end of the couch, and after finishing his tea, he said, "The Armenian spoken in Fresno has deteriorated so much. It is as terrible as my English."

"Your English is far from terrible, and your Armenian is very pure," she flattered him in her own refined Armenian. "Fresno may be a wasteland, but your poetry is keeping our language alive."

"I don't know, Mariam. We are brutalized! It is not good here in Fresno, and it was even worse in Turkey. I think maybe I should stop writing poems. I have stopped before."

"Please, no. You're an Armenian, not a Turk, and even an enlightened Turk should not give up writing because his people were brutes. Not at all."

Yes, he thought, someday he might find such an enlightened Turk, his twin, his brother – a new Nazim Hikmet.

He would write a poem about this, and he hoped that she would send it to Nor Or – the New Age, the Boston Armenian journal. And it did feel like a new age. Conditions were improving in Soviet Armenia. Mariam was right; he must write whatever he could write. And anyway, he found now that he loved to do so, to sing in his poetry and to play, to improvise; certainly he liked it more than making speeches in meeting halls or at the Armenian Progressive League picnics.

"Don't worry so, Armen," she said and silently reached across the couch to give his hand a squeeze. He knew he was acting preoccupied, but she did not mind. Mariam was so kind and gentle to him. He held her hand in his now, and for a minute they sat together quietly on the couch. Then he said he must pick up Juliet soon at the psychologist.

"I hope she feels better," she said in a calm voice. "And I hope Artemis is doing well."

As he drove back to Dr. Hopper's, Armen thought about Mariam. She would never let him grow passionate with her, and though she supported his writing, she was not the inspiration for his writing. No, Artemis was his muse, and she had been ever since they first met at a progressive picnic in 1927. As soon as he heard her voice, it called to him. It was true that she had changed, and this altered the angelic feminine gentleness he had always heard in her. Her voice commanded now in ways he had never imagined. The love he had discovered on his wedding night had continued for over a decade, but in the early forties, after her hysterectomy, she began to decline any invitation. Now it was not weeks but years between the times she would allow him, and he felt helpless to reach her.

Today was August 15th, his fifty-eighth birthday. He was getting old, and his spreading psoriasis was worse than ever now because the business was failing. Artemis had aged too; fine veins stretched over her legs and buttocks. He still felt desire, but she did not; he could not help it, yet all she allowed was the little comfort of simply holding his Angel. Was it not possible still to know the unconsciousness of desire? To experience a lapsing of hatred and opposition? When Garo married Lily, his question began to find an answer; it was then he found room to breathe again and sing and write. Especially when Pauly was born, the bitterness between Artemis and him somewhat diminished, and he wrote his tender love song to her, an apology really. Now, as he approached the psychologist's office building, he recited the poem aloud to the car dashboard.

Departing with a grieving and afflicted heart, I climbed
A path up the mountainside and sat on this rock ledge.
I abandoned you and rushed up the path like a mad deer,
Yet I still dreamt of our past decades and your words of love.

On the rock I waited for years, deaf, bitter, blind, alone.
Then an eerie blue fog descended on both valley and mountain.
A bird, a twig in his beak, passed by crying and cawing,
And the mild night breeze streamed like the lament of swans.

The lonely moon arose from behind the rock cliff
And kissed the mountain with the coquetry of a bride.
Reminded of you, I rushed from the rocks mad with grief
To whisper this song, aching for home and your dear words.

"Daddy, where were you?" Juliet asked as she opened the car door.

"Tsk. Sambo's."

"I saw Garo for a minute. His appointment was right before mine," she said. "He seemed upset."

Armen tsked again. He did not like speculating about people's moods, even with his dear Juliet. Of course, his son had a lot to worry him – his difficult wife, his failing business. Armen did not approve of venting your private matters. Sometimes, when he and Artemis sat on the living room couch watching television with Juliet, he felt awkward about the displays of affection on the screen. But such displays were part of America's culture now. He noticed how young women treated Garo when Lily was not there. They called him "Doll" or "Honey," and their hands would touch his arm, even his face.

An Armenian folk song came to him, and he began softly singing it, silly and lovely: "Kele kele kelit mermen: You walk and walk, and I would die to walk with you. I die for your beautiful spirit, my quail, my lovely little quail."

When he and his daughter entered the Garland Avenue house, Artemis hurried outside past them to the car, and when she returned, Juliet was at the stove lifting the lid off a pot of pilaf.

"Smells good," she said. The rich odor of butter and broth filled the kitchen.

"That's especially for you," Artemis said. "It's vegetarian."

"Didn't you put chicken broth in it?"

"No," his wife said blankly.

Armen was sure it was not true, and he realized Juliet watched him as he rolled his eyes. Instead of his usual tsk, he made a sound suspiciously like the noise of a chicken clucking, and his daughter laughed. He loved to see her face light up like that. He knew she would be fine when she went to Berkeley, as he hoped she would.

As he left the kitchen, he looked at Artemis who stood at the stove, calm and oblivious as she cooked his birthday dinner. It was irrelevant to him, but she always insisted on celebrating his birthday with the whole family. They would arrive at six, and it was now a quarter past five. The headache which had threatened him in mid-afternoon had not materialized, and so he decided to putter in the backyard garden for a while. The garden was his refuge, especially as the afternoon heat began to lift. The ash tree hovered above the lot, its blood-red flowers gone now and its leafy branches reaching for the sun, like an up-jutting olive tree. In the stretch of earth between the clothesline and the fence, he had planted ten-foot rows of tomatoes, eggplant, and peppers. He loved the rhythm of hoeing and irrigating. Working in the earth reminded him of his life in the village, before he followed his parents to Constantinople in 1911. He remembered when his dear grandparents would celebrate with great fanfare each grandchild's day of birth; those were the birthdays that mattered.

He recalled the morning in 1911 when his parents left him, his sister and brother, and the new baby Garo in the care of his grandparents, aunts, and uncles. The children and parents had walked together to the outskirts of town. Armen noticed that his mother's breasts were full from feeding baby Garo, who would now be in the care of their aunt, and he remembered her leaning to kiss and hug him tightly against her. In just a minute she would be leaving, and she softly cried: "It can't be helped, it is God's will." The terrible drought and the poverty that followed were taking their mother from them. He looked up at his mother's face with her deep-set blue eyes, and he saw her proudly hiding her tears for a moment behind her dark blue shawl. Then she said, "It can't be helped, Armen. You must be a little man, and help your grandparents. Never bring amot down on them. Guide Arsine. Help with Ervant and Garo. And you must do well in school."

Later that day, he had walked at dusk from their house, past the withered plum tree and next to it the akhor for animals. He walked out to the mulberry groves, nearly leafless from the drought. Each spring since early childhood, he had watched his father and uncles lumber out into these fields, pruning and tilling and seeding. And each summer, amid the leaves and bursting fruit, the men would reach to pick and cut and harvest. To him they seemed like giants standing among the vines and mounted high on ladders among the trees. But now the once fertile valley was empty and dying.

All around Armen the trees had yielded only a scattering of shriveled nuts and fruit. The olive trees had lost their tint of green; they stood ashen beneath the mountainous horizon of Duman Dagh. The withered trees and dried out fields and the distant mountain were his jury to be confronted with the evidence of injustices. The cows had waddled about and gazed calmly up at him as his voice rang out.

He spoke to the valley and the sky, beginning with the story of the winter rains in early 1910. First there were weeks upon weeks of storms. The family was huddled around the ojakh's flames, where their mother was cooking lentils, and she suddenly shouted: "Something is wrong. Run! Run children, run to the akhor!" All fourteen members of the extended family rushed to the door, and the mud bricks surrounding the hearth sagged and fell inward onto the dung fire. Through the hole formed in the wall they could make out the eerie half-lit rain-flooded fields; then, in a sudden roar, the chimney fell in and filled the hole with a heap of rubble and smoke. That night, the family brought their mats and bedding from the ruined house into the akhor, and they slept next to the pregnant mare with her udders sloping on the straw. Armen's bald grandfather, with his white handlebar moustache, kept whispering to their grandma in the night: "It is a bad omen."

As the family had rebuilt the fireplace, the rains ceased completely. The drought came. That spring, the buffeted, parched mulberry trees failed to bud, and the silkworms, without leaves to feed on, perished. Hail descended in early summer, and the grapevines and olive trees produced almost nothing. Without crops to pack and silk to comb and send to Bursa or Nicea, his family lived on what grain they had or could barter, whatever the cows and sheep produced, whatever beans and peppers and tomatoes could be grown in the yard's poorly irrigated garden. Last year his uncle Haig had fled to America from the terrible oppression in Turkey. Just now this morning his parents had left; his mother would find work in Constantinople and his father would work as a sailor on the sea.

Armen had turned away from the rocky sight of Duman Dagh, as the two cows stared at him in the yellow field. One cow's face was benign and slightly bloated, with black numb eyes. Armen walked the two of them toward the akhor. Inside the house, his grandmother was cooking, and soon the eleven remaining members of the family gathered for a paltry dinner.

It was a few months later that Baby Garo had died. He was being nursed by an aunt, but their poverty had dried up her breasts. All they had to give the infant was sugar water, and one morning he did not wake up. Armen could hardly bear it. And the terrible truth was that in Constantinople, his mother was serving as a wet nurse for rich Armenian families, as a slave to them, cleaning and cooking.

Finally after a year, their father had come to bring Armen, Arsine, and Ervant to live with their parents in Constantinople. When the ferry docked at the city wharf, a strange woman had approached on the landing; she had beautifully combed hair gathered in a bun and held by a tiara in back, and she wore a green, European-style dress of some soft fabric. "Armen," the woman had cried, running up to him and hugging the boy to her bosom. His mother's face was still graced by her dignity and her blue eyes, but her hands were transformed, hardened by her work dawn to dusk six days a week.

Then in 1912, his father sailed on a ship carrying olive oil to Venice, and when he returned, he was feverish, wracked with painful vomiting and diarrhea. Nothing would help, and Armen watched him die. He ran block after block from their building down the hilly avenues toward the shore. "No," he howled, over and over. He was twelve years old, and with a single blow he had become the head of their small family. "No, no," he kept chanting as he dashed across the scraggly beach to the shore of the Bosporus. Raw with shock, he began helplessly to cry. The swift current swept by him, and he stared, riveted by its lethal flow. He saw now that he must dodge death for the sake of his mother, his brother, and his sister. But how? He did not know, for in the lethal current he saw the face of death: it had singled his family out.

"Armen." It was Artemis' high commanding voice now, and it came through the screened window at the kitchen sink. "They're almost here. Come in."

Startled out of his memory, he stayed hunched over his hoe among the tomato plants, green and red. His body ached from all that weighed on him. He put the hoe down, slowly straightened his back, and walked into the house filled with the smells of cooking. Yes, the young people were coming. He washed up; when he emerged and walked to the living room, the doorbell rang.

"What have we here?" he said cheerfully to Tigran's wife at the door. Betsy held in her arms their three-month-old son, Adam.

"Happy birthday, Grandpa," Betsy said and leaned to kiss Armen's furrowed face.

Chapter 12
The blinding sun

JULY 29, 1959

She had to see her mother before the others arrived at the mortuary.

"I'm leaving," she told Armen. "You and Juliet can get a ride downtown from Tigran. I need to go there now."

And so she backed up their three-year-old cream and coral Ford Fairlane from the Garland Avenue driveway. When she came to Blackstone, it was busy this Wednesday morning. She stopped at the red light and looked at the King's billboard. "Eat like a King at discount prices" was illegible; the crown was stained, and the open mouth was peeling off.

"Businesses have their ups and downs!" Garo had said last year; he had been arranging one more pyramid of peaches, and the new assistant manager, a tall middle-aged man with a broad Oklahoma accent, had started shouting about meat to a screaming woman nearby. Garo had interrupted: "Lady, I like your spirit. Where are you from? In L.A. would they give you a new roast, no questions asked, like I'm going to do? And take a bag of these peaches. On the house." Then her irrepressibly optimistic son turned back to

Artemis and said, "A man can always repeat his successes, unless he's a fool!"

At the same time, Tigran had grown bitter and pessimistic. Early on he had started a rainy day account in Betsy's name. A friend of his, Don Wolf, who had become an assistant manager at a Safeway, had told him the markets' days were numbered. Artemis remembered him from one of Tigran's barbeques last year; Don had worn nicely pressed khakis, a beige tucked-in golf shirt, and a thin Indian necklace of turquoise and tubular beads, like pale shards of bone. Upper management at Safeway did everything it could, short of blackmail and murder, to drive King out of business, including insider deals with distributors and hiring away personnel. A month ago, the King chain had filed for bankruptcy and closed.

"Finally," she mumbled against the silence in the car as she drove toward downtown.

Two stores survived. One was in Clovis, just northeast of Fresno. That had been an ill-fated store, and yet it survived. Lily's younger brother Eddy had embezzled thousands of dollars there, and it was also where Chick Leone had been transferred when he collapsed in the meat freezer, a vodka bottle shattering in his hand as he hit the floor. That Clovis King was the only store Ronnie Arslanian would agree to save, when Garo had gone to Big Mike's son for help in May. Ronnie began paying the mortgage and appointed Garo managing partner. But Artemis knew the arrangement would not last. Nothing lasted.

She drove now into Fresno's downtown grid of lettered and numbered streets. The other store they saved was not far away, a little, dingy market on Belmont, which Armen had originally incorporated in Artemis' name. The Stars and Stripes Market was its name, and it had been too much trouble to change it. The small store catered mostly to winos and the neighborhood Orientals, Mexicans, and Okies. She and Armen and Juliet began working long hours there this summer. Their daughter, encouraged by her

English and art teachers, had wanted to apply to the University of California at Berkeley. "You're dreaming," Artemis had said; "we can't afford to send you away to college!" And last winter, they had sold Juliet's MG.

Artemis had been working the afternoon shift last Friday. It was two o'clock on a windless July day of baking heat, and she had lowered the shades to reduce the glare. For the last half hour, no one had come in for Muscatel or Thunderbird or a loaf of Rainbow bread, and she found herself sweeping the aisles. Armen would relieve her at five, in a few hours. Suddenly he opened the store's front door. There was a lit pipe in his hand, and his face was a frozen mask.

"Your mother is dead," he said. He had walked to the cash register and sat down on the stool behind the counter.

Now it was Wednesday morning, and she drove up to a large white clapboard house one block away from St. Paul's Armenian Apostolic Church. The small parking lot was drenched in morning light and lined on one side with dark green cypresses reaching up toward the glaring sky. She knocked on the locked door, and once she was let into the stuffy room, she walked past the rows of vacant seats. There was almost no sound; even her breathing seemed distant. Ever since Armen had said "Your mother is dead" five days ago, she noticed it had become hard to hear people's voices, the television, the car's engine, or nature's sounds. Even little Pauly's voice had seemed muted. Everything was muffled.

The scent of the roses, red and white, by the casket was mixed with a distant chemical odor. She looked into the open casket and saw the shrunken corpse. Her kindly mother had disappeared. The pretty, pensive face had become a mask encased in makeup. There seemed to be arcing sparks of light in her halo of grey hair, as if Lucine had been electrocuted, not felled by a stroke at 68. An aura of static penetrated the silence: this spirit has vanished, it said, this husk seeks earth, this flesh is dead and can give you nothing. Whatever it is you seek, I want only burial and earth. You are alone, and I have gone, am no longer present. Artemis stood there alone. All she could perceive was the baked and silent world she had inherited, from her first memories of the hot farm, the death of her little sister in a cauldron of steaming water, the years with Armen on the sun-drenched land, the homes that went up in flames consuming even Armen's poems, through to the most recent conflagration of their hopes. Always it was the same; nothing lasted.

What did it matter that they had lost the stores and their sons were full of blame and bitterness? What did it matter that two markets survived? What if Garo abandoned the Clovis store in frustration, and the other made a meager living from the long hours she and Armen and Juliet spent there? Did it matter that a new generation of Ararats had begun their journey, her Pauly and now Adam, Tigran's and Betsy's toddler? And what did it matter that Armenia was coming into its own, that socialism was thriving?

She stood frozen above her annihilated mother. Nothing lasted. Nothing counted.

At the other end of the long room, a door opened, admitting for a moment the glare of the midmorning sun and a wave of already superheated July air. Her sister Satenig, so much like their mother, approached, crying. She embraced Artemis with her heavy arms, fattened on her husband's grilled meats. Nick, bullish and teary-eyed, followed, along with their three children. They all loomed over Artemis, and she sat down on a chair near the coffin. Satenig sat by her. "Honey, you're so pale," she said, and Artemis mumbled in response. The door in back kept opening now, letting in more and more heat and glare; the room filled with the procession of mourners, yet all remained muffled, at a distance.

Anoush, her youngest sister, came up to her, confident, pretty, and full of tears, followed by two sons and her gentlemanly husband, Steve Samuelian, wealthy now after years of poverty. Uncle Souren Haroutian – boney and ascetic, with his long violinist's fingers – arrived from their old Kings Canyon house where he still lived his lonely bachelor life. Her long-suffering father had died last year at ninety: Uncle Zorab, the pig, had died in the nineteen-forties. Of the three brothers, thin and aged Souren was the sole survivor on that hardpan farm, the land impossible to cultivate. The family's little store had been sold long ago.

Tigran walked in, stern and efficient, followed by his Betsy, who carried little tow-headed Adam and quietly smiled at each relative she passed. Juliet came in with them, sad and silent. Then Armen walked in, putting his emptied pipe in his pocket. He gave her a nod and a characteristic tsk. His side of the family arrived, the contingent of the arrogant and stubborn: first his mother, Zabel, her hair cotton-white and pulled back in a bun, and then his sister Arsine, her back ramrod-straight, followed by Arsine's children and her husband Nubar, who looked burnt brown, having spent all these years pruning and cultivating and smoking in his fig orchard.

Their friends arrived. Big Mike Arslanian, openly weeping, came with his elegant Zephur and his son, Ronnie, who wore a beautiful black, pin-striped suit. The Balians were there, Mike and Sirun and their children, Gloria and young Joey, who in adolescence had grown a foot taller than his father.

Suddenly her Garo entered like a clap of thunder, late and unstoppable.

"Ma," his kind irrepressible voice called to her as he walked down the aisle toward the front, with his Lily in tow, pregnant again and holding little Pauly's hand.

Artemis, rousing herself from her numbed state, rose to intercept them. Her perfect grandson must not see Lucine's corpse.

"I'll take Pauly, while you look," she said with peremptory formality and led the two-and-a-half year old back down the aisle and out of the funeral parlor. It was time anyway to make their way by limousine to the church.

She kept Pauly by her side from then on. When they entered the dusty sanctuary of old St. Paul's, the little boy sat between her and Armen on the wooden pew. Her grandson looked about the sanctuary as they listened to the choir's sorrowful turns of melody, the Armenian mass for the dead. His eyes were as wide and lively as hers must be numb and narrow.

Lily's father, the priest at the anti-Soviet Tashnag church, Holy Trinity, sat in the back, deigning to attend but not participate. His knife-like face looked superior, and he sat surrounded by his daughter Bea and his son, Eddy, who seemed to cower there, aware that the Ararats had not forgiven either him, for embezzling from their Clovis store, or his father for hiding the loot in his own account, to save his son.

John and Lucaper Hatchaturian had driven down from San Francisco, as had other old leftist friends from out of town; they sat next to a contingent of Armenian Progressive League friends. And there among the others, she spied that strange Mariam Saroyan, a dark, dumpy, over-eager woman, who admired Armen to the point of idolatry.

Artemis noticed everything but felt nothing. Among the big crowd, she saw Juliet's friends and Tigran's friends. Cagey Don Wolf and Gretchen, his wife, had come, as had Tigran's new boss, Haig Garabedian; Tigran's work for him was a mystery to everyone. Garo's assimilated friend George Kallen and his wife were there; George had changed his name from Kevork Kalounian, and he owned a successful bar in the Tower District. Former employees came too. Chick Leone, supposedly sober now, brought his wife. The last Olive store manager, Moe Cleetus, crazy like a fox, came, and so did Lisa O'Shea and another ex-cashier.

Later, there was the graveside service. Artemis felt stupefied, and as soon as the new priest finished, she wandered away from the small tent protecting the mourners from the late morning sun.

She held Pauly's little hand in her own, and the two of them wandered up and down the dusty paths in the field of monuments and headstones, all incised with Armenian lettering and some of the dates going back to the nineteenth century. The blinding sun beat down on her bare head and her black dress, and her grandson wore a little cap against the glare and heat. The dust their walking raised hung in the air and settled over everything around them. The air was so dry and overheated, the earth and grass were baked a dead grey-brown, and a slender veneer covered the graveyard's rock and sand and gravel. The odor of the rising dust and the sun-burnt earth mixed with the odd smell coming from the graves and tombs. An acrid taste lingered in her mouth as they moved from tomb to tomb and the air inundated them. Now both her father and her mother resided in this burning expanse.

She stared at a small, broken headstone; its dates showed that a child had died at four. A wave of horror engulfed her. She began to drown in scenes of dying children, not only her sister Lucaper, who toddled to her death in boiling water, but also Thalidomide babies and mutant babies with their genes deformed by radiation. She gasped and helplessly squeezed Pauly's hand.

"Grams?" he piped up.

"Oh, my sweet boy, I'm sorry. We'll stop in this shade. Are you hot, my Pauly? I am hot myself."

They stood now in the shadow of a familiar large carved tomb.

"Zha zhis?" her grandson said.

"What's this?" she corrected. "It's a monument. It's for a great general. He died a long time ago, but Grandma remembers meeting him. His name was Andranik, and he was a great Armenian hero. There is no greater man."

"Does he live here now?"

"No. He died."

"But Grams, zhis is where the dead people live."

She lifted his slender body up in her arms, and his cap fell to the dirt lane. "Yes, this is where the dead people are buried," she said. She held his hair to her face, breathing deeply, regaining her sense of his god-like sweetness.

"Artemis!" she heard Armen's distant voice. She looked up and saw that her husband stood next to her, touching her arm. His lined face looked worn and worried; the lines seemed not wizened but exhausted. "I've been looking for you. Artemis, your face is red! It's too hot. Tigran and Garo want to go."

She lowered little Pauly to the rocky path and held his hand; Armen reached to hold her other arm. The three of them made their way through the labyrinthine cemetery, occasionally having to retrace their steps. The blind leading the blind, she thought, and finally they saw the limousines waiting for them. She could hardly hear her sons' complaints or Lily's hysteria about Pauly, hot and hatless. Instead Artemis sat between the window and Armen in the back of one long black car. Though a nearly soundless cushion insulated her from everything around her, still she needed Armen's company next to her. They drove out of the lot of the Armenian cemetery, the Ararat Cemetery, it was called, the last and final Ararat. Approaching Highway 99, she saw Roeding Park to her left and its semicircle of Greek columns; winos stretched out on the benches where Armen had courted her, over thirty years ago. "La chair est triste, hélas:" when he recited that poem, she had not fully known how sad the flesh could be, alas.

The limousines pulled up to the large Church Hall next to St. Paul's, and they unloaded the family at the sidewalk. It was one in the afternoon, and there would be speeches as well as the traditional meal inside, the hokijash or food for the soul. Artemis walked with Armen through the thick July heat toward the Hall door. There was distant shouting, and the couple slowed.

Nearby, Garo stood inside a tense circle of his friends; she saw George Kallen, the bar-owner, and Big Mike's Ronnie, and two former managers. Next to them stood Tigran with Don Wolf and some others. Garo was in the center arguing with Eddy the embezzler, Lily's brother. Despite her numbness, she knew that some disastrous act might occur. She had always had a second sense about crises before they occurred, always saw the warning signs of resentment, revenge, falsity, arrogance, self-loathing, delusions of grandeur. But why would they fight now? Her mother had died. Nothing else should matter that much now. She heard Tigran's voice, but whatever warning he spoke was muffled and distant.

Suddenly the circle broke apart, and there were shouts and cries. Garo was lifting Eddy, holding and shaking his brother-in-law in the air. She gasped as she saw the wildness and the rage that had fastened on her dear son's face. She knew his temper, but she was stunned to see such violence in him. He seemed on the verge of throwing Eddy across the sidewalk into the street.

The church hall door flew open, and Lily rushed through. "Garo," she screamed, "put my brother down!" The small woman began to beat her husband's chest and arm. Garo started yelling back and then let his brother-in-law go. Eddy fell to the pavement, landing on his feet and swearing as he backed away toward the sidewalk.

Armen tugged at Artemis' arm. "Enough," he said, "come." It was so hot. They entered St Paul's Hall. At the door, they met Lily's father, the Holy Trinity priest, who had just emerged and stood in the sun. Suspicion was etched on his grey face with its vaguely Mongol eyes. He mumbled respectful condolences, but when Eddy strode up and began babbling to him, Artemis and Armen turned away and entered the Hall.

Circular tables were set all around the room. The warm air was stirred up by big, standing fans. Friends and relatives were seated or standing about. Armen led her toward a big table for the immediate family, and she sat next to her sister Satenig. A distant hum of conversation enveloped the room. It was as if cotton had been put in her ears. Sweet Satenig leaned over and spoke to her, squeezing her hand and asking Artemis if she was okay.

Soon everyone was seated, and St Paul's new priest – an intelligent looking young man – gave the invocation. The lunch for Lucine Haroutian's soul was served. Women in their sixties and other church volunteers came out of the kitchen with platters for each table; there was roast chicken, rice pilaf, and summer salad of cut up tomatoes, cucumbers, red onions, and parsley in golden green olive oil and lemon juice. Armen, sitting next to her, talked with the priest, who wanted the church library to buy the volumes of a new encyclopedia just published in Armenia; could Armen help, with his ties to Soviet Armenia? Juliet sat not far away with her brothers and their families, and yet all of them were distant, as if Artemis were in an isolation chamber. She saw Pauly, who sat on one side of Lily, and gently waved at him. Garo, on the other side, was heartily eating and talking with the others at the table. Lily's father, brother, and sister were nowhere to be seen in the hot Hall.

After the dessert pastries – baklava and layer cake – people began to tap the tables for silence, and Armen rose next to her as the tapping reached a crescendo. He placed all ten fingers on the table cloth in front of him and began to speak, thanking everyone for coming and for sharing this homage to his mother-in-law.

"A mother never dies," he said. "She is like a great, gentle evergreen planted firmly and forever in our hearts even as her human form has fled."

She could not focus on his muffled words. She felt stripped down to this numb, unhearing person. He went on, and she began to think of her mother, her gentle touch, her loss of her baby daughter, her struggle to be kind in the face of the withering insults from her brothers-in-law and poor Papa's bitterness. She remembered how her father had sat at the great Andranik's hokijash meal; she wondered if he too had felt this cushion of silence blotting everything out. Paralyzed by stroke, he had been unable to speak of his dead general, and her mother had kept patting his trembling hand.

"Artemis," her sister said now in her ear. She could barely make out Satenig's words. "You must speak, you're the eldest child." But how could she speak – it was impossible. She looked up, and all the silent, assembled faces were looking at her. Armen sat down, and

Satenig was gently urging her to get up. It was as if she were lifted against her will from her seat between her husband and sister. In the noiseless Hall, she could hardly hear her own voice as she spoke.

"I can't say all that is in my heart. Our mother was the gentlest person, even though she had so much to be sad about. Imagine. She saw her own little Lucaper drown to death in boiling water. The poor thing. And yet she was always so gentle. Always a comfort to others, always helping." Someone coughed at a back table. "I'm not able to say all I want to. All I can say is that she was the kindest and sweetest woman I have ever known."

A person was crying in the back of the stifling Hall, and some of the people around her were quietly weeping. As she sat down, she realized that she could once again hear clearly.

PART THREE

American Lives

Chapter 13
Fathers and Sons

DECEMBER 24, 1960

—•—

The odor of chopped onions, parsley, and raw lamb filled his wife's kitchen. He lit his pipe and joined the table where Garo's Lily and his grandson Pauly were already sitting. Artemis occupied the entire opposite half of the circular table, filled with the paraphernalia of her cooking.

"Garo's taking care of Annette, while I do last minute shopping," Lily said.

"You're not nursing her any more, are you?" Artemis said as she kneaded fine bulgur into ground lamb.

"You know I stopped months ago. It ruins the shape of your breasts."

"I was nursed until I was age four, Pauly's age," Armen said with a smile. "I would tell Mama, 'You ate too much onion, Mama.'"

Pauly laughed, and Lily rolled her eyes at her mother-in-law.

Artemis was intent on making kufta and ignored him. There was a plate for snacking in front of Lily, containing shriveled oil-cured olives and pickled carrot and pepper tourshi, and a slab of blue cheese. Wide crackery lavash rounds were broken in pieces and slightly moistened. At his left temple, he felt a pulsing in his head return. He ate a bite of cracker, to see if that would help.

"Anyway, I'm so busy preparing for tomorrow."

"Christmas presents!" Pauly said.

Armen imagined closets full of toys and her refrigerator bursting with food.

"You get presents tonight too," Artemis said, "when you come here."

"Ooph, how do you do it, Artemis?" Lily said. "I'm just run off my feet, but look at you, making kufta at the last minute."

"Tigran loves it. Thank you for bringing me butter; it's for tonight's pilaf. I had no time to shop, and Armen has a little headache."

Pauly bit into a carrot tourshi, and his lips puckered. "Oh, toutou!" he said, using the Armenian word for sour.

"Do you know," his grandfather asked, "the phone number of the tourshi factory?

"No," the little boy said.

"Oh-oh two-two."

"Oh-oh two-two," Pauly said, giggling.

"And do you know," Armen said, "what the sourpuss ballerina Mademoiselle Froufrou wears when she dances, her little skirt?"

"No," Pauly said, smiling.

"Sourpuss Mademoiselle Froufrou wears a tutu," Armen said, his face deadpan.

Lily laughed at the idiocy of his pun, and he was pleased.

"What's the secret of your kufta? Is it from your mother's hometown?" Lily said.

"Harput," Artemis said. "The secret is in the por, the inside of lamb kufta. It has lots of chopped onions, mint, walnuts, pine nuts, a little lamb fat, and allspice – that's the secret."

"Pauly," Armen said, "let's look at the garden."

"Just five minutes," Lily said. "I have to be home by four."

He held his grandson's hand as they walked out the side door. The afternoon temperature was about seventy, ten degrees warmer than usual for the Valley winter. By the clothesline, Armen had turned over the earth where he had grown his summer tomatoes, peppers, eggplant, and goutah cucumbers.

"Guess what I'm getting for Christmas, Gramps," Pauly said. Though he was almost four, his grandfather still saw the baby's fresh sweetness in the boy's face, his auburn hair, his eyes with their long lashes.

"What do you get?" he said.

"A basketball hoop!"

"How do you know?"

"I peeked."

"Tsk, tsk," he clicked his disapproval, but he could not help smiling. "In my village when I was your age, I played with a stick in the yard – or sometimes with our lamb or our donkey."

"I'd love a little lamb," Pauly said. "Maybe Daddy will buy me one."

They walked toward the brick barbeque in back, past the big ash tree with its small clusters of berries about to fall from its leafless limbs. On the other side of the barbeque and the patio was the pool, which was covered for the winter by an oval tarpaulin the color of gray faded grass. They came to the barbeque with its single tile of a rooster embedded in the chimney. Armen was thinking about Lily's spending too much money, as he quietly smoked his pipe. He knew that her over-spending was the result of her deprivation; she was five when her mother died of pneumonia, and during the Genocide, her father had endured the murders of his parents and all his brothers and sisters. Could Armen ever tell such things to his grandson as he grew older? Of course, the bright little boy was only four years old now.

"Pauly, I remember when I got my first book," he said, smoking by the barbeque. "I wanted to learn to read so much. One day when I was just a little older than you, two Turks came with a cart, and they took away half of our hay. Afterwards my father came inside the house and showed me a big shiny coin. 'This is for your first primer!' he said. When they bought the book for me, everybody in the neighborhood gathered in a circle and stared at the book, and they cheered. My Mama was so proud."

"Were you still nursing?" Pauly said, his eyes wide.

"No, that was earlier," he said, emptying his pipe in the barbeque pit. "The next year, I went to school in the village. I saw at your house you have a beautiful new book about the Trojan War."

"Yes, Gramps. Mama reads it to me. It's about Achilles and Adamemnon."

"Yes, Pauly, Achilles and Agamemnon. You know, my village was not far from where that war took place, from Troy."

"You lived near Troy!"

"It was just about the distance from here to the beach in Santa Cruz, one hundred and fifty miles."

"Wow."

"My village teacher told me that a man had just discovered Troy's ruins there, from thousands of years ago."

"Pauly," his mother called from the door. "Time to go."

The grandfather gave the boy a kiss goodbye and waved to Lily. He stayed in the yard and refilled his pipe from a pouch of Half and Half. When at age seven he had learned the history of Asia Minor, he had realized that human beings could slaughter other human beings, without hesitation, in the millions. How could he tell Pauly such a thing?

"Armen."

Artemis' thin voice called from the kitchen window.

"Angel," he said.

"Get the mail," she said. "The mailman just came."

On the left side of his temple, he felt a constant pain, a shadow headache. For years, his head had periodically ached as if a fever held him in its grip, except there was no fever. And the psoriasis on his stomach and limbs had itched and flaked more than ever this winter, though at this moment it did not itch. As he walked into the house, he blotted out all these morbid thoughts, and by the front door, he opened the flap to the mail chute.

Some of the mail tumbled to the floor. He stooped painfully to pick it up, then walked across the wide Oriental rug on the living room floor, and sat on the couch. There were some bills, which Artemis would see to paying, and an end-of-the-year Life magazine with the face of President-elect John F. Kennedy on the cover. Yes, just like the thaw in the Soviet Union with Khrushchev, a thaw had begun in the United States with this election. Of course, Kennedy and his brother were both terrible anti-communists, but they were not as crazy as the John Birchers or that red-baiter Richard Nixon, and at least Nixon had lost. Armen had voted as usual a straight Democratic ticket.

He looked at the outside of several Christmas card envelopes; he would let Artemis open them. He saw that one was from her sister Anoush, whose card always arrived on Christmas Eve. Others were from friends, but his eye caught sight of one with gold-embossed printing and the return address of the Soviet Consulate in San Francisco. The envelope had been opened and its loose flap tucked back in. As he took out the season's greetings card, he wondered if the FBI surveillance would get better or worse under Kennedy. For decades, they had opened his mail and attended his speeches. The worst was five years ago when two agents had parked across the street from their home and had waited and waited. After an hour, he felt so harassed that he told Artemis to go and invite them in for a cup of coffee. They sat with him and his wife in the living room. "I am not your enemy," he had said. "I am a businessman, and I am a proud Armenian. My homeland happens to be in the Soviet Union, and thanks to that, the Turks cannot finish off the Genocide of the Armenian people, which they tried in 1915. One and a half million people were killed. I was there. So I believe in peace and friendship of America with Soviet Armenia and with Soviet Union. This does not make me your enemy. I believe in justice for the workers and the poor, the downtrodden, the oppressed, but I do not want to harm you or overthrow you. I want nothing to do with all that. America is my country too!"

"We understand, Mr. Ararat," they had replied. "We don't want to upset you. We're just doing our job." After that, they had parked further down the street, near the ditch, and then they disappeared altogether.

Now Armen opened the card from the Soviet Consulate. An official had signed the consul's name and written: "All best wishes to a good friend of Soviet Armenia." He was always treated nicely by the consul and his staff, though he was no longer active in the party. This summer he had opened the house to a couple of Russian diplomats who were chaperoning an extended visit of Armenians to Fresno. Educated diplomats, they wanted to help Armenia and were in a position to do so. And once a month, he would drive to San Francisco or Los Angeles, and at the embassy he would enjoy their vodka and caviar; the diplomats were intelligent and more interesting than anyone in the Fresno Armenian community. Of course, they also found him useful, but he did not mind. Whoever led the Soviet Union – whether Lenin or Stalin or now Khrushchev – had always been a great defender of Armenia; that was the main thing, and he celebrated it in poems he was writing about his homeland.

He wrote very literate and beautiful poetry in Armenian, and he was sure that it did not make him a hack writer to be willing to serve the cause of Armenia. Who would reject such a calling? The progressive Ramgavar Armenians published his poetry, and they were grateful when he gave his eloquent speeches. Soviet Armenia had arisen from the ashes of genocide, and he cared deeply for that homeland, almost as much as he cared for his children and for their children, even though they lived in capitalist America. Of course, he himself had to earn his living here. Who, though, in America had even dreamed what genocide was?

This summer Armen had written a poem in Armenian about all this and dedicated it to a brilliant young visitor from Armenia. Dr. Abrahamian was a rising and gifted cancer researcher from Yerevan, the capital, and the U.S. State Department had let Armen drive him and two accompanying Soviet diplomats up to Yosemite Valley National Park not far from Fresno, where the high mountains and monumental rocks had been carved by ancient glaciers.

The doctor began to speak to him about Yosemite's Sierra mountains and about Mt. Ararat, which was visible from Armenia but in a no man's land just over the Turkish border. He spoke eloquently of geography and loss, as if Armen Ararat, who lived in the American diaspora, understood everything his gifted visitor had experienced. Of course, this was not necessarily true, but Armen was touched and flattered by the doctor's trust of him. For a moment, he had wondered what the young doctor, sick for home, truly thought of this capitalist bourgeois country he was visiting. But it did not matter to Armen; what mattered was the pleasure of being the doctor's host, of making this young Armenian comfortable as he spoke his confidences and confusions.

A few months later, he wrote his poem for Dr. Abrahamian, and he used the doctor's words about Yosemite for his title: "These Mountains Are Not Ours." Sitting now in the living room, with the pile of opened letters next to him on the couch, he spoke it to himself.

These majestic, ice-carved mountains are not ours.
They have not lived with grief.
Through our mountains, conquerors have passed
Setting tree and bush aflame.
Our mountains have lived with loss,
And our salt tears petrified into its rock cliffs.

Deer and hunters have passed through your mountains,
But on ours, trees and bushes have turned to ash.
Buried beneath the bones of our trees, though, lay sleeping seeds,
And after the melting of spring snow, the smell of
A thousand wild flowers mingles with the odor of ash,
And a thousand colors rise from the petrified ledges.

He stopped reciting as he heard Juliet coming down the hall from her bedroom. She walked into the kitchen and talked with Artemis. Soon she came into the living room.

"Can you believe what Mama just said?"

He made his irritated tsk with his tongue and looked up at his daughter. She had become a woman, with flowing deep brown hair, the skin of her face smooth and cream colored. This fine young woman should not be here, he thought, trapped in their home in the boondocks, but at a university like Berkeley. Someday they would find the money to help her escape.

"She said it would be rude if I took the car for an hour at ten tonight, after everyone leaves! I just want to hear a folksinger at the coffeehouse."

Artemis was in the doorway, listening.

"Look, look, there she goes again making things up," she said in a bristling defensive voice.

"But that's what you said," Juliet protested.

"Listen to her! I just said...."

Armen stopped listening. He knew Juliet was not making it up. His head still hurt, and he had to get better for tonight. After a minute, Juliet stalked out, and Artemis sat down in an easy chair. She stretched and flexed her legs in front of her, in a sort of self-styled yoga.

"You look sick," she said. "They're coming in half an hour. What's wrong with you?"

"My head, Angel. I'm dying."

"I will bring you a jigger of Raki. Just one. It will help." Her voice was soft now. On a small bronze tray, she brought him the small glass of the liquor with its medicinal smell and anise flavor.

"Poor thing," she said and went to get dressed for Christmas Eve dinner.

He sat sipping the Raki on the living room couch, with the pile of mail placed now on the side table, and the liquor made its way into his blood and aching brain. It was kind of Artemis to bring him some Raki, but he was always a little wary of her. For no apparent reason, her mood could change. And between them there could sometimes be a kiss, a caress, but nothing more. She was a disappointed woman and had little patience for him. At least there was Mariam Saroyan, who loved to hear him read his poems and insisted on making a copy of each one he showed her. "For the archive," she said.

He carefully stood up now and walked to the family room and out the sliding glass door. There, in the still mild air of the Fresno twilight, he sat on a patio chair. He would smoke his pipe and wait for Tigran, Garo, and their families to arrive. He did not blame Artemis, for how could anyone fathom all the losses which made up their lives? His youthful world was swept away by the unspeakable violence of the Genocide. Yes, he loved to write about Armenia, and he loved his family here, but the truth was that all his farms and businesses were lost now in America. Even his faith in socialism was nearly gone. He was exhausted from having witnessed too much failure and too much suffering.

Suddenly in the Fresno twilight, tears began to form in his tired eyes. Sitting on the patio thousands of miles from his first, most terrible losses, he held his pipe in his lap and began to sing in a private, forlorn voice the classic version of an Armenian folk lament. "Take away my sadness, my sweet: Keler tzoler im yarea, arevidagin." As he softly sang, he wondered at his sense of exhaustion, and he saw that it was enough that he survived each day.

"What a beautiful song," someone said.

Armen looked up and saw Betsy, Tigran's wife, at the glass door, slid open now. His thoughts slipped away as she approached with little Adam, Tigran's blond three-year-old son. Betsy leaned over to give her father-in-law a warm kiss on the cheek. Dressed in Christmas green, she was a pert and charming girl.

Sitting up now, he gave his youngest grandson a hug and kiss. "Sweet Adam is a big boy!" he said.

"Who wrote the song you were singing?" Betsy asked.

"The great Gomidas," Armen said in a detached voice.

"I just love to hear you sing Armenian songs," she said. "You have a beautiful voice."

"It's my sister who has the beautiful voice," Armen said. Her compliment was just a gesture, he knew, and yet she had made it with such natural warmth. "As a child, Aunt Arsine studied with Gomidas in Constantinople, and we both sang in his choir. She still has a beautiful soprano voice. Even now she sings for her family after holiday dinners. At St. Paul's, she leads the sopranos."

"How interesting!" she said. "I'd love to hear her."

"Hey, Pop," Tigran said at the screen of the open sliding door. "It's getting cold out there. Come in and play tavloo with me. Let's shut this door."

"Okay, son."

Armen stood and followed Betsy and Adam across the patio to the door, and she waved for him to enter before him. It was as if Betsy were the hostess, and he were a guest in his own house. It was out of respect, he knew, but she definitely had her own ideas about how to please everyone around her. She had wanted to come with him to Yosemite to help host Dr. Abrahamian, and he remembered feeling baffled by her insistence, but there had been no room in the car.

He stepped into the brightly lit family room; the television was on, but the sound of the football game was mercifully turned down. Tigran had poured his father and himself some Seagram's Seven, and he was setting up the wooden backgammon box on a low table. He sat on a straight chair and gestured for his father to sit in the easy chair on the other side of the board. Then he threw the dice hard, on the wood.

"Outa!" he shouted as the dice showed eight, and he handed them to Armen.

"Chors," Armen named the four he threw, and he took a sip of the whisky. Tigran, with the higher number, took the first turn, shouting each number he threw – meg, yergook, yerek, chors, hing, vetz, yota, outa, ina, dasa – striking his circular wood pieces on the arrows he ticked off and slapping the chit down with another shout where it landed.

"You play like my father did," Armen said in his neutral voice, "lots of sound effects." They played a close game, and Armen maintained his poker face despite the heady feeling from his drink; the pain in his head had receded. He enjoyed the combat, the skill and adrenaline of it. A memory came to him of his father playing noisily in a fishing village on the south shore of Lake Nicea. Armen, ten years old, was accompanying his father to sell silk in Iznik to the east of their town. Later, he rode atop a donkey that the men had loaded with heavy packs of layered silk; they had even placed some pouches inside his shirt around his chest and stomach. Soon, his spirits had begun strangely to lift and soar into the canopy of sky above the water and land. It was as if he had risen from the donkey's back and taken a position high up in the white sky next to the sun. Far below were the deep blue lake and the sun-flooded road. The vista shimmered as he had never seen before, and simultaneously the golden fields seemed so close he could smell and taste them. When they arrived in Iznik, the Nicean men joined his father in lifting both Armen and the packs of silk off the donkey. They unbuttoned his shirt and removed the flat pouches that lay against his skin. The packages were filled with hashish that his father had won at the fishing village. This was the first time they had used him as a courier. He stumbled through a hallway, and suddenly there before him had been a beautiful wall. The leaves and buds of the Iznik tiles flowered before his eyes; the red and green and blue had unfolded against the luminous white of the wall.

"I'm beating you, Pop."

"You can't know. Chance governs the dice."

"Not this time. You're dead," Tigran said coldly.

Armen threw the dice hard against the wood. "Ina!" he said, sounding like his son. With luck he could still win; let come what may, he thought.

"How many times did you die today, Pop?"

"My head, Tigran. I was dying today,"

The front door swung open, and with a rush of energy Garo strode down the hall into the family room.

"Hey, Teeg! Pop! I play the winner!"

"Garo," Tigran said, "did you leave your family at home?"

"Naw, they're in the front yard. They're just slow."

The father and his oldest son returned to the game. After some lucky throws, Tigran won.

Suddenly Pauly burst into the room. He let Armen give him a big hug and then said, "Tavloo! Let me play."

"Come and give Uncle a kiss," Tigran said. "Now go find Adam, and play with him."

Lily came in looking exasperated. She was beautifully dressed in a black and red dress. In one arm, she held a casserole of yams and in the other one-year-old Annette, whom she handed to Garo, who handed her to Tigran to be kissed, who handed the sweet baby to Armen, and when Juliet came down the hall, Armen handed his granddaughter to his daughter.

He sat on the family room couch, as his sons played a new game. Each son shared something with him, but especially Tigran with his coolly critical tone. He had not yet found what he wanted to do after the bankruptcy and had recently switched jobs, beginning work as a private investigator. Garo, big as he was, seemed more like Artemis, a romantic, but with unstoppable energy; he was managing the Clovis King's, which Ronnie Arslanian had helped save from the bankruptcy. The sole significant thing his two sons had in common with him, Armen thought, was that both boys had married difficult women, and these women did not truly know their husbands. Otherwise, his own world was invisible to his sons, the world of his past, of his values and imagination. And he felt invisible in their world of American sports and television and Republicans for friends. At least neither son, though, had changed his Armenian name, and for that he was proud of them: Tigran and Garo Ararat.

"Time for dinner," Betsy said, entering, and then she went in search of Adam and Pauly.

They all trooped into the dining room. The table was laden with dinner: a baked ham, "wedding" pilaf with dates, apricots, almonds, and raisins, a large bowl of Harput kufta, yams Lily had brought, green beans in a Harput tomato sauce, yogurt with cucumber, sour tourshi and olives. Armen sat at the head of the table, with Tigran and Garo on either side of him. In the chaos, their voices were the clearest to him. Artemis kept sitting and then standing, helping everyone to their food. She filled a plate of food for Armen and brought it to him. Then she sat at the other end of the table between Juliet and Pauly, and she talked with Lily about little Annette.

"Yesterday, I was casing a bar," Tigran said between bites of food, "the usual thing – watching a cheating husband. Art Simonian walks up to my table and says, 'Hey there, Sam Spade!'"

"Edie's Dad?" Juliet said from the other end of the table.

"A big sweet man, but not the brightest bulb."

"People call him Churchill," Armen said, remembering the name he had bestowed years ago on heavy, jowly Art at the Ramgavar Club.

"Sure," Tigran said, "he's like Churchill, if you leave out the intelligence and the eloquence. So I'm hushing him up, but Winston blabs away he read in the Armenian Courier that I'm a private eye.

With the guy I'm shadowing two tables away, he slaps me on the back, and again he says, 'Sam Spade!'"

As the buzz of laughter diminished, Tigran asked for a refill of kufta, and everyone began to eat in earnest. "Can you beat that for stupid? He doesn't even understand he's giving my cover away."

There was a lull, and Armen raised his glass of red wine. "I make a toast now to the new generation! To little Annette, whose beautiful French name reminds me of the ancient Armenian city of Ani. To Adam, who has a most impressive name too, for it is said that Adam was the first man. And to Paul: he has the name of a great writer who exposed injustice in every society he lived in, Rome, Corinth, Ephesus, which was not far from where I was born." He glanced down the table in Artemis' direction and said: "I raise my glass also to my dear wife of thirty-two years. I love her with all my hearts. Her Harput kufta is the best in Fresno, in the United States of America, and in the world."

The adults clapped noisily, and Artemis looked down at her plate, with something between a smile and a frown on her face. The kids whispered, "All my hearts?" Later, after the table had been cleared, Armen – patient and exhausted – sat on an easy chair in the living room where the family was congregating. Artemis came from the hall, carrying a hand-held Super-8 camera, attached to mounted flood-lights. She had bought the little movie camera during King's last profitable year.

"Presents!" she said as she plugged in the lights and wound up the small camera.

Pauly and Adam whooped and jumped and ran in a circle on the wide oriental rug. "Juliet, you take the pictures while I organize the presents."

"Oh, Mom," she said, but Artemis pressed the apparatus on her daughter. Juliet hesitated but then raised the camera to one eye and began filming the circle of adults and children, stopping at each person. When she came to her father, Armen looked benignly at the glaring lights, but he felt it was like being interrogated. Of course, Juliet would never do that; she was like him, more political than any of the others and more likely to be interrogated than to interrogate. But there she was, filming him and all of them, making a visual record of Christmas Eve, 1960.

Artemis handed around the presents, the children's first. As they unwrapped their gifts, Pauly scrambled up, stood in the middle of the burgundy Persian carpet, and began to sing slightly off-key, strumming a little ukulele he had been given.

"One o'clock, two o'clock, three o'clock, rock! Gonna rock around the clock tonight!" he piped and strutted around the rug.

Amid the noise, Armen slowly unwrapped a blue tie, a ceramic ashtray, a tin of Half and Half tobacco, and a very nice bottle of cognac. Draping the blue tie around his neck, he thought for a moment of a noose. Without warning, the image of sixty hanging bodies flashed before him. Then suddenly the floodlights were on him again.

"Armen, look up!"

Momentarily blinded, he stared at the glare and dangled one end of the loose tie in the air. He did not know, at least not in that moment, that she was looking at him with a kind of pity, that she felt she had allowed her sixty-year-old husband to look like this disheveled clown in public, like Charlie Chaplin. Suddenly her heart broke, for it was her fault.

Chapter 14
Genocide Commemoration Day

APRIL 24, 1962

—•—

"Are you getting enough sleep?" his mother said, sitting across the kitchen table. It was noon, and Tigran had come for his favorite lunch, her derev dolma, the tender grape leaves filled with flavored ground meat.

"Ma, this is good," he said, hunching over his plate; there was garlic yogurt spooned on the dolma with a wedge of red onion on the side.

"You're working too hard," she said, and he heard the tension in her voice.

"It's a tough world out there, Ma," he said.

"I see dark circles under your eyes," she said. "Are you taking your vitamins?"

"For god's sake, I'm thirty-two years old," he said, but he did not finish what he was going to say. He would be going back after lunch to his work managing an appliance distributorship, and then he had an appointment with Ronnie Arslanian, to clean up the fucking mess about Garo. Ever since they were children, Tigran had had to save the kid brother from the shit he got into. And he got little credit for it. Garo was still Ma's favorite, her beautiful Garo-boy. Tigran was tired of it, as if he did not have enough shit himself, with the separation from Betsy and her keeping little Adam. It was killing him.

"It's too bad you have to work so hard," his mother said.

"I hate to tell you, Ma," he said, "but we lost the stores, we lost all our money, so we're broke. Just like when you take everybody else's money, you're rich." He knew this bit of wisdom by heart, though his parents always somehow managed to forget it.

At eight in the morning, he had driven to the Fort Washington golf club and played a round before going to work. Two residential developers, an Armenian – one of the Arslanians' competitors – and an Italian, plus their Jewish lawyer, Leo, paired off with him. These guys were rich, but he had them for breakfast. His golf game was good enough to bet on, and that's what he did. These three guys were ten years older than him but genial enough for being spoiled brats and getting their ass kicked by him every other week. They came back for the sheer love of gambling and pitting themselves against his skills. He felt no hesitation in taking them to the cleaners, and he knew they would not hesitate if the tables were turned. They were developing half of northwest Fresno between them, so they could afford to lose at golf.

Tigran loved the game. A natural athlete, he knew he could have sailed through college on varsity scholarships. He loved the spirit of competition. He had played shortstop like the best of them, a real hustler who once stole seven bases in a single game. It was a shame he hurt his leg and then had to leave college to help Pop in the supermarket. He could have gone on to law school and made a great lawyer, like Leo, who was sharp as a tack, even if his golf game was for shit. But now it was Juliet going to City College, which was okay. The brat had a wicked tongue on her, which was okay too, for he always got her goat. A few years ago, when he was working for

Haig Garabedian, she had asked, "What do you do for him?"

"I put his business back on track."

"How do you do that?"

"I just like to take a failing business," he had said evasively, "and save it."

"Too bad you couldn't do that with your own business," she had said.

"You're so good with advice," he had said. "Do you ever look in the mirror? You could lose about a hundred pounds."

The problem was that his sister was deluded about how smart and talented she was, even the slimmed-down, college educated version of her; people like that were a dime a dozen, and her future prospects were zero, as far as he could see. Ma and Pop could hardly make a living from the Stars and Stripes Market, and yet she wanted to go to Berkeley. Of course, it was true that Juliet helped out with a daily shift in the store.

"Does Juliet still want to go to Berkeley?" he asked Artemis as he ate the last bites of his lunch. He had memories of babysitting her, even changing her diapers, and then helping his mother take care of her when Ma went nuts in the Forties. Come to think of it, both women were delusional; mother and daughter were both nut cases.

"Maybe next year," she said. "You want some more?"

"Thanks, no. You're a hell of a cook, Ma," he said. "You know you spoil her, when you should be reining her in, teaching her about the real world."

"They say it's $45 a semester tuition at Berkeley."

"Yeah, but she's going to need room and board and books. That's a hell of a lot more than $45."

"But she has her heart set. And she's a smart girl, Tigran," Ma said, "even if she's a little nervous."

"My little sister's a spoiled brat," he said, "and you know what I say. Once a brat, always a brat."

"She's working her shift, but she'll be back at one," Artemis said, neutral and oblivious. She spooned a few more dolmas on his plate.

"Ma!" he said and got up from the table. "I'm going back to work." He left the extra dolmas on the plate, gave her a kiss on the cheek, and walked from the kitchen through the dining room to the living room where he was temporarily bunking on the couch.

As he drove to his showroom, down Shields and right on Blackstone, all he could think about was Adam and the fact that he loved his beautiful three-year-old son so much and that Betsy had him over a barrel. Last year, he had watched her practically throw herself at one of Pop's fancy Soviets, some visiting doctor from Armenia. But it was six months ago that she really cheated on him. At first he said nothing, and what was worse, he did nothing. Though he was working then as a private eye, he could not bear hunting down whoever it was Betsy was seeing on the side. Finally he had glimpsed the two of them in the window of a coffee shop in the Tower District. The guy looked like a two-bit salesman, some swarthy Italian.

"I saw you with your friend," he said when she got home. "You're fucking him while you're married to me."

"Fucking him?" she said, and when he heard her stewardessy voice repeat his words, something gave way in him. He had started to rush at her, a stream of curses coming from his mouth, but suddenly he heard sweet little Adam crying from his bedroom. Betsy said, "Take your things, and leave. You'll end up hurting your son." Disgusted with himself and appalled at her, he agreed to leave. That was almost two months ago, late last February, and he could not stand that he only saw his son on weekends. She had him by the balls, and he did not know what to do. This month, he had finally started surveying the available women and dating some. Shit, what did it matter now that he did a little cheating himself; a man should have some pleasure. Tonight he had a new date, with someone who knew his sister.

For an hour and a half, he led a training session for some newly hired salesmen, and then he drove from his office back up

Blackstone to Shaw. His appointment with Ronnie Arslanian was at his development office in a strip mall he owned near Shaw and Fresno. Ronnie's father, Mike Arslanian, loved Tigran's father, and Pop called him Big Mike, for he was a big man and had quite an aura. There were rumors that Big Mike had comfortably retired after years in the Detroit Mob, and for that reason, Tigran was wary of Big Mike's son. He wondered how it was possible that every one of his development deals turned a profit, from Clovis east to 99 and north of the city on Shaw; someone had to be pulling some strings.

Ronnie was hard to read and had never become a friend of Tigran, who thought of him as a phony, a bullshit artist. But he was pleasant and very respectful to Pop and Ma, a handsome, polite guy, but sometimes he would not give you the time of day, like he was above everyone, like his shit didn't stink. When the Ararats had gone bankrupt, though, he had provided the money to save the Clovis store; at the same time, he was profiting, of course. Tigran by then had given up on the markets, but Garo was obsessed; he had gone to Ronnie and asked him to take over the Clovis mortgage, and now Garo was running the store as manager and silent partner. But lately the two of them were not speaking to each other. Garo couldn't understand what was happening, and he asked Tigran if he would find out.

A secretary buzzed him into Ronnie's interior office. They sat down under the fluorescent lights and exchanged news about their fathers. Tigran was wary and waiting for him to broach the subject.

As if he were asking about the weather, Ronnie finally said, "How are your brother and sister?"

"They're fine," Tigran said.

"Garo seems to have something up his ass lately."

"He does?"

"A month ago," Ronnie said with a calm smile, "I told him about an opportunity that was presenting itself. Your brother starts storming and cussing me out, like he's crazy."

"He says you're not talking to him now."

"Your brother will not go nuts in front of me," he said, and there was a moment's pause.

"You said an opportunity."

"Yeah, an opportunity... next year I'm going to tear down the Clovis store and build a mall on the property."

"And what about Garo?"

"I was going to offer your brother a settlement."

Tigran felt suddenly furious that Garo and the whole family relied on him to be the go-between, the sane one, and he was fed up.

"How much?"

"How much do you think?"

"I'd say fifty thousand."

"Garo will get 25 K."

"You don't want to seem cheap."

"You don't want to seem cheap?" Ronnie repeated unsmiling. "You Ararats are fascinating. You're not nuts. You're just spoiled cowards. You come here on behalf of your brother and ask me for fifty thousand dollars, without a thought of what you might do in return for such a sum. Your family thinks you're so pure and smart that you just deserve it. There are much smarter and purer men than you, Tigran, churchgoers who give vast amounts to charity, the most respected men in the community, and do you know what they would do for such a sum? They would rip out your brother's guts. They would gouge out your child's eyes."

Ronnie stared coldly at him, and then he continued, "Think again before you call me cheap."

"Cheap? Who said cheap? You're a fucking crook."

"Get out of my office," he said, "before I decide to give Garo nothing."

In the silence, then, Tigran got up and left. As he walked across the parking lot, it was as if he were ricocheting like a pool ball. His fists gripped his steering wheel, as he turned out of the lot onto

Shaw. His body contracting in the driver's seat, he felt that he had been exposed, as if all his caution and intelligence were pointless.

He had to get a grip on himself. For a moment he had let Ronnie's shit reach him, but his inner core remained as taut as a fist. To reach that core, he would have to kill him. The fucking arrogant son-of-a-bitch! His empire of cheap ugly strip malls and pathetic tracts were a blight on Fresno. Ronnie was willing even to threaten the family of his father's best friend. It was criminal. Greed like his was sweeping everything up in the city, and for all he knew in the whole state, and it was brutal. It wrecked everything in its wake, making everyone feel sick and irradiated, like an A-bomb had dropped. He knew that Ronnie was powerful enough to destroy all the Ararats and would, if they were not careful. The father, Big Mike, was a sweet man, but they said he had done god-awful things in Detroit. Like father, like son.

At Blackstone, Tigran mistakenly turned right instead of left at the busy intersection, north instead of south.

"Fuck!" he shouted in the empty Chevy. He swerved to the curb and stopped the car, and his fists pounded the steering wheel. His brain and body were unconsciously directing him north, to the little tract house he had bought off of Barstow, to the fucking bitch he had left in February, and to the three-year-old son he so desperately missed. He had no idea what to do. Swerving back into traffic, he turned into a side street and then headed south on Blackstone, gripping the wheel so hard that his hands ached. It was impossible to go back to work this afternoon, so he drove back to the house on Garland.

He parked his car on one side of the carport, to leave room for his parents' yellow Ford. One or both must be out of the house, so he might have it empty to himself. As he opened the door, the entry way felt strange, as if he had never been in the house before.

Dizzy and confused, he heard some puttering around in the kitchen when he went inside.

"Shit," he said under his breath.

"Hello?" Juliet said and looked up at him as he entered. She was sitting at the kitchen table. A canvas was tilted in front of her on the table, and she had dipped a brush into some blue pigment on the palette by the painting she worked on. It looked like an oriental rug with a scene of some people in the middle.

He felt faint. The painting's geometric border shifted and trembled and blurred, and his knees buckled.

Juliet was leaning over him. "Tigran!" Juliet called out to him at a distance, and then she held a cool, moist towel to his forehead. "Tigran, can you hear me?"

He was overwhelmingly weak, but he forced himself to get up slowly from the floor. "I'm okay," he said.

"You're sure? You fainted."

"Yeah, I guess I fainted." His sister was holding his hand and arm and leading him to the family room couch. "I'm okay now."

"I'll get you some iced tea from the frig. You're sure you're okay? Should we call the doctor?"

"Don't worry about it, kid," he said. It was annoying that he needed her help, and he felt embarrassed that he had passed out. It was that fucking Ronnie Arslanian.

When she brought him the cool drink, he said, "Let's not bother Ma about this, okay."

"What happened?"

"It's nothing," he said dismissively and sipped from the cool glass of tea. "I'll just take a little nap." He put the glass on the side table and stretched out on the couch. After a minute, he felt a blanket placed over him and gave a vague grunt. After an hour of dreamless sleep, he slowly awoke and went to the bathroom.

He heard activity in the kitchen and walked in.

"We were quiet so we wouldn't wake you," Artemis said as she cooked at the stove. "You needed your sleep. I knew it at noon." Armen was smoking his pipe at the kitchen table.

"Sure, Ma," Tigran said. "How you doing, Pop? Did you die today?"

"Not today, son. I am decent today."

"In that case, how about celebrating with a little Raki," Tigran said.

They took their two small glasses of Raki and ice to the family room and sat sipping the clouded liquor, Tigran on the couch and Armen on the easy chair.

"I saw Ronnie Arslanian today," Tigran said coldly.

"A nice, polite boy," Pop said.

"He's an asshole, Pop. A real son of a bitch."

"Why do you say that?"

"Take my word. I'm sure he's in the mob."

"I never believe those rumors," Armen said. "Ronnie is a nice boy with a good father and mother." Pop looked out the window, absorbed by the early spring sunset flooding the room through the glass door. Pop looked like an old man already, and for sure he did not want to think too hard about Big Mike or his son. Hell, maybe he was right not to look too closely into things; it was his secret of survival. His anger began to lift, and he no longer cared so much that Ronnie had zeroed in on him with his insults. Suddenly he was himself again.

"Hey, Pop, I played golf this morning, and I see this old guy putzing around on the course with some friends as old as him – I mean they were older than you, Pop! So, in the men's room, this old geezer is at the urinal next to mine. He looks down at his pecker and says miserably, 'I never thought I'd outlive you, you son-of-a-bitch.' Now that's funny."

His father was smiling, but his sixty-year-old face was otherwise impassive, like the lined mask of a man much older than himself. "At least," he said, "with mine I can still pee."

Artemis walked in and said dinner was ready; then she went down the hall calling Juliet's name.

On the table was a feast of food, which Ma said she made special for him, and he fed himself with gusto. There was a salad, a steaming bowl of the remaining derev grape-leaf dolma, a plate of beautifully braised artichokes with dill and onion, and a casserole of baked souboragi, with the sheets of lasagna-like dough layered with a rich mixture of cheese, parsley, and melted butter.

"Are you going out?" Artemis asked him.

"Yeah."

"Where are you going?"

"Out."

There was silence for a time as they ate.

"I saw Sandy at City College," Juliet said in an irritated voice. "She says she has a date with you."

"What of it?"

"She's a lot younger than you," Juliet said. "She's my age."

"That pasty Americanitsi?" Artemis asked, but no one answered.

"So you want to go to Cal," Tigran said to his sister.

"Yes," she said.

"When?"

"Next year, in the fall."

"Fresno State isn't good enough?" Her wasting money on bullshit like that was the same as Pop with his fancy Soviet Armenians. "You'll just waste your time and Pop's money, I bet, listening to folk music in Berkeley dives. It's bullshit."

"Bullshit?" Pop said. "Berkeley is bullshit?"

Tigran did not answer. To hell with it, he thought.

"Are you going out tonight?" he asked Armen.

"Yes," Artemis answered for him. "We're going to St Paul's, the church hall. Daddy's giving a speech. It's the forty-seventh anniversary of the Genocide."

"April 24th, 1915," Pop said.

"I don't know how you people can get so excited about all that stuff," Tigran said.

"It's history," Ma said.

"I'm just saying it gets obscene."

"It gets obscene?" Ma said. "Over a million Armenians were massacred by the Turks in one year."

"Enough Armenians in misery!" he said.

"I give my speech to support Soviet Armenia," Pop said, "the phoenix arising from the ashes."

Tigran had had enough for one day. Anyway, there were other things on his mind.

In the bathroom, he showered and dressed. Putting on a dab of cologne, he looked in the mirror and saw his tan healthy skin, his clear blue eyes and dark hair. No, he was not a zero, not a fool or an idiot. He put on his soft wool sports jacket, a fine check alternating grey blue and rusty brown; it shimmered a bit in the mirror. Conscious of the impact of his looks, he had decided not to sit on the bench while Betsy played the field. He could not stop thinking about her, though. Nuts, he said to himself, she was nuts. Then, looking in the mirror, he stopped himself. He was not going to think about it tonight.

He drove down Shields and headed for the nearby lounge where he would meet Sandra. Next to Manchester Mall, the bar was owned by Don Wolf, his friend from the store days; he had quit managing for Safeway last year and started this new business with some silent partner. Tigran did not know who it was, though he knew a lot of people in Fresno. Ever since he was a teenager and an early member of the Armenian Triple X fraternity, Tigran had made friends easily, not because he was a bullshitter, just the opposite. People could count on him to be solid, realistic, discrete. They had not called him Sam Spade for nothing. His closest friends were the earliest ones, the Triple X Armenians, who were dedicated to protecting each other and the community. The Rock, his friends called him with pride – but then with an added ironic grin once he fell for Betsy, the divorcee.

He walked into the big lounge room, noisy for a Monday night, and he saw that Sandra was not there yet. He sat at the darker end of the bar and ordered a beer and a shot. Don Wolf walked up and sat on the stool next to him. Around the neck of his beige shirt, Don wore an odd southwest style string tie with a turquoise clasp. A tall, hefty man, he always wore neutral colors and an odd complacent expression. He was a regular American – an Americanitzi, Ma would say. His parents were Germans from the Volga region, and he had recently married a German girl.

"Like your tie," Tigran said. "You wearing moccasins next?"

"Hell, yes," Don Wolf said.

"And in that get-up, you want me to go to Candlestick to watch the Giants with you next month? You'll be heading for North Beach, Wolfie."

"Nothing like a string tie to stir your imagination."

"But seriously, it's a beautiful team now – with Mays and Cepeda, and Willie McCovey coming up fast. I love that guy," Tigran said. He had known Don for five years, and he enjoyed the friendship.

The two men walked over to the pool table and began a game. Tigran smashed the triangle of set up balls, and they ricocheted wildly around the green felt. He felt in control and kept razzing Don about his southwest outfit.

"I heard," Don said, "Garo's talking about buying a bar."

"That's news to me," Tigran said. He shot hard with his cue, and the ball missed. "You opened this place last year, and George Kallen opened his the year before. What's with all these saloons? It's like the Old West."

"Well, it's Monday night, and we're pretty hot. And you're here, Tigran," he said and smiled.

"Hi," Tigran said, as Sandra walked up to him. She was pretty conventional looking – pale skin, turned-up nose, light brown hair – except that she slightly swaggered when she walked, as if those hips were a little out of control. She wore a revealing pink sweater and a tight skirt to just below the knees. She was a little shapeless down there, Tigran thought; she had better think twice before she wore it again.

Sandra said she would have what he had, a beer and a shot, as they sat on the stools near the dark end of the bar. After a while, she had several drinks and seemed pretty tanked. Her arm was around his shoulder, and her other hand was on his thigh. He did not want her pawing him, and he did not want her, period. He wanted to leave.

"Hey, Sandra, I'm feeling a little sick. Like I'm coming down with the flu or something. I'm sorry about this. I gotta get home. Are you okay with it? You can drive yourself home, no?"

"Sure," she said, slightly slurring the word. Her face was a little puffy, and he could not read her expression. He waved to the bartender and had him pour her a cup of coffee. Finally, he paid their tab and left.

He drove back down Shields, and when he got to Garland, it was 11 p.m. There were no street lights because it was county property – the neighborhood was a developer's wet-dream: no need to worry about the expense of lights or sidewalks. So it was dark except for a sliver of moon, a few stars, and houselights. There was a little smog in the air, but not as bad as LA, at least not yet. From the street in front of their house, he could see the glow of a reading lamp in Juliet's room, and the flickering from the local news on TV in the family room. He parked and stayed sitting in the darkened car.

Sandra was almost a dozen years younger than Tigran, but it was not because of her age. Over the years, he had known women much younger and much older. And it was not only because he kept thinking about Betsy, about trying again with her despite her being unfaithful – for Adam's sake and for his own. Thinking about that had not prevented him from making it with other women during this month. No, it was because Sandra was unreal; she had no class.

Juliet was a real person, a brat but real. Why would she be friends with Sandra? It was as if there was no person there, just her need to fuck, and a dumb fuck it would have been. The thing was that Betsy had charm; she was an impossible, disloyal, confused person, but she was a person. Sure he liked sex with her, but he also liked just being with her, even if she was nuts. Anyway, he hated bars. Why the fuck would Garo want to own one, he thought as he sat in his car.

Inside the house, his mother questioned him: why did he stay in his car, why didn't he come in right away? She must have detected the fear in his voice before dinner when he told her that Ronnie Arslanian was in the mob. Something was terribly wrong, she replied; how could a nice Armenian boy like Ronnie become ruthless and brutal, like a Turk?

Chapter 15

Armenia

OCTOBER 26, 1962

The Aeroflot rattled, rolled, and pitched down the runway in Yerevan, and finally the jet was airborne over the capitol.

"I can't believe this takeoff?" Tigran's wife said. "It's even worse than our arriving flight." Betsy looked pale and stunned in the aisle seat next to Artemis. She had reconciled with Tigran six months ago.

"They say Aeroflot is safe," Artemis said, sitting by the window.

"So much for what they say."

Suddenly in the midst of ascending the plane plummeted what seemed a hundred feet. For several seconds Artemis floated fearlessly on a wave that crashed through the sky.

"Oh my god," Betsy said. Her face was gray, and she stared straight ahead. Slowly the plane recovered and flew steadily and calmly.

"There should be colors," Artemis said. The plane's interior was a uniform industrial gray and terribly cramped – the walls and seats, the ceiling and floor. Without replying, Tigran's wife closed her eyes.

"When we arrive home," Artemis said, "the flight will be nothing but a memory."

Outside the window Artemis saw the land tilting and turning below her. To the right was Ararat, Armenia's mountain, which was located tragically on Turkish soil. It was snowcapped and grander than she had imagined when she drew it – was it thirty-five years ago? As it receded from view, she thought she saw on one side the glint of a NATO missile complex, just a hundred miles from Yerevan. American nuclear missiles were installed there in Turkey, pointing at Armenia and the rest of the Soviet Union. People had been discussing the Soviet-American missile crisis, and no one knew much about it, but all the Armenians she met wondered what the difference was between those American missiles on Armenia's border and the Soviet missiles in Cuba. Just now before their departure, she had phoned Armen in Fresno to make sure he would meet her and Betsy at the Fresno airport. He had been so worried about Kennedy's gamble over Cuba and the possibility of nuclear war.

The nuclear crisis confirmed her sense that everything was unstable now. It was not only a question of the plane's unsteady ascent, and it went beyond Fresno and Garo and his business and family. The Aeroflot kept jerking about, rising and falling as if dangling on a string. Everything about her life seemed to dangle like that. She was suspended between departure and arrival and unable to answer the most fundamental questions about her life. To whom and for what was she truly responsible? Who truly were the people she loved?

Earlier in the year, Garo announced at a family dinner: "I have something I want to tell you all. I'm going to buy a bar."

"A bar?" Armen had said. "But what do you know about running a bar - there's very little profit margin in it, son, very late hours, and not a good element."

"Pop, it would be a great business – and a great location. The Garret's for sale at Olive and 99, on the property the Simonians own."

Armen sounded his tsk.

"Do you really want to suck up to those drunken fools, Garo, and pour them drink after drink?" Tigran asked. Her sweet Garo looked hurt and began explaining his reasons.

He had talked about owning a bar ever since the stores had failed. Now that the Garret was for sale, Garo would buy it with the severance payment from that Ronnie Arslanian. Her son was a good farmer and a natural athlete, but she knew he wanted to do something different from anything Tigran or any of them had done. A bar, though? Armen had told her for years how savage Fresno could be. The Armenians controlled bookmaking, the prostitutes were owned by the Volga Germans, who also ruled the police and the downtown politicians, and the Italian builders ran the other rackets. Fresno was a corrupt town, yet Garo wanted to own a bar here, a dangerous business that catered to Americans drinking and carousing. And there was worse; she had forced Tigran to tell her the truth: that the money Ronnie bought out Garo with was tainted, that Ronnie was a racketeer. Maybe Big Mike's son would try to muscle in on Garo's business. There were evil people in this world, and Garo was so innocent; he could be terribly hurt if she were not sufficiently vigilant.

In these three years since losing the Kings markets, her sense of crisis had grown more urgent, especially since her mother's death. The sight of her mother shrunken in the coffin had permanently changed Artemis. A door had opened to what lay beyond her ordinary life, and a new, painfully suspended sense of herself lived alongside her normal temperament. The Byron passage she had memorized in youth came back to her. "I live not in myself, but I become portion of that around me." What could help her endure all the troubles and death around her? The people she loved did help, above all Garo and his family, but also Tigran, Adam, and even Betsy – and of course Juliet and Armen.

She thought of all her efforts to help her husband. It was for him that she traveled to Armenia, even if Betsy had arranged for the tickets through her work at the travel agency. The U.S.

government had refused Armen permission to travel there, and Artemis had brought with her a portfolio of his poems for publication in Yerevan and Moscow. Most of them were about Armenia, imagined from the distance of the California Diaspora, and they were much praised by the literary people she met. Arrangements were being made, and as his wife, she was treated with great respect by writers and politicians alike.

They saw Armen as the face and progressive voice of the Armenians in the United States. Of course, she knew what they did not about him, that he was gifted in writing but a lightweight in action, a bankrupt and a weak man. "I know you'll enjoy when I'm gone," she had said bitterly at the airport when she departed, "because you'll never change. You think life is just about having a good time. And your daughter takes right after you." The bitterness between them ebbed and flowed in a peculiar pattern, and she realized there was something fateful about it. Partly it had to do with Garo, whose spirit she had nurtured and encouraged since the beginning. She would lay down her life before she would permit Armen to sully her creation with his idle detachment.

Outside her window now, Armenia had disappeared beneath the endless sea of clouds. She had been thrilled to see the nation and glad about how far it had risen above the excruciating poverty during World War II twenty years ago and, even worse before that during the decades of early struggle. Walking and driving through the thriving capitol, she had felt pride mixed with a certain shock at being where everyone was Armenian, without exception or variety. Abovian Street, lined with busy shops, was Yerevan's main boulevard, and at one end was the central square with hotels, restaurants, and government buildings all clad in the pretty rose color of their indigenous tufa stone. An old party friend, Margo, had emigrated from California in the forties and lived in a small apartment off Abovian. She had hugged, fed, and regaled Artemis and Betsy with her family's attentions. Margo was an administrator for the state television, and she spoke with great intensity about the nation's earlier poverty when there had been little food and less heat and people wore newspaper beneath their clothes against the cold. Artemis remembered receiving letters from her written in tiny script on cigarette paper. Now, however, there was some abundance, and a new political warming that allowed Americans to visit.

The Soviet thaw under Khrushchev was allowing the new generation of writers to express themselves. Of course, Armenians had always managed to express or at least insinuate an unruly sense of independence, sometimes to their peril. One evening in Yerevan, she had been introduced to a coolly charismatic young Russian poet on his "annual visit," and Voznesenski had said, "In Moscow, saying you heard something on Radio Armenia is like saying you heard the truth." She was introduced to several Armenian poets, including kind and serious Kevork Emin and two gifted women, Maro Markarian and Sylva Gaboudikian; they were all a decade younger than Artemis. They read their works in friends' living rooms, and the poems were both proud and critical of Armenian life, sympathetic and questioning all at once. She wondered if this thaw would affect Armen's poetry; probably not, she thought.

Of course, in all these writers, there were limits, and all of Armenian life here was haunted because so many of the best people had been murdered in the Genocide forty-seven years ago. The old survivors were identifiable on the streets of Yerevan from the sadness on their faces and the weakness in their stride. Also, there was some reversion to village ways, even in the city. Men and women alike hooted and scoffed at the sight of Margo driving the new car the family had bought. This last week, on a visit to the lovely highland village near Gerghard, with its Early Christian church carved into a mountain, she noticed how gaunt were the farmers and their families, how brutal their lives seemed. Most American-Armenians, including her husband, made these mountain villages into some sort of romantic ideal, and they blinded themselves to their actual poverty. Even her Byron had not been immune, and she admired him less now than in her youth.

High mountains are a feeling, but the hum
Of human cities torture: I can see
Nothing to loathe in nature.

The years she had spent on remote farms had taught her that there were unforeseen consequences to a life close to nature. As for the hum of human cities, she had loved her visit to Paris, which was filled with beautiful art and the vital sound of people determined to master the time they had before their deaths.

"Are you awake?" Betsy asked softly, her voice pleasant now and relaxed.

"Yes," Artemis said. She turned to take in her daughter-in-law's charming smile. "You took a nice nap. You needed to sleep."

"Hopefully it'll be smooth going from now on."

"I was just thinking about that village of Gerghard with the stone-carved church."

"The carved saints and their serious looking eyes! Was that your favorite place we saw?"

"The church was beautiful," Artemis said, "but I liked Yerevan best. And it was wonderful to visit people in their homes."

"People were so gracious," Betsy said with her smile.

"Remember Kevork Emin reading his poems at Dr. Abrahamian's."

"What a great apartment. But the doctor's wife seemed sad. I wonder if their marriage is troubled."

"I'm sure they're happy together," Artemis said, surprised at Betsy. "I like them both very much. There was even a Russian poet they invited that evening. Dr. Abrahamian is so open-minded and intelligent: a genuine Armenian intellectual. Armen really respects him."

"He's quite cosmopolitan for a cancer researcher," Betsy said, and then she started talking about other people they had met.

Artemis remembered Betsy's crush on the doctor two summers

ago, but she was sure that her daughter-in-law's speculations about the doctor meant nothing. She would not betray Tigran now after he had forgiven her and they had gotten back together. It was true that when they were touring, sometimes Betsy would disappear; she would say she went shopping. She was given to flirting and infatuations, and perhaps she was trying to draw the doctor into some relation, even if not physical. Maybe something was missing in Betsy, some sense of loyalty, but this lack fascinated Artemis, for it seemed to release an unusual power over people in her. She could smilingly flout conventions and obligations, and that even increased her charm and impact. During their Paris stopover on the way to Armenia, one afternoon an English-speaking Frenchman staying at the hotel had invited them out for dinner in the evening, but early that evening Betsy explained that her "friend," as she now called him, had been able to make reservations only for two. Artemis wondered whether it was so terrible for Betsy to manipulate people with her charm and to live chiefly for herself.

"Can I tell you a little secret about Tigran?" Betsy said.

"What do you mean?" Artemis answered tensely, but Betsy's smile, her leaning toward her, and her lively warmth were irresistible. "All right, tell me."

"Tigran is going to that psychiatrist you found, Dr. Hopper. I probably drove him to it."

"What?" Artemis said, distressed mostly because she had not known. The doctor had helped Juliet and Garo, but why Tigran, who was like a rock, so steady and strong? "How do you know?"

"I saw one of Tigran's sleeping pill bottles with Dr. Hopper's name on it. I asked him about it, and he said, 'I don't go to talk; he's just prescribing pills for insomnia.' But I know he sees him every Wednesday at noon; it's in his appointment book."

"Well, psychiatrists are trained physicians," Artemis said.

"Do you know he sleepwalks? Or used to, before he started taking the sleeping pills. Since when we got back together, I've thought he's depressed, bothered by something, but he won't talk about it. You know he's thinking of moving us to Sacramento to start a new business."

"He is!" Artemis said. "When did he say that?"

"Last month. He probably didn't want to tell you until it's a sure thing."

"Tell me what he's disturbed about!"

"I don't know. Maybe it's just the seven year itch."

How could Betsy tell her such things now, in the plane, things she had not suspected? She felt dizzy, and she thought maybe the Aeroflot had begun again to pitch and plummet. Nauseated, she thought how contorted her body was, her taut legs on the verge of snapping, her swollen feet, her nose and pasty skin and thinning hair. She was shaken by revulsion. What was disturbing her son? Could it be Betsy's behavior? Was it that evil Ronnie Arslanian, with his false politeness? Or was it the corruption that had invaded Fresno? She felt she had been whipped back and forth, as if the plane had abruptly changed course. Looking out her window to steady herself, she saw the sky filled with clouds; the horizon had vanished; the airless cabin threatened to suffocate her, and panic gripped her. She felt that some sort of violent change had occurred just now, a distortion in the very structure of things – maybe a nuclear explosion somewhere had shaken the Earth.

"Artemis, are you okay?" Betsy said in her warm, almost unctuous voice. "You're so pale. I didn't want to upset you so. I waited to tell you until now."

"I need to rest," she said, trying to control herself. She lowered the primitive window shade on its roller, so that the altered sky was no longer visible.

Closing her eyes, she began inwardly repeating the mantra: Tigran will be fine. Tigran will be fine. In this way, she tried to overcome panic and allow herself to believe that he would not move from Fresno. She forced herself to think about memories of her visit. The evening meal the doctor and his wife had served included delicious mezes of Russian caviar and cheese-filled beregs, then shish kebab, and for dessert a wonderful cake – layered and buttery gatta. Artemis was moved by the Abrahamians' generosity, by their serving their best food and gathering such fine friends. Yet like so much in Armenia, the evening felt haunted; the doctor and his wife and friends all seemed aware of how diminished their lives had been and how the shadow of the Genocide remained with them still nearly fifty years later. That evening, three marvelous poets read from their work, and each poem struggled with a similar shadow – first, Voznesenski had recited his ferocious "I Am Goya" with the doctor translating, then Gaboudikian her sensitive "No One Answers," and finally Emin his "Siamanto's Prayer." Kevork Emin had a flowing moustache above a sensitive mouth. Tears had come to her eyes as she listened to his lament for the Armenian poet murdered in the Genocide. One passage – about Armenia overrun by its invaders – came to her:

What sort of aloof being would conceive
Of creating a hell on our high plateau
And imagining it would be a heaven,
Safe and protected next to Ararat?
Who, instead of a genuine nation,
Gave us this ancient rutted road –
Instead of fertile fields, these rocky crags,
Instead of sweetly flowing springs, spilled blood?

Slowly, as her mind approached unconsciousness, the speeding jet began to fill with images from her dreaming. Her old father and her beloved mother occupied the seats adjacent to hers, and on the faces of her dead parents were expressions of such tender sadness and heart-breaking loss. Behind them sat more of the dead, their bodies preserved as in life but stiff as if the fuselage contained a wax display, except that behind her the cabin extended as far as she could detect, stretching back and back forever and completely filled with the seated dead in their vast array of poses: weary, brutal, desperate, yearning, or massacred by fire or bomb or bullet or sword.

Chapter 16

Juliet in Berkeley

NOVEMBER 11, 1962

Lights flickered outside. There was a wide window by the side of her bed, and she looked out over the bay and the ocean beyond. The water lapped gently at the window's edge. Now she saw. She was in an apartment facing the Golden Gate. Beautiful azure water was ebbing and flowing as a ship plowed the waves nearby, and she lay in the arms of a young man. What a pleasure to be with him, a blond folksinger, twenty-one like herself. They had made love before, but in Fresno, where he would be living, if this were not a dream.

The Sunday morning sun streamed in the window, warming the bed. As she woke up, she vaguely remembered dreaming. Her Murphy bed was at one end of the living room. Edie and Sandy, her roommates, were asleep in the twin beds of the bedroom in this small Berkeley apartment. She needed to get up, but the sun warming her limbs drew her back, and she lowered herself once again under the sheets and covers. She remembered the Renaissance Coffee House in Fresno's Tower District, where she loved to listen to folk music, and spend her spare time during her two years at Fresno City and then State College. Four months ago, however, at the end of June she had moved to Berkeley. The first man she made love to had been the blond folksinger named Joey, who sang in the Renaissance. In May she told him she was going to leave for the Bay Area. She liked him, but she was going to make a new life in Berkeley, away from Fresno.

Juliet loved the university, and she gulped down these first months here as if she had been deprived of nourishment she needed. She loved her art, English, and history classes, and there was simultaneously her discovery of Telegraph Avenue's bookstores and coffee houses. She liked the Mediterranean Café with its air of strong coffee and conversation and where everyone dressed in peasant skirts and buckskin and Beat black and jeans. The café's elevated ceiling was like a high canopy filled with a haze of cigarette and pipe smoke. The students looked and sounded like beatniks, the beatniks sounded like students, and professors often wandered in. A folk musician strummed a guitar at a table in back. She loved the taste of croissants with coffee. What a pleasure it was to be in her early twenties in this amazing town. "We happy few," she thought amid all the talk and smoke of the café. She wanted to spend the rest of her life here with her books and professors, friends and lovers, the ocean and bay, the freedom to grow her hair to her waist, the admiring glances, the music. She wanted to get her PhD in history and teach here, or she would live as an artist in San Francisco and paint her Matisse dreams and Armenian fantasies. She had no desire for marriage, which she feared would trap her. She would never leave the Bay Area. And she loved the friends she was making in Berkeley – Sophie, the intellectual German-Jewish New Yorker, Alan the Trotskyite, Gary the handsome Anthro grad student with a crush on her, Jeremy the Negro art major, Bob the homosexual journalism student.

The clock read 9:30, and she lifted herself from the bed, went to the bathroom, and then to the kitchen. She had to get ready because her mother and father were driving up from Fresno this Sunday morning, and they planned to arrive by ten. It was the first time she would see her mother since her trip to Armenia last month; there was a lot to tell her, she had said, about Armenia and about Tigran's wife, with whom she had traveled. From the refrigerator, she took a crisp red apple and began taking bites as she went around straightening the living room. Edie and Sandy were sleeping late, as they did most mornings, for they were not students and were still looking for jobs. She didn't envy their laziness, though she sometimes felt Sandy envied her for making friends so easily in her classes and at the Mediterranean. Sandy Jones had once dated Tigran, when her brother was briefly separated from Betsy. She was a rusty-haired, pasty-looking girl, a sometime student at Fresno City College, who seemed to go through a boyfriend a week. Sandy had always tried to adopt Juliet's bohemian look, growing her thin hair long and piercing her ears a few days after Juliet had.

Edie Hatchaturian, her other roommate, was a close old friend and a fine sweet person, whose parents owned the property where Garo was going to lease a bar, the Garret. Edie was not very interested in art, but she always supported Juliet and complimented her about her expressiveness in art and everything else. Before they left for Berkeley, Juliet had tried to help Edie with her worsening psoriasis, getting her to go to the same specialist who treated Daddy. And she had persuaded her to go for counseling to Dr. Hopper, as well. Juliet herself had continued to see him and had lost thirty pounds over the last two years. Moving to Berkeley, she was ready to lead a new life.

At 10:10 a.m. she heard her parents on the porch, talking in Armenian. They knocked, she opened the door, and there they were – her father wore a gray sports jacket over a plaid shirt, his face was lined but calm as usual, his hair mostly gray, and her mother seemed thinner now after a month in Armenia, her hair dyed light brown, her face eager. She almost sprang from her raincoat as she entered the apartment. There was the sound of a piano filtering from the apartment next door, a classical piece. It was Sammy, one of their neighbors. The music, the sunlight flooding from the porch and the windows, the proximity of forty thousand fellow students – Juliet loved it all; her world and her parents' seemed in a sort of balance now on the crisp, breezy November morning.

"I brought you Harput kufta," her mother said, holding a bowl with its top wrapped in aluminum foil.

"That's so nice, Mama," Juliet said and smiled.

Artemis headed for the kitchen, opened the refrigerator door, and seemed to inventory the contents as she placed the bowl on the bottom shelf. "So much fruit," she said. "Are you eating enough protein?"

"Yes," Juliet said.

Her roommates drifted in from the bedroom. Edie wore a bathrobe; Sandy wore short baby-doll pajamas and seemed oblivious to Armen's looking away, embarrassed.

Opening the refrigerator, Sandy said, "What's in the nice bowl?"

"It's kufta," Juliet said.

"It's Juliet's favorite," Artemis said. "They're lamb meatballs with walnuts in a juicy filling."

"Yum," Sandy said. "How sweet of you!"

Armen struck a match to relight his pipe.

"Why don't you smoke outside? These girls don't like your smoke," Artemis said

"That's okay, Daddy."

"It is fine," Armen said. "I take a little walk, to Telegraph and back."

Juliet remembered a story he told about his semester at Berkeley almost forty years ago. She realized that maybe she was doing what he had wanted to do at her age, but she couldn't be sure because Mama hardly ever let him talk about things like that.

"May I use your phone? I have to call Lucaper in San Francisco?" Artemis said. They would be staying overnight at the Hatchaturians.

"Something's wrong with our phone, Artemis," Edie said.

"Maybe you can call at the drugstore down the street," Juliet said.

"What about your neighbor's phone?" Artemis said. "I heard nice music from the porch."

"You don't want to bother them," Juliet said. Often in passing, she had greeted the two students who lived there. Last week, she was eating an ice cream cone while walking across the parking lot on one side of their apartment building, she had glanced up, and there was one of the students, doing dishes at the kitchen window. It was Sammy Weisberg, with his wildly curly red-brown hair, his kind handsome face, and his shoulders slightly slumped from studying. His smiling eyes were looking at her through thick, black horn-rimmed glasses. They had waved at each other.

"I'll ask them," Artemis said. "They must be nice people."

She and her mother walked together across the porch and knocked at the door. The piano stopped, and Sammy opened the door, smiling and saying hello.

She spoke before Artemis could and explained that her mother needed to use a phone, but theirs was out of order.

"Use ours," he said.

"What nice music you play," Artemis said as she dialed. "What was that?"

"Schubert. A Schubert sonata."

On the phone, she began talking in Armenian during his response.

"It's beautiful," Juliet said.

"Is it too loud? I hope it doesn't bother you."

"Not at all. We only hear it on the porch. It's really nice."

Her mother finished and picked up a coin that was resting on the telephone table. "Oh, here's a quarter for the call," she said. Sammy looked confused.

"Not necessary," he managed to say, but Artemis had turned and left. Her mother's behavior was absurd, and Juliet looked apologetically at Sammy. But he just smiled broadly at her, and once again she was struck by his kind eyes.

"Juliet," her mother called from the porch.

Daddy, pipe in hand, was stepping onto the porch. "Berkeley has changed," he said as Juliet emerged from the other apartment.

"We met a nice student just now," Artemis said. "I think he's a nice Jewish boy. He looks like a genius with so much curly hair. He should get a haircut."

"Tsk," Armen clicked his tongue. "There are so many more students than before."

Soon Juliet sat in the backseat of the Ararats' car as Armen drove. The nearby dorms loomed across from her apartment house, and Artemis saw students waiting in long lunch lines outside the cafeteria. "Look at that," she said, "it's terrible to have to line up like that for lunch. It was the right thing not to live in a dorm."

On Bancroft, they passed new campus buildings and shops crowded with people.

"It's all new," Armen said. "Everyone is so young, and there are so many students."

"Why do you keep saying that?" Artemis said. "We know."

They made their way west toward Spenger's, a fish restaurant facing the bay. Last month, on the morning of her twenty-first birthday, when Artemis was in Armenia, someone had knocked on the apartment door. She opened it, and there was Daddy, who took her to lunch across the Bay to Alioto's Grotto Number Nine on Fisherman's Wharf. She was so surprised. As they drove across the Bay Bridge to San Francisco, he had sung Armenian songs. She felt how sweet and devoted he could be.

"Do you know," Juliet said in the car now, "what Edie's mother does with fine art prints?" Her father began to smile. "She takes old black and white photos of Armenian doings, cuts her face out of them, and pastes them onto the faces in the color prints of women in ball gowns – sometimes two on one painting, both the piano player and the listener. She's very sweet, but even Edie thinks it's strange. They're all over the house."

In the restaurant, Artemis talked about her trip to Armenia and the rebirth of the country. She opened her purse as they waited to be seated. She brought out a pair of amber earrings. "Juliet, you have pierced ears," she said. "These are for you."

Gold filigree held orange amber delicately flecked with brown. Juliet was amazed at the beautiful offering, and there was no hesitation in her voice when she said, "Thanks so much, Mama. They look so expensive."

"Things are cheap there. Betsy bought so much jewelry!" As they ordered their lunch – lobster for Armen, crab Louie for Artemis, and sautéed salmon for Juliet – Artemis talked on about what Tigran's wife had bought and then how she behaved in Paris and in Yerevan with Dr. Abrahamian. "She's such a charming person," she said as she ate her salad, "but she flirts too much."

"Have you told Tigran about it?" Juliet asked, but Artemis did not reply.

"I love gossip," Armen said, and Artemis started speaking of Tigran's business dealings.

They finished lunch, and she realized it would be impossible to stop her mother from going on and on about Tigran unless they distracted her.

"You were gone during the Cuban Missile Crisis last month," Juliet said.

"It wasn't reported, but there was a lot of talk."

"It was terrible. There was a silent vigil on the sidewalk by campus, at the end of Telegraph. They were cloudy days, and it was so bleak. The color seemed bleached out of everything." She had talked with Sammy at the vigil. How pale his face had been.

Juliet let the waitress take her plate away; she had eaten half of her salmon, a diet portion.

"You eat like a bird," Artemis said. "Something must be wrong with you."

"Today is Armistice Day," Armen said.

"Yes, Veterans Day," Juliet said, frowning but otherwise ignoring her mother's comment.

"America does no honor to veterans. This missile crisis is silly. America has missiles in Turkey, a few miles from Soviet Union, from Armenian soil. But Soviets are not allowed to do the same in Cuba. America is a bully."

"Maybe now we'll remove our missiles from Turkey," Juliet said.

"Tsk," Armen clicked his tongue.

As they walked back to the car, the November breeze had moderated, and it was pleasant. Juliet sat once more in the back seat and slightly lowered the window.

"Why did you open the window?" Artemis said irritably as they started out.

"Do you want me to raise it?"

"Never mind," she said curtly. Then she said, "Duncan called. He says hello."

Juliet sat there ambushed. He was the young man who had attempted to assault her at their house on July Fourth seven years ago. Some months after that, she realized that he worked at the Clovis King; his name was Duncan, and he was an Armenian from Beirut. A few years later, when she graduated from Fresno High in 1959, he had brazenly called her and asked her out, casually apologizing for what he had done four years before. She told him she never wanted to speak to him. She refused his calls and ignored him when she happened to see him. But he had begun to phone her parents, ingratiating himself with them, and Artemis knew very well that it felt to Juliet like he was stalking her.

"I don't want to hear Duncan ever mentioned again," she said as she sat there incensed.

"He's such a nice young man. I told him you were having a good time in Berkeley."

"You told him I live in Berkeley! I told you he was stalking me," Juliet said, on the verge of breaking down. "You probably told him my address."

"Not really."

"You did!"

"Just the street. It's not important. He's a nice man."

Her thoughts raced. This recent call to her parents must be his first in quite a while, for a year ago something had happened to stop Duncan. Big Mike's son Ronnie Arslanian had interceded, the man her family lately said was a pariah. One evening last November, Juliet had been studying at a table in the Renaissance in Fresno, and suddenly she was surprised to see Ronnie standing by her, commanding in a tailored suit.

"Juliet, don't be startled," he had said in a soft voice. "I want you to know that I'm aware someone working at Clovis has been harassing you. He boasted about it at the store, but he won't be bothering you anymore. I've taken care of it." With a smile, he simply left, and outside he got into the back of a parked Cadillac, which drove away in the darkness. She had been surprised and wondered about his motive. Ronnie was such a typical Fresno Armenian, with his nose job, his slick Americanness, and his blond American wife, let alone his reputation now for ruthlessness. Everyone assumed he was in it only for himself.

"I'll bet you've kept talking to Duncan, haven't you?" Juliet said. Artemis made no reply. "You did. You're so rude and irresponsible."

Suddenly her mother turned pale, and her voice became thin and raspy. "You're the rude one! Coming to Berkeley and doing whatever you want! People always say you're such a selfish irresponsible girl. And why do you always wear your hair in your eyes?"

"You're horrible!" Juliet said from the back seat. She had hoped her new life in Berkeley would insulate her from feeling so vulnerable. And the most horrible thing was that Artemis saw herself as the victim! It was impossible for Juliet to stop her or to tell her anything about what Duncan had done years before.

The three of them sat frozen in the car, parked in front of her apartment.

Chapter 17
Garo's Garret

OCTOBER 30, 1964

It was a restless unease Garo felt – charged, even panicky, hard to define. The thing that helped was company, friends, visitors, and acquaintances. They warmed him, made him feel supported, so that the vague panic he felt receded. It was a vulnerability, he knew, and yet from childhood on, the pleasure of being with people had been a key to being alive; it sustained him.It was past four in the afternoon, and Lily was puttering in the kitchen. Chick Leone sat with his wife on the living room couch while Garo did his Royal Canadian exercises in front of them; he could feel the rafters of the house shaking. He had hired the Leones to work for him at the Garret, Chick as a bartender and Diane as a waitress; their shift would start at five. They had been at his and Lily's home for a few hours, lazing around and shooting the breeze. Lance Fetzer had been there earlier; the hulk of a man had started hanging around the bar since it opened last month, on Garo's thirty-second birthday. Lance looked belligerent, but he was a sweetly genuine young man in his mid-twenties, and Lily had asked Garo to help straighten out the big kid, who had been there, singing happy birthday to him. This month he almost seemed to be living at the bar. He felt sorry for Lance. And the fact was that he felt sorry for Chick Leone, too. After the stores failed, Chick could not be kept on as an assistant manager at Clovis, and he had ended up working in produce at a Safeway. So earlier this year, as Garo interviewed potential employees while he had the Garret refurbished, he hired Chick, with his soft red face and impossible resume of past jobs, as well as his pretty wife, Diane. He knew Chick had been a lush for a time, and he was definitely a bullshitter. He invented careers the way a garden sprouted weeds.

"Let's count up the years, Chick: eight as a minor league player, ten as a major league referee, five as a scout, plus seven as a CIA spy, five as a restaurant manager, the past six years in Fresno. And you're forty years old! It's impossible. You'd have to be at least seventy. From now on, I call you Methuselah." And he teased him too about his name. "You just don't seem like a Chick. Where'd you get that name? You're no spring chicken, and you're not Czech. Is it a Sicilian thing or something?" But there was a deep sense of loyalty in Chick; it was something Garo valued highly, and it had to be reciprocated.

"Hey, Champ," Chick said, "Diane and me'd better get to work."

"Wait a second," Garo said. "I want to show you what I've been working on." He went to the closet and got out his golf club. He had worked on perfecting his golf swing and was proud of it. He walked to the center of the living room. "Watch this," he said, positioning himself as if he were about to hit a shot. He pulled back the driver so it was high in back of him and swept it forward, in a powerful arc, just brushing the rug, as if he were hitting a perfect long shot.

"Beautiful shot, Champ."

"I've been working on it."

When they left, Lily sat down with a cup of coffee at the long table, already set for the family's dinner. Sitting there, she was such a lovely woman, he thought, and in her pink dress, she did not even show her pregnancy yet, her third. Garo remembered when he first saw this petite French-Armenian girl, a few years after her father, the Holy Trinity priest, had brought her from Marseilles when she was a teenager. She had captured his heart immediately.

Now she took out her cigarettes and began smoking.

"I don't see how you can smoke so much, especially when you're pregnant," he said. She was a good housekeeper, but it made him sick that his wife smoked almost two packs a day; all her cleaning and freshening could not remove the odor of smoke from the house. She was like Pop with his pipe, and Mom like Garo hated all the ashes and the odor. His mom and pop were due to come over for dinner later today.

"I don't see how you can try out a golf club in the house," Lily said. "What kind of a person shows off his golf swing in the goddamn living room?"

"Oh, come off it. It did no harm," he said and sat down at the other end of the table.

"You practically ripped the carpet. It's a pathetic old carpet, but we can't afford to replace it."

"We'll get a new carpet and a lot more than that! In a few years, I'll be a millionaire – ten years, tops."

"In ten years, you'll be history," Lily said. "No one keeps a bar in Fresno that long."

"That's bullshit. You have to keep your customers guessing. You have to reinvent yourself, reinvent the bar." She didn't see that all you needed to keep people coming was to be creative.

"You reinvent yourself! That's bullshit."

"It's not bullshit!" he said. "We'll bring in live acts. We're going to serve Armenian food."

"So, you're going to bring Frank Sinatra to Garo's Garret!" Lily said. "And what will you pay him with, dolma and pilaf?"

He could feel that thing growing in him that was different from panic or anxiety. It felt like what his brother did to him. He tried counting to ten.

"If you convince him to come, I guarantee you he can put his slippers under my bed any time."

"What the fuck!" Garo exploded.

"You're brilliant, Garo. Live shows! You think you could ever afford that? You're such a big man now? Well, I have news for you. Tigran's the real man in your family."

"You bitch," he yelled. He took the dinner plate in front of him and hurled it, barely missing her slender shoulder. There was the splatter of crockery shattering.

"Cocksucker!" she said, with a slight French accent in the last syllable. "How can you do that!"

"It was easy," he said, grabbing a second dish. "Like this."

He hurled it at her, and she had to duck to avoid it. He vaguely sensed that Pauly and little Annette were watching now from the living room, and he rose from his chair, unsure what he would do – cease completely, or kill her. Lily got up too, and the pregnant woman grabbed a shoe from a bag she had picked up at the shoe repair. A foot shorter than his six feet, she held the stiletto heel in her hand and came at him. He turned to avoid her blows, and he felt a dull stabbing at his broad heavy back.

All the while, she unleashed a stream of curses in all her languages: "Cocksucker! Fucking bastard! Salaud! Vidany gov! Sickdir pesevang!"

The front door swung open. There were Armen and Artemis.

Lily stared at them as if they were strangers, and then she rushed down the hall. "Pauly, Annette, come with me," his mother said in a sweet voice, and his parents ushered the children out the side door to the backyard.

He could hardly recall what they were fighting about. There was just pure dissatisfaction. He didn't know what to do about it. He sat back down at the table, but then he remembered the broken dishes.

Getting up, he took a broom and dustpan, and swept up the shards and flakes of crockery. As he did so, Lily came in, her clothes changed into brown slacks, a light brown sweater, and slippers.

"Ooph," she sighed, "I don't know anymore."

She went into the kitchen, opened the side door, and called out: "Pauly, Annette, Grandma."

He saw that her pretty face was placid now, and that was enough for him. He relaxed and followed her out to the backyard. She kneeled next to Annette and held the four-year-old in her slender arms.

"How are you doing, sweetie pie?" she said, and to her in-laws, in a quiet, matter-of-fact voice, "Sorry you had to see that."

Armen nodded and said nothing, but Artemis started talking about how everyone was under a lot of pressure nowadays.

Garo tousled his son's hair, hoping to cheer him up, but the seven-year-old looked wary. His daughter ran to him now, and he swept Annette up in his arms. "Anni, sweet Anni," he said and gave her a big kiss. He felt bad about the kids seeing them argue, but he was so overwhelmed that the sense of guilt and regret faded.

"Artemis, do you want to come in and help me with dinner." The children followed the two women into the house.

"How's it going, Pop?" he said.

"I'm okay, son."

Garo led his father around the yard to the very back, where Garo had tended a summer garden. Now in late October, he would soon be turning over the earth, a ten by twenty plot of brown-black soil. The loam looked dark now in the diminished light of evening.

"What happened, son?" Armen said, his voice calm and his lined face impassive.

"I can't stand it, Pop. Something came over us. She's a wonderful mother and a lovely girl, but it's like nothing satisfies her."

"Tsk," his father clicked his tongue.

"We never have enough money, she says. She hates this house, it's shabby and it's small, she says, especially now she's pregnant again. Nothing I do is right, Pop; she hates the bar, my playing golf, everything I do!"

"Wives," Pop said. "They like to complain."

"What was the name of that Levon's wife? Ardashes? You remember those stories about them, how they seemed normal in public, but people heard horrible screams from the house at night. They were your age."

"Yes."

"Tell me, how did she kill herself?"

"One day she shot herself on the front steps of the house on Dakota."

"It's a wonder that more husbands and wives don't do away with themselves. Or each other."

"They barely survived the Genocide, Garo," Pop said. "Now Levon wanders around his yard, day and night. He mumbles, he talks, and no one listens."

"What a shame."

"Dinner's ready," Lily called from the side door.

At the dinner table were platters of buttery pilaf and lamb chops. Artemis had prepared a bowl of salad, with parsley, fresh basil, tomatoes, cucumbers, lettuce, and Lily had added her own variation of cut-up avocadoes and crushed garlic in the dressing of olive oil, lemon, and vinegar.

As they sat down and started to eat, Lily asked if the men wanted beer; only Armen took one.

Lily brought up Tigran and Betsy after a bit. "When they were separated two years ago, do you know who she had a fling with?" Artemis looked tense, and Pop did not even look up. "It was with Ned of all people, the manager of that Italian restaurant on Blackstone."

"DeMelto's!" Pauly said.

"Ned has a wife and children!" Garo said.

"Gossip. We shouldn't be talking about this right now," his father said, glancing at the children.

"Sure, we should, Pop," Garo said. Tigran was not as perfect as he pretended to be, and anyway, it was reality.

"How is the bar?" Pop suddenly asked.

"Garo's Garret is going great! One month and counting," he said with pleasure. "I'm thinking of building a stage and bringing in live music." he turned to Pauly. "Hey, Buddy, you should hear the 45s I put in the jukebox now – the Beatles, the Righteous Brothers, Marvin Gaye, Bill Haley."

"Wow," Pauly said, wide-eyed.

Then Garo turned back to his father, wanting to connect somehow with him. "How's Juliet doing at Berkeley?"

"She is very happy there," Artemis answered for her husband.

A rare smile opened on Armen's face. "I drove up two weeks ago and took her to Fisherman's Wharf for her birthday."

"You've done that before, haven't you?" Lily said. "What a sweet thing to do."

"She was surprised."

"That's great, Pop," Garo said, "She always makes me laugh! Remember when she teased me about trying to teach Pauly golf when he was two. I told her, 'You got to get them early.'"

Artemis started talking about how much weight Juliet had lost, and then dinner came to an end. After some dessert of fruit and ice cream, Garo told his little son to come out to the yard with him. He took his golf driver and a golf glove with him. There was a sort of osmosis, he felt, by which his skill and enthusiasm could pass directly into Pauly; the boundary between father and son needed to disappear.

"Watch this, Pauly."

He took a golf ball from his pocket, put it on some tamped down soil in the back of the long yard. He could see Lily and Armen looking on through the lighted kitchen window. As Pauly watched him, he felt that he was the complete master of his backyard universe. Concentrating, in a golfer's stance, he raised the club in back of him, held for a moment, and swung it down in the smooth arc he had been practicing. The ball lifted in the air, traversed the yard and headed for the house, hitting the roof near the top and skittering off and back down to the darkened yard.

"Garo." He barely heard his name yelled through the kitchen window.

"That was beautiful, Dad."

"You'll be doing that soon, Buddy. But now we'd better head inside. We don't want to get your mother madder than she already is."

At seven in the evening, his parents went home to the Garland house, and he drove his old Buick down Clinton to his bar, a block from the cars and trucks whooshing up and down US 99. He wondered whether his neon sign attracted enough attention, or if he should put an ad on the billboard next door: Garo's Garret plus some catchy phrase like the one he had thought up for Kings. He was proud of his bar's exterior, even if the man he trusted to do it never completed the job. You could hardly tell. There was a pitched, shingle roof rising high above the façade of stones – big pieces of slate grouted with mortar. It was only one story, but it looked like two, as if a garret was up there, even though it didn't exist. The parking lot was pretty full, which was a good sign. As he walked toward the bar entrance, he loved anticipating what he would find inside, all the music and conversation. His warmth and energy would pour unobstructed through all the people gathered in the bar.

Inside, he saw half the tables were already filled with little groups – couples, friends – and more than half of the bar stools were occupied. Chick Leone waved from behind the bar as he moved from customer to customer. A cool blue aura encompassed everything, giving the bar an almost futuristic look. Maybe he should repaint the interior a soft brown; that would make the Garret warmer, still a cool place but more welcoming. He would do that.

Behind the bar, he fielded people's greetings as he inspected the glassware to make sure it was sparkling and the bottles to make sure they were in the order he had established – Bourbons together, brandies, gins, rums, Scotches, tequilas, vodkas.

He chatted with two old football buddies from high school, who were also in their early thirties and fixtures, really, at one end of the bar by the TV, turned down so as not to intrude on the records playing on the speaker system. He loved having a good mix of music and was always finding new music or rediscovering neglected greats. There was a new single he loved by the Beatles, "I Wanna Hold Your Hand," and he played it several times a night.

There was a girl at the bar whom he had talked with a few times in the last few weeks. She was the cutest woman in the Garret. A Marilyn Monroe blonde, she sat sort of side-saddle on one of the stools. Her name was Linda. A couple of men were hovering around her, but she was looking right at him.

"Garo, have a drink on me," she said.

He felt drawn by the heat and sweetness of her glance. "Sure, anything for you, Marilyn," he said, and she laughed.

"I'm going to take you up on that, handsome."

"We'll see," he said. Occasionally he had a shot of brandy, but not much more. He did not need it to feel a buzz; all he needed was the embrace of the bar and its collection of customers, of swingers and family types, of girls and old geezers and kids just turning twenty-one, friends and strangers. It had become clear to him that people really liked to be with him, especially the girls, who seemed to more than like him. His response to their come-ons had been to tease and hold them off.

"Hey, watch this," Phil, one of his old football buddies, said as he stood to reach the TV and turn it up. A little girl filled the screen, and in her hand was a daisy; picking the petals off it, one by one, she was unaware of the massive mushroom cloud from a nuclear explosion busting behind her.

"Wow, if that doesn't win Johnson a few votes," Phil said, "I don't know what will. But you know Goldwater brought it on himself with all that saber-rattling about Vietnam." The people drinking at the bar seemed dismayed.

"That's just politics," Garo said loudly. "Nobody's gonna use a nuclear bomb. We're going to end up all living together, the way it should be."

"Whadayamean we'll all live together?" a middle-aged businessman, a newcomer at the bar, said. "You a commie?"

"I'm a capitalist and I'm a communist," Garo said, improvising in front of his customers. It was possible to be both. Let's face it, he thought, his father had been both. He had joined the Communist Party and yet had broken the unions at his stores. "I think we should all live in peace."

"Even those dirty Armenians?" the man in a business suit sneered.

He had grown up hearing those slurs against his people, and now that thing, immediate and explosive, again arose in him.

"Shut your fucking mouth. What do you think I am?"

"You, big guy! You're white."

He leaned over the polished surface of the bar and put his face close to the man. He flexed his big hands on the counter. He despised bigots, and he felt his face begin to redden.

"Bud, you're not going to want to come here anymore." And he was about to say, "Get the fuck out of here" when the guy's face collapsed and seemed a dozen years older than he was.

"Hey, sorry," the man said. "No offense 'ntended."

Just then Lance Fetzer entered the bar with a biker friend. This distracted him, and he walked to their booth. Lance was taking steroids to bulk up because he wanted to be a boxer.

"Hi, Garo," Lance said, sitting across from his biker friend. Both men had tattoos on their thick arms, and Lance's friend had a brutal scar from a knife cut on one forearm. Their muscled bodies hardly fit into the space of the booth.

"Lance," Garo said. "Introduce me to your buddy."

"This here's Hank."

"Hi, Hank," he said in a genial voice, but he suddenly punched the air in front of the young man's face. "Watch it," he said.

"Hey," the man shouted and reached in his jacket pocket, but then he saw that Garo was smiling and teasing, and he thought better of getting whatever was there.

"Hank, I want you to know we never fight in the Garret. Lance knows," Garo said.

"Never," Lance said and poked his friend's black leather jacket.

"Great," Garo said; he looked at other tables and patrons and moved on to them.

He wanted to examine the receipts from the day so far, and he walked then to the back hall, passing the toilets. He knocked and looked in each door to make sure the bathrooms were equipped and cleaned up for the night crowd. In his office, he closed the door, sat down at the desk, and filed through the day's receipts. The bar was doing okay, but he hated having to keep track of all the details of cash in and cash out. Pop needed to sell the Stars and Stripes Market and come work as the bar's accountant, but he said he needed to wait until he could collect his full social security in three years. Garo wondered if he hesitated because Tigran was always criticizing the bar. Last year, Tigran had seemed so furious after he used his $25,000 settlement from Ronnie Arslanian to buy the Garret. Tigran told everybody it was the last time he would take care of his kid brother; he was washing his hands of anything to do with the bar.

He had visited only once, at the bar's opening last month, and even then it was with Betsy and only for ten minutes. "What's with the unfinished exterior?" he had said. "And slate of all things! First off, it looks lousy unfinished. Second, it looks like you want to be some sort of lord of the manor!" And then he said that the blue interior looked like "an indoor swimming pool without the fucking water." But the worst was when his brother said, "You better watch out, Garo. Everybody says this town is getting wilder and wilder – shit being fenced everywhere, guns, stolen goods. The mob could muscle in on the Garret, and before you know it, they'll own a piece of you."

He could not tell whether Tigran was warning or insulting him. He wondered whether his older brother truly loved him anymore. Ever since they'd had that knock-down, drag-out fight as teenagers, Tigran never let his guard down, and for years there had not been a moment of just pure generous heart from him. That hurt. But Garo's response had been basically to rebel. Tigran was pissed off because the bar was unlike anything he'd ever done. Of course, Tigran enjoyed bullshitting with acquaintances, but people knew he really couldn't care less about them. He would act like a man's man, but that was phony too because actually Tigran disapproved of most of the people he met. Just the opposite of Garo.

He sat alone in the back office, feeling restless and anxious. Juliet used to joke that anxiety had to be in their mother's milk. She would imitate Mom's voice: "Don't go outside, you might fall in a ditch. Don't cross the street, you'll be hit by a truck." He wished he could laugh now, but he felt somehow sealed off, even with the bar pleasantly buzzing and crackling and all that reveling humanity several yards away. Sitting a little panicky at his desk, he heard knocking at his door. A voice was calling, and he said come in.

Linda with her Marilyn Monroe face and hair opened the door and then shut it behind her. Her voice was tender and undefended, as if she were forlorn because he left. "Are you stalking me?" he teased her when she said she asked Chick where Garo disappeared to. He felt his panic lifting, though everything seemed oddly to be occurring at a distance from him. She floated toward him, saying sweetly that she did not want to seem like a fool, but she really liked him. She called him sweetheart, and suddenly she was kneeling at his side and laying her head on his lap. Again she said she really liked him. He wanted to object, but he was already aroused. She unzipped him and took him into her mouth, and a joy he had not experienced before took hold of him. He felt amazed at being entitled to such a sense of power and pleasure. This blonde goddess, he thought, knelt there making love to him, and it was as if his body had become the statue of a god, endowed with a grandeur beyond the human being he was.

Sounds of an argument came from beyond the door – and someone was saying "c-note" and "shit."

"Linda, honey," he said softly as he pulled himself from her. "Something bad is going on out there." He could not hear what she replied, for adrenalin pumped through his veins. His focus was completely on what was happening in the hall.

He tucked himself in, swung the door open, and roared, "What's going on here!"

Lance's biker friend was giving a hundred dollar bill to a sallow young man, who was handing him some sort of heavy package, the size and heft of a gun.

"Sons-of-bitches!" he shouted into the close space. "Don't you fence your shit in my bar!" He reached to grab both men, the money and heavy bag fell to the floor, and he had hold of Hank, the biker, but suddenly the fence held a switch blade up to Garo, and yelled, "Let us go, fucker!"

He let loose of the biker, who fled. He faced the man with the knife and suddenly lunged forward to tackle him. He felt something slash, but he grabbed both the man's arms and steamrolled him with his body, smashing him up against the men's room door. The knife clattered to the floor.

"You fucking scum," he said. "I'll kill you if I ever see you in here again."

He heard Chick Leone in the main room, saying, "Settle down, everything's under control. There's no problem anymore."

Garo pushed the young man out the back door and threw him onto the asphalt parking lot. "Get out, scum," he said. The man scrambled to his feet and ran to his car. "You'll pay for this, motherfucker," he shouted at Garo, but it meant nothing to him. He felt at that moment as if he were floating above the cement steps and the hall as he made his way back to the bar. He picked up the package and the hundred-dollar bill and then put them behind the counter. Everyone was talking, and he smiled broadly at the waving hands and curious faces. He searched the crowd for Linda, but he realized with a confused longing and regret that the beauty must have left.

"A drink for everyone. On the house!" he said, and there was a roar of pleasure. Diane Leone came over and told him the back of his white shirt was slit, but not the undershirt beneath; there was no blood. "That's okay," he said.

Lance Fetzer saddled up without his friend, who was nowhere in sight. He said, "I wouldn't never have brought Hank, if I'd known what he was doing. Garo, I swear. And if you'd asked, I would've nailed both of them. You know, honestly, I'd be honored to be your bouncer."

Garo smiled at the heavy man. "The bartenders can handle it, Lance, but thanks for offering." Maybe someday he would need the hulk of a man as a bouncer, except it would be hard to trust him. Lance had quite a reputation. They said that the big Volga-German had disfigured a man's face with a can opener. Why? For no reason at all. It was a terrible world out there now, Garo thought, filled with predators and thieves of all types, and he wondered why such a sorry lot would gravitate to his bar. He realized it had been a close call; sure, there was the occasional crap game he had to stop, but nothing like this before. Maybe Tigran's doom-mongering was right. But maybe it was this way everywhere.

Looking out over the tide of friendly faces, he was suddenly confused. Was it a dream to try to create a sanctuary here, where people could escape from the trouble in their world? Nobody could deny his impact on people; he was a strong, big-hearted man, and his spirit filled the bar. People loved being with him, and he loved being with them. He was sure that they would flock to Garo's Garret.

Chapter 18
Honeymoon

JUNE 19, 1965

—•—

The stores they passed on Blackstone had grown shabbier over the years, and the billboards were more blatant than ever as they drove south down Fresno's main boulevard of commerce. They turned east on Belmont toward the Stars and Stripes Market, which Juliet saw coming up on the right. The one-story store, saved from the Ararats' bankruptcy six years ago, was unchanged. Through the wide windows and glass double doors, the aisles were visible with a row of produce bins to one side. The sign running above the windows was the same, though the building seemed a newly painted tan. Through the glass, Juliet saw her father sitting on a stool at the checkout counter with its cash register and cigarette shelves. He looked so stoic, perched alone inside what seemed like a vacuum-sealed box. Armen's hair was completely grey, and his pipe seemed locked in his mouth. No Saturday customers were in the store.

She opened the passenger door to get out of the car and stood in the noon heat, which eddied from the sidewalk and the wide street. Her husband, Sammy, came around from the driver's side of the old, coral and white Ford. Here they were in suffocating Fresno. She was upset that the first days of her marriage had to be spent here, but it was a relief that her parents had been glad to celebrate her getting married last Tuesday in the Bay Area. And she felt calmed by Sammy, by his kind presence, curly headed and smiling. They walked into the market together. He was giving his new father-in-law a break to go home for lunch. Sammy wanted to help, and so he spent two hours in the store from noon to two each day since coming to Fresno. Though it was not quite a honeymoon, she was moved by his willingness to help. And it was obvious that her father and mother were grateful.

"Business is slow," her father said, "but who knows? It might pick up."

When she saw Sammy sit on the cashier's stool, she felt sad, though she tried not to show it. In years past, she had spent so many hours sitting there herself, with time standing still, reduced to ringing up the occasional dollars and cents. It hurt her that Sammy too had to experience this emptiness in Fresno. But tomorrow morning, Sunday, they would be leaving by train to return to Berkeley.

"He is very nice," her father said as they drove home, "to help out."

"He's a good person," Juliet said.

"He is going to apply to graduate school?"

"He already has."

"Ah ... In English, no?" Armen said.

It was unclear whether he was impressed or doubtful about it, but she let it pass. She was thinking about the neighborhood they drove by in the front of an old movie theater in the Tower District; there they passed the Renaissance Coffee House, where Ronnie Arslanian had appeared out of nowhere in November years ago to say he had warned Duncan away from her, though no one knew about any of it, except now Sammy.

At the beginning of this year, though, Duncan had appeared in Berkeley again and began to stalk her. Once he had cornered her and grabbed her in a campus glade she walked through. She raised a fist and was going to bash his face, just as she had done a decade ago, but first she started screaming, and suddenly he disappeared. That evening she decided to call Ronnie Arslanian in Fresno. He was surprised to hear from her, but when she explained what Duncan had done, he had listened carefully and said, "Don't worry about it, Juliet. He'll not be bothering you anymore. You'll not have to see him again." She had no regrets about calling, but she had not told any of this to another human being until a few months ago when she had told Sammy, and she had felt so relieved.

They arrived now at the Garland Avenue house. At lunch, she and her father and mother sat together around the kitchen table. There were plates of string cheese, olives, lox (which Mama had bought special for her new Jewish son-in-law), and a salad of sliced red tomatoes, green basil, and pungent red onion, all bathed in cider vinegar and olive oil. Juliet could see on the kitchen counter her mother's preparations for their barbeque dinner this evening. Once again, Auntie Arsine and Grandma Zabel were the focus of her talk, and she went into exhausting detail about Arsine's call this morning and how stubborn and selfish she was. Auntie had invited them over in the evening, knowing full well they could not come, because tonight Garo was bringing his family over and Tigran was driving his family down from Sacramento, to meet Sammy.

"Tigran has a whole sales staff in Sacramento," Mama said. "He's under a lot of pressure selling vacuum cleaners." As they ate, her talk kept shifting back and forth from Betsy and Tigran to her resentments of Auntie and Grandma.

Looking out the kitchen window, Juliet resisted the temptation to roll her eyes.

"You look so nervous. Your face is all screwed up," Mama said. She twisted her mouth into a grimace and said, "You look like a person who has no control over her face."

"At least that's better than having no control over your brain," Juliet mumbled.

"You're just a nervous girl," her mother said. "I thought marrying a nice man like Sammy would help, but you're just the same nervous person as ever."

Her father sat unspeaking, fiddling with his pipe.

"Mama," Juliet said, making an effort to speak clearly and calmly, "I have lived through things you know nothing about, I have experienced things you know nothing about, and I will never be able to tell you about them. I love you, Mama, but I can't trust you. Your words have hurt me too often."

She stood up, and as she walked out, her mother said to Armen, "What nonsense is she saying now?"

"Tsk," her father clicked his tongue.

In her bedroom, Juliet closed the door and sat trembling on her bed, but she felt relieved that she had not blown up at her mother's craziness. Instead, she had said what she felt was the truth. It would never change her mother's behavior, but it could help to change herself.

There was knocking now at the door, and someone tried the doorknob. She opened and found her father there. "Is it time to leave?" she said.

"No, it's time to keep daydreaming," he said in his usual deadpan voice.

On the drive back to The Stars and Stripes, they made perfunctory conversation and again fell silent. She thought about how her father was really a bystander, so passive, dismissive, and occasionally puncturing. Of course he inhabited a world apart with his poetry and his singing, and there was the idealistic propaganda he wrote and spoke to the comrades. In recent years, too, he had been telling stories about the past to little Pauly, Adam, Annette, and this week even to Sammy, about his love of literature and politics in youth.

They drove up to the Stars and Stripes, and she saw her husband through the window. He was sitting where her father had sat inside the glassed-in box of a store. There were only a few customers, he said as Armen sat down on the cashier's stool. A few derelicts had bought wine; some poor barefoot children and their mothers bought bread and milk.

Once in the car, Sammy sat at the wheel, started the ignition, and turned to look at her. "Let's not go home right away," he said. "I think you can use a break. And so can I." He looked a little numb. It was the result of two hours in the empty box of a store, and she knew it would be hard to go from the near silence of the market to the babble of her mother's conversation and complaints.

"Let's go to the Renaissance. I'll show it to you."

So they drove back to the Tower District and parked on the street near the coffee house. The stores there seemed dusty and neglected, as if the neighborhood were about to be abandoned.

"The café seems a lot smaller than three years ago," Juliet said as they entered and ordered coffee at the counter. They sat at one of the shaky tables. It looked completely different to her, with its brown painted walls and new chrome chairs. During her City College years, it had been warm and mysterious to her, but now that she'd lived in Berkeley it seemed dark and characterless.

"Tomorrow we should be at the train station by ten thirty, no?" Sammy said.

"I can't wait to leave," she said. "It will be so nice to be in the new apartment."

They began discussing how they would place their desks, the rickety chairs, and the double-bed mattress, and their conversation focused on their life in Berkeley, as if they were not in the Renaissance but already two hundred miles to the north. They talked about when they first met three years ago in 1962, and they lived in adjacent apartments in a building on Durant. When she moved the next year to her place on Channing Way, Sammy had begun bicycling down to her apartment at least once a week. She learned that his father, a pathologist, had gotten a new job and moved up from L.A. to the Bay Area; Sammy spent each Sunday with his parents and his older brother Albert at their big house on Benvenue near the Oakland border. But on Friday or Saturday nights, they would be together. He was different from any other man she had known intimately. He was sensitive to the tragic things in life, but there was also such a strong impulse to affirm in him.

They had started living together earlier this year, and he had helped her set up a studio for her art in part of the bedroom. There was a nearly completed painting on her easel there, awaiting their return. Fresno, 1946, would be its title; on one side of it, her mother stood ironing, and two boys – her brothers – played tavloo on the other side, with Tigran throwing dice into the air as Garo watched. On the wall in the middle of the canvas she had painted a mirror, which reflected her father reading and a child, Juliet, looking directly forward at the viewer. The painting was embroidered with vivid patterns, ornamental detail, and the unusual flat perspective Juliet loved in Armenian illuminated manuscripts or in Matisse canvases. The wall, her mother's dress, and the Oriental rug border were all bathed in shades of red; it was the color of pomegranate, watermelon, strawberries, and tomatoes. Along the bottom was a row of Armenian witnesses, the faces of ghosts and elders.

Now, they finished their coffee and drove the short distance to the Garland house. When they parked the Ararats' old Ford in the carport and walked to the front door, Artemis rushed through the entrance.

"Where were you?" she said irritably. She brushed past Sammy, went to the car, and seemed to peer closely at the odometer. "I needed help."

"I'll help you," Sammy said.

"It's only three thirty," Juliet said defensively. But Artemis was already explaining to Sammy about the barbeque. For a while, Juliet watched her husband listening patiently to his new mother-in-law. He could help make the marinade she used for shish kebob: finely chopped onions, parsley, and a little tomato, olive oil, cider vinegar, salt, pepper, and a few dashes of Lea and Perrin's. In the barbeque pit, she wanted him to use no starter fluid, only twigs, crumpled newspaper, a cache of dry grape boughs and stumps, and some briquettes. Speaking to Sammy, Artemis seemed so at ease with him and to appreciate his patience and responsiveness.

At five, Juliet drove alone to pick up Daddy, and as she retraced the usual route to the store, she thought about Sammy's family. He had said his parents were strange, difficult people; he loved them but had hoped she would never have to meet them, even if they started to live together, which they did.

They began spending time with Sammy's brother at the campus café, laughing and talking about their June plans to elope, which Albert encouraged. Early in the month, Mrs. Weisberg realized that her youngest son was serious about a girl, and she insisted that the doctor and his wife meet her. And so a week ago she and Sammy were invited for dinner.

She had walked into the Weisberg home for the first time last Friday evening. Her immediate impression was of how different its minimalist décor was from Fresno Armenian homes, which were stuffed with furniture, rugs, and knickknacks.

Dr. Weisberg seemed immediately to like her, and while he shook her hand, he said with surprise to no one in particular, "Why, she's charming!" After their dinner of garlicky lamb roast, rice, and brownies for dessert, Sammy's mother had questioned Juliet in the kitchen.

"You are two years older than Sam, aren't you?" she said.

"Is that a problem?"

"It isn't customary."

"No," Juliet had replied, "actuarially, though, I should be seven years older than Sammy, because women live seven years longer than men now."

The two women joined Albert in the living room and listened to Sammy and his father finish playing a violin-piano sonata; she felt she was witnessing an unusual, oddly tense yet tender ritual. It was a Schubert sonatina, they said afterward. Then Dr. Weisberg went to the bookshelf and took down the first volume of the Encyclopedia Britannica.

"Let me show you what I was telling you about," he had said with an insistent sort of civility. Sitting with her on the couch, he read aloud a paragraph from the entry on Armenia, which speculated that perhaps the Armenians were a lost tribe of the Jews, for there were so many parallels between the two groups. The doctor treated Juliet with a European formality and politeness, which seemed to keep her at a careful distance; it was as if they were not seated next to each other – as if the doctor, gracious and stiff, positioned himself across a large hall from Juliet, in a world apart. She looked at Sammy sitting nearby and saw that he was using all his patience to keep from showing any distress. She had not realized the complexity of Sammy's situation; how could such a natural and kind man have blossomed in this place?

After the dinner with the Weisbergs over a week ago, Sammy and she agreed that instead of eloping they would be married the following Tuesday at the Alameda County Courthouse nearby in Oakland. Juliet called Fresno and found that her mother was visiting in San Francisco. The day after, a fogless Saturday, Juliet and Sammy drove the Weisbergs' Rambler across the Bay Bridge to the Hatchaturians in the Sunset District.

In Lucaper's sunlit kitchen, Mama had sat across from them, a coffee cup in her hand. "I have some news, Mom," Juliet said – that they were going to get married next Tuesday, Mama spit out the coffee she was about to swallow all over little Lucaper, who immediately rose to mop up the splatter. Then, with a sort of springing vitality, Mama emanated a controlling and, thankfully, not hostile energy. She called Armen to summon him to San Francisco, and they all spoke briefly on the phone. She drove the couple to a jeweler downtown and bought them both wedding bands. The two sets of in-laws met for the first time at the Courthouse; Albert and Lucaper were the witnesses, and afterwards, there was an extremely polite champagne breakfast for everyone at the Weisberg home. The next morning – it was four days ago – they drove down to Fresno, with Sammy next to her in the back seat. Artemis refused to have the air conditioning on, for it might give them sinus headaches.

Now, Juliet and her father returned home from the Stars and Stripes. It was shortly before six, and soon Tigran walked into the Garland house with Betsy and Adam, their blue-eyed seven-year-old tow head. Tigran greeted her and Sammy as if he saw them every day; Betsy gave them each a warm hug, and Adam imitated his father by briefly shaking Sammy's hand. Almost immediately, everyone proceeded to disperse – Betsy to the kitchen, Adam to the backyard, and Tigran to the family room to challenge his father to a game of tavloo. Juliet and Sammy followed Tigran, who looked up and frowned as he set up the board. "It's hot in here," he said; "Ma should turn up the air-conditioning." Then he spoke only the numbers of the dice he threw; he seemed to offer acceptance but no curiosity about the new family member.

Juliet went into the kitchen and found Betsy sitting like a princess in shorts, her legs crossed next to the round table. She was saying something about Garo's wife but stopped and asked Juliet how married life suited her, and when Juliet said fine, Betsy's "Great!" sounded both positive and perfunctory. Juliet volunteered to help her mother, who labored at the counter, but Artemis said everything was taken care of.

There was knocking at the front door, and when Juliet went to answer, Garo and his family roared into the house. They all hugged her and Sammy, too, even the children – Pauly was nine now and a sprite, Annette was a sweetly polite six-year-old, and little John a wildly energized three-year-old.

"Hey, kid," Garo said to Juliet in the kitchen, "sorry we couldn't see you and Sammy earlier. Maybe we can all go out for breakfast tomorrow."

"No!" Mama said. "There isn't time before their train leaves."

"When is the train?"

"Eleven," Juliet said, surprised that Garo cared.

"Well, we could all get up early."

"You can't get up early!" Artemis said. "You'll be up all hours at the bar."

"Aw, Ma, give me a break. I just want to see my little sister and brother-in-law again. Just lay off."

"You won't be able to get up. You have to sleep." The two of them continued to bicker, but then Tigran shouted for Garo from the family room, and Juliet followed him out of the kitchen.

"Let's play," Tigran said.

"Hey, Juliet, I gotta play," Garo said. "You'll be here for Christmas, no?"

"I think so. That'll be fine," Juliet said. Garo turned on the TV baseball game – the Giants – and sat down to play.

She looked out the sliding glass doors to the patio. The late afternoon sun poured over the cement. There was no shade because the ash tree was gone; Mama had had it cut down last year. Too many falling leaves and berries, she had complained. Juliet saw the severed stump and dead roots and felt the loss of the sheltering canopy of leaves. The kids were playing raucously by the pool; Betsy, in a one-piece bathing suit and with a late spring tan, was in the pool and watching them. Juliet saw Daddy and Sammy sitting on patio chairs; they held small glasses of Raki with ice, and Juliet could tell that her father was telling her husband a story. Smoke poured from the red brick barbeque chimney decorated with a single tile depicting a crowing bird, and on the grill she could see the shish kebob skewers that Mama had just put on.

Dinner would be in a few minutes, and Juliet went to the bathroom. As she washed up, she looked in the bathroom mirror. She was a twenty-three-year-old woman with large dark eyes and almost untamed dark brown hair, a woman who had little place in this house and had found a place somewhere else altogether. Tigran, a dozen years older than she, seemed at best indifferent to her. Her mother's favorite was Garo, ten years older, but he was so distracted and spread so thin, though he was a generous person. When Armen had finally been able to visit Soviet Armenia in the late summer last year, they were so anxious about Armen's visa that they had forgotten to leave her a check for the $50 tuition at Cal.

She had called up Tigran at his vacuum distributorship in Sacramento, saying: "You know Mama will reimburse you as soon as they come home." "Sorry, Juliet," Tigran had said, "I don't give money to people who ask for it." He resented her so deeply, she realized; he must have thought he was the one who should have been encouraged to go to college. So she had driven that afternoon two years ago to Garo's new bar business, the Garret, which he was fixing up for its opening in late September. "Sure, kiddo," he said immediately, "take it in cash." And he unpeeled two twenties and a ten from a wad in his pocket. "Don't even tell Ma."

Now the barbeque dinner was served. All the family members were talking at once.

"Dad," Garo said at one point, "when are you going to sell that miserable Stars and Stripes? You could come and do my books for me."

"You should, Daddy," Juliet said across the table.

"There weren't a lot of customers at the market, today," Sammy said. "Why not?"

Through the evening, she was glad that Sammy seemed at ease with the family, even when Daddy, Mama, Tigran, Garo, Lily, and she would begin speaking Armenian. Like Daddy, though, he had little interest when Tigran and Garo talked sports or gossiped about people he'd never met and probably never would.

After dinner was finished, there was the cleaning up and then the good-byes. Mama inspected whether Juliet had correctly stacked the dishes in the dishwasher, rearranged them, and turned on the machine. Finally, in the family room, Mama sat down on the couch and sipped water from her personal hygienic Pyrex measuring cup. She and Daddy watched the late local TV news. Sammy and she said goodnight and walked to her bedroom, making sure to shut the door behind them. Once in bed, he held her closely under the sheet, and they began to make love. She felt how their bodies seemed to have absorbed the dry heat of June in Fresno.

She sensed someone's eyes were on her, and when she turned her head, there was her mother standing in the doorway.

"Why is Sammy on top of you?" Artemis said. In her exhaustion Juliet had forgotten to lock it.

"We're just going to sleep," Juliet said as Sammy slipped off her.

"Keep the door open, or you'll choke in here," she said. "Don't you know the air needs to circulate through the house? Good night."

They restrained their laughter when she left. Sammy got up to lock the bedroom door, and when he came back to the bed, laughter kept returning to them. It was an initiation all around, she thought, for him and her, for the bed and room. One thing was for sure, they would never again forget to lock their bedroom door.

Afterward, Juliet found herself unable to sleep. Outside their windows, an iridescent light from the moon and stars filled the still night air. The room itself seemed bathed in an odd greenish black fluorescence. She could hardly wait to return with Sammy to Berkeley, for she was aware of the presence in this house of an obscure shame; she did not know whether other Armenian daughters felt it, but it was certainly present in this home.

Before she moved to Berkeley, she and her parents had attended the showing of a documentary on the Armenian Genocide, at the Art Cinema in the Tower District. When they had arrived, Juliet saw to her shock that in the lobby there was an art show of drawings and paintings from Fresno State, and some of them were of her in the nude. Her mother and father and their friends just walked by the pictures without recognition, without any comment at all. In the college art classes, she had felt no hesitation modeling; it was for her a part of building a new life, and it seemed an obvious extension of the seriousness of painting itself. There was an art professor at State, Molly Firenze, who loved to employ Juliet as a model in her classes, and she had said: "You're so interesting and so still; you're so at ease." And it was true. At the university, people seemed to accept her body as part of the art-making process, for they were, male and female alike, focused on their efforts to draw and paint. In the darkened Tower theater, Juliet watched the tragic images suspended on the screen – Armenians marched out of their villages by Turks on horseback, villages burned and in ruins, village children starved and beseeching the still photographer before them – and all the while she had felt an inextricable knot of feeling: terrible outrage before this record of the Genocide and immense relief that the images of her body had escaped her parents' censure.

Chapter 19
A daughter's daughter

JUNE 5, 1969

"Do you think Betsy and Tigran will stay together?" Lily said.

"Tigran will keep them together," Artemis said, "even if she has a little problem."

They were sitting at a wrought iron and glass kitchen table, which was situated not in the kitchen but on a platform above the sunken family room of the big new house Garo had built for Lily and himself. It felt as if they were on a stage, illuminated by a metal chandelier of electric candles. Garo was working at the Garret until dinner time. It was four-thirty in the afternoon.

"I'd say it's more than a little problem for Tigran," Lily said, taking a puff of her cigarette. Then with a slight smile, she said, "You have to admit at least I don't chase after other men."

"Of course you don't," Artemis said in a serious voice. She sipped from a glass of lemonade but then sat back to relieve a new pain in her hip. Her daughter-in-law, a petite thirty-five-year-old, could be difficult. She had grown up poor, a priest's daughter in Marseilles and then Fresno. Even now that Garo had bought her this big new home, she still seemed to feel deprived, and she put terrible pressure on him. What fights they had! Sometimes Artemis worried whether Lily truly loved Garo, yet she admired her daughter-in-law for her honesty and for her loyalty, too. Once Lily decided on something, nothing could dissuade her.

Little Annette, who was tanned already in early June, came in from the hall. After Artemis hugged her, she sat between her and Lily.

"Oh, thanks for the box of peaches," Lily said.

"Garo will like them, and Annette will too," Artemis said, smiling at her placid, ten-year-old granddaughter.

"We're almost finished with that flat of nectarines Uncle Ervant brought from Chowchilla," Lily said.

"Good," she said. "This new box is Uncle Nick's first harvest; Auntie Satenig brought them. We could never eat so many."

Uncle Ervant, Armen's poor brother, was paroled earlier this year into Garo's custody; he had served thirty-five years for murdering a policeman, though Artemis knew it was self-defense. He had spent a few months on the run after escaping in 1950 but then put in almost twenty years of good behavior, and he was now paroled to his nephew. Artemis was proud of Lily for accepting Garo's uncle with such an open heart, and she would never forgive Armen's sister for having nothing to do with Ervant for all of these years.

"When is Juliet's baby due?" Lily asked.

"Any time now."

Lily turned to her daughter. "Auntie is having a baby soon."

"Is it a boy or a girl?" Annette said, thoughtful and curious.

"Auntie Juliet and Uncle Sammy won't know until it is born."

"Annette," Artemis said, "when the baby is born and I go to see it, you could come up with me to Berkeley. What do you think?"

"That would be nice," she said in her contemplative way.

"Lily, she could come when Armen and I drive up."

"I wish I could come. But I just don't have the time," she said with an edge not of resentment but of realism. "You sure you'd like to, Annette?"

"I want to go with Grandma."

John John, Garo and Lily's third child, came running from the hall. "Gramma!" he yelled and almost leapt into her arms, except the hefty six-year-old was too big for her to lift; as she hugged him, he clung to her, soaking up her affection. He was a wonderful boy, she thought, but so different from Pauly, who was curious about everything Armen and she tried to offer their grandchildren. John John was bright and spontaneous, yet he always seemed a little uninterested and distant. "Did you bring them?" he said, for she had told him on the phone about the fruit.

"Look on the washing machine," Artemis said.

He walked to the laundry room. "Peaches!" he shouted triumphantly, and his voice echoed a little in the big family room opening out next to them. Across the room was a new green and brown pool table, and near it were the sliding doors to the backyard, with a swimming pool, fruit trees, and a vegetable garden on the side of the house. In the middle of the family room was a half-circle of oversized sofas and stuffed chairs next to a big TV and the adobe façade of the fireplace. Everything about the new house was oversized and especially this sunken family room with its vaulted wood-beamed ceiling. The extravagant design seemed to dwarf them all, and even though it was Lily's idea, the big room reminded Artemis of Garo. He had such an impact on people and so much energy; it was almost beyond control, and he was still a little unrealistic. He sometimes seemed to think that he could make people adopt his views, even Lily, and they would argue so.

She had never told Garo what Lily had said to Betsy. That was last year, just when Garo's family moved into this wonderful new house. Betsy had come to Artemis and told her. Lily had said that she did not think she really loved Garo, and that she was forced into marriage by Garo's insisting so much. She had kept this terrible story from her son, just as she had protected Tigran from Betsy's infidelities. Sometimes you had to lie to get what was best for everybody. It still disturbed her, but that was the way life was. People had to be protected.

John John came in now holding a peach, about to bite into it. Artemis said, "Wash it first and get a napkin."

"You heard your grandmother," Lily said slowly, as if it were suddenly an effort to speak.

Through the sliding glass doors, Artemis saw Pauly and Armen walking toward the house. A half hour ago, Armen took his eldest grandchild outside to inspect the vegetable garden, and now Grandpa put a hoe away in the garden shack, walked across the yard, and entered the air-conditioned house with Pauly.

"Pop says the tomatoes would have died in this heat, if we hadn't hoed and irrigated!"

"Ooph," Lily said and poured herself more coffee, which she always had to have while smoking her cigarettes, "it's such a hot day for June."

"Very hot," Armen said as he sat by them. Pauly came with a peach he washed.

"Do you want some?" Lily asked. Armen said yes. Their sweet granddaughter went to the kitchen and brought back a bowl of washed peaches, some small plates, knives, and napkins. As they cut up their fruit, Lily said, "God, smell how great they are?"

"Delicious," Artemis said.

Pauly stood by her, listening. He bit into his sweet peach and caught the juices dripping from his face with a napkin. He was so handsome, she thought, with his auburn hair and wonderful brown eyes and the juices bursting from his peach. She was amazed that it was possible for her – with all her flaws and her sixty years of struggle – to have such a beautiful grandson. He was just entering adolescence, she sensed, from the way he looked and held himself. He was truly an Ararat, standing there quiet and slightly apart from them, proud and even a little rebellious. He would be thirteen soon, and she thought she saw in him the man she knew he would become, so proud and intense like Garo – and perceptive, too, like Lily.

"Garo will be home soon," Lily said.

"We have to go to Tigran's," Artemis said.

"Tsk," Armen clicked his tongue, but as usual she was not sure whether it was a sign of not wanting to go, or of disapproval of her for stating the obvious.

"Did you hear," Lily said, "Garo's installed strobe lights. Only the latest thing for him."

Artemis knew he was always hatching new plans to improve the bar, and sometimes he drove down to L.A. or up to the Bay Area to book new acts. He had such sparking, creative energy, but she worried all the more whether he had it under control, whether he truly knew what he was doing.

After they said goodbye, they drove a few blocks to a wide street of huge mansions, Van Ness Extension, with big flat lawns and puny shrubs, where orchards of peach and fig had once stood. Finally, Armen turned east to drive to Tigran's house, off of Barstow.

Artemis had visited the bar with Armen. She didn't like its atmosphere or that Pauly went there on Sundays to help his father clean it up. Customers and hangers-on were sitting around, including that big hulk of a man named Lance, looking like a 300-pound hoodlum – because he took too many steroids, Garo told her. And there was that drinker from Kings, Chick Leone, who was the bartender. Garo walked around the bar, and his voice sounded larger than life as he started to tell customers how terrible drugs were, how rotten their effects on your morals and on your whole system. A stream of invective against them flowed from him – above all he hated the smugglers, who were flying in their loads of drugs from Mexico. He would kick the shit out of anyone who dealt drugs or made deals in his bar. Artemis felt that her son seemed even taller than the nine inch difference between them. In fact, everything seemed bigger and louder there, the Rolling Stones on the sound system, her son's voice, and the customers'.

She had gone down the hall to the women's room, and when she came out of the stall to wash her hands, there was a horrible beetle sitting in the center of the mirror; it was a cockroach the size of a fist. It wouldn't budge, and its size horrified her. Was it alive? What was it? She screamed. Garo came running, and as soon as he saw it, he smashed it with his bare hand. She could not stand to watch him wash up at the sink, and trembling she went to sit in the back office with Armen. It had been a reminder: she must never allow herself to be unprepared for evil, which could emerge anywhere, in a flash.

When Garo joined them in the office, Artemis had said: "There's something wrong, Garo. I feel it. And something is bothering you. All the drinking, the drugs ..."

"Mom, you're just a little upset. Everything is going to be fine. Anyway I'm not the only person in Fresno who wants to deal with the problem. A lot of people think the way I do, and we're going to do something about it." Artemis had looked into his eyes, and she knew they were withholding something from her, as if he imagined terrible things raining down on Fresno and its citizens.

"How can we help Garo?" Artemis wondered aloud now as her husband drove down Van Ness Boulevard toward Tigran's.

"We are helping him," he said in his detached voice. He had begun doing Garo's accounting four years ago in the late summer of 1965, after a robbery one evening at the Stars and Stripes. Artemis had been sitting at home reading when he called her from the store. "I've been robbed," he shouted and hung up. She called the police, and the operator said, "I'm so glad you called, lady, because your husband called us and then hung up; we have no idea who or where he is." The robber had murdered six liquor store owners, it turned out, up and down the state. When the man stuck up the Stars and Stripes, Armen told him he did not blame him; the capitalist system was at fault. The murderer said, "Shut up, Pop, or I'll kill you," but instead of shooting him, he tied him up and locked him in the restroom. Her husband couldn't believe that such a thing would happen here, in America; within a month, Armen had sold the store. To supplement his Social Security, he began working half days at Garo's Garret, doing the books in the office down the hall in back.

Armen turned off Barstow and drove up to Tigran's white ranch-style house. He had kept this tract home, and she knew he had rented it out during their years in Sacramento. Their eldest son was always like that, conserving his property and money, unlike their youngest. When they knocked, Betsy answered the door and with warm hugs ushered them into the living room. Tigran said "Hi" from the easy chair he sat on, watching the TV news. There was something strange about the house, which had been brand new when the couple bought it nine years ago. Now, its exterior – nondescript to begin with – seemed oddly run down, and the air-conditioned interior seemed bare and unoccupied. It was as if Betsy and Tigran were tenants, not owners. There was a single Victorian print of a blushing woman above the fireplace mantle in the living room. She sat on the couch, and Armen sat in a recliner. From his easy chair, Tigran turned down the volume with a newfangled TV remote.

"Do you want to sit where Daddy is sitting?" she said to her son.

"No," Tigran said.

"But you could trade with Daddy. It's more comfortable for you."

"I'm sitting where I'm sitting."

"But it's a recliner."

"This is my house, Ma. I'll sit where I want."

"But you'll be more comfortable."

"Hey, Ma," Tigran said abruptly, "did you bring any of those early peaches Uncle Nick gave you?"

"Oh, no," Artemis said quickly, "they were rotting. You wouldn't want them."

Just then the doorbell rang, and Tigran got up to answer. It was strange about the peaches, but she just could not feel as generous toward Betsy as toward Lily. Betsy followed Tigran silently to the front door, and Artemis realized she seldom heard them converse. Artemis wondered about what was happening between them. Eight years ago they had separated, and after a few months they had reconciled; then seven years ago Betsy and she had traveled together to Armenia. She still thought about Betsy's behavior on that trip in 1962, when she disappeared for hours in Yerevan or during their stay in Paris.

Now Betsy reentered the living room. With a wide, fixed smile, she ushered in a dark-haired hard-looking well-dressed woman with a German accent. She was introduced as Ursula, and she was Don Wolf's wife.

"I think we met before," Mrs. Wolf said.

Tigran walked in with Don, who wore his usual beiges and his strange necklace of small turquoise and onyx stones. As soon as he entered, Artemis felt agitated, for Wolf was one of Garo's rival bar owners, and she heard that he was building a big new bar near the Ararats' Garland home. He was a Volga German, like Fresno's police chief.

"Everybody knows each other," Tigran said as they shook hands and sat down. He got them all beers or iced tea, and Tigran asked how Don's bar business was going. On the TV, there were images of protesters in a park near the Berkeley campus, of masked police marching down a street, and of a National Guard helicopter spewing tear gas over the area. Someone had been killed by the police, but it was unclear whether it was a protester or a bystander.

"Governor Reagan gave the order to shoot to kill," Don Wolf said. "I'm glad he did."

Armen looked incredulous and said, "The protesters' cause is noble."

"Noble? My ass!" Wolf scoffed. Artemis was appalled by the man's mocking, and she was frightened by what she heard on the TV because Sammy and Juliet, who was pregnant and about to give birth, lived only a few blocks from the Berkeley campus.

"They're just a bunch of confused kids," Tigran said.

"That's not what Reagan thinks," the bar-owner said, "or Nixon. They say that Commies are leading the so-called protests. Just when the president has Kissinger trying to negotiate with the Gooks, he has to deal with Bolsheviks camping across the street from the White House. I say, get rid of them by any means necessary. We're in a war, Tigran."

"I don't trust Kissinger," Ursula said, sitting on the couch next to Artemis, who was going to agree with her, for the Soviet criticism of Kissinger was growing more and more pointed. Juliet's Sammy looked a lot like a young handsome Kissinger, she realized, and she decided to point it out to him next time she saw him.

"He's a Jew," Ursula continued. "You can't trust Jews."

"That's not true," Artemis said. She was surprised and disturbed. "We've known a lot of nice Jewish people over the years. And our son-in-law is Jewish."

"One of Jesus' brothers," Armen said in Armenian to Tigran.

"The Jews, the Jews, the Jews. That's all you hear about now. We Germans suffered just as much as they did! When I was a girl in Germany during the War and afterwards, we would search in the rubble looking for clothes, even food. We had to cut out pieces of rubber tire for shoes. We suffered a lot."

"You can't compare that to genocide," Artemis said.

"Hi," Adam said, having just come in from the hall. His cheery smile and wavy blond hair made Artemis feel her face light up. She had no more desire to talk to Ursula.

"Come on in, Adam," Tigran said, in a firm, fatherly voice.

"Adam, come over here!" she said.

Slender and spry, the twelve-year-old came to her, and she hugged him. While the others talked, she asked him about school and about his plans for the summer vacation. He answered her eagerly, as if he were somehow responsible for pleasing her, for healing a difficult situation, and she felt a surge of sympathy for him. Betsy announced dinner, and they all went to the dining area between the living room and the kitchen. On the table were plates of bratwurst and hamburgers and a potato salad made with mayonnaise, which was Betsy's specialty and very different from Artemis' potato salad with lemon, olive oil, and chopped parsley dressing. It was odar food, and it was no wonder that Tigran visited her and Armen for her home cooking at least once a week and that he preferred her potato salad. Adam sat between Armen and Artemis on one side of the table, and they all began talking and eating.

Later, after dessert – scoops of vanilla ice cream on an apple pie from the super market – Artemis walked to the kitchen, following Betsy and Ursula, who gossiped together. Through the open door to the living room, she listened to Tigran and Don Wolf.

Wolf began to criticize Garo. He sounded superior and condescending, and she was not sure whether his tone was just his usual manner or whether he was trying to belittle her son.

"Garo doesn't understand what he's dealing with at the Garret."

"What do you mean?" Tigran said.

"You can get any drug you want there. The place is hot."

"Those are just rumors".

"No, no. My sources are good."

"So now you have drug pushers for friends, Don?"

"I just don't think Garo understands what's happening."

"I'm sure he's taking care of the problem," Tigran said. "If it exists."

Overhearing them, suspicion swept over Artemis. She remembered Lily's birthday party in their new house; there had been so many people from the bar mixed in with their friends – even Dr. Hopper had been invited, but so were the barmaids from the Garret and the huge bouncer Lance Fetzer. He and the barmaids all walked around as if they had a secret, as if they were carefully not saying things they were not supposed to say.

Don said loudly now, "Lance boasts about having Garo wrapped around his little finger. That bouncer is bad news. He's as cruel as anyone in this city, but Garo has no fear. I think a little fear might do him some good right now. The police are taking their cut, right under Garo's nose!"

"I don't want to talk about this," Tigran said. "Garo's doing what he needs to do. Dealing with Ronnie Arslanian years ago wised him up. And if that didn't, I don't know what will."

"Arslanian," Don Wolf said. "I told you he has a little stake in my bar. Why not? He's already bought up most of north Fresno and Clovis. And he paid a mint for his mansion on Van Ness Extension."

"Every asshole has a seat," Tigran said.

When the Wolfs left, Artemis could hardly bring herself to shake their hands. Don Wolf was sly, deceptive, and superior acting. You never knew what a man like that was capable of. As soon as the front door closed, Artemis confronted Tigran.

"If there are drugs at the bar," she said, "we have to help Garo."

"Ma, Garo doesn't want to be helped! Leave the man alone. No, Pop?"

"But," Artemis said, "he has to be told about the reality of the situation."

"And you know 'the reality of the situation'? We're talking second-hand gossip here, boasts and bullshit."

"You boys have to face reality!" Artemis said loudly in a thin panicky voice; she felt suddenly clammy and pale.

"Ma, if reality came up and shook you by the hand, you wouldn't know what it was."

"Tigran, you have to do something about it." Her voice had become raspy and high pitched, but she did not care how it sounded; small as she was, it filled the room. "You have to help him!"

Desperately agitated, she did not listen to his reply. She certainly knew what was real and what was not. Tigran said they were just rumors, but he could not know for sure. Poor Garo, every part of his life was under terrible pressure now. One way or another, she had to make sure he was safe.

At 9:30 that evening, the Ararats arrived at their Garland home. The phone was ringing as Armen opened the front door, and Artemis ran to answer it in the family room.

"Hello," she said, out of breath.

"Artemis," it was Sammy's voice, "Juliet gave birth today. It's a baby girl."

"A baby girl! Oh, my!" she said, feeling a great upwelling of relief. "I'm so glad. Is everyone okay? Juliet is breast-feeding, isn't she? And what is her name?"

He answered that all was well, though it was a long and painful labor. The baby was named Lucy, after Artemis' mother. As she listened, she felt a great release of tension and a sense of wonder at the great unwinding of time's cycle, now that her daughter had a daughter, and her name was Lucy. And partly it was Sammy himself, who had helped Juliet to be not so nervous; he was so soothing and thoughtful.

"I'm bringing Annette up with me this weekend," she said. "We'll stay at the Hatchaturians'."

After she told Armen the news, it was not too late, so she called her daughters-in-law. Then she sat alone on the family room couch. Sammy was a scholar, a graduate student, and he lived in a different world from hers, but he was kind and human. Of course, he was a bit of a dreamer, with his love of the arts. She remembered the present he gave Armen last Christmas Eve. It was on the bookshelf now, a folder of poems in English, which Sammy had selected and typed up himself. She had read it more closely than Armen had, she thought, and she remembered some of it still. There were passages from Shakespeare – "When to the sessions of sweet silent thought, I summons up remembrance of things past" – and there was one of her favorite poems by Byron, "So we'll go no more a roving." She still liked Byron, though she did not take him seriously now; for one thing, she did not want to think about the relations he might have had with his sister or with youths. Sammy's brother was a poet, Juliet had said and once implied that he was a homosexual. It baffled her that there was such strangeness in the world, especially among artists and writers, and she wondered why that was.

Now Artemis began preparing herself for bed. Armen said he could not sleep and was staying up. They each had a separate double bed, a luxury they had afforded when they had the stores, and the beds were separated by several feet. When she got under her covers, she felt her aching hip and thought about how contorted her body must look. She tried to relax, but an edge of worry prevented her from sleeping.

Her sweet Garo always wanted what was best for everybody, even for those drunkards at the bar. And now were there smugglers, dealers, and drug addicts there? What a mistake! And yet she realized that in many ways her son was like her, in his caring and his vulnerability, too. She must be vigilant and help him.

Armen must be sitting at the kitchen table writing his poems in his careful Armenian printing; usually he was the one with insomnia, who would drive to Denny's or Sambo's for waffles at 3 in the morning, or stay up all hours writing poems. His poetry had its admirers, even some Soviet Armenian poets whom they met on their recent trip to Yerevan and who hoped to visit them in Fresno. There were his Fresno fans, too, like Big Mike Arslanian, Ronnie's father. And, of course, Mariam Saroyan continually complimented and flattered him. Could Armen be unfaithful to her, she wondered? She did not really know who he was. Yes, he was a poet, but he was also a restless and lax man. She did not miss him in her bed, and yet there was no one else for her. Resentment began to grip her. She felt agitated and turned onto her stomach, then again onto her back, and she stared at the ceiling.

She remembered a line from Shakespeare in Sammy's folder. "Say what you feel, and not what you ought to say." But sometimes a person had to hide and lie, for people needed to be protected in this world. But maybe she had failed to protect her Garo, her Tigran and Juliet. Was it possible even that she had harmed her sons and daughter? But how could such a fate befall her! A horrible sense of outrage at her lot in life came to her, and she shuddered. Lying there under her blanket and sheet, she knew that she was pale as a ghost. She should have married someone else, a man of great will and strength, a heroic warrior from the turn of the century – if only a man like that still existed – someone who knew when to lie and when to tell the truth, someone who understood how to deal with her pain and rage and who knew how to protect her children.

Chapter 20
Christmas Day

DECEMBER 25, 1970

—●—

It was a foggy day, and he could see no more than twenty yards ahead as he slowly drove their new white Chevy sedan through great pools of fog. Moments of sudden sun sometimes penetrated the earthbound cloud, and such dazzling brightness would light the foggy air, so that he could suddenly make out the roadside firs and eucalyptus shrouded in white diaphanous mist. Heavy rain had fallen on the San Joaquin Valley for a week, and now fog had descended. As Highway 99 approached, he heard but could not see the freeway and the cars whooshing by. Turning off Olive, he pulled into the parking lot of the Garret. It was 9 a.m. Christmas morning, and Garo had called to ask if he would meet him to count the bar receipts from Christmas Eve. It was odd that Garo would leave his house so soon after his family opened their Christmas presents, but he accepted without hesitation his son's sudden need; without saying so, he cherished Garo's energy and enthusiasm. They were like his Angel's best qualities, without the hurt, the disappointment, and the resentment.

Garo's Grand Prix was not in the parking lot yet. Armen opened the locked back door with his key, and locking it behind him, walked through the empty hall to the office, which he opened with a second key. Just down the dark hall were the restrooms, uncleaned after last night's Christmas Eve crowd and now vaguely foul smelling.

He switched on the office light and then shut and locked the office door. As he opened the combination safe and brought out the canvas bag of money to count, his movements were mechanical and sure, shaped as they were by the trust between him and his son, let alone all his years in the markets. Carefully, he counted the money and entered in the ledger amounts representing profits far beyond what the Kings had achieved. The Garret was Garo's great success. It was true that something unusual was happening to the business, not really the drinking and carousing or even Garo's "friends," who scurried about like flies. No, it was more like the drugged compatriots of the Volga German bouncer Lance Fetzer, who brought in the parasites dressed in black leather but then drove them away when Garo or Chick, the bartender, discovered them selling drugs in the bathroom. And it was worse than that. Even Tigran had had to get involved.

In the past few years, Armen knew that Garo occasionally met with rival bar owners, like Tigran's friend Don Wolf, who had opened a new bar half a mile from the Ararats' home. Garo told him that at those meetings, he would ask the bar owners why, there in the Central Valley, drug dealers and smugglers were operating more and more freely in Fresno's bar scene. The other owners told him not to pursue it. But that only made him want to find out more. At first he accused the Volga-Germans who ran so much of the city. Nothing happened in Fresno without the permission of one of them, Police Chief Hank Morton, a born-again fanatic who was married to the town's main Madame; her whorehouses lined the south side. Chief Morton told people that Jesus reigned in death but Hank reigned in life, keeping the politicians in tow, the Central Avenue whores whoring, the pimps and crooks and pushers working, let alone the garbage collected, the sewage processed, etc.

Garo told Armen even more. One night at the bar last month, his son had talked with an old Armenian gambler, who was fleeing from the mob in Fresno and fearing for his life.

"Do you know who's the main drug lord in Fresno, in charge of all the shit coming into the Valley – weed, seconal, reds, whites?" the Armenian gambler had said to Garo. "It's Ronnie Arslanian. That guy is more evil than all those Eyetalian hoods put together."

That was a month ago. Now, as Armen sat counting the Christmas Eve intake, he had a hard time believing what the frightened gambler had said. Since the Arslanians had gotten so rich, some envy and resentment had cropped up among Armenians. Armen seldom saw Ronnie's father, but when they did meet, Big Mike was always very respectful and flattered him about his poetry. The combination of generosity, warmth, and competitiveness in father and son was baffling, but he doubted they would be involved with drugs. After all, as developers, they could buy and sell tracts of land the size of entire villages in the Old Country!

But Garo believed the story to be true and began sharing it not only with Armen but with people outside the family. He knew his son was gathering evidence against Arslanian to go to the Feds and if necessary to testify to a grand jury, "to blow this thing wide open." Threats began to be made, but not by anyone associated with Ronnie; for example, a pair of police officers came into the bar one evening and began arresting the underage and the stoned. "This is nothing," one of them took Garo aside and said, "This is nothing compared to what'll happen if you don't shut the fuck up." Two weeks ago, Armen was there when a Hells Angel, one of Lance Fetzer's acquaintances, had said, "Don't you see you're gonna get hurt?" When Lance found out, the bouncer had apologized for him in his high, polite voice, which sounded mocking to Armen.

As the father, he felt he must tell Tigran what was happening. Six days ago, on Sunday morning, he had arranged for his sons and him to meet in the bar's back office. None of them told the wives about it. He had never told Artemis about many things – so many nightmare memories of Turkey and so much of the thinking that went into his poetry, let alone about Mariam Saroyan. So last Sunday's meeting did not seem like a particularly remarkable omission.

He had watched as Tigran listened to Garo pour out the story of what was happening. Then Tigran said, "There's a time to shut up. You need to cool it with this vigilante shit."

Garo looked on the verge of exploding, but he had not answered back or said anything for a minute.

"This is not just about shutting up," Armen had spoken up. "Tigran, you must help your brother. Go talk with Ronnie."

"Shit!" Tigran said, staring at Armen. "Once was enough, Pop. What do you want me to do, beg? We'll get nothing from him." He paused and then went on, "Anyway, why would the Arslanians be involved with drugs? They have so much money, it's coming out of their ass. Years ago, maybe they'd hide a rug to claim the insurance. But drugs? I don't believe it. Not then, not now."

"You're dead wrong, Tigran," Garo said finally.

"Son, I beg of you," Armen had said.

The next day, it was last Monday, he sat in his living room chair listening to Tigran recount his second meeting in a decade with Ronnie Arslanian. That morning, he had been kept waiting by Arslanian's secretary in the strip-mall office building on Shaw, and then she ushered him down the hall. There was an open unlit office he passed, and he thought he saw Big Mike lounging there with his back to the doorway; his wispy crown of white hair was visible in the darkened office, and the heavy man sat absolutely still as if he were waiting for something to happen. Tigran thought how stupid and futile this visit was, just like the last time he visited this building. He entered Ronnie's large office. The white walls had only a few family photos on them; one showed Ronnie's two blond children and his odar wife. Ronnie himself was sitting behind an executive desk. Big Mike's son did not rise to shake hands. Instead he nodded coolly for Tigran to take a seat.

"It's been years," Tigran said, calm and non-committal, but Ronnie made no reply.

"Garo," Tigran forged ahead, "he's been shooting off his mouth and..."

"My father," Ronnie had coolly interrupted, "respects your father very much. And for my part, I've always wished Juliet well. It's good your sister left Fresno. It must have felt like a prison to a girl with her talent. I probably should take my wife and children away from here, but we've invested a great deal in the city." His gaze froze on Tigran, who wondered how he could possibly plead Garo's case once more to this impenetrable man.

"There have been many rumors over the years about the Arslanian family," Ronnie continued. "They grow like a cancer, from envy and spite. Drugs are now one more rumor. People in this town cannot stand that Armenians are successful, Tigran. You play golf like a professional, and you can beat any player in Fresno; are you allowed into their country club? My father and I own developments worth more than all the city's drugs combined, and these rumors are just another way to get back at Armenians. But even Armenians buy them and spread them. Your brother seems to believe them – not only about us, but also about the police. And he repeats them. Of course, they're only words, and Garo likes to talk."

Tigran understood what Ronnie was saying to him, but he was not sure what Ronnie might be implying.

"Garo's like a kid in a lot of ways," Tigran said. "He blurts out what he thinks. But I've talked to him, and he understands now. Our father respects your parents, Ronnie, and Garo understands that, too."

"Fresno is like the Wild West," Ronnie spoke again in his inexpressive voice, "It's like a town in the Deep South. It's a violent, racist city. Yet your brother is a man who likes to gossip and spread rumors, who likes to talk and makes threats. Do you Ararats know what a savage place this city is? Does Garo?"

"I've just told you, Ronnie. I talked to him," Tigran had said, suddenly insistent. "He's shutting up."

Ronnie had stared blankly at him. "That's all then," he said almost inaudibly and turned to a file on his desk. Without looking up, he added, "Tell Juliet hello from me."

Armen had sat frozen in his easy chair, listening to Tigran finish: "No goodbye, Pop, not even as a fucking afterthought."

"Hi, Pop," Garo said now as he opened the door and swept into the Garret office. "Sorry I'm late."

"I just finished the books, son. Take a look at the figures here," Armen said and pointed at the totals entered in the ledger book before him.

"Lily made me stay and watch the kids open all the presents!" He glanced down at the Christmas Eve totals. "Not bad at all," he said and then added energetically, "I'll just clean up the mess from last night. See you this afternoon. Christmas dinner!"

The fog had lifted outside. On his drive home, he thought about his two sons, how much Artemis and he worried about Garo and Tigran, who always had to try and help Garo, as he had last Monday. And he received so little in return; there was no truer son, and yet he did not get the respect due him? Last night, when all the family gathered once again for Christmas Eve on Garland, Tigran had looked so tired, and on top of everything he was preparing to raise his twelve-year-old Adam on his own, for Betsy and he were finally going to get a divorce. Tigran had turned forty earlier this year, and he was already looking used up. Poor man had always had used things, used houses, used cars, used women, and now he seemed so tired and used up. Armen remembered how uneasy and drained he himself felt in his forties, when World War II raged, let alone how tired he had felt with his Mediterranean disease. And he could not have guessed how tired his body was now at seventy, how it ached and ached. There was a war raging still in Vietnam. America was a violent society willing even to kill its young men in the Vietnamese jungles; it was beset by assassinations, and there was the violence on university campuses, at Kent State and Berkeley. And he felt, too, that in Fresno there was the same savagery as in Turkey.

Driving home through the lifting fog, he thought of Artemis' censure of him: "Why don't you talk with your sons, guide them, help them survive in this terrible country! You're such a selfish man – you never take responsibility, and I have to do it all. You always just let things happen!" She was right to protest and punish, for he was unfit for life in America, and despite all his poetry and politics, he despaired that nothing could relieve his paralyzing exhaustion. There was nothing he could do to fill the emptiness of their lives in America.

Now he parked in the Garland Avenue driveway, and immediately Artemis raced out of the house with her pocket book and her coat on against the late December cold.

"You're late," she said hurriedly. "I want to drop by and see Adam before we go to Garo's this afternoon." It was eleven a.m., and they were due there around one.

"Okay," he said and walked past Sammy and Juliet's Ford parked there – it was the Ararats' old car, and they had recently given it to their daughter and son-in-law, who had driven down from Berkeley this Christmas with their Lucy, one-and-a-half years old now. It occurred to him that, with his wife gone for at least an hour, Sammy could drive them all to say hello to Mariam Saroyan, the friend who collected his poems and sent them off to be published.

In the house, he made the suggestion to Juliet, and she objected that she was tired, for she was now seven months pregnant with a second child. He said, "It won't be for long, and I want you and Sammy to see her." And so she agreed. Sammy drove them east to Mariam's house, talking with Juliet in the front seat. Armen sat in the back next to little Lucy in her car seat. The babbling granddaughter grabbed his finger when he put his hand on the bar holding her in. As he gently babbled back to her, teasing in his deadpan manner, he felt the delight and pleasure of amusing the innocent baby.

The car stopped in front of Mariam's small one-story bungalow surrounded by a rose garden, withered now in winter. They rang and waited in the cold bright December light. Finally, Mariam Saroyan – dark haired still at sixty-five – opened the front door. She seemed thrilled that they were there. Her raspy alto voice climbed in pitch, as she hugged the three of them, and it reached a chirping soprano lyricism as she marveled over little Lucy, who was half awake and about to take a nap. Inside the musty house, it was dark, but then their eyes got used to the living room. Old rugs decorated with birds of paradise covered the floor. Worn velvet upholstery covered the furniture, and the lamps were decades old and fringed in faded gold.

They ate little khorabia almond cookies and drank tea from chipped china cups, as Juliet's little daughter slept, reclining in the small bassinet they brought from the car. As they ate and chatted, Armen felt pleased that his daughter was extending herself to his friend.

"I love your father, but of course our relationship is completely platonic, Juliet," Mariam said toward the end of their visit. "I respect Artemis and their marriage. Yes, sometimes we hold hands, but that is all. I love your father's poetry, and I keep it here, in an archive. I will always have it for him, and for you."

"That's very nice," Juliet said.

"You know Armen and I were born in the same village near Boursa," she said, holding her tea cup delicately in her hand. "Armen was the lucky one, though. He had moved to Constantinople by 1915. He saw bad things, but nothing like what I saw. My mother told me to hide in the attic, and from a little window, I watched while the neighbors and my parents were forced to dig a big hole.

Then the Turks took all the babies from the neighborhood. They threw them in the pit, poured kerosene over them, and lit a match. I wish I had no ears to hear the sounds, no nose, no eyes to see it. The Turks became nervous at all the screaming and started shooting everywhere. They mounted their horses, with their swords slicing and guns shooting, and the next thing I saw they pushed Mama and Papa into the flaming pit."

Mariam paused and mumbled, "Ooph" and then looked at Sammy. "The Jews have suffered like this, too." She turned to Armen's daughter and raised her cup of tea: "Before you leave, let us have a toast, to celebrate your family: your Sammy, your little Lucy, and the baby to come! I will get some Raki, or would you prefer Scotch?" she asked Sammy, as if she were an elegant society hostess.

When she brought the Raki, everyone toasted, though Juliet had only a sip from Sammy's glass. Armen watched as his friend seemed to give herself over to savoring the anise liquor, and her face cracked into a warm smile now at the sensation, as if to say there was still some pleasure left – in poetry, in friendship, and in this heady liquor.

On the way home, Armen again felt aching and tired, and he dreaded the possibility of his wife being home already. As he played in a desultory fashion with the little granddaughter next to him, he listened to Sammy and Juliet talking in the front seat of the car about living in Berkeley last year, when Lucy was born, and how hard it had been for Sammy to teach as a graduate instructor because the National Guard occupied the city and protesters had stopped the university from erecting a building on what became People's Park, off Telegraph Avenue.

Armen leaned forward in his seat. "Why protest for a park, tsakis?" he said, using his endearment for his daughter and now for Sammy as well.

"I wondered about that, too," his son-in-law said as he drove. "Especially since the war is still going on in Vietnam."

"I admired the protests and sit-ins about voting rights," Armen said, thinking back over his decades of politics. "It is a new generation, so different from the Fifties; it's more like the Thirties. But why protest for a park now, or for dirty words? Why not protest against American imperialism, poverty, injustice?"

"Yes, exactly," Sammy said. "But there are protests against the war, too."

Of course, Sammy was right; there were protests now against everything. Armen leaned back, thinking about Berkeley's Free Speech Movement six years ago. Truly that was about protesting against racism and segregation. He remembered driving up to visit Juliet for her birthday in October 1964 and visiting the Berkeley campus that night. He had parked and walked with her onto the central plaza, which teemed with thousands of students chanting and listening to speaker after speaker. The two of them had made their way to the stairs of the Student Union at the edge of the crowd, and Armen saw wave upon wave of heads, some bare and some capped, and he heard the agitated rumbling of the crowd and the amplified voices of the leaders who stood atop a marooned police car in the middle of the plaza. Visible in the nearby lot of the Sproul Hall administration building were helmeted policemen standing with their terrible batons at the ready. The police had already arrested one leader who sat handcuffed in the cruiser marooned in the center of the mass of students. The injustice of that arrest and the sight of the police stirred the crowd's outrage. It was as if the possibility of police violence loosed a wildness, like a sparking electric arc, into the chilly air. Everything was illuminated by the orange glare of the clustered outdoor lamps dotting the plaza, and Armen had suddenly been transported fifty years back, to seeing the vast crowd of Turks roused by the sight of the hanged Armenians on Beyazit Square in Constantinople at the start of the Genocide in 1915.

Now when Sammy parked the car in the Garland driveway, Armen could see that their new Chevy had not returned yet.

Instead of relief, he felt a peculiar pressure in his head and told his daughter that he would take a little nap before going to Garo's. In the bedroom, he sat on the edge of his double bed, took off his shoes and pants, and before slipping under the covers looked at the sliding doors of the closets built into a wall of their bedroom. Inside the closet, two thirds of the space was taken up by Artemis' clothes. The mirrored doors reflected back gray-red patches on his legs, his short bull-like body, his lined unsmiling face, and the gray hair on his head. Then he got into bed and fell into a deadened dreamless sleep.

"It's time," he heard vaguely. "Get up, Angel." It was Artemis puttering about the bedroom, sliding the mirrored doors open, taking a dress from the closet and laying it on her double bed. She had used his endearment for her.

"Angel," Armen said sleepily, "come here and let me hold you for a minute." She sometimes consented to being close, but only rarely.

"No, no, I haven't time," she said and placed at his feet on his bed a clean shirt from his side of the closet.

"'I have no time,'" he said in a high soft silly voice, but she did not respond. He got mechanically out of bed and put on his pants and the shirt she had chosen for him. After a while, they all got into the Ararats' new sedan, with Lucy sitting in the car seat they brought from the old Ford. Armen drove them through the now bright crisp day to Garo's big house a block from millionaire's row on Van Ness Extension.

Without knocking, they went in through the side door near the kitchen, for it was by the driveway, and the family almost never used the formal front entrance. Sound came from beyond the utility room where they entered, an erratic roar of conversation. There were a dozen people in the big family room; some sat around the wrought iron kitchen table overlooking the room, with its high ceiling and stone fireplace. Garo and Lily were having a Christmas open house, and Armen knew that these people would leave before dinner began at two. He saw some of his son's friends, some of his best customers, and some of his workers, including a few barmaids, the Leones, and the bouncer Lance Fetzer. Garo was playing pool with his friends, and when he saw the family arriving, he raised a glass of eggnog and shouted his greeting across the big noisy room. Pauly stood by the green pool table, looking out of place, and Armen walked down the few steps from the kitchen into the cavernous room, which would dwarf any Bacchanalia. He nodded at everyone, headed for his grandson, and suggested they look at the garden outside.

As they emerged into the cool afternoon, he felt once again that Pauly and his other grandchildren were a gift he had never imagined receiving, a beautiful surprise arriving just when the stress of life seemed overwhelming, with the Kings' bankruptcy and Artemis' continuous troubles.

"Dad got me a weight set for Christmas," Pauly said and pointed to the shiny barbells and weights, which were carefully set up on the covered patio. "It's state-of-the-art."

"Will you work out with your father?" Armen said as they walked from the patio and pool to the side of the yard.

"I might," Pauly said in a tentative voice. He would be fourteen in a week. His voice had not changed yet, but adolescence had begun to show itself a little bit in him. For one thing, he could be controlling and even cruel to his sister, Annette. But the wonderful promise in Pauly was still intact.

Before them was a plot of soil that they had turned over for the winter, and there were a few grape vines, dormant on their stakes. Armen took a pruning shears from the tool shed. "Do you see what we will do?" he said. "You must prune very carefully." "Why do we have to prune?" Pauly began asking his grandfather and listened to his replies with an earnestness that deeply moved Armen. When should the vines be pruned? Where do they need to be pruned and at what angle? What happens to them after pruning? Pauly had a capacity to focus, and he saw beyond just owning things; to Armen, it promised that his grandson would not succumb to the greed and emptiness in American life. Of course, his intense focus could hold dangers, but Armen thought he would have the strength to overcome any self-centeredness or obsessiveness.

"Hey, Pauly, Pop. Come back inside," Garo shouted across the yard from the sliding door. "It's cold out there."

"Just a minute," Pauly said, but soon they returned to the house. The big television set was blaring in the family room, and most of the guests had left. Garo was busy talking with his old high-school buddy Phil, while the Leones and Lance were offering some parting shots. It all seemed like madness to Armen, and he calmly led his grandson in search of the rest of the family. His son-in-law was giving some last minute help to Annette in the kitchen, but Artemis, their daughter and daughter-in-law were not there. So Armen and Pauly walked down the hall, and they heard little John John somewhere, singing along with the Beatles' Rubber Soul. In the master bedroom, they found the three women huddled over the end of the bed, with their backs to the television, which was strangely on without the sound. Juliet was changing her daughter's diaper; she handed the wet diaper to Lily, who looked over her sister-in-law's arm and pointed the diaper at Lucy's private parts.

"Shame, shame," Lily said with a tight-lipped smile.

"Don't say that!" Juliet said as she finished diapering.

"I was just kidding."

"It's not funny. It's like something from the Old Country!"

Armen felt uncomfortable being there, and he saw that poor Pauly looked embarrassed. They turned to leave.

"Daddy," Juliet said suddenly, holding Lucy in her arms, "I didn't know you were here." As Armen said hello to them, Artemis suddenly interrupted.

"You shouldn't act so superior, Juliet," she said, "biting off Lily's head like that!"

"It was nothing," Lily said.

"I've come to realize," Artemis said icily, focusing on Juliet, "that we should respect our people's history in the Old Country. You just don't realize that all of us are survivors of the Genocide." Juliet looked shocked at her mother. Armen felt badly for his daughter, having to endure his Angel's patronizing words, which discounted what Juliet knew. "Don't get on your high horse! The Genocide has cast a terrible shadow on all of us, and especially Daddy, who was there!"

"Hey, what have we here?" Garo said as he burst into the room and reached to lift the little girl from Juliet's arms. "Go on. I didn't mean to interrupt," he said and began making nonsense sounds in response to the words Lucy spoke. But Artemis and Lily dispersed, heading for the kitchen to put Christmas dinner on the table. Pauly left, and Armen stayed to listen to his son; when Lucy said Gaga for Garo, he said Lulu for Lucy, and she laughed. She said teetee for TV, and then Garo said Gragra for Grandpa. "No," little Lucy said, "that not Gragra, that Papa."

Soon they were all called to come to dinner, and once seated everyone served themselves the usual holiday meal: platters and generous bowls of warm sliced ham, celebration pilaf with dates, almonds, apricots and raisins, a souboragi with tender wide noodles laced with parsley and melted cheeses, ambrosia with fresh fruit, and a Caesar salad. Garo sat at the head of the table, and next to him sat Armen. Across from Armen sat Juliet, Sammy, and Lucy in a high-chair. Lily was at the other end with Artemis and the three children.

Garo jumped from topic to topic. Dr. Hopper, who just turned sixty-five, was thinking of retiring from his psychology practice. Nixon had better stop his bombing of Vietnam or face rioting in our streets. And by the way, the Balians' Gloria was finally getting married to an Armenian guy from Watertown, Massachusetts. The guitarist Jimi Hendricks had just died because of the evil scourge of drugs, which were threatening Fresno, too: cocaine, marijuana, crystal meth, and in his case heroin!

In the midst of all the words pouring from Garo, Sammy mentioned that there would be a classical concert he wanted to see on CBS at four.

"You can watch it in the bedroom," Lily said, for a moment stemming the flood of her husband's kibitzing. "That way you'll be able to listen without distractions."

His son-in-law was grateful, and Armen was pleased. Garo's flowing energy and impulsiveness, his needs and dreams, were a constant source of distraction in the family, and it was a saving grace that Lily had the capacity to focus and be realistic – sometimes, of course, to a fault, when his son and she would argue so viciously.

After dinner, Sammy went to the master bedroom to see and hear on TV two musicians from the Soviet Union, the violinist David Oistrakh and the pianist Sviatoslav Richter. Sammy had told everyone Richter was one of the greatest pianists. After a while, Garo said he was going to see if Sammy was okay, and Armen followed him down the hall, curious about seeing two Soviet musicians. Beautiful sound filled the big bedroom, and Sammy said it was Beethoven. The pianist's Germanic face reminded Armen of Don Wolf. Garo just stared at the two Russians on the screen and at his brother-in-law, who sat on the floor with his back to the bed a few yards from the television.

"I wish we could always live this way," Garo said, "where everybody does what they love most – that would be a real community. Then, I'd be happy." His smile shed a warm aura over the room. As they listened to the music for a minute, Armen was impressed by the weathered inexpressive faces of these Soviets making such stormy music, and he was touched by his son's words, though he knew that it was wishful thinking on Garo's part. For one thing, there was such tremendous training involved in producing this beauty, not to mention the fact that no matter how much these two musicians were revered in the Soviet Union, the life of an artist was a solitary one. Nevertheless, he thought, Garo's wishful thinking was so good-willed. The whole family relied on him to be this way because it helped them endure the defeats in the stores and now the dangers and difficulties at the bar.

Garo and he walked together out of the bedroom and into the empty hall, where the light of winter dusk hardly penetrated.

"I can't take it anymore, Pop," Garo said, and they stopped walking. "I don't know what to do with those sons-of-bitches – the drug users are pathetic, the dealers are maniacs, and the smugglers are your upstanding citizens. You won't believe it, but a bunch of land developers came to me to say they're taking care of it. 'Don't trouble yourself about drugs anymore.' Do you see what's going on? The police protect the whole operation. Last night two plainclothes guys came to the office; they wanted to give me another 'friendly warning,' and they said: 'If you want to stay out of shit, don't step in shit.'" Worried and dismayed, Armen stared at his son as Garo's words flooded fast and quiet from him. "I should just quit, Pop. You know I wanted to be a farmer. It's our birthright, isn't it? – planting and pruning and hoeing those grape vines in the hundred ten degree heat, and your sweat dripping down your face tastes like the burning sun. Now that's a life for an Armenian. But Lily says no." Armen made his tsk sound, and he could see Garo's mouth narrowing into a tight smile.

They walked back to join the rest of the family. Soon the day ended, and at seven, Armen drove them back to their Garland home. There Juliet rocked Lucy to sleep, and then they sat around the kitchen table playing gin rummy. Eventually, after the local news on television, they all went to bed. He had kept to himself what Garo said; mulling it over, he slept fitfully. At one in the morning, he silently rose and went to sit alone at the round table in the kitchen, turning on the side lamp.

Here was where he worked late at night on his poems, going over and over them. And this was the room where Artemis cooked such fine food, her raw meat chema, her derev grape leaf dolma, her braised artichokes, her salads and pilaf. Lately, another Fresno Armenian writer had been coming over to visit them; he loved Artemis' cooking, especially the artichokes with onion and dill and her aromatic quince compote. After a recent visit to Yerevan, William Saroyan had sought Armen out and became a friend. The Ararats wined and dined William, along with his egotistical painter friend Shaunt, but what had Saroyan done in return? Unfortunately, he was an ungenerous spirit. Yet Armen still hoped Sammy would have a chance to meet him, for his son-in-law was studying literature at Berkeley. Last year Armen had glanced through the folder of poems in English Sammy had typed up for him: "You men of stone." It was a nice gesture, though Armen felt less and less able to read anyone but Armenian writers, so Sammy's folder remained on the bookshelf in the television room. "Speak what you feel, not what you ought to say."

Armen took one of his own poems from a corner shelf. The light from the kitchen lamp illuminated the pieces of paper that he had covered with his careful script. They were the eulogy he had written for his mother's death four years ago, in the bitter winter of 1966. It recited the pain and endurance of poor Zabel, who never stopped working as she moved first from a Turkish-Greek fishing village with its palms and flowering orchards of olive and nut, to the Bursatsi village in the mountains where she married and Armen was born near Duman Dagh, to Constantinope where they survived the Genocide, to the miserable heat and sun of Central California fields and Fresno. What did we give to our mother in return for her labor, he asked, to the kind village woman who with self-denial and many sacrifices had reared us, educated us, and stood by us throughout her life? Our grief and some bouquets of flowers, that was all. What if those flowers could speak?

He turned to the page with the poem he was working on now, prompted by his latest trip to Yerevan: "I am a pilgrim seeking the blue road of brotherhood, far from the hurtling engines of American greed." As he reworked the words and phrases, Armen began to hum a folk tune about the winter winds blowing from the mountains and descending on the valley, Hovern Engan. He was not sure he believed what he wrote now, all this indictment and celebration. But words were still his deepest habit and compulsion. He would not know who he was if he did not write. His memories were decaying, and though he experienced such joy in his grandchildren, he felt himself continuing to break apart under the pressure of his exhaustion. It would soon be the end of another year and really the end of an era because the promise of this decade of youthful protest was yielding now to cynicism in America.

His eyes slowly closed, and his head began to sink to his chest now. He felt a bone-deep tiredness. He must try to sleep. He rose, switched off the light, and walked through the dark house to the master bedroom. Artemis snored in the other bed, but it didn't matter to him. He had his own noisy breathing to think about as he took off his robe and slippers and got into bed. A wave of exhaustion carried him toward sleep and a deterioration he couldn't stop. How absurd even to try. What did they say about the decaying atom, that it had a half-life? He had a half-life. He wanted to tie himself to a dangling rope and be pulled up to the sky, but he could not think of a deity who would hold the rope. He imagined the sunny slopes of Duman Dagh in Turkey where his mother worked in the fields, and then California's sun-drenched Central Valley where he farmed decade after decade and where once again his mother labored. He roamed the fields of his past, encountering everything with his disintegrating consciousness. Soon Armen Ararat would disappear into a poof of decaying particles. He imagined the hanging dead in Turkey and then his flight across the world. He imagined another life in Paris as a student at the Sorbonne, welcomed by a crowd of Armenians in their thousands; they filled the Champs Elyssés, and there were palm trees in the Tuilleries, hung with spit-roasted lambs to feed the crowd, and all the sweet Armenian girls cried out,

"We love you, Armen Ararat." Which was reality and which was a dream? He knew that he was on a bed on Garland in the city of Fresno, the name of which meant the ash tree. And he knew that he had dreamed such dreams for seven decades now. Artemis too had been dreaming her dreams for all these years, and now Garo, Tigran, Juliet, Paul, Annette, John, and Lucy – all of them were also dreaming their dreams.

Chapter 21

In the end is my beginning

JANUARY 2, 1972

—•—

The painting was oddly familiar to her. In it, a dark haired young woman was standing with her head tilted to one side; she looked like one of Degas' wonderful ballerinas, except that the nude in the large painting was more abstract. Peering in at the side of the canvas was a strange deer with horns and fawn eyes, which reminded her oddly of Pauly with his beautiful eyelashes and his growing physique. The painting was one of Shaunt's somewhat abstract figures, in the exhibition that Artemis and Armen walked through this Sunday evening. Some of the paintings by William's friend had an Armenian character; there were big abstract village landscapes, and giant warriors seemed to have leapt, wielding swords, from the frieze of an ancient Armenian church. The colors were muddy, but sometimes blue or orange streaks emerged from the tans and dark greens.

For a few minutes, the artist himself followed them from picture to picture, talking mainly with Armen, in Armenian. Shaunt's head was tilted up, his nose in the air with a sort of arrogance, or maybe it was a defense. This was a joint show of works by Shaunt and by the Fresno State art professor Molly Firenze, who was a nice friend of Juliet's. The title of the exhibition was "Images from Europe and the Caucasus: Two American Painters," and tonight was the opening at the University Art Gallery.

It was Shaunt's abstract nude that remained on her mind. "Armenian Girl" haunted Artemis, though she could not quite figure out why. It was partly the calm frankness of the woman's nudity, as if her nakedness were nothing unusual. Artemis felt some discomfort, even sadness before such ease. It was hard for her to accept her own flawed body, but she yet hoped that her children and especially her grandchildren would accept theirs. "Armenian Girl" reminded her of a Picasso painting but also, somehow, of Juliet. There was something about the expression, the thick dark hair, and the stance. How ironic that art should accidentally mirror life. Yes, that was why she felt haunted by the painting. She hoped Juliet would see it someday, so that she could see a bodily ease that she could not imagine her daughter attaining, for she was even more nervous than Artemis herself.

"Do you want to go?" Armen said. They had been there for half an hour, and he seemed restless. Amid the people who milled around the gallery, they had had short conversations with a dozen other Armenians.

"We haven't seen the other room," she said. In it were the paintings by Juliet's friend Molly.

"Yes," he said curtly, and she did not know if he meant it as disagreement or assent. They drifted toward the passageway to the other room, and as she led the way into it, Professor Firenze waved to them and walked over. She was as short as Artemis, with dark hair and a kindly face; her skin looked strangely smooth as if a layer were missing.

"I'm so glad you came, Mr. and Mrs. Ararat."

"Juliet wanted us to see your paintings. She speaks of you so warmly," Artemis said. "It's too bad she couldn't come down from Berkeley for the opening."

"I know. But with the children, she really couldn't," Molly said.

"Juliet loves to paint," she said. "But it's so impractical."

"That's true, but she's good. How are little Lucy and Jason?"

"Jason is ten months old now! Very sweet. And Lucy is so cute, so sensitive. She's two-and-a-half years old now. You never had children, did you, Molly?" Artemis added, and the professor made a self-deprecating gesture.

"I have two wonderful nieces and a nephew in San Francisco," Molly said, and as she went on about her extended family, Artemis thought that the paintings on these walls must be her children. That was the answer to the question Artemis had asked; she always posed realistic questions like that because she knew from long experience that reality had to be questioned, or it would catch you off guard.

As they made their way among the knots of people in the room of Molly Firenze's paintings, Artemis was fascinated by the largest painting dominating one end of the room. It was a three-part work, a triptych, or so said the legend on the wall; it showed three generations of women. On the middle and largest panel was the face of the oldest woman, Italian looking with her dark brown hair streaked with grey. Each of the side panels showed the face of what seemed to be her daughter and, on the other side, her granddaughter. The faces, with their beiges and browns against a plain blue sky, were disembodied; they bore amazing little wings, which crowned the sides of the hair, as if these were Medieval or Renaissance angels. What struck Artemis most was the feeling of the oldest face, the mother's, isolated in its rectangle of blue. Her smile seemed so lonely – ethereal, virginal, and alone. The sad separateness of the matriarch cut her to the quick.

Armen tapped her arm. "I'm sick, Angel," he said. "Let's go."

"Where is Molly Firenze?"

"Tsk," Armen clicked his tongue.

"I want to say goodbye to her."

They found Molly in the other room of the university gallery, near Shaunt's abstract nude. Artemis thanked Molly and told her how much she liked her "Triptych," and Molly thanked them for coming.

"Isn't that a good painting?" Artemis said appreciatively, pointing to "Armenian Girl." "It seems so familiar."

Molly smiled and looked expectantly at her but only said, "It is familiar, isn't it?"

"To be so at ease like that," Artemis said. Baffled by Molly's manner, she wanted to ask her more questions.

"Yes, God help us all," the professor said with ironic self-deprecation.

Just then Shaunt walked up to her and Armen and burst into a discourse on his and Molly's paintings. Before he could finish, she and Armen said goodbye and left. Outside in the car, Armen pulled out of the parking lot and turned onto Shaw. Dense fog obscured everything in the dark winter night.

"I feel sick," he said as he drove slowly. "I'm dying, Angel."

"Again?" she said, irritable after her conversation with the two artists and feeling that she had contacted the life of painting, which she had hoped to live herself. "Even if you die tomorrow," she said, "I would have to live nine more years to live as long as you have." Armen did not reply, and as he navigated carefully through the darkened fog-bound streets.

She thought about what she had seen in the gallery. Art and also music and poetry could move her deeply, to the point of making her feel haunted and even threatened. Art's power could be like the irrational forces which so easily disrupted their lives – that's what Kevork Emin, the poet from Armenia who had just visited them, had told her. He had been staying with the Ararats and left just a few days ago. At Christmas dinner, Shaunt, Silly Willy Saroyan, and some Armenian Progressive League friends had eaten with them, and after dinner, Kevork read some poems. She vividly remembered especially one of the poems: Armenia was small but powerful like a thrown stone, like a mountain stream swollen with snowmelt, like a shot bullet, like a fine poem, like sprouting corn or seasoning salt, like a coal nugget compressed into diamond, like scattered stars; it was small but powerful like a radioactive atom of uranium.

On Christmas Eve, Kevork had met her children and grandchildren, and he had especially liked Garo. Afterwards, he had said he was so moved by Garo, who had seemed sad about something he would not discuss. And Kevork had been exactly right. She knew because of what happened two months ago, when she drove up to Berkeley with Garo. Her son had wanted to interview a rock group about performing at the Garret. He took her and Sammy to a place called the Longbranch near the border between Berkeley and Oakland; Juliet had stayed with the children, but Artemis wanted to see what Garo had been talking about. As the loudness came blazing from the stage, she felt so odd standing there, a dwarf, with her big son and her graduate student son-in-law. For a moment, she thought her ears were exuding acid, but they were dry when she reached to touch them. The band was called the Tower of Power and was made up of horns and guitars and drums. The force of the sound was more powerful than any she had heard before. The horrible sound was proof that there were powers in this world larger than anyone could imagine, certainly bigger than any politician could wield. Garo seemed to sway to the rhythm, if one could call that blast rhythm.

After the show, Garo had driven them to a hamburger joint on University Avenue in Berkeley, and she and Sammy had sat quietly at a table with Garo who talked with three Mexican-American rock musicians sitting across from them. She listened to Garo boasting about the Garret, what a responsive audience they would have, what perks in addition to payment, and all the while the musicians seemed to look on, irritable and greedy. Her ears were still buzzing, and she could not really follow their words. All she saw was Garo's mood, his stunning combination of intensity and exhaustion, as he sought to convince these sullen singers to perform in Fresno. Suddenly she heard him shout, "If you're looking for drugs, just stay the fuck away from my bar!" She was stunned to hear him shout like that. He was more desperate than she imagined he could be.

The next day, after they met Juliet's in-laws for breakfast, Garo had driven her back to Fresno, and on the ride, she had interrogated him.

"Give me a break, Ma."

"I don't want you to be so upset, Garo, so desperate."

"Don't worry, Ma. I'm doing something about it. Me and my anti-drug group, we're changing things in Fresno. Now, let's just have a nice calm ride home?"

"Are you taking care of yourself?"

"Well, I have bouncers."

"Bouncers! That Lance Fetzer is a Volga German, like Don Wolf!" she had said.

"I'm just joking, Ma. Stop worrying. I don't want to talk about it anymore."

Now, she and Armen arrived back home from the art exhibit. He unlocked the front door, and the phone was ringing. She ran to answer it, but the line was silent, and she felt a strange wave of anxiety pass over her. Tigran's son must have fallen asleep early. Adam had developed a cold after Christmas and was still ill. She walked down the hall, quietly opened the door, and saw her fourteen-year-old grandson sleeping. His aura of calm and sweetness touched her, and she hoped that Tigran's and Betsy's divorce would not harm him too much. Tigran and Adam began living in the back bedroom when the divorce came through – in Juliet's old room. That was almost six months ago, and now in January he planned to move to an apartment with his son.

She returned down the hall, still uneasy, and in the kitchen she saw Armen sitting at the table with the aspirin bottle, a glass of water, his pipe, and an ashtray. She said she was going to read in the family room, but first she needed to take a shower. In the bedroom, she took off her clothes and put on a nightgown and robe from the mirrored closet. In the bathroom, she went to the toilet, then turned on the water to warm, and took off her robe and nightie. Under the streaming heat of the shower, she felt her body begin to uncoil, though only up to a point. As she lathered her thinning grey golden hair (she used just a little dye), she never forgot how vulnerable one's body was. She remembered once more her baby sister Lucaper's puckered purple body boiled alive almost six decades ago, an accident that none of her mother's vigilance or her own could have kept from happening; even now she felt ashamed to be alive. She mechanically lathered her symmetrical body, arms and breasts, stomach and private parts. Hers was a sad body, and anger began to well up in her. She had endured three painful childbirths and decade after decade of work, and now as she washed her legs and feet, she felt helplessly enraged. With the hot water needling her back, she thought that this was the human lot, to have a poor forked body and be forever vulnerable and unable truly to work your will in the world.

Suddenly she was overcome with shock. She realized what Molly Firenze was going to say about Shaunt's painting of the nude "Armenian Girl." It was familiar to her for good reason. The painting was of Juliet, her obstinate daughter. Shuddering with shame, Artemis quickly finished her shower. Juliet was leading a counter-life. How could she pose for Shaunt! How could she lead an artist's life, being a Bohemian and studying art and painting and modeling! Artemis had once imagined such a life for herself, but Armen – demanding, desperate, restless – had whisked her away when she was nineteen and deprived her even of attempting it. Had she not married him, though, she would not have had her children and her beautiful grandchildren. She quickly dried herself, dressed, and tightly buttoned her robe around her, and in the television room, she sat down on the couch. Trembling a little, she began paging through Time, absorbing nothing of what she read.

A car's headlights appeared out of the foggy darkness and shot through the front window. From the TV room, she could hear the car park and now footsteps up the walk. She was about to get up, but her husband was already in the foyer, and she heard Armen shuffling his feet there. The key clicked in the lock, and the door opened. It was Tigran. His voice mumbled something, and a strangled cry came from Armen. Then her son walked in, his face hard and colorless. She felt her own face freeze white; her shoulders and chest tightened, and the tightness made her shake.

He mumbled something.

"What?" she said. "I can't hear you. Why do you mumble?"

"Garo..." She couldn't hear the rest.

"What?" she spit out, stern and urgent.

"Garo, Ma, Garo is dead."